"You are also the only individual that has had the opportunity to make an in-depth study of the Plainfolk," the young President of the Board of Assessors told Steve. "What you have to tell us will be invaluable in planning our campaign to repossess the overground."

Brickman thought it appropriate to reply at this point with a sober nod. He had had a long time to prepare for this moment; now he was ready with a carefully edited version of what had happened to him after he'd been knocked out of the sky by a Mute crossbow bolt. This was definitely not the time to mention that it was the M'Call clan who had provided tools and assistance in building Blue-Bird—the aircraft in which he had made his escape.

"All we wish to do is share the knowledge you have gained during captivity in the hope that it will provide us with a greater understanding of the enemy," the dark-haired young President went on. "The overground is ours by right. It's been promised to us by the First Family. We don't have to share the blue-sky world with anybody."

YOU ARE THE FIRST TRACKER
EVER TO SURVIVE CAPTURE
BY THE MUTES...

THE AMTRAK WARS
BOOK II
THE FIRST FAMILY

PATRICK TILLEY

BAEN
SCIENCE FICTION
BOOKS

THE FIRST FAMILY

A Baen Books Original

Baen Publishing Enterprises
260 Fifth Avenue
New York, N.Y. 10001

First printing, April 1986

ISBN: 0-671-65567-1

Cover art by Richard Hescox

Printed in the United States of America

Distributed by
SIMON & SCHUSTER
TRADE PUBLISHING GROUP
1230 Avenue of the Americas
New York, N.Y. 10020

To my sons,
Pierre-André, who solved the
problem of the wagon-trains
and
Bruno-Christian, whose photographs
gave me the key to the
overground.

THE TRACKER PRAYER

(Offered thrice-daily to images of the President-General)

Hail to the Chief!
All-seeing Father, Leader and Sage
With our hand on our heart
We praise and salute you.
Glory be to the First Family!
Gift of Ages Past, Rulers till the end of Time
Bedrock of Amtrack, Founders of the Federation
Guardians of the Earth-Shield
Chosen Saviours of the Blue-Sky World
Creators of the Light, the Work and the Way
Keepers of all Knowledge, Wisdom and Truth
In whom the Seven Great Qualities are enshrined
And from whose sacred life-blood
our lives spring

All-seeing Father, Leader and Sage
Chief among the Chosen, Creator of Life
This day you have given us we dedicate to you
Let your wise counsel guide our thoughts
Let your power strengthen our hands and hearts
So that we may strike down those who oppose Your Will
Teach us to follow the glorious example
Of the Minutemen and the Foragers
So that we may serve you better through all our days
The life you gave us we gladly offer up again
Use it as you will so that, by the manner of our dying
We may honour their great sacrifice
Just as you will honour ours
at the Final Victory.
Amen

ONE

DEKE HAYWOOD stretched back in his chair, linked his hands above his head and yawned cavernously. He squinted through one eye at the digital time/date display on one of the battery of tv screens that surrounded him: 17.20 hours, 14 November 2989. Another forty minutes to go before Glen Wyler took over the watch. And another eleven years to the end of the century: 3000 AD; the long-awaited moment when—according to the First Family—the Amtrak Federation was due to repossess the blue-sky world. Deke couldn't see it happening, not in his lifetime anyway. That particular dream, like so many of the current operations, was badly behind schedule. Deke was careful to keep his thoughts on the matter to himself. It did not pay to comment on any shortfall in the Federation's performance. Like all Trackers, Deke had been bludgeoned from birth by one, constantly reiterated, fundamental truth—"It is only people who fail; not the system."

The desktop console that required Deke's attention while on duty was a three-sided affair with twenty-four tv monitors ranged in two rows around it. The monitors were linked to remote-controlled cameras mounted overhead, on the top of the windowless watch-tower. These were the ever watchful eyes of the way-station. Through them, Deke and the other VidCommTechs kept the surrounding area—

1

known as the station precinct—under constant surveillance; twenty-four hours a day; 365 days a year. Their
purpose was to provide early warning of a precinct incursion by hostiles; armed bands of Mutes—the perpetual
enemies of the Federation. It was not necessary to sit
glued to the screens. Each camera had an image analyser
and was programmed to react to a range of specific shapes
and movements. It knew what the area it covered looked
like down to the last pebble and if it saw anything on four
or two legs or a rock or bush that had moved out of place it
alerted the duty crewman by means of an audio-visual
alarm.

Normally, Deke looked forward to his four hour stint as
Duty VidCommTech but today, the overground had failed
to deliver the special kind of action he craved. Never
mind. Deke had devised his own back-up entertainment.
Swivelling round in his chair, he slid open the bottom
drawer of a stack under the left wing of the desk, inserted
his forearm and retrieved a video cassette lying right at
the back in the dead space between the underside of the
drawer and the floor.

Deke pushed the video cassette into the nearest record/
play slot, slipped a lightweight headset over his ears,
started the tape running and brought the picture up on
the screen in front of him. It was a dawn sequence, a deep
rose-pink sky overhung with ragged clusters of pale violet
clouds. A thin soft-edged line of deep chrome yellow
appeared and spread swiftly north and south along the
horizon, heralding the rising sun. The sharp clear sounds
of the illicitly-made electronic sound track cut through the
muzzy boredom that clogged his brain and made his spine
tingle with its forbidden rhythmic beat.

Reared at Nixon/Fort Worth and originally a lineman
aboard the Rio Bravo wagon-train, Deke had been caught
in an Mute ambush on his third operational tour and badly
wounded in the legs. Although this automatically qualified
him for a home base assignment Deke had applied for
retraining as a VidCommTech (OG) and had gotten himself
posted to the Tracker way-station at Pueblo. His eagerness
to get back to where the action was had been warmly

commended by his superiors and had earned him ten plus points at the next quarterly assessment. This, in turn, had resulted in a welcome boost to his credit rating. The added privileges that came with an upgraded ID-card could always be put to good use but the real pleasure came from the knowledge that he had beaten the system. Had the Assessors known the real reason behind Deke's wish to return overground they would, without doubt, have been a great deal less generous.

Deke was a covert cloud-freak. He had become addicted on his first trip aboard the Rio Bravo and, since reaching Pueblo, had been using the facilities in the watch-tower to secretly record the more spectacular sunrises and sunsets on videotape. He had, of course, only been able to do this when he was alone. Though most Trackers might have considered it is distinctly bizarre way of passing the time, looking at clouds did not, in itself, contravene any of the statutory codes of behaviour laid down by the First Family; on the other hand, making unauthorised video recordings certainly did.

Deke was not quite sure whether it was a Code Two or Code Three offence but, either way, getting caught could be bad news especially if—as in this case—the videotape included a sound track featuring a proscribed form of music known as "blackjack." Hence the need for a secure place in which to stash the tape—not an easy thing to find in a Tracker way-station or indeed anywhere else, for there were few doors and even fewer of them could be locked. In the Federation, the emphasis was on group identity, group activity and shared facilities; privacy, in the normally accepted sense of the word, was deemed to be unnecessary; personal possessions were regarded as unimportant.

Deke was different to the majority of Trackers at Pueblo who lived, ate, fought, slept and screwed around in small, close-knit groups and looked forward eagerly to the next overground sweep, or an incursion by hostiles. They needed that extra shot of adrenalin generated by combat to feel fully alive. Deke had gotten the same buzz during his time on the wagon-trains but his real kicks came from gazing

upon sun-tinted towers of cumulus, the dark menacing
bulk of thunderheads, the delicate tracery of alto-cirrus,
teased out by the wind like the tails of horses—one of the
many extinct animal species. His four-hour solo stint in
the watch-tower had become very precious to him. He
liked the solitude, the privacy—even though neither word
concept was included in the official Tracker vocabulary.
The videotape, with its illegal sound-track, was his alone;
his most precious possession. The last thing Deke wanted
to see while on duty was a bunch of screaming lumpheads.
An alert packed the tower with people and blew his chances
of adding another cloudscape to his collection.

Despite being a code-breaker Deke was still a good
soldier. His leg injuries had meant being downgraded to
line-support status but he still wore his Trail-Blazer badge
with pride. Mutes were still the enemy. He had simply
lost interest in body-counts shortly after glimpsing his first
sunrise. He'd gone on dutifully to do his share of killing
and had even made sergeant at the end of his second tour
but from that first, glorious golden moment only clouds
had counted. Indeed, it became an almost fatal obsession.
At the back of his mind lurked the knowledge that, had he
paid more attention to the ground instead of looking at the
sky he might not have led his squad into the ambush from
which only he had emerged alive.

Today, like most days, there had been no PIs. Which
was good news as far as Deke was concerned. The bad
news was that, this time round, there had been very little
to look at, and absolutely nothing worth recording. The
sky on the bank of screens in front of him had been
depressingly empty of cloud. The airborne drifters whose
multi-hued, ever-changing forms fired his imagination had
wandered over the far horizon leaving behind a bland hazy
canvas; a smoothly-graded wash of colour which began
right of screen as pale violet blue and changed impercepti-
bly to pale yellow on his left.

Deke reached over the back of his chair and picked up a
cup of java from the table behind him. Java was the
synthetic, third millenium equivalent of the pre-Holocaust
drink known as coffee; a minor historical fact Deke had

uncovered during one of his occasional dips into the video archives. As he blew on it and took a trial sip he saw, out of the corner of his eye, a brief flash of light in the top right-hand corner of the screen fed by Camera One—fitted with a six hundred millimetre telephoto lens and known to the watch-tower crews as "Zoomer."

Deke knew that the pin-point flash of light he had glimpsed on the screen could only be caused by sunlight bouncing off the wings of a Federation Skyhawk—but he was puzzled by the lack of prior radio contact. Wagon-trains putting up air patrols always informed way-stations if any of their aircraft were likely to enter its precinct—a notional circle drawn around its overground location with a radius of ten miles. It was not just a matter of courtesy. Under a procedure known as PAL (Precinct Air Liaison) tower crews, when notified of overflights, would monitor the appropriate radio channel for any distress calls and, by maintaining a sky watch for the duration of the patrol, could provide invaluable help in any subsequent search and rescue operation.

Just when Deke thought he must have been imagining things, Zoomer zeroed in on a small, blurred, bluish object. Whatever it was was now inside the extreme range of the lens. Using the keyboard, Deke called for maximum resolution. He was confidently expecting the blur to resolve itself into the familiar shape of a Skyhawk but to his surprise the object on the screen did not have the normal three-wheeled cockpit pod, cowled pusher engine and the inflated delta wing with the coloured-coded tips that showed which wagon-train it belonged to. No . . . this might be a flying machine but it had not rolled off the assembly line at Reagan/Lubbock. This was a cee-bee rig with a single-ply wing braced by a tangle of wires and struts. The pilot was slung underneath, lying on his belly in a strap harness with his legs straight out behind him and the wind blowing round his balls; his hands rested on a large triangular strut in front of his face.

Deke hit some more buttons to bring the optical rangefinder into sync with Zoomer and noted the read-out: distance, three miles; altitude, twelve hundred feet; esti-

mated airspeed, fifteen to twenty miles an hour. Returning to the keyboard he instructed Zoomer to hold focus on
the approaching craft and keep it in the centre of the
screen. As he watched, it became clear that the pilot was
steering the craft by swinging his suspended body from
side to side while pushing or pulling on the lateral section
of the triangular strut. It was still too far away to allow him
to distinguish any small details but he could see the pilot's
red and white bone dome with its dark face visor. The
craft itself was unarmed but there was no way of knowing
what its passenger might have up his sleeve.

Deke knew that similar red and white helmets were
worn by wingmen aboard The Lady from Louisiana—a
wagon-train that had made a supply run to Pueblo in the
spring and which, later, had been badly mauled in some
heavy action in Wyoming. He also knew that the same
type of helmet was worn by Tracker renegades—small
scattered bands of thieving scavengers who roamed the
overground in search of abandoned items of equipment
and stores. Sick individuals, wasted by the lethal radiation
that blanketed the overground. Deserters who had abandoned their kinfolk and comrades, broken their oath of
loyalty to the Federation and betrayed the trust of the
First Family; a Code One offence and the ultimate crime.
It was little wonder that, when captured, such anti-social
elements were usually sentenced to summary execution
without trial.

In the verbal shorthand used by Trail-Blazers, renegades were usually referred to as cee-bees—derived from
the term code-breaker (any individual who, by their actions, contravened the Behavioural Codes laid down by
the First Family and contained in the Manual of the
Federation).

Deke was aware that if the pilot *was* a renegade he was
crazy to come anywhere near a way-station. But then you
had to be crazy to *be* a renegade in the first place. His was
not to reason why. In one swift movement he pressed the
eject button, retrieved his videotape, stowed it back under
the bottom drawer and hit the Precinct Incursion button.

It glowed red under his finger as, five floors below, a high-pitched electronic bleeper sounded in the guard room.

The head and shoulders of Lieutenant Matt Harmer, the duty officer appeared on the visicomm screen. "Okay, gimme the sit-rep." Harmer was a pugnacious individual with an undersized chin. To compensate for not being cast in the heroic mould he had worked hard to develop the rest of his body and the less attractive side of his nature. He was, in other words, a lean mean gung-ho sonofabitch who could drive nails into rocks with his fist.

Deke told him about the approaching unidentified flyer and relayed the picture from Zoomer onto the screen in the guard-room so that Harmer could decide on the appropriate response.

Harmer faced up to Deke, his eyes studying the flyer on the adjacent screen. "Looks like he's heading right for us."

"Has been since I first picked him up," replied Deke.

"You reckon he's from some renegade outfit?"

"Don't know where else he could be from. What I can't figure out is why he would be calling on us."

"Maybe he's lost his way." The duty officer gave a harsh laugh. "Never mind. Once he's down he'll find it's only a short walk to the wall. Do you have an ETA?"

"Yeah. If he keeps coming he'll be overhead in about eight to ten minutes."

Harmer turned away and spoke rapidly to someone off-screen. "Jake?! We've got a single hostile intercept. Unidentified—but could be a cee-bee—coming in from the north-west. By air. Don't ask how, just listen! I want Units Three and Four suited up and on the ramp in five minutes. Stand by to take Three out on the South Side. I'll take the North Side with Four. Okay, go for it." Harmer pivoted on his heel, threw his right hand towards a control panel adjacent to the visicomm screen and hit the button triggering a Level Four alert—the next-to-lowest state of readiness.

In the watch-tower, a klaxon mounted on the wall facing Deke emitted a series of long bleeps. Since, as the duty VidCommTech, he was already seated at his post no further response on his part was required but elsewhere, as the alarm sounded throughout the way-station, specific groups of Trackers stopped whatever they were doing and ran along subterranean passageways to man the gun positions around the perimeter of the way-station and other key points within it.

Harmer faced up to Deke Haywood's screen image. "Anything else to tell me?"

"Only that maybe you should try and bring him down in one piece," suggested Deke. "Grand Central will want to know whether he's a one-off loonie or whether those bad hats have gotten themselves an air force. Hard data like that could put the station in line for a commendation."

"My thoughts exactly," said Harmer. "Gimme a voice hook-up on Channel Five and put Mary-Ann in the picture. I'll get back to you when I've loosened a few teeth. Meanwhile, don't lose him."

"Wilco," replied Deke.

To "loosen a few teeth" was Trail-Blazer jargon for an overground sortie; a macabre reference to one of the nastier phases of radiation sickness in which the gums became swollen and ulcerous and bled continuously. Mary-Ann was the unit's nickname for Colonel Marie Anderssen, the thirty-five-year-old way-station commander.

Built overlooking the Arkansas River near the pre-Holocaust site of Pueblo, the way-station under Anderssen's control was the most northerly of the Federation's overground bases; the subterranean home of a one thousand-strong pioneer battalion made up of men and women in almost equal numbers, aged twelve and upwards. In its overall physical shape, it resembled a concrete iceberg: one-tenth of it was visible above ground, the other nine-tenths was buried safely within the earthshield. The exposed section consisted of a stepped, eight-sided bunker with each of the three layers over-hanging the one beneath like an inverted ziggurat. Weapon ports set in short but massive reinforcing spurs at each corner allowed all exits and entrances to be covered with enfilading fire.

Dotted around the bunker at a distance of one hundred yards was a ring of turrets set at ground level like a mini-Maginot line—with one important difference: the guns in this defensive line had a three hundred and sixty degree field of fire. Now that Harmer had sounded the alert, these turrets—which looked a bit like those of 20th century tanks buried hull-down—were occupied by four-man gun crews.

Rising from the roof of the bunker was the circular watch-tower. Eighty feet high and thirty feet in diameter, it looked like an unfinished lighthouse perched on a rock being eaten away by the surrounding sea of red grass. The upper floor, where Deke Haywood sat and to which Colonel Anderssen now directed her steps, was known as the Tactical Command Centre. Like all external structures, the tower had ten-foot-thick walls lined with lead. There were no windows. External surveillance was via remote-controlled tv cameras and there were also a number of periscopic sights that could be uncovered in the event of a power-failure; an event regarded as both unlikely and unthinkable but against which elaborate precautions had been taken.

Below ground-level, where the soil and bedrock afforded an extra layer of protection against the lethal radiation that still lingered in the air, the main walls were only half as thick and the lead lining—always in short supply— was dispensed with. Here, arranged on five floors, were the living quarters, mess halls, power-house, air filtration and ventilation plant, and all the other service and engineering facilities necessary to sustain life inside the way-station and to permit its progressive expansion.

As in all way-stations, and other parts of the Federation, the overall level of technology was curiously uneven. The electronic equipment was highly sophisticated, in marked contrast to the accommodation and the life-style which was spartan and heavily work-oriented. The image it conjured up was that of a group of male and female Green Berets equipped with late-20th century weapons and communications equipment transported back in time to occupy a pre-Civil War army fort on the Mexican frontier. With one important difference; the sour belly pork and black-eyed beans had been replaced by processed soya-based ration packs.

The door of the small tower lift slid open. Colonel Marie Anderssen stepped out followed by a junior aide and three VidCommTechs. Deke Haywood leaned on the table to help pull himself out of his chair and made a visible effort to take the curve out of his spine. Anderssen acknowledged the gesture with a nod and stepped up onto her high chair. Glen Wyler, Deke's relief, and the other four Trackers who crewed the Tactical Command Centre came pounding up the stairway in their rubber-soled boots, threw their colonel a hurried salute and took their places.

Anderssen laid her yellow long-peaked cap aside, ran both hands through her short, greying, wavy hair and studied the picture Deke had put up on her VDU. The unidentified craft was still heading directly for the watchtower. "Is this it?"

"Yes, sir," replied Deke. "Picked him up three miles out. He's been heading straight for us losing altitude steadily ever since."

Anderssen turned to the junior aide. "Who's duty officer today—Harmer?"

"Yessir!" snapped the aide. A real eager-beaver.

Anderssen turned back to Deke. "Post-alert reaction?"

Deke told her about the two squads that Harmer and the guard commander, Line-Sergeant Jake Nolan, were taking overground.

"You're voiced through on Channel Five."

One of the VidCommTechs now handling the North Side cameras spoke up. "Harmer just went up the ramp."

Deke put a lateral composite on Anderssen's secondary screen showing both squads fanning out around the North and South flanks of the bunker, fingers on the triggers of their three-barrelled air rifles.

Anderssen put on her light-weight headset and moved the slim mike arm into line with her mouth. "Blue One, this is Sunray. What is your PTR? Over."

PTR was verbal shorthand for Planned Tactical Response—Grand Centralese for what veteran Trail-Blazers in the shambolic heat of battle usually referred to as "Plan X."

Harmer's voice came back over the speakers. "I've got

the perimeter guns tracking him. Both squads have him in their sights. If he so much as sneezes, he's gonna—"

"Hey, Matt! Ease it down a little," said Anderssen amiably. "We may have to ship this one to Grand Central for interrogation."

"That's what I figured, sir. I managed to rustle up four sky-hooks. If he comes in low enough we're going to try and snag the wings as he goes past. But it could be tricky. This is the first time we've had an airborne PI."

"That's right," replied Anderssen. "I don't mind if you bend him a little. Just don't bring him back looking like a diced meat dinner, okay?"

"Blue One, Roger, Out," said Harmer.

You stroppy bastard, thought Anderssen. One of these days I'm gonna roast your balls and feed 'em to you one slice at a time . . .

The sky-hooks Harmer had referred to were grappling irons and lines that could be fired 250 feet into the air by compressed air rams that looked like small infantry mortars. They had been designed for scaling sheer rock faces but, apart from a few test firings, had not been put to any practical use. This, thought Harmer, could be the moment. And if it worked, it would be difficult for that grey-haired, hard-assed bitch in the watch-tower to avoid giving him full marks for ingenuity.

Harmer had positioned his two pairs of sky-hooks to the east and west of the way-station bunker. If the ragged blue sky-ship kept on the same course, he had to pass on one side or the other. That would be the time to nail him. Two sky-hooks placed twenty feet apart would be fired towards the ship as it approached, would pass over its wings then, as the ship flew on and the line ran out, the hooks would bite and then—el cruncho.

The airborne intruder drifted steadily lower, circled the perimeter defences at five hundred feet then, seemingly undisturbed by the eight six-barrelled gun turrets that were tracking him, dived down towards the north face of the watch-tower. As he neared the crouching linemen, he came lower still, putting him within range of the skyhooks.

Lieutenant Harmer could see the pilot quite clearly.

His ship might be homemade but he was dressed in the standard red, brown and black camouflaged fatigues worn by all Trail-Blazers on over-ground sorties—like those of Harmer and the linemen around him. The blue-winged craft veered to the west of the tower. Keep coming sucker, thought Harmer exultantly. This is where you get yours! He used his helmet radio to alert the two linemen manning the skyhooks on that side of the bunker. They aimed the slim mortar barrels holding the grappling irons up at the oncoming plane and fired within a split second of each other. There was an explosive whoosh as the barbed hooks soared skywards then an angry whipping sound as their lines, arranged alongside in open containers, uncoiled with the speed of striking rattlesnakes.

The intruder took immediate evasive action. As the two lines snaked upwards on parallel courses, he stood his craft on its right wingtip, side-slipped neatly between them and banked tightly round the watch-tower.

Harmer bellowed into his chin mike. "Brennan! Powers! Aim your lines to cross over! Take him as he comes around your side!"

Once again, the intruder evaded the soaring lines. He pulled up into a stall, dropped a wing to turn back on his tail then flew a tight circle around the ropes at the narrowest point of the 'X'."

Despite his anger at being outfaced, Harmer was impressed. It was a great piece of flying—especially without a motor. "Okay, you flashy sonofabitch," he muttered grudgingly to himself. "So far so good. But the wind's dyin', and the sun's going down—which means that soon, there'll be nothing keeping you up there. So enjoy it while you can, friend, cos I'm gonna be there when you touch down and I swear you are gonna get the shit kicked out of your ass all the way back to Pueblo."

The intruder banked around the watch-tower. He was now down to about a hundred feet. Harmer saw that the dark visor of the red and white wingman's helmet had been raised revealing a tanned face. He was unable to discern its individual features or whether it displayed any aggressive intent. The owner of the face waved to the armed men spread out in pairs below, then pulled something out of his breast pocket and threw it out to his right.

Two smallish dark objects tied closely together and attached to a fluttering blue streamer curved out of the sky and plummeted earthwards.

Harmer's trigger finger itched unbearably as the blue-winged ship passed silently overhead. He swore under his breath then barked into the mike mounted inside the chin guard of his helmet. "Hold your fire! Hold your fire!"

The intruder passed overhead and circled the tower again, his face turned towards the remote controlled tv cameras mounted on its roof.

Inside the Tactical Command Centre, Colonel Anderssen watched the same manoeuvre on the big screens mounted around the walls like windows; saw the pilot wave again as he flew past.

Anderssen spoke into her radio mike. "Sunray to Blue One. What did he drop?"

Harmer's voice came back in her ear, and over the speakers. "Nolan's retrieving it now."

One of the smaller telephoto lensed cameras was already onto Nolan. Deke Heywood switched the picture through onto Anderssen's console.

Nolan came on the air. "It's a flat rock, a piece of wood and a strip of blue solar-cell fabric from a Skyhawk. Hold on—there's something carved on here—'8902 Brickman, S.R.'—" Nolan turned the small roughly hewn piece of wood over. ". . . Don't shoot."

Deke turned to face Anderssen. "There was a wing-man called Brickman on The Lady from Louisiana. I met with him a couple of times when they made that supply run back in the spring. The reason I remember is because my guard-mother is also from Roosevelt Field and—" He waved away further explanation. "What I'm trying to say is—if it's the same guy, he's kin to the Provost-Marshal of New Mexico."

Anderssen knew enough about realities of life within the Federation to know that it was not wise to make irreparable errors of judgement when dealing with the kin of State Provost-Marshals. She spoke into the bar mike of her headset. "Sunray to Blue One. Matt, tell your men to lay down their guns and wave him in."

In response to their signals, the airborne intruder unhitched his legs from the rear harness straps, swooped down over the heads of Harmer's men, turned steeply and landed on his feet facing them. Using his helmet radio Harmer ordered the two squads to pick up their weapons. Holding his own rifle at the ready, he adopted a grim expression and doubled towards the blue-winged rig.

The flyer was holding it up by means of the control bar while he undid the straps around his chest and he was either unable to see Harmer's forbidding countenance behind the plexiglass face plate of his helmet, or was totally unfazed by it. He grinned broadly as Harmer approached and thrust out his hand. "Hi, how're you doing? Is this Pueblo?"

Harmer halted one pace from the outstretched hand, restrained the urgent impulse to sink the butt of his rifle into the grinning face and replied with a silent nod.

The flyer stepped clear of the blue-winged craft, punched the air vigorously and loosed a raucous rebel yell. "YeeehahHH—I made it!!" The exultant gesture lifted his feet off the ground. As he bounced back down he asked, "What day is it today?"

"Thursday, November 14th," replied Harmer, before he could stop himself. *Enjoy it,* he thought. *It could be your last.*

Line-Sergeant Nolan moved in to stand alongside Harmer. Nolan was a grizzled block-buster—a name given to Tracker pioneers who break ground and do the initial excavations for a way-station. At thirty-eight, he was ten years older than the lieutenant. He laid his rifle back over his shoulder but kept his fingers curled round the pistol butt and trigger. In his left hand he held the small stone-weighted slab of wood with its blue streamer. He ran his eyes over the flyer. His camouflaged fatigues were as patched and as clumsily sewn as the wings of his ship. "Our friend here looks happy . . ."

"Yeah," growled Harmer. "His brain must have gone

gammy." He spoke over his helmet radio to the linemen who now surrounded the motorless sky-ship. "Okay move this thing inside. Use the freight ramp."

The flyer called out to the linemen as they took hold of the ragged, fabric-covered wings. "Hey, fellas, go easy with that, okay? The White House may want to put it in the museum at Grand Central."

Harmer gripped his rifle so hard he almost squeezed the barrels out of shape. He found himself wishing he hadn't acknowledged Mary-Ann's instruction not to "damage" their visitor. "Shee, jack me," he breathed to Nolan. "This guy's got some nerve, hasn't he?"

"He's still treading air," replied Nolan. He addressed the flyer, his voice coming through the small external speaker grille on his helmet. "Okay, mister, we seem to have an identity problem here. You've got FAZZETTI written on your bone-dome and it says BRICKMAN on this piece of wood. Which one are you?"

The flyer pulled off his red and white helmet and snapped to attention. "8902 Brickman, *SAHH*! Posted wingman aboard The Lady from Louisiana April 20th, shot down while on active duty north east of Cheyenne June 12th, and now reporting for reassignment!" Freed from his helmet, the young man's wavy golden hair slowly unwound and fell about his neck and shoulders.

Lieutenant Harmer stared at the seven thin rat-tail plaits tied off with blue ribbon—three over one ear and four over the other—then exchanged a disbelieving glance with Nolan. Never, in all the years since he donned his first uniform at the age of three had Harmer been confronted by such an incongruous sight. "Columbus wept! Look at that hair! He's decked out like a fucking Mute!"

Nolan handed Harmer the weighted piece of wood, eased the rifle off his shoulder and aimed it at Brickman's chest. "Okay, mister, unstrap that knife you've got around your leg and drop it on the ground in front of you."

Brickman went down on one knee and began to unbuckle the straps that went through loops around his right trouser leg.

Harmer looked at the carved legend on the wood then

lobbed it into the hands of nearest lineman. "Kotcheff! Run that in to the Colonel!"

The lineman doubled away towards the bunker. Brickman stood up and dropped the knife and its scabbard at Nolan's feet. Harmer covered him while Nolan picked it up and read off the name stamped on the hilt. "Naylor's knife and Fazzetti's helmet. What else have you picked up on your travels?"

"Nothing."

Nolan slipped the knife into a side pocket on his trousers and jabbed the barrel of his rifle at Brickman. "Okay. Both hands on the back of your neck, fingers linked together."

Brickman raised his hands level with his shoulders then hesitated. "Don't you want to know what happened to me?"

Line-Sergeant Nolan waved the barrel of his rifle towards the bunker. "Just shut your mouth, and do like I said, mister."

The procedures for dealing with renegades had been made clear to everybody at Pueblo. Defaulters were not permitted to converse with the arresting party. Once the defaulter's identity had been established, he was to be addressed only with clear, concise orders. When captured the defaulter was to be searched, chained and hooded, and held in solitary confinement until he could be brought before the senior officer of the arresting unit. If the defaulter could not be so confined, a temporary speech restraint was to be applied; he was, in other words, to be gagged. If the orders given to a defaulter were not promptly obeyed he was to be "physically admonished." If the defaulter became violent, or attempted to escape from custody, he was to be subjected to "prejudicial constraint"—i.e., shot; another example of Grand Centralese.

Brickman raised his hands a little higher. "Hey, guys, listen—let's get one thing clear. I'm not a ren—" he broke off and tried to turn away as Harmer lunged forward, his rifle a moving blur.

The hard rubber butt of the lieutenant's rifle slammed into Brickman's right arm just below the shoulder muscle, hitting the nerve centre a paralysing blow. The force of the blow was calculated to cause the maximum pain without breaking any bones. Harmer followed through with the barrel, bringing it down hard on the left side of the neck where it joined the shoulder—another nerve centre. As Brickman arched his back under the blow, Harmer swung the rifle butt in for a kidney punch and stomped his heel down hard on the calf muscle of Brickman's right leg.

"Easy, Lieutenant," muttered Nolan. "The Colonel wants this one for questioning."

Brickman sank slowly to his knees, clutching his right arm. He gasped for breath. his face contorted with pain. Nolan had to hand it to him. A lot of guys would have been squealing by now. Harmer kicked him in the stomach, knocking him sideways. Brickman rolled onto his back. Harmer straddled him, stuck the rifle butt against his throat and pinned his head to the ground. "Okay, *mister*, it's *your* turn to get something clear. Nobody of junior rank addresses officers and senior noncoms at Pueblo as 'Hey, guys'. Secondly, I don't appreciate flying pieces of lumpshit like you from that fancy Academy trying to make my boys look like a bunch of assholes. And thirdly, "—Harmer dug the butt harder into Brickman's throat—"I don't like soldiers with ribbons in their hair. Do we understand one another?"

"Loud and clear, *sirr!*" gasped Brickman. He lay there tense but unresisting, trying to master the pain hammering through his body, his eyes fixed on Harmer.

Harmer knew that look; knew what it meant. He'd seen it often enough in the mirror. It came from hard-asses who didn't know when to quit. He lifted the butt of his rifle clear of Brickman's throat hoping he might say something. Anything that might provide the excuse to put a few dents in that pretty-boy face.

Mary-Ann's voice sounded quietly in his ear. "Sunray to Blue One. Okay, Matt, you've made your point. Just stand him up and walk him in. And make sure he doesn't trip up on his way down the ramp."

*   *   *

The first interview with the airborne intruder was held in
Mary-Ann's underground office, a sparsely furnished room
in the section known as Central HQ. Colonel Marie
Anderssen sat behind her desk flanked by her two senior
battalion officers, Major Roscoe and Major Hiller. The
piece of wood bearing Brickman's name, with its stone and
blue streamer, lay in front of her, laid parallel to the
standard issue combat knife he'd been carrying. The third
item that had been placed on the desk for her to look at
was the red wingman's helmet with the broad white lightning flash on either side. On the front, above the closed
dark bronze plexiglass visor, was the name "FAZZETTI"
and above that, the red, white and blue star and bar
insignia of the Federation. There was no blotter, scratch-
pad or document tray. Trackers didn't write things on
paper. They typed on keyboards and read tv screens. Set
at an angle on the left hand side of the desk was Anderssen's
personal monitor and keyboard; the indispensable link
with the rest of the Peublo way-station, and Grand Central.

Anderssen pressed a button that put her through to the
junior aide in the outer office. "Okay, wheel him in."

Lieutenant Harmer and Line-Sergeant Nolan entered,
saluted, and stood on either side of the door as Brickman
was marched in, closely escorted by two linemen. The
manacles round his wrists were attached by chains to steel
leg cuffs fitted below each knee. The chains were long
enough to allow a prisoner to bring his forearms level with
the ground when standing, and to be able to eat or wipe
his ass when sitting down; the chain linking the cuffs
below each knee allowed him to walk but not run. His
head was covered by a black hood tied with a draw string
around his neck.

Nolan filled the room with his voice. "Defaulter and
escort—HALT!" The heels thudded down in unison. "Ess-
corrrt, disss-MISS!"

Anderssen nodded as the two linemen saluted, about-
faced and marched smartly from the room. Nolan removed
the prisoner's hood and stepped back, heels thudding
together as he came to attention.

"At ease, gentlemen," said Anderssen. "You too, Brickman."

Brickman, blinked rapidly in the bright light and gulped air. Anderssen studied the young man. Like Harmer, she found the long hair with its seven ribboned plaits rather hard to take. In the Federation the haircuts fitted in with the general Marine boot-camp atmosphere; crew-cuts or short bobs were the only styles allowed. Only Mutes had long, weird hair-dos; Mutes and cee-bees. But that was something the base barber could fix inside fifteen minutes. Anderssen mentally deleted the hair and noted with approval his tanned, well-boned face with its strong lean jaw, his clear blue eyes, square shoulders and slim-hipped body. This was the kind of man she liked to bunk down with in the few off-duty hours she allowed herself. This one was strictly off-limits. Never mind. There were quite a few of them at Pueblo; rock-hard jack-dandies that knew how to thump the tub. Not all as good-looking as this boy, but close enough to pass muster in the half-light.

Anderssen fingered the piece of wood on which Brickman had carved his name, looked up at him and nodded at the video monitor. "We've been on the wire to The Lady. They confirm that an 8902 Brickman, S.R. was posted aboard at Nixon/Fort Worth on the date you claim. The same wingman was also listed PD/ET on June 12th following an engagement with a strong force of Plainfolk Mutes northeast of Cheyenne. Naylor and Fazzetti, wingmen from the same section were also listed PD/ET the same day."

"PD/ET" was Tracker shorthand for "Power down/Enemy territory"; a crash—with predictably fatal results—during combat operations over Mute country.

Anderssen entered a three-digit number on the keyboard. Deke Haywood's face appeared on the tv monitor. "Deke—have you managed to raise Grand Central yet?"

"No, sir-ma'am. We're still having a problem with that. I've had to route the signal via Roosevelt/Santa Fe."

"Okay. Let me know the moment you receive that voice- and palm-print data." Anderssen cleared the screen and looked up at Brickman. "In the meantime, we'll as-

sume you are who you say you are." She looked past him
at Lieutenant Harmer. "Did anything else turn up during
the body search?"

"No sir-ma'am. All there is is what's on the table."

Anderssen's eyes met Brickman's; noted the shrewd,
intelligent gaze that met her own; direct, unflinching. "No
ID-card?"

"No sir-ma'am." He spread his palms in an apologetic
gesture, arms moving as far as the chains would allow. "I
lost everything except the clothes I'm standing up in."

Anderssen cast an eye back to the tv monitor where the
details supplied by the wagon-train were displayed. "You
went down on June 12th . . ." she mused. "It's now November 14th. Where have you been and what have you
been doing for the last five months?"

It was the question Brickman had been dreading as he
had sheltered in the high places on his journey south,
waiting for a threatening storm to pass, or for a favourable
wind. Perched precariously on mountain ledges, he had
thought long and hard about this moment, working out
exactly what he would say, how much he would reveal.

He had done so because he knew his reply was bound to
lead to a great many other questions; questions which,
depending on his answers, could transform his interrogation into a matter of life or death. He could not tell the
whole truth because many of those in positions of power
would find his story not only incredible but also totally
unacceptable. What had happened to him, the things he
had witnessed, what he now knew to be the truth ran
contrary to everything he had been taught as a child of the
Federation; what he had discovered challenged even the
received wisdom of the First Family.

Anderssen frowned. "Did you hear what I asked you?"

"Uh, yes, sir-ma'am." Brickman took a deep breath and
jumped in the deep end. "I was taken prisoner by the
Mutes. Plainfolk. The clan M'Call."

Colonel Anderssen exchanged a glance with her two
battalion officers then addressed Lieutenant Harner and
Line-Sergeant Nolan. They looked as surprised as she did.
"Matt, Jake—"

Harmer and Nolan leapt to attention.

"You didn't hear the defaulter answer my question. Is that understood?"

"Loud and clear, sir-ma'am!" they chorussed.

"Okay, wait outside. I'll call if we have any problems."

Harmer and Nolan saluted and left. Harmer didn't slam the door but he shut it with sufficient vehemence to convey his annoyance at being dismissed just when things were getting interesting.

Anderssen had her reasons. If what Brickman had said was true, the fewer people that knew about it the better. She ran her fingers along the streamer of blue-solar-cell fabric, smoothing it flat against the desk top, then looked up at Brickman. "Mutes don't take prisoners."

"They do now," replied Brickman.

Anderssen turned to Major Hiller. "Jerri—get a chair for this young man. And grab a couple for yourselves. Oh, and here—" She handed the red and white helmet to Major Roscoe, "—put this junk somewhere."

Roscoe cleared Anderssen's desk, laying the bits and pieces on a shelf.

Anderssen gazed at Brickman squarely. "I'd like to draw your attention to the two framed Unit Citations on the wall behind me. They were awarded to this battalion because, here at Pueblo, we run things by The Book. That means, until your story checks out, you will be held as a suspected cee-bee, subject to the conditions and restraints laid down in the Manual. In other words you will be kept in chains, in solitary confinement, and you will be hooded whenever you are removed from your cell. The lieutenant in charge of the welcome home party is a good man but inclined to be over-zealous. Apparently, it was something you said. I will not permit any unwarranted maltreatment but you should know that I and my fellow officers share his dislike for code-breakers. If that's what you turn out to be, you'll go the wall—either here, or at Grand Central. If it's here, *I'll* be there to give the order to fire. Is that understood?"

"Loud and clear, sir-ma'am!"

"Okay. Sit down." Anderssen's face softened a little. "You look like you had a rough trip."

"It was worth it, ma'am." Brickman sat down, keeping his back straight and his head up like a freshman during Induction at the Flight Academy.

Interesting, thought Anderssen. The usual disciplined reaction to authority but a distinct lack of awe. A typical NewMex wingman. But there was something else that was different about this young man. A winner, certainly. But it was more than that. Anderssen found it hard to define but, if pressed, she would have said that Brickman exuded a subtle air of natural superiority, of latent unstoppable power. The kind that could take a man right to the top.

The light on her tv monitor flashed as Deke Haywood appeared on screen. "Brickman's ID-data just came down the wire from Grand Central. I've put it on the converter. We can run a voice- and palm-print match anytime from now."

Anderssen pressed the button that put her picture on the screen in front of Deke. "Okay, I'll get back to you on that."

"There's just one thing, ma'am. His record contains a Level Nine entry."

Anderssen caught her breath. "Okay, put it through."

Information transmitted over the video networks controlled by COLUMBUS was graded into different levels of confidentiality. The level of access was controlled by the magnetically coded ID-sensor card carried by every Tracker. The card was upgraded with each promotion, or when an individual was awarded extra privileges or assumed a post with extra responsibilities. As a colonel in command of an important way-station, Anderssen had Level Nine access.

Deke wiped himself off the screen and put up a section of the file on Brickman transmitted, via Roosevelt/Santa Fe, by COLUMBUS, the giant, omniscient computer that functioned as the brain and the central nervous system of the Federation.

Anderssen pulled the box hood out of the casing around the tv, blocking off the screen from her two battalion officers, now seated on either side of the desk. Pulling out her ID-card, she slipped it into the slot provided and spoke to the machine. "5824 Anderssen. Print-out please."

There was a brief pause as the network matched her voice print to the one on file then a new bottom line appeared on the screen.

It consisted of two letters, a four digit serial number, then two more letters: ST-3552-RX. Brief, but highly significant. "ST" stood for "Selective Treatment"; "RX" for "Refer to Executive"; the number merely indicated Brickman's position on the "ST" list.

Anderssen pressed the Card Eject button, causing the ST code to vanish from the screen. She put her ID back into its protective wallet and slid the box hood back into the casing. It had been a close call. Fortunately, good old Deke had spotted that Level Nine entry before she had gone any further. An "RX" rating meant that no administrative action affecting the subject was to be initiated without reference to the White House at Houston/GC.

The First Family had plans for Steven Roosevelt Brickman.

TWO

COLUMBUS had been programmed to alert the White House to any enquiry relating to personnel records carrying an "RX" tag. As it sent the data down the line to Pueblo, it simultaneously reported the fact to Central Records Control—a unit under the direct supervision of members of the First Family occupying twenty floors, each the size of a football pitch, containing line after line of tv screens and keyboards that were manned round the clock. Notification of the Triple-R—a Restricted Record Request— was flashed on the screen of an operator in the section dealing exclusively with the Selective Treatment List.

The White House was quick to confirm its continuing interest in 8902 Brickman, S.R. The transmission of his voice-print data was followed by a "Your Eyes Only" videogram to Colonel Anderssen. Brickman was not, repeat not, to be interrogated. No one from his home base was to be allowed near him or to learn of his presence. Apart from the briefest orders or instructions, no one else was to converse with him. Once positively identified, he was to be examined by the way-station doctor who was to report on his general state of health. He was then to be held incommunicado until arrangements could be made for his transfer. Until that time he was to be treated as a suspected code-breaker—with two exceptions: he was not

24

to be "boxed," and he was not to be "physically admonished." To use a pre-Holocaust term, Brickman was clearly a hot potato—a vegetable that no one in the Federation had tasted for nigh on a thousand years.

Anderssen was not, by nature, nervous but she knew she would not rest easy until Brickman was off her hands. She had been right to dismiss Harmer and Nolan at the first mention of imprisonment by the Mutes. If the news got out, it could have an adverse effect on the morale of combat units. It was, she supposed, only natural that Grand Central would want to analyse all the implications first, but—godammit—she was a front-line way-station commander! Surely she should be allowed to know what was going on out there?

Anderssen paced around her private quarters trying to control her frustration. No wonder that mother Harmer had slammed the door. She knew how he felt. She turned and slammed both fists down hard on the long table at which she occasionally dined with her fellow officers. It helped restore a measure of outward calm. All in good time, she told herself. Grand Central would assess the facts then FINTEL—Field Intelligence—would circulate a report to all interested parties. The fact that Brickman claimed to have been held prisoner for nearly five months before escaping was not going to change anything. It hadn't stopped bands of Mutes attacking work-parties around Pueblo during the summer. And it wouldn't stop Trackers killing Mutes.

Brickman's achievement in building an aircraft from cannibalised parts was remarkable but if, as Marie Anderssen surmised, he had put it together under the noses of his captors, it meant that the Plainfolk Mutes were ever dumber than their Southern brothers, the scattered remnants of which had been rounded up and herded into work-camps; the penultimate phase of the pacification programme for the overground: the ultimate phase—annihilation—would come when there was no more Mute poison in the air.

Anderssen knew the words of the Fourth Inspirational off by heart. It was a video she often drew comfort from in moments of doubt; those moments in the twilight gloom,

alone in her bunk, when she began to wonder, to ask . . .
she shook the memory from her mind, turned towards the
big picture of the President-General that hung on the wall
beyond the far end of the table and let his message echo
through her mind. Yes! That day *would* come! When the
way-station bunkers would empty and everyone in the
Federation would emerge from their bases within the
earth-shield to repossess their birthright: the blue-sky world
the Mutes had stolen from them.

That was the promise made by the First Family, founders of the Amtrak Federation and generation after generation of Trackers had laboured and sweated unceasingly to
help make it come true; had willingly laid down their lives
on overground operations. Their efforts had not been wasted.
The dream which inspired those who had gone before was
almost within grasp. The children of the children born to
the guard-mothers of Anderssen's generation would live
under the open skies; would see sunrise, moondark; would
feel the rain on their faces—not just see it splash against
their visors or hear it drum on their helmets; would cleanse
the overground; would wipe every last Mute off the face of
the earth and build the New America.

It was more than a dream. It could happen. But not
until the mass of Trackers who resided in the earthshield
were able to overcome their dread of the vast open spaces.
Not to worry. The First Family was working on that. The
Amtrak Federation had come a long way since its founding
father, George Washington Jefferson the 1st, had gathered the faithful Four Hundred around him and nursed
them through the Long Night—the traumatic aftermath of
the Holocaust.

In the beginning, the Federation had consisted of nothing more than a few scattered holes in the ground on the
southern edge of the nation state once known as the United
States of America. That country had been burned to the
ground, sacked and ravaged by an unstoppable horde of
Mutes—deformed, half-idiot mutants who in an orgy of
destruction had unleashed a poisonous cloud of radiation,
which had killed millions of Good Ole Boys—the affection-

ate nickname for the Trackers' ancestors—and forced the handful of survivors to take refuge within the earthshield.

The recovery had begun deep in the earth under the shattered city of Houston, in an underground base built to house and power COLUMBUS. Renamed Grand Central by George Washington Jefferson the 1st, the first President-General, it became the permanent home of the First Family. Although none of the pre-Holocaust states now existed as legal, social or economic entities, their historic boundaries and names had been retained. Texas, the focal point of the Federation, became known as the Inner State. As time passed the underground empire had expanded, establishing bases under Oklahoma, Arkansas, New Mexico, Louisiana, Mississippi, and Arizona. These were called the Outer States. Kansas and Colorado, the latest additions, had been designated New Territories, in 2886 and 2954, the year Anderssen had been born. New Territory was an oblique way of saying that the state was not yet under Federation control. There was a small, growing Tracker base in the earthshield under Wichita, Kansas, that would eventually house a full division; in Colorado, there was only the way-station at Pueblo manned by Anderssen's pioneer battalion. The Federation might have laid claim to the whole of Colorado but, for all practical purposes, Pueblo—situated in the southern quarter of the state—marked the frontier; the northern limit of the Federation's over-ground fief. Beyond that lay enemy territory. Mute country or, as they themselves liked to regard it, the Land of the Plainfolk.

The trouble was, the Mutes didn't recognise frontiers. For a race that was supposed to be sub-human, they were both cunning and tenacious. They had this unshakeable idea that the overground belonged to them. And so they kept coming back and getting themselves killed. Anderssen assumed it must be because of the brain-damage that had been passed down from their ancestors. Too dumb to learn. But not dumb enough, reflected Anderssen. Their inability to remember was one of a long list of Mute failings that had been hammered into her since Junior Leaders school but the bastards still knew their way around.

Groups of lumpheads would infiltrate the so-called "paci-
fied areas" of the Outer States and make sneak attacks on
overground work-parties, supply trains and guard posts in
the mills and process plants. The network of way-stations,
set up at strategic points was supposed to halt these
incursions.

Over the centuries since the Holocaust, Mutes had shown
themselves to be totally immune to the radiation that
blanketed the over-ground; in fact, they seemed to thrive
on it despite the mounting yearly body-counts filed by
Trail-Blazer expeditions. Mutes lived, on average, twice as
long as Trackers and were said to outnumber them by over
fifty to one. At the last census, in 2985, the Tracker
population was just under 450,000—which meant that, if
FINTEL had gotten its facts right for once, there were
over twenty-two *million* Mutes spread across the landscape!

Privately, Anderssen found it hard to believe. She was
not insensible to certain attractive aspects of the overground
but, in general, it was a vast, forbidding place. She had
been out there, many times over a period of years, and
had never seen more than five or six hundred Mutes at
one time. Someone on her staff had found a good name for
it. The Big Open. The place was empty! That had been,
and still was, her overriding impression. A silent land,
where danger lurked, ready to trap the unwary; a sleeping
land, waiting patiently over the centuries for the return of
its rightful owners. If there were twenty-two million Mutes
out there you wouldn't be able to walk ten yards without
tripping over one of them.

Anderssen's doubt were not shared by Grand Central.
Faced with such alarming estimates of the size of the
opposition, it was not surprising that the top priority task
of the Federation's overground forces was to bring the
total Mute population under control by continuing the
programme of pacification that had been launched soon
after the Break-Out in 2465. Pioneers from way-stations
like Pueblo and Trail-Blazers from the roving wagon-trains—
like the one Brickman had served on—played their part by
conducting what, in Grand-Centralese, were called "fire-
sweeps"; scorched-earth operations in which every possi-

ble resource that might provide Mutes with food and shelter was methodically destroyed and every animal within range of the patrol's guns was killed. Mutes, themselves, were at the top of the target list. Whenever the tactical conditions permitted, the young males and females were rounded up to replenish the labour force in the overground work camps; the rest, the old and the very young, were liquidated.

It was a grisly, messy business in which Anderssen herself had participated while working her way up through the ranks. But it had to be done. Everyone knew that. That was what they had been raised to do. In the Federation you obeyed orders. You didn't ask why. Anderssen was a typical product of the Federation. She was a good soldier; a tough commander. But sometimes she asked herself questions for which there were no easy answers. Questions she had tried repeatedly to dismiss but which kept returning to niggle away at her iron resolution.

Occasionally, the pressures would pile up and become too hard to handle. For those particularly difficult moments when even the honeyed voice of the P-G intoning the Fourth Inspirational was not enough to take the heat off, Anderssen had her own private escape hatch. Taped to the back of the big portrait of George Washington Jefferson the 31st was a precious cache of rainbow grass taken from a cee-bee who had gone to the wall for being dumb enough to be caught trying to smuggle it into the way-station from a wagon-train making its usual quarterly supply run. Officially, the evidence was supposed to have been burned after the summary trial but way-station commanders, if they are sharp, can sometimes fix these things. Anderssen came into this category. Despite her outward, solidly conformist, slightly plodding demeanour, she didn't miss a trick. In the underground bases within the Federation, even line-colonels had to keep looking over their shoulder. Everyone had to. But in the front line—despite what she had said for Brickman's benefit— you could bend the rules a little. Well—some of the rules. As Anderssen would occasionally remark in private—why the heck else would a guy break her ass to make colonel?

Only Major Jerri Hiller, Anderssen's closest companion and the only other woman at Pueblo above the rank of lieutenant was in on the secret. Anderssen had shared the illicit grass with Hiller for close on a year now. It was a Code One offence but she had enough on the blue-eyed Major to know she would not turn rat-fink and call in the Provost-Marshals.

Mutes smoked rainbow grass in pipes. Anderssen didn't have one. Most Trackers who smoked grass rolled it up in a certain kind of dried leaf. Anderssen also had a supply of those. The inch or so of dead space created by the frame backing made an ideal hiding place. The President-General's holographic portrait was a permanent fixture in every living- and work-space throughout the Federation. And while similar pictures were addressed thrice-daily by Tracker pioneers intoning the Prayer to the First Family, no one actually *looked* at it. And it was extremely unlikely that anybody would think of moving the one in Anderssen's office.

Unless you were the colonel and needed to get to something behind it.

Anderssen lifted the picture frame out of its four wall clips, pulled off the pouch taped to the back then repositioned it. Under the benign gaze of the white-haired President-General, she carefully rolled a leaf around a portion of grass to make what Trail-Blazers called a "reaf," took a hot wire coil from the same pouch, plugged it into a power socket till it glowed red then lit up. She took a deep, calming draw, raised the reaf to Jefferson the 31st in an ironic salute then sauntered through to her sleeping quarters. Dropping the light level down as far as it would go, Anderssen stretched out on her bunk in the semi-darkness and burned off some more grass. She felt a lot happier. The frustrations that had built up inside her after getting the "hands-off" order on Brickman began to fade. What the heck! Let those gold-braided sacks of lumpshit at Grand Central find out the bad news. Maybe it might take the crease out of their pants.

The wall of her bed-space began to change colour and curve outwards. A pleasant numbness spread through her body. The unending pressure of her tightly regimented, claustrophobic existence eased; the problems of maintaining the high level of motivation and discipline required by Grand Central ceased to exist; the blood-stained images of dead lumpheads and mutilated Trackers that littered her own private landscape of death no longer pressed on her inner eye. The octagonal light panels in the low ceiling glowed and sparkled of their own accord; moved upwards away from her—as if she was inside an expanding balloon— then exploded silently into a thousand pieces. The fragments receded; became a carpet of stars.

It was the moment known to Trail-Blazers as "tunnelling out"; the Happy Time . . .

Two days later, following another videogram from Grand Central, three silver-blue Skyhawks with red-tipped wings and a similar craft camouflaged in red, black and brown like the wagon-trains approached Pueblo from the north east and asked for permission to land. Seated in his alloted place at the main console, Deke Haywood tracked them with a wide-angle tv camera; saw them circle above the watch-tower in tight diamond formation then drop down, one by one, to land into the wind on the south side of the bunker.

Deke's interest was aroused by their appearance. Pueblo had received an equipment update depicting the new Mark Two Skyhawk that was being tested operationally, but this was the first time Deke had seen one for real. Instead of the sweptback inflated wing, these new aircraft had rigid constant chord wings with a straight leading edge, a cruciform tail mounted on a boom above the pusher engine, and a streamlined transparent cover over the previously open cockpit. The whole appearance was sleeker, more powerful, more deadly. The camouflaged aircraft—the last to land—was different again. It had a tubby fuselage pod and as it came into close-up on screen, Deke saw it was a side-by-side two-seater.

The aircraft had been flown off the illustrious Red River wagon-train. Better known by its semi-official nickname of Big Red One, its combat record over the last eighty years was unequalled. It was the Federation's number one killing machine and every Trail-Blazer with an ounce of ambition aspired to serve aboard her at some time during their overground career.

Wyman, the fair-haired, crew-cut wingman leading the airborne guard detail, saluted Anderssen with impeccable precision and handed over the small, floppy-disc file containing a copy of the orders concerning Brickman's transfer. Anderssen passed the disc to Jerri Hiller who loaded it into the drive slot of the electronics module that sat under the VDU, ran a validity test, then screened its contents.

Anderssen quickly scanned the one page movement order. The four wing-men from Big Red One were to be Brickman's escort as far as Roosevelt/Santa Fe. Buried deep under the desert of New Mexico, it was the nearest base linked by shuttle to Grand Central. Brickman was to ride, hooded and chained, in the two-seater. At Santa Fe, Brickman was to be handed over to the Provost-Marshal's office from where he would proceed to Houston/GC. The skyship he had constructed in captivity was to be sent back aboard the next wagon-train calling at Pueblo.

Steve Brickman leapt to his feet and stood to attention as the door to his cell opened. Three Deputy Provost-Marshals entered; a fourth held himself at the ready in the corridor outside. Two of the Provos carried out the routine check to see that the manacles on Steve's wrists and legs were still securely fastened; the third, toting the standard lead-weighted rubber truncheon, stayed two paces back ready to deal with any trouble.

Following his initial interview, Steve had found himself in the way-station hospital where he was ordered to strip. After an initial, violent hose-down, he had been thoroughly scrubbed from head to foot by two masked, rubber-gloved para-medics. They had allowed him to undo his blue ribboned plaits and wash his own hair. He had then been examined in almost total silence by Pueblo's surgeon-captain. Afterwards he had gotten the same blank wall treatment when he had been issued with clean cotton undergarments, a new pair of combat boots, and a set of black fatigues—the mark of a defaulter. They had a broad diagonal yellow cross on the front and back you could spot a mile off—and which also made a good aiming point. Once dressed, he had been immediately put back into chains and taken down to the cells.

Steve hadn't given any trouble then and wasn't planning on causing any now but he was fast becoming extremely pissed off. He had expected a cautious reception at Pueblo but once he had landed and made his identity known he had not expected to be treated like a renegade. Christopher Columbus—he'd come back of his own accord, hadn't he?!

One of the DPs produced the hood and slipped it over Steve's head, plunging him into total darkness. He felt himself grasped by each arm. "Okay, move it."

Steve was aware of retracing the same route he'd been marched along before. It led to Anderssen's office. A right turn out of the cell, one hundred paces, a flight of twenty stairs, left turn, thirty paces, into an elevator and up. Could be three floors . . . hard to tell. Out of the lift, another thirty paces straight ahead, right turn, into some kind of outer office. Stop. Voices, murmuring muffled, tantalisingly indistinct. A second door opening. A faint fragrance permeated the air inside the hood. A sharp command from someone close by. "Okay, mister—straighten up!"

The same voice formally reported his presence to Anderssen and he was given the order to stand at ease. Steve did the best he could; the chain between his wrists was not long enough to allow him to put his hands in the regulation position behind his back. He heard his escort march out. As the door shut behind them, the hood was loosened and removed in one swift movement by Major Roscoe, leaving Steve blinking rapidly in the bright light.

Anderssen was seated behind her desk, flanked by the blonde, broad-hipped major she had previously addressed as "Jerri." The last time around, Steve had noticed that the major was packing a size fourteen ass into size twelve trousers. The result was some badly overstressed seams and the kind of shape that could make your attention wander. Steve could not help thinking that, for a unit that was supposed to be run by The Book, it was a curious departure from the rules of dress which stipulated that the standard-issue unisex jump-suits and fatigues should be loose-fitting.

"Good news, Brickman," said Anderssen, with a touch of disdain in her voice. "Grand Central has taken over your case. You ship out today for Roosevelt/Santa Fe. By air." She saw the change in his expression. "Don't get excited. You're travelling as a passenger."

Passenger? Steve's curiosity was aroused. Since when had there been two-seater Skyhawks?

Anderssen stood up. "Good luck, Brickman. I don't know what it is you're supposed to have done but I hope you get away with it."

"Thank you, sir-ma'am."

Anderssen nodded at Major Roscoe. "Okay, black him out."

Roscoe pulled the hood down over Steve's head and tightened the draw-string. The door opened, boots thudded across the floor, and Steve was seized by the arms and quick-marched out of the office.

Anderssen turned to her pet major. "Jerri, I know Brickman was decontaminated by the medics soon after he got here but I don't want to take any chances. Christopher knows what kind of contagious filth he might have picked up from the Mutes. I want this office sterilised along with every other place he's been. Especially his cell. Make sure the floor, walls and ceiling are steam-cleaned and swabbed with disinfectant. The mattress, the quilt, and anything else he's been handling should be burned." She inspected the front and backs of her hands and wrinkled her nose in distaste. "If I'd known beforehand where he'd been I would never have touched any of his things. Must have had at least six showers in the last two days. Almost scrubbed myself raw." She looked up at Hiller. "What did he use to eat with?"

"Don't worry. It was all disposable. And the air in that cell block is vented separately to the main supply."

"Okay. Get on it—including anything I've forgotten."

Anderssen paused reflectively. "Actually, after he'd washed out those goddam plaits that long hair of his didn't look so bad."

"No," said Hiller. "I quite liked it."

Anderssen reached out and ran her fingertips through the hair over Hiller's right ear. "Maybe you could try growing yours a little longer."

"Yes," said Hiller. She smoothed her hair back into place. "I'll think about it."

Steve lost his bearings after leaving Anderssen's office but he knew he was outside the bunker when he felt the earth under his feet and the smell of the grass filtered through the light-proof vents in his hood.

"Okay," said a voice. "Put your feet together and bend your knees forward. We're gonna lift you into the aircraft." Three pairs of hands grabbed hold of him and hoisted him into the air. Another pair of hands guided his feet down under what he visualised was the instrument panel. He felt them touch the floor. "Okay, siddown."

Steve sat. Hands pulled the straps of the safety harness over his shoulders and thighs, clipped them into the quick release buckle then adjusted the tension so that he was held down firmly.

"Now put your wrists together," said the voice.

Steve offered up his manacled wrists. Another chain was passed around his wrists, drawing his wrists, drawing his hands tightly together and towards the right-hand side of the cockpit. He heard the snap of a padlock closing. "Okay. Don. he's stowed away nice and tight."

Don . . .?

Steve aimed his head up to the right. "What happens if we have to get out in a hurry?"

A hand patted him on the head and a new voice said, "I guess it means that you don't, good buddy."

Terrific . . .

"Okay, let's go," said the first voice. "We've done the map plot, so you know the course heading. We'll fly a loose diamond at three thousand feet. 70 per cent power after climbout. You lead, Don. I'll take the number two starboard station. Joe, number three to port, Tony, you sit on our tail."

Steve heard the others murmur their assent. "What's the Santa Fe channel?" asked a third voice. Steve caught his breath as he recognised it. Come on—it couldn't be . . .

"Tower frequency is Channel Ten. I'll give you the switch when we clear Pueblo."

Steve felt someone settling into the left-hand seat. He spoke into the enveloping darkness. "Is that you, Don? Don Lundkwist?"

"Yeah, that's me," said the voice, with a hint of surprise. "Who's under there?"

Steve laughed. "It's me! Steve! Steve Brickman."

"Christopher Columbus," muttered Lundkwist. "I thought you were dead! Listen, hold it down—we'll talk later." The electric motor burst into life with a loud *vrooomm* as she pressed the button on the dash. A few minutes later they were airborne.

How amazing, reflected Steve. Of all people. His escort on the first leg of his journey was to be Donna Monroe Lundkwist. The last time he'd seen her had been in his shack at the Flight Academy on Graduation Day. Lying naked alongside him on the bunk. With his guard-father asleep right beside them in his wheelchair.

A quarter of an hour into the flight, after they'd levelled off, Lundkwist removed Steve's hood. As his eyes adjusted to the light he saw to his surprise that they were seated under a streamlined plexiglass canopy. All the Skyhawks Steve had ever seen were open-cockpit models. He took in the view. The weather was good, the sky blue, with scattered alto cumulus and you could see for ever. In an ordinary Skyhawk, Steve might have been frozen stiff but with a closed canopy and the blower on, they were snugly insulated from the cold, mid-November air. "What do they call this thing?"

"A Skyrider," said Lundkwist. She was wearing a white bone-dome with a bold red figure one on either side and she had the dark face-visor raised. Her shoulders were squarer, her face leaner and harder than when he had last seen it. She smiled. "You may find this hard to believe but even with the hood on I thought there was something familiar. I felt sure I recognised the hands . . .

"You got a good memory."

"For some things, yeah . . ." Lundkwist gave him a sidelong look then broke away to search the sky ahead.

Steve eyed the silver-threaded Minuteman badge sewn on her tunic, the top award given to the most outstanding senior cadet. It was a sharp reminder that he had been the victim of a shadowy conspiracy. Steve Brickman had set out to come in first in his year at the Flight Academy and for three years he had totally dedicated himself to pursuing that goal with relentless determination. Brickman *knew* that he was the best cadet in his year but instead of being awarded the two highly prized graduation honours and top marks in the final examinations they had gone to Lundkwist. Never mind. He had mastered his disappointment but he had not forgotten or forgiven his humiliation. He now had a new goal that would be just as rewarding. He planned to destroy Lundkwist—and all the others who had conspired to give her the prize that had been rightfully his. Sooner or later, one by one, they would all get it.

But she would be the first.

He smiled at her. "Good to see you."

"You too. The word at Fort Worth was that you'd powered down last June."

"Just goes to show you shouldn't believe everything you hear. Steve nodded towards the black hood that now lay on his lap. "Are you sure it's okay to take that thing off? Supposing the other guys see me—and make trouble?"

Lundkwist smiled. "Relax. Rick Wyman said it would be okay. In fact he suggested it. We're all from Big Blue—right?"

"I hadn't thought of it that way. Thanks." Big Blue was the graduates nickname for the Flight Academy at Lindberg Field—buried fifteen hundred feet down under the sands of New Mexico.

Lundkwist eyed him. "Incredible. We knew we were picking up a wingman but I had no idea it was going to turn out to be you under that hood. Christopher—the idea

of you as a cee-bee is really hard to take on board. It just
. . . doesn't make sense!"

Steve shrugged. "It must be somebody." He gazed out
through the canopy and wondered if Lundkwist's presence
was just pure coincidence or whether—because they knew
each other—she had been sent to pump him. Maybe even
the removal of his hood as a gesture of solidarity was all
part of the business. Whatever the answer, if Lundkwist
was hoping to trap him into revealing some code-breaking
indiscretion she would discover it had been a wasted journey. During his five months as a prisoner of the Mutes,
something had snapped. His previous automatic, almost
robotic, responses to the military style discipline that gov-
erned the thoughts and behaviour of everyone within the
Federation had gone. He had realised it from the moment
Harmer, the pudgy-faced lieutenant had rushed out of the
way-station with his heavily armed men and had tried to
haul him in on a line.

From early childhood, Steve had become adept at concealing his true feelings. He had used that skill to exploit
the system to his own advantage but he had, nevertheless,
believed in the system wholeheartedly. That certainty had
now evaporated; his time with the Mutes had exposed the
Federation's weaknesses; had made him aware that he
wanted something other than what it had to offer. He was
not yet sure exactly what that "something other" was. He
only knew that he wanted things *his* way. Now that he was
back, he would say and do the right things but, from here
on in, it would be nothing more than an elaborate game.

Even so, Steve was under no illusions. This was no
inconsequential battle of wits or abstract triumph of will.
He was about to pit himself against the collective might of
the Federation and the all-pervading power of the First
Family.

This game was for real; a deadly contest in which the
slightest false move could cost him his life.

"I've got your gear in the back. Naylor's knife and
Fazetti's helmet. Did Lou—?"

"Yeah. He went into the meat business." And not just
metaphorically, thought Steve. Every time Steve had seen

that helmet it conjured up the image of Fazetti's impaled head. In all the time he'd been a prisoner, he'd never found out what the M'Calls had done with the body and he'd tried not to dwell on the possibility that bits of Fazzetti might have ended up in one of the thick hot-flavoured stews his captors had fed him with.

Looking back over his shoulder, he surveyed the aircraft formation on their starboard wing and noted the dramatic change in its appearance. "What are you guys flying—Red River Specials?"

Lundkwist smiled. "The Mark Two Skyhawk. Part of a batch delivered for field trials."

"What happened to the rifle mount above the cockpit?"

"We've got a fixed, forward firing set-up called Thor instead. Six revolving barrels, motor driven and drum fed, delivering twelve hundred rounds a minute."

"Smokin' lumpshit! Is this one armed too?"

"No, this is just a delivery truck."

Steve jerked his head towards the cockpit canopy. "This must be great for keeping out the rain. How well does it stand up to Mute crossbow bolts?"

"Depends on the range. It won't stop a bolt hitting it more or less dead on—say eighty or ninety degrees—but if the strike is at an angle of seventy degrees or under it tends to bounce off. But that's not all, we've got light-weight armoured panels made from some new composite under the floor, around the sides and the behind the seat."

Steve gazed around the cockpit and shook his head. "Pilot armour, six-barrelled guns, canopies—" He glanced back up over his shoulder at the ribbed starboard wing, "—a totally new method of construction. It's too much to handle."

"You're forgetting you've been out of circulation for five months."

"So what? Come on, Don, you know as well as I do they haven't even changed the *nut* sizes on the Skyhawk in the last fifty years! And now suddenly, all this—" Steve swept his eyes over the cockpit. "Doesn't it strike you as amazing?"

"Yeah, fantastic," said Lundkwist. "But I don't see what

you're getting at. You know what Federation policy is—'If it works, you don't change it.' Going up against the Plainfolk Mutes showed us the old Skyhawk was too vulnerable. You guys aboard The Lady found that out the hard way."

"Yeah . . ." Steve thought back to the bloody battle in the flooded river bed.

"And we lost a few guys during the summer too. That's what's so wonderful about the First Family. Right from the very beginning, they've always provided us with the right tools, the right equipment and technology to enable us to the job they ask of us."

"They've certainly been busy," admitted Steve. "How many of the wagon-trains have got the new model your friends are flying?"

"Right now, nobody else but us. They're still gearing up the new production line at Reagan/Lubbock."

Steve eyed her with a touch of resentment. "So meanwhile, the rest of the guys are flying garbage . . ."

Lundkwist smiled. "You know how it is with Big Red One. It's the outfit that gets the best of everything."

"Don't remind me."

Lundkwist checked the sky around them then glanced back at Steve. "How did you get into this mess?"

"Good question. I got shot down over Wyoming and was made a prisoner by the Mutes. It's a long story but finally, after five months, I managed to escape."

Lundkwist frowned. "But—"

"Yeah, I know what you're going to say. 'Mutes don't take prisoners.' That's what everyone keeps telling me."

"And you mean you were out there, with them, for *five whole months?* How come you're still in one piece?"

"That's another good question. You tell me. Trouble is I have a feeling that if you came up with the right answer you might find yourself at the top of the Most Wanted List."

Lundkwist looked across at him. "I'm not quite sure what you mean."

"Neither do I. Forget it."

"So how did it happen?"

"Gus White and I were fire-bombing some Mute

cropfields north of Cheyenne. I got hit by a cross-bow bolt, lost control—and spun in from about three hundred feet."

"How did you manage when they, uh—touched you?"

"How d'you mean?"

"Well, y'know how it is with lumpheads. They have diseased skins. You got hit by a crossbow bolt and fell out of the sky. Was that when they grabbed you?"

"Yeah. I broke a few things here and there and couldn't move. A couple of them pulled me out of the wreckage and took me to this old, uh, lumphead who was some kind of medicine man. He patched me up."

"Ughhh, shit . . ." Lundkwist's face wrinkled up with disgust at the idea. Trackers were raised from birth to believe that skin to skin contact with Mutes could cause their own flesh to rot. Gangrenous open sores; swollen leprous limbs. There were videopics on the Public Access Channel to prove it. Some of the radiation-sick renegades she had seen executed on tv had been infected that way too.

Steve had felt exactly the same when Mr. Snow and Cadillac, his two principal captors, had tended the injuries caused in the crash. Now though, the picture that came into his mind was of Clearwater; her perfect face; her firm flawless body entwined with his on the soft layered animal furs in the moondark. "I know how you feel," he said. "I try not to think about it too much."

Lundkwist shook her head. "Five months out in the open breathing bad air, with a mess of Mutes pawing you. How did you survive? What did you eat?"

Steve shrugged. "I ate what they gave me. Had no choice."

Lundkwist looked disgusted. "Makes me feel sick."

"Made me feel sick too. For the first week I couldn't keep anything down. In the end I had to force myself. It was the only way to stay alive."

"But—all that stuff out there—it's poisonous! It's not just the bad air that can kill you. It's in the water, the grass—everything!"

Steve turned back to Don. "What would you have done?"

Lundkwist thought it over. "I don't know. What you did, I guess. But it must be awful having to eat when you know you're killing yourself with every mouthful. Are your sure you feel okay?"

Steve shrugged. "I'm here talking to you now. My brain feels like it's in one piece. What can I tell you?"

"I really don't understand it. It just . . . doesn't make sense."

"I've discovered there are a lot of things that don't make sense, replied Steve. "Don't let it worry you."

"Sure but . . ." Lundkwist looked concerned, ". . . even though I can see you're still coming on like a hard-assed sonofabitch I'd like to think you were gonna make it."

Steve gave another shrug. "I've made it this far. What happens to me from here on in depends on what they're cooking up at Grand Central."

"What's so funny?"

"I was just thinking about when I last saw you, how worried you were about not making seventeen."

"Yeah." Lundkwist's grin was tinged with sadness. "You wanna know something? I'm getting to think like you. It's not good to get too close to people. It hurts too much."

"Not only older but wiser," observed Steve. "Happy birthday whenever."

"July 4th."

Steve nodded. "Must remember to make a note of that . . ."

In Anderssen's office, Deke played back the videotape he had made of Steve's arrival at Pueblo, plus general coverage and close-up details of his flying machine and the standard mug-shot footage taken soon after he had been hustled inside but before he'd lost his beribboned plaits; the last segment showed Brickman as seen by a concealed camera in his cell.

Seated behind her desk, Anderssen watched the run-through in silence. She looked up at Deke as the screen cleared. "Do you think we ought to trim out that bit where Harmer lays into him? She dismissed the question with a wave. "Ahhgh, what the heck! Leave it." She checked her watch. "Just make sure that goes down the wire to Grand Central in the next hour."

"Yes, ma'am." Deke removed the cassette, threw a casual salute that he knew Anderssen would accept when there was no one else around and headed for the door.

"Oh, Deke," said Anderssen.

Deke paused with his hand on the door. "Sir-ma'am?"

"I've got a little problem. A couple of days before Brickman arrived I asked Major Hiller to run a check on our inventory of videotapes—including the ones currently on issue to the watch-tower. She checked the racks and we seem to be one short. Did you know that?"

Deke felt a slight chill creep up from the base of his spine. He framed his reply carefully. "No, sir-ma'am. We log the movement of all tapes. I can't understand how one could have been removed from the tower without—"

Anderssen waved him down. "I didn't say it had been removed from the tower, Deke. I said it wasn't on the *racks*." She smiled. "If you are going to make unauthorised recordings, you really ought to find some better place to hide them." Anderssen paused and eyed Deke in silence, prolonging the agony. "It's not that I have any particular objection to clouds. It could always be argued it was a batch of sky searches that you forgot to wipe. But you might have some problems justifying that sound track to the Provost-Marshals."

"Yes, sir-ma'am. Are you . . . putting me on report?"

"It's something I have to consider, Deke. Handling blackjack is a Code One offence. You do realise that if your case were to reach the Assessors, they will not accept a plea of mitigation. Code One sentences cannot be modified, or commuted, and the accused has no right of appeal."

"I know that, ma'am. My action is indefensible. I only hope that it does not reflect on your command."

"So do I," said Anderssen. She eyed Deke and shook her head. "I just never had you down as a guy who would stick his neck out." She opened a drawer, took out the code-breaking cassette and laid it on the desk. "Okay—who else has been handling this stuff at Pueblo?"

"No one, ma'am. I found the track by accident on a

brand new, unused videotape. We always run our own quality check by doing what we call a reel-to-reel scan before using 'em in the tower. This one was part of a consignment that was shipped in from Grand Central last July. They come as sealed packs of ten, one hundred to a box. The stores issued me with ten—I broke open the wrapper myself. The batch inspection ticket was still on it."

"Sounds plausible. Last spring Commander Hartmann told me he'd gotten an FYO ordering him to reload a shipment of videotapes he'd just delivered to Amarillo. Later, I heard that a couple of guys at GC had gone to the wall for handling spiked tape. There may or may not be a connection. In any case, they're certainly not the only ones involved." Anderssen laid her hand on the cassette. "Okay—let me get this straight. Was it this one that came in with the blackjack on it?"

"Yes, ma'am."

"Has anyone else heard this?"

"No, sir-ma'am."

"And you are definitely not pushing this stuff? I don't want you to feed me one story only to discover you've been hauled in and that the Deputy Provos have beaten a totally different one out of you."

"There's no question of that, ma'am. I know there's been talk about some outfits where guys are trading this stuff off against grass but nothing like that is happening here. There's no network."

"There'd better not be. If there was, I'd bury every mother-fucking one of you."

"If there was anything like that going down the wire, I'd know about it, ma'am."

Yeah. Like you know all about your stalwart Mary-Ann smoking grass. Oh, Deke, you asshole, thought Anderssen, without malice. She turned the cassette over between her fingers. "You realise, of course, that this could be a set-up, don't you? If it came in on a blank tape, sooner or later someone was bound to find it. Maybe it came from some internal renegade outfit but suppose it didn't? You know what devious bastards those Provost-Marshals are. They've got guys back at GC who do nothing else but dream up stings like this. I have to report it, Deke—just to cover my own ass."

Deke wavered on his crippled leg then drew himself up straight. "Yessir-ma'am!"

Anderssen waved him down. "Relax. I'm talking about the tape. I don't want you struck off the roster. Shit . . . you're the only guy within a hundred miles of here who can tell those dummies in the electronics pool how to fix all this junk." She handed the video cassette to Deke. "It may be marked in some way, so this is the one that has to go back. Clean everything off it except the sound track. And wipe my prints off the case. When you've done that, report what you've found to the duty officer. Shock, horror, outrage, loyal indignation. You know the drill."

"Yes, ma'am."

"And if you want to save your pretty pictures dupe them onto some other tape—but find some way of fiddling the stock returns, and Deke, please, *don't* stick it back under the drawer. It's so fucking obvious! Use your imagination."

"Yes, ma'am. Thank you, ma'am."

"Okay, don't waste time saluting, get on it." Anderssen waved him away.

Deke headed for the door.

"Wait a minute—"

Deke froze, and turned round awkwardly, his heart beating overtime.

"I think it would be a good idea if you ran me off a copy of that sound track. Just for the files, you understand."

"Of course, ma'am . . ."

Anderssen smiled. "I think it's important that I should have some idea of what it is we're trying to stamp out, don't you? After all, we may get another spiked shipment. If you are a doctor trying to stop a contagious disease from spreading, you have to be able to recognise the symptoms—right?"

"Absolutely . . ."

"Do you know where this music is from, Deke? Who it's by?"

Deke hesitated. "Well, it's hard to be certain. There are

so few facts available but I'd say it was definitely vintage material. My guess is it's pre-Holocaust—"

Anderssen sucked in her breath. "As old as that . . .?"

"Oh, yes, the real thing. Probably the work of a man called Vangellis."

Anderssen nodded. "This conversation didn't take place, Deke."

"I did not hear, or say, a word, ma'am."

"Good," said Anderssen. "One last thing. You've got two tapes there. One of Brickman, and one of clouds. For Christoper's sake, don't send the wrong fucking one down the wire."

THREE

THE FLIGHT from Pueblo to Santa Fe—a distance of just under two hundred miles—was accomplished without incident and a minimum of dialogue with the rest of the formation. Wyman, the Red Riverman who was flight leader, radioed once to announce that they were crossing the state line dividing Colorado from New Mexico. Steve glanced down but, from three thousand feet, could see nothing of particular interest.

The point to which they were heading—the Roosevelt/Santa Fe interface—was situated approximately halfway between the pre-Holocaust centre of that name and Albuquerque, another sixty miles farther south. The actual base, housing a ten thousand strong division of Trackers, lay buried deep within the earthshield. Level One—which was regarded as the ground floor—was over fifteen hundred feet below the surface. Each level was a horizontal slice of space one hundred and fifty feet thick, subdivided into ten floors, or galleries numbered 1–10 from the bottom up. Thus One-1 was street Level, and Ten-10 was the ramp access floor; the interface with the overground. Tracker bases did not always contain all ten levels. Many of the smaller subdivisions were built on Levels One to Four—know as the Quad. Below Level One were other layers known as the A-Levels containing heat pumps, ventilation

47

units, bio-processing and plant nutrient tanks, garbage
disposal and sewage lines. Labelled from the top down in
alphabetical order, these were the exclusive province of
Service Engineering and Maintainance—Seamsters. Steve
had never made a serious effort to find out how far down
they extended. Graduates from the top combat academies
and other Federation high-flyers regarded the A-Levels as
the absolute pits—hence the pejorative term "Zed-heads."

As was customary, the base had been assigned the name
of the nearest important pre-Holocaust centre as its
overground marker, in this case that of the ancient state
capital of New Mexico. Perched five thousand feet up on
the high ground east of the Rio Grande, the original Santa
Fe was now nothing more than an untidy maze of low,
jagged, broken walls overshadowed by a profusion of red
bushes and trees. Here and there, where fragments of
decaying façades rose ten, sometimes twenty feet into the
air, a frameless window gaped hollowly, like the eyeless
socket in a shattered, sun-bleached skull. Albuquerque,
like so many of the larger urban centres, had suffered a
more violent fate. The sprawling site it had once occupied
was now cratered like the surface of the moon. The act of
obliteration had altered the course of the Rio Grande,
which now flowed sideways into a chain of circular lakes
before emptying back into the snaking riverbed that ran
southwards to the sea.

Despite the fact that he had flown patrols from The
Lady for three months before being shot down, Steve had
never seen the Roosevelt Sante Fe interface from the air.
As they approached, it gave him a curious feeling. Roosevelt Field—to quote its official designation—was not only
the nearest shuttle stop to Pueblo; it also happened to be
Steve's home base and with which he was permanently
identified by his middle, divisional name. It was here that
he and his younger kin-sister Roz had been reared by his
guardians, Jack and Annie Brickman.

Following the usual practice, his given name—Steven—
was the name of one of their own guard-fathers—in this
case, Annie's. Roz had been named after Jack's guard-
mother. Annie had been reared at Nixon/Fort Worth.

Before pairing off with Jack, her kin-folk name had been Bradlee. The Bradlees were well connected—what was known as "being wired in"—and several, like Annie's kin-brother Bart, who was State Provost-Marshal for New Mexico, had won promotion to similar positions of power.

Brickman was a less illustrious kin-folk name but both could be traced back through the generations to the Four Hundred; the very first Trackers who, under the leadership of the First Family, had formed the nucleus of the Federation and whose names were now enshrined on the Roll of Honour. The list had, in fact, originally contained five hundred and eighteen names but, like so much of the Federation's history, such minor details had been glossed over in order not to mar the general presentation. Just as the Old America of the pre-Holocaust era had been created by a group of pioneers known as the First Four Hundred, so would the descendants of the second Four Hundred build the New.

Just before they banked eastwards, Steve took a last look at the chain of circular lakes occupying the point on his map labelled Albuquerque. The sight caused him to reflect on what Mr. Snow had told him about the War of a Thousand Suns. What he had learned had shaken his previous unquestioning belief in the Federation's account of the Holocaust. How could the Mutes who, despite their mysterious powers, were at best untutored savages with a primitive lifestyle, have wrought such changes in the earth? Where could they have gotten such destructive power? Steve was becoming increasingly convinced that the War of a Thousand Suns and the Holocaust were two irreconcilable interpretations of the *same* event. If so, what had *really* happened? And who was to blame?

Lundkwist's voice interrupted his train of thought. "Gonna have to black you out. We'll be landing in a few minutes." She banked the Skyrider over to port and began to lose altitude. As they dropped down towards the final approach and landing, Steve drank in one last deep draft of the overground through his eyes, drawing its image hungrily down into his memory like a defaulter gulping in his last breath as he stands against the wall. Below, the great sweep of the earth, its hills and hollows, peaks and plains filled with vivid colour; countless shades of red, orange, yellow and brown, overlaid by a changing cloud-cast pattern of sunlight and shadow. Above, the glorious blue vastness that stretched away unseen beyond the curtain of haze that veiled the outline of the distant mountains.

Lundkwist picked up the hood. "Okay, lean your head over this way . . ." Their eyes met. "Good luck, Brickman. Hope we meet again sometime in, uh—more promising circumstances."

"We will," said Steve—and was plunged into darkness.

The Santa Fe interface was a whopping great flat-topped slab of concrete similar in its general appearance to the bunker at Pueblo. The main difference was the 150 yard concrete landing strip that had been laid down alongside. Lundkwist put the plump-bodied Skyrider down on the white centre-line. Wyman, and the two other Red Rivermen touched down a fraction of a second later to make a perfect formation landing. Rolling forward, Lundkwist saw several work-parties of Mutes alongside the strip, toiling under the guns of masked helmeted Trackers. One of the guards waved to them as they went by. The Mutes, the nearest of whom looked ragged, grubby and unkempt and who all wore knee and wrist shackles, appeared to be involved in extending both the width and the length of the landing strip. Lundkwist wondered why. Depending how they were loaded, the take-off run of a Skyhawk was between fifty and seventy-five yards and it could land in less than half that distance. Was the First Family paving the way for an even bigger and more powerful machine than the new Mark Two?

Shepherded by the three Skyhawks, Lundkwist made a right-angled turn off the strip onto the fan-shaped area that sloped down to the ramp access doors. At Lindbergh Field, the site of the under-ground Flight Academy in southeastern New Mexico, the interface had four such ramps, arranged in the form of a huge cross. Here, as there, the ramp was bordered by converging walls that increased in height as they ran in towards the massive reinforced concrete doors, cutting her view of the over-ground down to a wedge-shaped slab of sky.

Although Steve could see nothing, he sensed the walls hemming him in; could feel the deadening weight of the huge doors that were about to engulf them. Once again, as on his first solo, he was swept by a wave of apprehension but this time, he was firmly in control; there was no panic. The two days and three nights he had spent inside the Pueblo way-station had helped him begin what was clearly going to be a long and difficult readjustment. The first few hours of his solitary confinement in the cell block had been unbearably oppressive. He'd felt as if he was about to suffocate but, somehow, he had managed to talk himself through the worst moments. After a while he had been able to isolate himself mentally from his surroundings. Squatting cross-legged in the manner of his Mute captors, Steve had sought the calmness he had observed in Mr. Snow and Cadillac, his principal guardians and guides to the ways of the Plainfolk. Gradually, his thoughts had turned inwards, dwelling first on the Talisman Prophecy that had been revealed to him by Mr. Snow, and then on his possible role in the events it foretold. His life had been spared because his captors believed he had been chosen to play an important part in the future of the Plainfolk. But they had not told him whether it would be as their friend or their enemy . . .

The bond of friendship and understanding he had forged with Mr. Snow and Cadillac, the two wordsmiths, still held; his feelings for Clearwater would, he was sure, never alter. But even with her image burning bright in his mind, older, deep-rooted emotions had begun to stir. His flight in the Skyrider, the sight of the sleek new Skyhawks had reawakened his fascination with hardware; the instruments of war. *This* was where the real power lay—in the techno-logical superiority of the Federation. He could not ignore the forces Mr. Snow had unleashed upon The Lady from Louisiana. Forces that had almost wrecked the wagon-train and which he himself had seen Clearwater summon inexplicably out of thin air. But had not the old wordsmith confessed that a *single* bullet from a Skyhawk had almost killed him before the clan's attack on the wagon-train had gotten underway?

As they sat waiting for the concrete curtain in front of them to rise on its battery of huge hydraulic rams, each as thick as a man's body, the thought now uppermost in Steve's mind was to get through the inevitable interrogation as quickly and cleanly as possible and be reassigned to overground duty aboard The Lady. He did not yet know how he would react if he were sent into action against the Plainfolk clan who had held him prisoner but it was not something that Steve saw any need to lose sleep over. The dilemma, insofar as one existed, would eventually be resolved, as always, to his best advantage . . .

With the inner ramp door closed safely behind them, the Red Rivermen deplaned and while Wyman logged their arrival with the ramp control office, Lundkwist, Minelli and Reardon hauled Steve out of the Skyrider and checked he was still securely hooded and chained. Lundkwist saw a group of six Deputy Provost-Marshals walking towards them from the far end of the ramp access bay. They wore the usual dark blue jump-suits and white helmets similar to a wingman's bone-dome but the visor—of mirrored silver—had a curved bottom edge like a pair of sunglasses. The helmets had "PM" painted on the front in big red letters and a band of the same colour going right around it. This white-red-white sandwich had led to a Deputy Provo being known as a "meat-loaf"; a derisive title bestowed by certain groups of Trackers who, despite the constant exhortations, were less responsive to the laws of the Federation than they might be.

Emerging from the ramp control office, Wyman hurried over to where Lundkwist and the others were waiting with Steve. "Good news, guys, they're rustling up a cup of java for us in the ramp control office. I've been in touch with Big Red One. We've got permission to cancel out for an hour before the return trip."

"Great," chorussed, Lundkwist, Reardon and Minelli.

"Okay, this way, mister." Steve felt two people take hold of his arms and march him forward. He knew

Lundkwist was on his left from the supportive squeeze she gave him.

Rick Wyman led the way towards the DPs, handed over the hooded defaulter with the minimum of ceremony then turned his back and walked away, followed by the other Red Rivermen. Nobody looked back in case the gesture was misinterpreted. Provos were bad news.

Steve felt the sudden hostile atmosphere just as surely as he had felt the enveloping concrete. Bodies closed in on either side and behind him. Someone kicked at his heels, forcing him to almost lose his balance. Several hands slammed into him, pushing him back upright and he was simultaneously assaulted by a chorus of hard-edged voices.

"Stand up straight, you cee-bee bastard!"

"What are you—a sack of lumpshit?!"

"Beaver-lickin' Mute-sucker!"

"Get your gammy ass into gear!"

"Okay, move it!" He was seized roughly by both arms. The tip of a Provost rubber truncheon was rammed sharply into the base of his spine just above his ass sending a sickening wave of pain flooding through his back. Steve stumbled forwards.

"Pick it up, pick it up!" yelled a harsh voice. "Head up, get those shoulders back!" The jabbing tip of the truncheon began to beat time on his kidneys. "Left-right-left-right-left-right-left!"

When the hood was pulled off, Steve was still standing, but only just. His back was on fire and his thighs felt rubbery. He looked over his shoulder and saw the door closing behind him. Glancing down, Steve saw that an additional chain had been looped over the one linking his knee shackles. He was now padlocked to an anchor point in the floor of a small office, facing an empty desk with a swivel chair behind it. Apart from the usual ventilation grilles, the fawn-coloured walls were completely bare. There was nothing to indicate where he was or what the function of the room might be. His ears and stomach told him he had come a long way down in an elevator and then been hustled on board a wheelie. He had recognised the characteristic whine of its electric motor. Near the end of the

trip he had felt the wheelie tip forward and run down a
slope. The only one he knew of at Roosevelt Field was the
freight ramp coming up out of the TransAm station under
New Deal Plaza. Since he was due to ride the shuttle from
there to Grand Central, it seemed the most logical place
to have taken him to.

The door opened and closed. Someone paused behind
him, placed a hand briefly on his shoulder then walked
past and went behind the desk. Steve took one look at him
and closed his eyes with a feeling of relief. It was Bart
Bradlee, State Provost-Marshal of New Mexico, dressed in
his spotless white uniform—the antithesis of Steve's black
cee-bee fatigues—decked out with gold braid and dark
blue rank insignia. Good old Uncle Bart. Twenty-nine
years old, his close-cropped hair already going grey. Not a
soft, or lenient man, and certainly not a barrel of laughs.
No . . . Bart was a hard, humourless, gold-braided piece
of lumpshit who did everything by The Book.

But he was still kin.

Bart laid his plaited, leather-covered swagger stick on
the desk, made sure it was parallel with the edge, then
laid down his white Stetson in front of it with the badge
facing him. "How do you feel, boy?" Bart's eyes were fixed
on the stetson, making sure that its fore and aft axis was at
right-angles to the swagger stick.

"A lot better for seeing you, sir."

Bart looked up and eyed him severely. He was obviously upset by Steve's dishevelled shoulder-length hair.
"Wish I could say the same . . ."

Steve gave it the old "down-home" touch. "I'm not a
cee-bee, sir. I keep telling people that, but no one seems
to want to listen and I can't figure out why. I mean, you
know me better than that! The way Annie raised me and
all! What the heck! I think too much of my kin-folk to ever
turn renegade."

Bart nodded but looked unconvinced. "The report says
you were taken prisoner. Five months . . . that's a long
time to be in the hands of those animals, boy." Bart came
out from behind the desk and circled Steve slowly, his
hands clasped behind his back.

Steve held his head up high, braced his aching back, and hoped that Uncle Bart wasn't going to lay into him. What with the pudgy-faced lieutenant at Pueblo, and the Deputy Provos, there weren't many parts of his body left to bruise.

"Time for them to raise up a lot of bad thoughts inside you. The kind of thoughts that mixes a man up so that, pretty soon, he doesn't know right from wrong." Bart paused and brought his mouth close to Steve's ear. "You know what The Book says about the Mutes, boy?"

"Yes, *sir*! They are creatures of darkness—"

"That's right. Creatures of darkness . . . that can poison your body and infect your mind. Not my words, Stevie. Those words are from the lips of the First Family—whose wisdom has protected us down the ages." Bart circled round in front of him, his piercing, pale blue eyes fixed on Steve's face. "Have they poisoned *your* body, Stevie?"

Steve tried to keep his eyes focused on an imaginary point behind the State Provost-Marshal's head. "I don't think so, sir. The surgeon-captain at Pueblo examined me. I don't know what he found but I, uh—feel pretty good."

Bart didn't seem to be listening. He moved to Steve's left and again brought his mouth close to his ear. "Have they infected *your* mind?"

"No sir!" There's no way they could ever do that, I swear! The whole time I was out there my mind was busy with one thing, and one thing only—and that was figuring out ways to get back here where I belong!"

As Steve spoke, Bart moved behind him and stopped once again, this time behind his right shoulder. Steve shot a quick glance in that direction and found the Provost-Marshal's face about an inch from his own, chin thrust forward, teeth clenched and bared, eyes open so wide there was white all around the pupils. Steve whipped his head to the front and stared hard at the fawn-coloured wall. In the past, in their more private moments, he and his kin-sister Roz had viewed Bart's fanatical loyalty and his pious mouthings from the Manual with amused irreverence. But now, as he stood there chained to the floor, Steve was suddenly struck by the realisation that good old

Uncle Bart had popped his rivets; jumped the buffers; had flipped his trolley. Christopher Columbus! A crazy State Provost-Marshal . . . the head of law enforcement for the whole of New Mexico, with the power to arrest, imprison, interrogate, pass sentence—even send people to the wall! Steve found himself trembling at the thought. It was frightening. But what was even more frightening was the fact that he suddenly felt an equally crazy desire to burst out laughing.

Bart emerged from behind Steve's shoulder, leant back against the front edge of the desk with folded arms, and ran his eyes over Steve from the feet up. Steve's face muscles ached but, somehow, he managed to keep a straight face.

"You say you feel pretty good. How good do you feel about the Federation, boy? How good do you feel about the First Family?"

Steve suddenly felt better. This was familiar ground. "Same way as I did before, sir. Thinking about them was the only thing that kept me going out there." The words came easily. Steve knew it was the kind of stuff Bart loved to hear. "Never once did I forget what they've done for us. The way they built the Federation from the bottom up. The way they gave us life, the will to live, the rules to live by and the promise of a better tomorrow. What we owe them is a debt that can never be repaid. But each of us can show our gratitude by living right and thinking straight, and by being ready and willing to make the ultimate sacrifice."

Bart thrust out his bottom lip and nodded approvingly. "Well said, boy."

"That's how it is, sir. Nothing's changed." Steve paused, then added with appropriate solemnity—"I still believe that the greatest honour that can be bestowed on any Tracker worthy of the name is to be called upon to lay down his life in defence of the First Family and the Federation. That's why I want to clear myself of any suspicion of misconduct and get back into action. I know one should never ask for favours but—can you help me do that?"

Bart replied with a shake of the head. "Your case is not under my jurisdiction, Stevie. Best I can do is to give you some advice."

"Well, I'm always grateful for that, sir," said Steve, with as much sincerity as he could muster. "I recognise that it was the guidance you gave me during those years when Poppa-Jack was away fighting Mutes that helped keep me on course."

Bart appeared to accept the tribute. "Maybe so. It's up to each of us to do what we can for who we can—starting with those nearest to us. I've never held back from helping you, Stevie. Not because you're family, but because I really and truly sincerely believe that you have that something special that can take a man right to the top."

Coming at any other time, such a glowing assessment would have been music to Steve's ears. Unfortunately, having just reclassified Bart as a Category One basket case, rendered his opinion on any subject totally valueless. Steve's awareness of his own treacherous intentions lent a certain irony to his reply. "Thank you, sir, I'll try not to disappoint you."

"You won't," said Bart. He straightened up off the desk and took a step towards Steve and fixed him with his mad blue eyes. "I want to ask you something, Stevie. Man to man."

"Go ahead, sir."

"I've heard and read about Mutes but you've got closer to 'em than any man I know. I've watched videos of what these animals do to our boys, but you've *seen* it with your own eyes. Those lumpheads are *killers*—am I right?"

"Yes, sir."

"So how come they didn't kill you?"

"I don't know the answer to that question, sir. They came pretty close to it more than once. Maybe if I hadn't escaped . . ."

"Yeah, sure, but in those five months you were with 'em didn't it ever cross your mind to ask 'em what made you so special?"

"No, I just kinda steered right away from that."

Bart eyed him doubtfully.

Steve felt obliged to offer some explanation. "Maybe the Plainfolk do things differently to the clans we've been fighting up to now. Or maybe they don't yet realise they've got a real war on their hands."

Bart gave Steve a twisted grin. "Come on, Stevie, you can do better than that. What did you do to save your skin—offer them some kind of a deal?"

Steve replied with a surprised stare. Crazy Bart was a lot closer than he realised. "No, *sir!*" he said firmly. "The thought of doing such a thing never crossed my mind but even if it had and I'd been foolish enough to try something like that it would have been a waste of time. There's no way Trackers are ever going to be able to do a deal with Mutes. It's like you said—they're animals!"

Bart chuckled and clapped him on the arms. "You're a heck of a boy, Stevie. I'm sure, deep down, you're bustin' to let it all out. But—" he smiled genially, "—I'm not upset at you holding out on me. After what you've been through it takes *time* to unwind. It's only natural . . ." Bart raised his right hand, palm open, fingers extended.

Steve knew that hand; knew it had been hardened by countless hours of karate practice; had seen it smash through a stack of half-inch-thick clay tiles. He braced himself but, instead of the expected blow, Bart patted him on the cheek. In a strange way, the amiable gesture was even more frightening than the use of brute force.

"Yeah . . ." chuckled Bart. "I bet if you and me were to sit down nose to nose for a while we'd end up jawing all night about the things you've been up to but . . ."

Steve went to reply. Bart motioned him to remain silent.

". . . we don't have time," he sighed. "That's why I want you to take note of what I'm about to say." He walked round behind the desk, picked up his swagger stick and stood with his legs astride, flexing the stick slowly between his hands. "When you get to Grand Central don't hold anything back. I want you to promise me you'll tell them every single thing that happened to you. Everything you did, everything you saw, everything you heard, everything you felt—no matter how strange or foolish it might sound, or whether it goes against everything you've been taught to believe in."

"I promise, sir."

"Good. I knew I could count on you, Stevie. You are going to be talking to some pretty important people. Put your trust in them the way you've always trusted me. Have faith and everything will come out right." Bart looked at his watch. "The shuttle from Johnson/Phoenix'll be here in fifteen minutes. Is there anything else you want to say to me?"

"Yes, sir. I'd like to ask how my guardians are. Is Annie—?"

"Annie's just fine."

"Is Poppa-Jack still alive?"

"Yeah, just about . . ."

"And Roz?"

"She's still at Inner State U."

"Do they, uh—know what happened to me?"

"They got the same news we all did—that you'd powered down in enemy territory." Bart shrugged. "Jack, well—being an old Trail-Blazer himself I guess it was no more than he expected. Annie was kinda cut up at first. I helped talk her through it."

"Fifteen minutes . . . I don't suppose—?"

"Not a chance, boy."

"In that case could you let them know I'm all right, sir? Would you tell them what's happened?"

Bart shook his head. "Nope. Can't do that either."

Steve stared at him. "Sir . . . I don't understand."

"It's very simple." Bart laid his swagger stick down at ninety degrees to the edge of the desk, picked up his stetson and used both hands to position it at the correct angle on his head. He then retrieved his stick and thwacked it against the palm of his left hand. "As far as they, and the rest of this base is concerned you crashed into a burning cropfield. Bang into the middle of a whole screaming mess of Mutes—right?"

"Right . . ."

"So that's it. What do I have to do—spell it out? Mutes don't take prisoners. You're dead."

"But, sir—"

"There are no 'buts', Stevie. Be reasonable. You can't expect Grand Central to start rewriting Federation history just on account of what happened to you."

Steve's satisfaction at scoring points off Bart was replaced by a feeling of uneasiness. "So . . . what are they planning to do with me?"

"You mean after they get through with you at Grand Central?" Bart spread his hands. "That's not for me to say, Stevie. The Federation's a big place. There's all kinds of things going on. Maybe they'll give you a new assignment. On the other hand . . . who knows? I guess it all kinda hangs on the way you shape up from here on in." Bart stepped out from behind the desk and gripped Steve's shoulder as he went past. "Let me give you a last piece of advice. We know all there is to know about you. Don't think you can fool the First Family. No one can. You think I'm crazy—"

"Sir, I—"

"Don't interrupt me, boy. How d'you think I got where I am? I can read you like Page One of the Manual. You know why I had you figured out to go places? It's because I've spotted a lot of me in you. I guess we've both got a bit of the same little something from the President-General. You're a survivor—"

Once again, Steve went to reply.

Bart held up a warning finger. "No. Don't deny it. It's a good thing to be. In the world we're trying to build we need men with the qualities you have. But don't *ever* make the mistake of trying to survive at the expense of the system." He gave Steve's shoulder a friendly pat. "One of these days, if you ever get where you're aiming to go, you'll see things a whole lot differently. And you'll think back to your good old Uncle Bart and you'll say—'Yup, there was a man who did what he had to do' . . ."

Steve swivelled round after him and felt the chains tug at his knees. "Sir—!"

Bart paused at the door, a faint mocking smile on his face.

". . . will Jack and Annie ever know?"

Bart's eyebrows went up, lifting his eyelids clear of his cold blue eyes as his mouth went down at the corners. "That all depends on the First Family, Stevie." He gave him a friendly poke with his swagger stick. "S' been mighty good talkin' with you. Be sure and take care of yourself now, d'ya hear?"

Steve watched the door close then turned back to face the empty desk and the blank walls with a long sigh. When he'd been up in the hills above the Wind River in Wyoming, he had been faced with three possible options. One—remaining a prisoner of the Mutes and probably getting himself killed, either because of what had happened with Clearwater or because of his unlooked-for feud with Motor-Head: two—escaping and becoming a renegade, a wandering outcast who, sooner or later, would die from radiation sickness: three—returning to the Federation and a hero's welcome. At the time, the third option had seemed like his best bet but, up to now, it wasn't quite working out the way he'd expected.

He heard footsteps and took a deep, calming breath as the door opened. Boots crashed on the floor. Once again he was seized from behind and everything went black as the hood came down over his head. There was a metallic jangle as the chain anchoring him to the floor was withdrawn.

"Okay, move it!" Someone struck him across the small of the back with a rubber truncheon. Not hard enough to break any bones or rupture any vital organs. Just hard enough to let him know he was in the hands of people who were not about to fool around.

Steve's calculated guess as to his location turned out to be right on the nose. After a couple of right and left turns down various corridors and through a number of doors Steve was halted on the east-bound platform of the subway station under New Deal Plaza. He recognised, from his previous trip on the same line with Roz, the faint echo-effect added to the voices and footsteps of people moving about and his nostrils picked up the same antiseptic odour through the two light-proof breathing filters of his black hood.

Running from Johnson/Phoenix, Arizona in the west, to
Le May/Jackson, Mississippi in the east and with direct
connections to Houston/Grand Central, the Trans-Am shuttle ranked as the major engineering achievement of the
Federation, rivalled only by GC's spectacular John Wayne
Plaza. The system of tunnels, driven through the earthshield
over the last three hundred years by generations of fourteen-
year-old Trackers during their twelve-month stint with the
Young Pioneers housed a single monorail track straddled
by a string of cars propelled at high speed by a linear
induction motor. Passing loops at each subway station and
at intervals along the line enabled a twice-daily service to
be run in each direction. The shuttle was usually loaded to
the roof with freight but there were always plenty of spare
seats. Trackers from the bases along the line did not travel
just for fun, only when required to do so. Everybody in
the Federation got to make at least one trip as part of an
organised group to visit the memorial shrine of George
Washington I at Grand Central, but anyone "riding the
rail" had to have a movement order issued by their local
Provost-Marshal's office. To deter potential code-breakers
the subway was regularly patrolled by pairs of the dreaded
meat-loaves who often boarded the shuttle to run checks
on passengers in transit.

A two-tone electronic chime and a recorded announcement signalled the imminent arrival of the east-bound
Central Liner for Reagan/Lubbock, Nixon/Fort Worth, and
Houston/GC. Steve felt a sudden draught swirl round him
as the incoming shuttle rammed a column of air down the
tunnel ahead of it. A tunnel he himself had helped build
during his time with the Young Pioneers. He wondered
what it was like in Arizona. Around him, his unseen escort
chatted in a desultory fashion, mainly about what they
might do in the short time they would be spending at
Grand Central. Steve had the impression that there were
four of them but he couldn't be sure. He heard the faint
hum of the shuttle as it drew nearer.

"Where's this one gonna ride—in the hot box?" asked a
voice.

"No, with us," said a second voice.

It was the first time Steve had ever heard the term "hot box." He wondered what it could mean and decided that it must be Provo slang for a cramped, poorly-ventilated punishment cell.

"Which of you has that disk with the medical report from the way-station?" asked a third voice.

"I have," said the second voice.

"Okay. Don't forget to hand it over. And Gazzara—forget any ideas you got about jack-assing the local yippies. I've keyed you in for a two-hour furlough to take a look at the Plaza and then it's back here on the first westbound out of GC. Comprendo?"

"Yes, sir!" said Gazzara—now identified as the second voice.

Steve committed his name to memory.

"You forgot the shrine, Sergeant," said the first voice.

"Fuck the shrine," replied the third voice.

"Yeah," said Gazzara. "We'll be standing in line all fucking day."

"Even so, we ought to pay our respects."

The noise from the approaching shuttle grew louder.

The Provo-Sergeant raised his voice. "Delaney—you got two hours. If you want to spend it waiting to see a fifteen foot high face carved out of white marble, that's okay by me."

Steve filed Delaney along with Gazzara for future reference.

The shuttle, banded along its length from the bottom up in red, white and blue, slid smoothly out of the tunnel and eased to a halt with its bullet-nose at the far end of the platform. The passenger and freight doors opened with a hiss of compressed air and there was a sudden bustle of activity as the loading and unloading process got underway.

A hand closed round each of Steve's arms but this time there was no baton blow in the small of the back. "This way, fella . . ." said Gazzara. His tone was less abrupt than before. Steve was walked a short distance up the platform then wheeled round to the right. "Okay, mind your head."

Steve ducked down and stepped forward. The surface

under his feet changed from unyielding concrete to the more resilient hard rubber tile flooring of the shuttle cars. He was turned again and felt the edge of a seat behind his knees.

"Okay, siddown." Gazzara was obviously the one that did most of the talking.

Steve did as he was told. He could tell from the shape and feel of the seat that he was in one of the normal passenger cars. There was a rattle of chains. Someone bent over him.

It was Delaney. "I'm hooking you up to the chair. Just relax and take it easy. Give us a break and no one'll give you a hard time. All right?"

Steve nodded in silent assent. "I need to go to the can."

"Arrghh, Christo!" spat Delaney. "Listen, uh—you'll have to wait a while. I'll get back to you after we pull out."

Steve sat back and tried to ignore the ache from his constricted bladder. He'd felt the need to urinate on landing but had been hustled away by the Provos, and somehow, at the end of his rather heavy audience with the State Provost-Marshal when Bart had asked him if he had anything to say, it had seemed a rather frivolous request to make.

Fifteen minutes after its arrival, the Central Liner headed out of Roosevelt/Santa Fe on the next leg of its journey—to Reagan/Lubbock, Texas, the base where the new Mark 2 Skyhawk was being readied for series production. The shuttle, which attained a top speed of 120 miles an hour, took around seven hours—including stopovers—to make the eight hundred mile run to Grand Central.

A short while after they'd gotten underway, Delaney unlocked the chain holding Steve to the seat and shepherded him along the aisle to the washroom. Delaney pushed open the door and followed Steve inside. "Hold it—I'll pull the hood."

Once again, Steve found himself blinking rapidly as his eyes adjusted to the light. He took a deep breath and glanced appreciatively at the D-P.

Delaney responded with a nod. "Knock on the door

when you're through. The orders are to keep you hooded until the handover at GC."

"I understand. Is it the 17th today?"

"Yeah . . ."

"What time is it?"

"1408. We should get to GC around 2100 hours. Okay?"

"Yeah, thanks."

Delaney shut the door behind him.

Steve stood against the wall-mounted urinal and unzipped the trouser section of his black fatigues. The muscles had been locked tight around his bladder for so long it took a couple of seconds to release the tension and a good minute to empty it. He closed his eyes and continued to breathe deeply.

Ever since he had entered the way-station at Pueblo, he had been struck at the difference between the air that filled the underground world of the Federation and that of the Plainfolk. After his crash, when he had recovered consciousness to find himself a prisoner of the Mutes, he had been unable to breathe without feeling nauseous. The smell of their bodies, their huts and their food made his bile rise and during the first week he had been physically sick several times. Yet within a month he had become totally acclimatised, so that now, the filtered, purified air pumped out and sucked in through the countless vents and grilles throughout the Federation seemed positively thin and stale; all the "flavour" had been processed out of it.

As he washed his hands, Steve tried to work out the reason for the noticeable change in the attitude of his escort. He decided that Delaney and Gazzara must be the afternoon shift. On the other hand, they might be two of the original bunch who, having temporarily vented their aggression, were now resting between rounds. Whatever the answer, Steve did not intend to probe the limits of their new-found amiability. He knocked on the door.

Delaney stepped inside and unfolded the hood.

"Thanks for giving me a chance to breathe," said Steve.

"Don't understand why you're dressed up in this gear in the first place," grunted Delaney. "A guy with your connections. If we get an empty car at Lubbock, I'll pull it again so's you can watch some tv."

"Terrific." Steve bowed his head so that Delaney, who was a little on the short side, could replace the hood without having to climb on the can. So that was it, thought Steve, as darkness enveloped him. His escort had unearthed the fact that he and the State Provost-Marshal were kin and were hedging their bets in case he was acquitted and came back into circulation. Good thinking, Delaney. I'll get back to you later, you little creep. You can help me track down those six guys who hauled me off the ramp . . .

Delaney sounded disappointed when the carriage didn't empty at Reagan Field. Steve did not mind missing the video being shown on that particular run and declined the offer to listen to the sound track over one of the headsets provided for passengers. "There are people around," he explained diplomatically. "I don't want you guys getting into trouble."

The truth was slightly different. Even before he had gone over-ground and discovered the world of the Plainfolk Steve had never been an avid viewer of Federation tv. Apart from the vocational and archive channels, the programming was as bland as the air being pumped by those Zed-heads in the A-Levels; blue-sky balladeers and processed inspirational pap interspersed with newscasts composed, for the most part, of mind-numbing trivia.

For Steve, the turn-off had begun somewhere around his sixth or seventh year and the inability to swallow this uninspired diet had increased as he grew older. Roz, who was two years younger, had confessed to having a similar rejection problem and it was this shared aversion that had led them to believe that they were somehow different; superior. This belief in their "otherness" had become *their* secret and throughout their brief childhood, they had been inseparable. By the time he was fourteen—the age at which, in the Federation, you were regarded as an adult— Steve, who admitted no other friends, was aware that the relationship between Roz and himself went beyond the bounds of kinship as defined by the Manual.

Leaving Roosevelt Field to begin his year of labour

service with the Young Pioneers, Steve had pretended not
to care about being parted from Roz. He had become
skilled at camouflaging his true feelings but soon after
starting work on the last lap of the shuttleway to Phoenix,
Arizona, he had been troubled by the discovery that, on
certain occasions, he and Roz were together even when
they were hundreds of miles apart. He had said nothing
about this to his sister but, in the few days he had spent
with her between leaving the Flight Academy and joining
his wagon-train, Roz had revealed that she had been in
mental contact with him during his first overground solo.
She had experienced the same heart-stopping sensation as
he soared off the ramp and caught his first glimpse of the
overground; had *seen*, deep within her mind, the same
great glorious sweep of earth and sky.

The strength of his feelings for Roz, which he had never
fully revealed to her or dared admit to himself, was only
surpassed by his response to Clearwater, the female
Mute—no, that was wrong—the Mute *girl* with whom he
. . . Christopher! It was too painful to think about. From
the moment he first set eyes on her on the night he had
been called upon to bite the arrow, he had been plagued
by powerful, conflicting emotions that, at times, had blotted out all other concerns. Ever since catching sight of her
perfectly formed face in the firelight he had felt an overwhelming need to be in her presence; a burning desire to
possess her physically and in every other way; to merge
her entire existence with his.

In plain Pre-Holocaust language, Steve had, quite simply, fallen passionately in love but, unfortunately, he did
not know what that meant. A far-reaching decision by the
First Family taken centuries before Steve's birth had deleted the words "love," "passion" and "desire" from the
Federation's video dictionary along with a great many
other potentially disturbing word-concepts such as "indi-
viduality" and "freedom." There was no place for such
ideas in a nation shaped by military discipline and empiri-
cal logic, nor was it necessary to admit the existence of
such intangible notions as those expressed by the words
"art," "literature," "religion" and "soul."

The removal of these words from the language deprived
Steve of the means to express his true feelings. He was
stricken by the age-old fever but was powerless to describe the symptoms. Worse still, his brief liaison with
Clearwater ran contrary to everything he had been taught.
Trackers were raised from birth to consider Mutes as
sub-human. If the mere thought of touching them was
considered abhorrent, then what Steve had done was so
unthinkable it was beyond rational consideration. Yet, in
the midst of this mental confusion, one clear thought
remained, piercing the fog of uncertainty like a white-hot
laser beam. Steve knew that, as a result of meeting Clearwater, his life had changed irrevocably. From now on, she
was part of the equation; his need to be reunited with her,
to possess her totally, would be the basis of all future
calculations.

Steve lay his head back against the seat and made an
effort to shut off all external sensations; the low murmur of
conversation, the monotonous hum of the shuttle, the
manacles encircling his wrists and knees, the stifling constraint of the hood. After a while he felt himself floating
away into the enveloping darkness. He wondered where
Cadillac and Mr. Snow went in their periods of stillness
and thought about the voices he had heard in the past.
Could they have been the mysterious Sky Voices which
Mr. Snow claimed to be in contact with? Could such
things actually exist? Clearwater's name came into his
mind. He tried to conjure up a vision of her but the image
that formed in his mind's eye was of Roz. He felt her mind
reaching out to his, bridging the hundreds of miles that lay
between them. A voice that only he could hear flowed
through his inner consciousness. A cool urgent whisper
that reminded him of the wind sweeping gently through
the tops of the trees. She knew he was alive. She knew he
was coming. He must be careful. They were watching her.

FOUR

AT HOUSTON/GRAND CENTRAL, Steve was handed over to another kid-gloved Provo escort. Still hooded and chained, Steve was hoisted aboard a wheelie, driven some considerable distance to another subway station and marched onto a second shuttle—this time for a brief twenty minute trip. The final part of the journey, which entailed stepping on and off a series of moving walkways and an upward ride in an elevator, left Steve completely disorientated.

Even if he had been able to see, it would have made little difference. His two previous visits to Grand Central had both been brief; the first, at the age of seven, as part of an organised group whose fixed itinerary had taken him through the shrine of George Washington Jefferson the 1st, and past the awe-inspiring façade of the White House; the second, eight months ago, when he and Roz had spent two days wandering around the recently completed John Wayne Plaza, and the spectacular new accommodation deeps. Neither visit had been long enough, nor sufficiently wide-ranging to enable him to acquire a precise mental map of the Federation's capital.

When the hood was finally removed, the only thing Steve could deduce from his surroundings was that he was now in some kind of medical unit. On the edge of his field of vision he could just discern two Deputy-Provos standing

69

behind him. He decided not to swing his body round to look at them more directly. Defaulters were expressly forbidden to make direct eye contact with their escorts; to do so, with any hint of aggression or defiance, unleashed an instant massage with rubber truncheons. That was why the lieutenant at Pueblo had cut loose with his rifle butt.

The second shuttle ride provided a tenuous clue to his possible location. Steve knew that the White House and AmEx—the executive arm of government—were both situated in closely guarded enclaves some distance from Grand Central. But there were also other specialist agencies located around the main base: Inner State U—the huge college campus where Roz was currently studying for her medical doctorate; the Life Institute where all Trackers were conceived "in vitro" and implanted in their host-mothers; the headquarters of the Provost-Marshal Division, known formally as "The Bureau" and informally as Meat-Loaf Mountain; and Columbus Circle, the home of the Federation's giant computer.

Steve had ridden on the special subway that linked the White House to Grand Central but that had been ten years ago. At the time he had paid little attention to the mechanics of the journey and could no longer remember how he'd gotten to it from Grand Central Station. He dismissed the problem from his mind. If the Family decided he was to be allowed back into circulation all would eventually be revealed; if they didn't, his whereabouts would swiftly become irrelevant. His illustrious career would end—this time permanently—with a nosedive down the nearest available shaft.

So much for the predictions of the Sky Voices . . .

A medic in a white coat came through the doorway and paused in front of Steve with his hands in his coat pockets. Pursing his lips he gave Steve the once-over then addressed the DPs. "We won't be needing the cuffs. Take them with you."

The two DPs unlocked the chains. Steve rubbed his wrists with a grateful sigh.

The DP who had unlocked the knee cuffs straightened

up and coiled the chains neatly around his hand. "What about the MO?"

"It's been initialised," said the medic. "Pick it up from the office on your way out."

Steve watched them walk out of the room then turned towards the medic and stood to attention.

The medic waved him down. "Relax."

"Thanks." Steve looked around the room. "It's kinda hard to imagine that I woke up this morning in Colorado— and here I am in Grand Central."

"Yeah . . . you've had a long ride. Feel like a shower?"

"That would be great."

"Did they give you anything to eat at Pueblo?"

"Yes, sir. I had breakfast. Cup of java and a B-side special."

"Nothing since?"

"No, sir."

"Okay," said the medic. "Here's what we'll do. While you're in the washroom I'll get rid of that cee-bee outfit and get you a set of blues—and then we'll go down to the mess deck and pin down some hot chow. How does that sound?"

"Fantastic."

"And go easy on the 'sir' bit. I just empty the test tubes round here." The pleasant-faced medic stuck out his hand. "The name's Chisum. John Chisum. Okay?"

Steve shook the offered hand firmly. "Glad to meet you, John."

"There's just one thing . . ."

Steve eyed him warily.

Chisum smiled, as if reading his thoughts. "You're gonna have to lose some of that hair before you walk onto the mess deck."

"I'd be happy to," replied Steve. "Every time those Provos get a look at me they start foaming at the mouth."

"Yeah, I know what you mean. Wonder what it is that makes a guy volunteer to be a meat-loaf? Maybe they breed a special brand of shit-head over at the Life Institute."

That cancels out one possible location, thought Steve.

And if the Provos collected his movement order on the way out, then he was not in the Bureau either.

Chisum pulled open a drawer of a counter unit set underneath a wall cabinet full of various surgical instruments and took out a pair of scissors and electric hair clippers. He plugged the clippers into a nearby socket. "Pull that chair over here."

Steve wheeled the metal chair into place and sat on it passively while Chisum chopped off the bulk of his hair with the scissors then used the clippers to give him an impeccable crew cut. "Makes a change from shaving the hair off guy's dongs . . ." he grunted. He waved his right hand in front of Steve's nose. "Wish I had a credit point for every one I've picked up with these pinkies."

Steve said nothing but deep down, he resented having to lose his long hair all because of some damnfool regulation. Once again he reminded himself he would have to keep a tight rein on his reactions. *You're back inside, Brickman. Play it cool and, above all, play it smart . . .*

Chisum stepped back to study his handiwork. "Guess that about does it . . ." He picked up the scissors, trimmed off a few stray ends then switched on the clippers again and moved in close to clean up the hair line behind Steve's right ear. "Listen, I know your kin-sister—Roz," he muttered. His voice was barely audible under the whine of the clippers. "D'you want me to tell her you're okay?"

An alarm bell rang inside Steve's head. What was this guy's connection with his kin-sister? "Won't that be dangerous?"

Chisum laughed off the question. He laid aside the clippers, pulled the towel from around Steve's neck and invited him to stand up. "Welcome back to the human race."

Steve felt his eyes suddenly fill with tears. Rising from the chair, he rubbed his face vigorously with both hands in an effort to conceal his emotions and berated himself silently. *Get a grip on yourself, Brickman! You mustn't let any of these people get to you. Especially the nice guys. They are the most dangerous of all . . .*

*   *   *

During the meal on the mess-deck, Chisum made no attempt to question Steve on his period of captivity. The conversation ranged in desultory fashion over Steve's life at Roosevelt Field, his three years at the Academy, and what it was like to serve aboard a wagon-train. Chisum was amiable, asked intelligent questions but was not over curious. By the end of the meal, Steve realised that Chisum had revealed virtually nothing about his own background.

As they pushed their plates aside, Steve asked the questions he'd been waiting to ask since the haircut. Questions he knew Chisum would expect to be asked. "Where am I?"

Chisum considered the question. "I think, at this stage, it's better for you not to know that. Better for both of us."

"What's the connection between you and Roz?"

Chisum shrugged. "Nothing special. Just good friends."

Steve waited but Chisum did not elaborate further.

"The thing is, no one's supposed to know that I'm back."

"That's okay, she can keep a secret." Chisum's eyes did not waver.

"Maybe, but . . ." Steve shook his head, ". . . there's too much at stake. If anyone found out it could really screw things up—for both of you."

Chisum shrugged. "I'll take a chance if you will."

"John, come on. You know what the score is. They're keeping me under wraps. Why stick your neck out? You don't owe me anything."

Chisum's eyes stayed on Steve's. "That's right. I *don't* owe you anything—and that includes an explanation. Okay?"

"Guess it'll have to be. Thanks anyway."

Chisum rose from the table. "She's a good kid. Gonna make a fine doctor."

"If she makes it."

Chisum nodded firmly. "She'll make it." He took Steve up from the mess deck to a small four-berth hospital ward, bade him good-night and announced he would collect him in the morning.

The ward was one of six set behind translucent partitions on either side of a wide corridor. Two white-coated orderlies sat at a lamp-lit table inside the door to the unit. The rest of the lights were turned down to twilight level. Steve took the only bed that was made up and slept soundly.

Over the next two days, Steve underwent an exhaustive medical examination covering virtually every part of his body—both inside and out. He was given a complete body scan, skin tissue, bone marrow, blood, saliva and urine samples were taken and he had the unappetising task of spooning a sample of his faeces into a small jar. His mental and physical reflexes were tested by a wide variety of devices ranging from electronic displays to a rubber hammer, and electrodes taped to his ribs and his newly shorn skull monitored his heart and brain.

Steve assumed he was being checked for radiation damage but, as at Pueblo, none of the medical staff explained the purpose of the tests, or communicated any of the results. His body was manipulated and examined as impersonally as one might examine a black box filled with transistors. Chisum, who he glimpsed occasionally, was his only contact with reality.

At the end of the second day, when he found himself alone with Chisum, Steve asked the medic if he knew how he was doing.

Chisum went to the doorway to check that no one was coming then opened up the taps of a nearby sink unit. He beckoned Steve to come closer. "I haven't seen anything official, you understand, but the word is you're clean." His face split into a broad grin. "You don't look surprised."

Steve frowned. "I'm not surprised because, personally, I never felt better in my life. But . . . are you saying they've found absolutely nothing wrong with me at all?"

"Yeah," replied Chisum.

Steve stared at him. "But . . . you and I know it's impossible to survive that long without some—"

Chisum didn't let him finish. "Yeah. Maybe that's why they're keeping you under wraps. I'll tell you something else, soldier—" He glanced again at the doorway and brought his face in close so that Steve could make out what he was saying above the noise of the running water. "You ain't the first."

The news was so surprising, it left Steve temporarily speechless. But, for some unexplained reason, it also had a deeper, more unsettling effect. His legs felt wobbly—as if the ground was crumbling away beneath him. Part of him seemed to be coming loose. There was the same roaring in his ears he had heard when Roz had told him about their mental contact during his first overground flight. Shaking uncontrollably, he made an uncoordinated grab for Chisum's arm.

Chisum evaded his grasp and backed off.

Steve found his voice but the questions came out in a hopeless jumble. "What d'you mean I'm not—who are these—how can—?!"

"Shut up! Sit down!" hissed Chisum. "Someone's coming! Forget what I told you, okay?!" He turned away abruptly and walked to the far end of the room as a medic who'd been involved in the two-day examination entered and came over to where Steve, dressed in a white hospital gown, sat limply with his hands in his lap.

The medic laid his hand on Steve's shoulder. "Okay, you can get dressed now." Steve didn't respond. "Hey, soldier—what's the matter? You're trembling."

"Just cold," said Steve weakly. He rose sluggishly to his feet forcing his head up and his shoulders back. The roaring in his ears began to fade. "Nothing's wrong. I feel fine, sir. Just fine . . ."

"Good," replied the medic. "Tomorrow morning you go before the Board of Assessors for your first debriefing session."

Later that night, while Steve slept restlessly in the empty hospital ward, Chisum used his ID-card to gain entry to a small conference room where a large, wall-mounted tv screen faced the open end of a U-shaped table with nine seats around it. As Chisum sat down in the centre seat at the base of the U, a camera mounted above the tv unit recorded his arrival and confirmed his identity by subjecting his electronic image to computer analysis. At the appointed time, the red, white and blue star and bar Amtrak logo disappeared from the screen and was replaced by the top half of a young, dark-haired woman sitting behind a metallic silver desk with a mirror-like finish.

Chisum rose respectfully.

The woman leant towards him, put her forearms on the desk and laid her hands one on top of the other. "Good evening, John." Her low-pitched voice was firm and well-modulated.

"Good evening, Fran."

"Take a seat."

Chisum sat down and assumed the same position as his interlocutor, hands crossed on the table in front of him.

Fran had a pale, oval face, a wide, firm-lipped mouth, and greyish brown eyes. Her short straight hair, parted on the right, was brushed in a sloping line across her forehead and swept back behind the ears. She was dressed in a silver jump-suit—the official work uniform of members of the First Family—with dark blue and white inserts that denoted her rank. Chisum, who had been in contact with Fran for some six months judged her to be about twenty-seven years old—it was hard to tell with the Family. Even though her location could not be far from where he now sat they had never met face to face, and since taking up his present assignment he had only learned two things about his Operational Director; her full name was Franklin Delano Jefferson, and she was Steve Brickman's controller.

"How is 3552?"

"Chipped, but not about to crack apart," replied Chisum.

"Has he communicated anything of interest regarding the period he spent in captivity?"

"Nothing at all. There exists the possibility of a potential relationship but, being a wingman, he is extremely self-reliant. I've tried to get him to open up but he exhibits absolutely no need for any significant degree of social interaction."

"It's true he does have an exceptionally well-integrated sense of identity," admitted Fran.

"I also have a strong impression the subject suspects I'm there to do more than clean out test tubes."

"It would be surprising if he didn't," replied Fran. "He's a sensitive, like his kin-sister. He's also a little paranoid. He suspects everybody. Did he ask about the result of the tests?"

"Yes. I replied as instructed. His reaction was very much as you predicted. For a moment or two I thought he was going to come apart at the seams. It was, uh—an interesting experience."

Fran nodded thoughtfully. "After the exposure he's had it's not surprising that some of the mind-blocks have worked loose. What do you think, John—will the conditioning hold?"

Chisum chewed over his reply. "I'm no expert but if you're prepared to gamble on my intuition, I think the answer is 'yes.' On the other hand, if it turns out I'm wrong, could he be reprogrammed?"

"Good question, John. It's something that's never been tried before. This segment of OVERLORD has been running for over fifty years but we're still very much in uncharted waters. Any attempt to reprogramme one of the current subjects may cause more problems than it will solve." Fran ran her fingers through the hair on her forehead and favoured Chisum with a warm smile. "Anything else?"

"Yes," said Chisum. "Despite his very high degree of self-control, I loosened some of the cement when I mentioned the name of his kin-sister. This was definitely a genuine emotional response. It's possible that the hard-soft-hard approach we decided to adopt is beginning to pay off. On the other hand he may be harbouring some feelings of guilt towards Roz—uh, I mean, 3801. I think we should seriously consider putting the two of them nose to nose. In view of the psychosomatic wounding she suffered when he crashed, I would expect her to know that he is still alive anyway."

"And here at Grand Central . . ." added Fran.

Chisum shrugged. "That wouldn't surprise me either."

"So what you're suggesting is that we let him go before the Assessors as planned, and if he proves a tough nut to

crack we put him together with his kin-sister then—once
she's involved—use her to apply leverage?"

"Exactly," said Chisum. "Meanwhile, I'll keep playing
the good guy. And, of course, my position would be enhanced if I could be instrumental in arranging for them to
see each other . . ."

Fran nodded. "I like it. Well done, John. I'll clear
things this end and get back to you. Stay tuned."

"I will." Chisum got to his feet.

"Good night, John."

"Good night, Fran."

Her image was replaced by the Amtrak logo—a blue
circle enclosing within its circumference a white, five pointed
star. Set on either side of the circle were two rectangular
white panels each split horizontally by an outward-pointing
red arrow. The circle and the panels were surrounded by a
border of the same colour and thickness. According to the
Manual, the white star symbolised Texas, the Lone Star
State, the Inner State where the Amtrak Federation was
born; the blue background represented the blue sky world
to which it would return. The red border around the star
and bars symbolised the overground frontier being pushed
ever outwards by the arrows—red like the blood that was
being spilt in the process. The two white rectangles trav-
ersed by the red arrows represented the Outer States that
had been won back from the Mutes—the cleansed overground.

As Chisum carefully repositioned the chair, he reflected
upon the realisation that the true genius of the First
Family lay in its infinite capacity to deceive. At some time
in the distant past, the Jeffersons—a self-perpetuating dy-
nasty whose interrelated members were currently believed
to number around five thousand—had succeeded in placing themselves at the apex of a pyramid of cunningly woven
lies and deceit that, over the centuries, had gradually
assumed the authority of received truth; had slowly hardened like the rock of ages within the earthshield, providing them with the solid foundation upon which they had
constructed their present unassailable position of power.

Brickman was a special case, but everyone else had been conditioned too. Even Chisum could not bring himself to fully believe that what he had discovered was the truth. That was one of the curses of being an undercover agent. Truth and untruth quickly become indistinguishable; assumed identities merged with the underlying self leaving you, in the end, with only one touchstone of reality—the fact that you were alive. And even that fact could quickly become obsolete. One big black mark was all it took.

Chisum left the conference room and headed back towards the quarters he shared with three other medics. Yeah . . . it was a hard world, sure enough. The only thing the First Family didn't control was the state of after-death. They could kill you a dozen different ways and at infinitely variable speed but once that old heart stopped pumping, you were—metaphorically speaking—out from under. Up and running.

Yes, sir . . .

Always assuming, of course, that there was some part of you left, and some place to run to. Chisum hoped there was. He had been thinking about the idea for years, ever since a Tracker—one of a gang of cee-bees he'd tracked down in a warren of pre-Holocaust tunnels below an overground site called Dallas—had shown him a book. Not *The* Book; not the Manual; not electronic pages from the video-archive but lines of words on yellowing, tattered rectangular leaves of a thin, fabric-type substance.

The old guy had told him it was paper. The nearest thing to it that Chisum had seen was plasfilm—the stuff maps of the overground were printed on. The book, which was called the Old and New Testament, contained a string of stories about what was supposed to have happened way, way back before even the blue-sky world had taken shape. Chisum, whose task had been to infiltrate the group, took time out to read great chunks of it. It hadn't been easy. Most of the pages which were supposed to be fixed together down one side had come loose, some were missing, or were torn. It was not surprising that the Federation had switched to putting everything on video. Chisum's over-

riding impression of the book was that times hadn't changed
much. There were lots of battles, bad times, good times,
people getting shafted—there was one guy, Job—Christo!
Now he *really* had a bad time! And then there were a lot
of guys making promises about a better tomorrow, a lot of
talk about right and wrong, and a place called Heaven, the
Kingdom of God. Like the blue sky world—only better.

When the group had been rounded up, Chisum had
hidden the book away behind some loose bricks in one of
the decaying tunnels. He'd meant to return for it but a
Provo demolition gang had blasted the gang's hide-out into
a heap of rubble. Chisum often told himself it was the best
thing that could have happened. That book could have
cost him his life. As part of an undercover law-enforcement
unit he knew what the rules were but, having discovered
that book, he could not understand *why* possession of it
should be a Code One offence.

From that moment on, Chisum had begun to examine
more carefully what he was asked to do: not to question
orders—that would have ben fatal—but to ponder the
reasons why people like him were necessary. Some of the
ideas in that old book still stuck in his mind, and one
persistent question had remained to nag him. Just before
the hide-out had been raided, the old cee-bee had let
Chisum in on a big secret: under another part of Dallas he
had discovered a big underground gallery containing thousands of such books full of all kinds of stories, pictures, and
facts about the pre-Holocaust world. Swore to it on the
P-G's life. This old man had actually spent two whole days
just walking *round* it! Rack after rack of books from floor to
ceiling; set in long lines that seemed like they went on for
ever. He had promised to show Chisum where it was but,
on the very day he was due to lead him through the maze
of tunnels, Chisum's team and their Provo back-up had
swooped in and bagged the whole bunch. That had been
five years ago.

Were those books still there? Chisum wondered. Lying
sealed behind the rubble? And did the First Family—who,
through the medium of the video archives, had only the

barest information to offer about the pre-Holocaust period—
know they were there?

The Board of Assessors that Steve found himself facing the
following morning consisted of five men and three women.
The ninth member—the President of the Board had not
yet arrived. Steve stood at ease in front of the chair that he
was scheduled to occupy for the better part of the next five
days and tried to guess the demeanour of the individual
board members as they took their seats on either side of
the President's hand-carved, high-backed chair. The table,
at which the Assessors would sit, was semi-circular in
shape, curving round on both sides of Steve's chair so that
he could be observed closely while under interrogation.

Raising his eyes, Steve caught sight of one of the ever-
present tv cameras and mike units that would record everything he said and every movement he made. The
videotapes would be carefully scrutinised later; every aspect of his performance would come under review. It was
the standard technique applied to all Trackers, regardless
of rank. Everybody below senior executive rank was inter-
viewed at three monthly intervals by two Assessors. An
individual's performance and attitude were evaluated and
he was rewarded or penalised with plus or minus credit
points. This process began at the age of five and continued
for most Trackers until the bagmen called. Steve had
always managed to do well in his quarterly assessments
but he had never faced a full board before. He glanced
discreetly at the board members and tried to guess their
ages. He judged them to be between thirty and forty years
old. The greying hair was no guide at all. Some execs had
white hair at twenty-five and, after a particularly hard
tour, a lot of Trail-Blazers ended up as silver-tops too. It
was said that, even if they were stark naked, you could
always spot an Assessor by the way they looked at you.
That piercing gaze. For some unexplained reason, Assessors almost always had abnormally intense pale grey or
cold blue eyes and an air of total dedication. They could
quote page after page of the Manual and were absolutely
fanatical about points of procedure, rules and regulations.

But while there were some word-perfect pedants who could not see the wood for the trees, there were other Assessors who were remarkably shrewd observers adept at spotting the slightest hint of evasiveness or insincerity.

A tv monitor was set into the table in front of each assessor on which data relating to the examinee could be displayed. Each member of the board was also provided with an electronic memo pad to make notes on. The pads could be plugged into the monitors, enabling them to send messages to one another without the examinee knowing what was being said. A number on Steve's side of the table identified the individual board members; 1–4 on his left, 5–8 on his right. The President's position needed no clarification.

A door on the left-hand section of the wall behind the table opened. Steve sprang to attention as the President of the Board entered and moved to her place directly opposite him. The eight Assessors waited deferentially until she sat down, then followed suit.

"Sit down, Steven." The President's voice was low-pitched, firm and well-modulated. Her dark hair, parted on the right, sloped across her forehead and was swept back behind the ears. Her eyes were greyish-brown. It was Fran. Franklin Delano Roosevelt, Steve's controller.

Steve had no means of knowing this, or that she was Family. Fran was dressed in the standard grey jump-suit worn by all members of the Federation's Legal Division. Draped over her shoulders was a loose-sleeved, three-quarter length sessions gown—part of an Assessor's formal dress. As the Board's President, Fran wore a vermilion gown with charcoal grey trim. The other members of the Board wore similar gowns with the colours reversed. Had she cared to consult COLUMBUS, Fran might have discovered that the shape and cut of the gowns recalled those worn by ivy-league college professors in the halcyon days preceding the Holocaust. The others—who, despite their Level 12 ID-cards, would never acquire the same unrestricted access—were destined to remain ignorant of this minor piece of sartorial history—and a great deal more besides.

Fran exchanged the customary greetings with the other members of the Board and checked that the monitor inter-com system was working satisfactorily. The preliminary questioning of the examinee, which followed a standard procedure, was conducted by the Board's President. The primary function of the eight Assessors was to observe the examinee and evaluate their responses, but individual members were permitted to seek clarification of an answer, or ask a supplementary question. Any Assessor wishing to do this sent a signal to the President then waited for the green light. Fran used this brief settling-in period to make an appraisal of Steve. Since taking over as his controller she had studied the videofile covering the relevant stages in his life from birth to date, but this was the first time she had met him face to face. As a woman, she liked what she saw but that did not affect her resolve to extract from him every ounce of information he possessed about the Mutes.

Fran leaned her forearms on the table, placed her palms carefully together and fixed Steve with her grey-brown eyes. The corners of her mouth tweaked up into a half-smile that belied the serious note in her voice. "Steven, before we ask you to describe your experiences, I want to emphasise that despite the circumstances surrounding your initial reception at Pueblo and Santa Fe, the Federation does not consider you to have defaulted in any way. In no sense are you suspected of dereliction of duty whilst serving as a wingman." Fran glanced round the table. "I think, in that respect, I speak for all members of the Board?"

The eight Assessors nodded and murmured their assent.

Fran turned her attention back onto Steve. "As you are no doubt aware from the degree of incredulity you en-countered at Pueblo and elsewhere, you are the first Tracker ever to have survived capture by the Mutes—and the only individual that has had the opportunity to make an in-depth study of the Plainfolk. What you have to tell us will be invaluable in planning our campaign to repossess the overground. It follows that—since your experience is unique—there can be no question of this Board seeking to censure any aspect of your behaviour, or any observations you might have to make about the period under review."

Fran paused and treated Steve to a sympathetic smile. "It must, to put it mildly, have been a very difficult time. Traumatic even."

Steve thought it appropriate to reply at this point with a sober nod.

"I can believe it," continued Fran. "However, we are going to ask you to relive each moment from the time you took off from The Lady with—" She broke off to consult the screen. "—with White, G.R . . . your friend Gus . . . until you arrived over the way-station at Pueblo. I want you to consider this examination as an extended version of the debriefing process you would normally undergo at the hands of your Flight Operations Officer. All we wish to do is to share the knowledge you have gained during captivity in the hope that it will provide us with a greater under-standing of the enemy. Do you understand that?"

"Yessir-ma'am," replied Steve.

"Good." The President smiled again. "The First Family has asked me to say that they are aware of the hostile treatment you underwent en route and will take steps to provide appropriate compensation. I understand that the State Provost-Marshal of New Mexico explained some, if not all, of the reasons why it was necessary for you to be hooded and chained."

"He has, sir-ma'am."

"The various physical assaults were regrettable, but—given the unforeseen circumstances surrounding your return—I'm sure you will accept that the incidents were due to an excess of zeal."

"It was a small price to pay for the pleasure of getting back home, sir-ma'am."

"I'm glad you see it that way," said the President. "At least no permanent damage was done."

None that shows, thought Brickman. That was a good line. Well done, Steven. But why all this preamble—plus what amounted to an apology by the First Family? It was unheard of. Why should *they* suddenly start caring about guys getting beaten up by Provos? The alarm bells inside Steve's head started ringing. The Board's President wor-ried him. She was, at a guess, closer to twenty-five than thirty. To be heading a full board of Assessors at that age meant that she was either very bright, or . . .

Or what?

Steve was aware of blurred images forming in his brain. The entity, the power, or whatever it was that lurked within was trying to tell him something but the lines were down between them. It was his own fault. He had fought it off, tried to shut it out, ignore it, bury it, for so many years it had retreated like some strange recluse into a distant room at the back of his mind, emerging only when it felt the need to do so. Steve tried to bring the images into focus but the dark messenger did not respond to his call and his inner eye remained clouded.

He suspects, thought Fran. She had spent several days wondering whether to take this opportunity to come face to face with Brickman and now cursed herself for making the wrong decision. She should have waited; should have chosen a less distinguished role. Something with a lower profile. Dammit! Never mind—too late to backtrack now . . .

"Ohh-kaay," she sang as she consulted the angled screen set into the table in front of her. "You and Gus White took off on June 12th to fire-bomb a Mute cropfield north-east of Cheyenne. Wingmen Fazetti and Naylor were to make a similar attack on a nearby forest—believed to be the location of a Plainfolk settlement. Why don't you take it from there?"

Steve had had a long time to prepare for this moment. He took a deep breath and began his carefully edited version of what had happened to him after he'd been knocked out of the sky by a Mute crossbow bolt. The daily sessions were divided into four two-and-a-half-hour periods with a thirty-minute break in the morning and afternoon and an hour for lunch. After just two periods during which he did most of the talking, Steve's jaw ached intolerably and his tongue felt stiff and swollen. The prospect of another forty-five hours under the same pressure left him distinctly uneasy. It was not just physical stamina he needed, the mental effort required was considerable too. Apart from the highly sensitive information he wished and, indeed, had sworn to conceal, Steve knew that, in his

own interests, he had to avoid making any value judg-
ments. In this kind of examination, the choice of words
and phrases was crucial; a careless remark, or an ill-thought
out reply could suddenly lead to an explosive confronta-
tion. And so he concentrated on the facts, expressing
neither approval nor disapproval of the Mute way of life,
and their strange beliefs about the world.

On the first day, after describing how he had been
dragged from the tangled wreckage of his Skyhawk, Steve
related how Mr. Snow had used plant leaves to dress his
wounds, and had forced him to eat dried shreds of Dream-
Cap, a pain-killing mushroom, when setting the bones in
his broken leg and how, with a self-imposed programme of
exercises, he had brought himself back to peak combat-
fitness in preparation for his eventual escape.

Asked about the wounds in his cheek, Steve described
how, to avoid being killed by a hostile faction of the
M'Call clan, he had been forced to take part in a Mute test
of warriorhood known as Biting the Arrow in which—under
the threat of instant execution—he had to submit to having an arrow driven through his face without flinching
before breaking it between his teeth. A memorable
moment—not for the pain—but because that was the night
he had caught his first glimpse of Clearwater.

He went on to describe the organisation of the clan
M'Call; the way their settlement was laid out, and the ease
with which the huts and their contents could be packed up
and carried over long distances; the clan's daily round of
activity, the food-gathering and distribution process, the
patrolling by posses of Bears and She-Wolves, and the
aggressive defence of their "home turf."

On the second day, when the questioning turned to
Mute tactics and weaponry, Steve scored a hit with the
Board when he revealed the existence of the Iron Masters,
the mystery men from the Fire-Pits of Beth-Lem who
furnished the Plainfolk with their powerful crossbows and
other edged weapons—what the Mutes called "sharp iron."
Pressed for more details he could only repeat the few
scraps of information he had been able to glean: the Iron
Masters' trading expeditions were made aboard "wheel-

boats" that came up the great rivers called the "Miz-Hurry" and the "Miz-Hippy." Steve was unable to tell the Assessors where Beth-Lem was located. When asked the same question Cadillac had been noticeably evasive saying only that "it lay in the lands beyond the eastern door."

On the third day, the main subject was wordsmiths. The Assessors were particularly interested in Steve's account of his relationship with Mr. Snow and Cadillac and, in particular, his explanation of the old Mute's key role as the clan's historian and walking encyclopedia and his position as chief tactician and adviser to the governing clan elders, and how Cadillac was being trained as his replacement.

"Are you telling us these wordsmiths are educators—that they can train any child to memorise nine hundred plus years of oral history?" asked Assessor 6.

"No, sir, not any child," replied Steve. "These wordsmiths are a breed apart. They are born with that capability. I don't know how, or what the selection process is, but I do know the M'Call's don't yet have a third generation whizz kid to replace Cadillac. Don't get me wrong. Outwardly these, uh—guys—look just like any other Mute. But beneath the skin and bone deformations they are remarkably gifted individuals."

Assessor 6 grunted. "Well, they obviously impressed you."

"Sir, these people are the enemy. If I were to ignore their undoubted potential to harm us I would be failing in my sworn duty to do all I can to protect the First Family and the Federation."

The young President of the Board smiled. "Well said, Steven."

Right, thought Steve. It was the kind of line that went down well with Assessors. But it also had an edge of truth. The irony was that Steve's apparent eagerness to tell all concealed the real truth: Mr. Snow's potential to harm the Federation was greater than they could ever imagine.

Steve fixed his gaze on the grey-brown eyes and beamed out his best honest-John look. "Ma'am, at the risk of incurring disfavour, I have to say that while—in term of brain-power—the two wordsmiths stood head and shoul-

ders above the rest, the average Mute was not as stupid as
I had been led to expect."

"Let me get this quite clear," said the President. "Are
you trying to tell us that the Plainfolk Mutes possess human
intelligence?"

"Yes," added Assessor 3, a blunt-featured man whose
neck was too wide for his face. "Are you saying these
animals are our equals?"

They were both loaded questions. Any discussion on
these lines was pure dynamite. Steve weighed his reply
carefully, conscious that an overlong hesitation would be
interpreted unfavourably. "The Manual states that Mutes
are sub-human, ma'am. Compared with our own life-style,
theirs is certainly primitive, many of their customs savage
and barbarous. But while they have no written form of
communication, they speak a language that closely resem-
bles Basic and, through their wordsmiths, they possess a
history covering a similar time span to our own. They
make music and they sing—"

"So do birds," said Assessor 3.

Steve accepted this interruption with a polite nod. He
knew that one of the techniques employed by Assessors
was to make seemingly stupid remarks in the hope of
triggering a contemptuous and ill-considered reply. It
worked well with examinees who thought they were brighter
than their interrogator. "Sir, I know they are commonly
referred to as animals—they are also called lumpheads,
four-eyes, shit-balls and dick-eaters. Not without reason, I
am sure. But I submit that the word 'animal' applies more
correctly to an overground beast incapable of communicating its thoughts, ideas and intentions to a human being
through the medium of syntactic speech."

"Do you think you can buffalo us by using long words,
boy?" snapped Assessor 3.

"No, sir," replied Steve. "I know that particular definition is not in the Manual but—"

"Maybe it should be . . ." The President came to his
rescue. "Go on, Steven."

"Ma'am—I can only speak with reference to this particular clan but what I'm trying to say is that, although the

Plainfolk are technological illiterates, the various craft skills they possess shows they *can* learn. Their apparent inability to remember does not prevent them from *absorbing* information. The problem they have is one of information retrieval. They can retain knowledge but they can't *express* that knowledge verbally. As a result, most of them appear incredibly stupid."

From the looks that passed between them it was clear that some of the Assessors did not like what they heard. Steve knew it was the wrong thing to do but some perverse impulse made him pursue this theme. He addressed the President. "Ma'am—I was asked if I regarded Mutes as our equals. In terms of their bodies and mental attitude, the answer has to be 'No.' If we ignore the small number of 'yearlings,' the physical differences are irreconcilable, their way of life totally alien. But if we apply different criteria—strength, stamina, manual dexterity, educability and—it has to be said—a latent intelligence, then my answer would have to be 'Not yet.' "

The President compressed her lips into a thin line.

Assessor 7, one of the other women examinees leaned forward. "Would you care to explain that last remark?"

"Ma'am, I am not disputing the wisdom of the Manual. But if I have understood it correctly, the information it contains on this subject was compiled as a result of operations against the *Southern* Mutes. I have only observed them as captives in work-camps and chain-gangs. The Plainfolk are still independent. An undefeated warrior race. And, from what the M'Call wordsmiths told me, they have every intention of remaining so. Our first advances into their territory have shown them what they are up against. We should not underrate them. They have the capacity to adapt, to acquire higher craft skills—even technology."

Assessor 1 snorted drily. "Technology! Where the heck are they gonna learn that—from us?"

Steve turned to his left. "Well, sir, that hadn't occurred to me but now that you mention it, maybe it's something we ought to be thinking about."

Assessor 3 exploded. "Have you gone soft in the head?!

Those gammy-assed shit-balls can't even tell the difference between a pick and shovel unless you whup it into 'em!"

Steve fought down a sudden urge to let this overbearing turd have it right between the eyes. To tell him and his nit-picking friends that underneath the swirling patterns of black and brown, Cadillac's body was as unblemished as his own; that with short hair and dressed in a jump-suit, the eighteen-year-old Mute could easily pass as a Tracker; that although uneducated by Federation standards the young warrior had an uncanny ability to learn at lightning speed—and was, in many ways, smarter than most graduates from the Flight Academy. Steve bit his lip and said nothing, mindful of his promise to Mr. Snow never to tell his masters of Cadillac's true physical state, or reveal the existence of Clearwater.

He turned on a winning smile for Assessor 3. "I have to admit there were a few who were kinda slow." Yes, sir . . . this was definitely not the moment to mention that it was the M'Call clan who had provided tools and assistance in building Blue-Bird—the aircraft in which he had made his escape. That would have led to some awkward questions which, in turn, might have forced him into revealing that, in exchange, he had taught Cadillac to fly. Despite the honeyed assurances of the dark-haired President, that particular piece of news would *really* have caused the shit to hit the fan.

"Steven," said the President. "I'm intrigued. Why should we teach the Mutes anything?"

"Don't get me wrong, ma'am. I'm not questioning Federation policy—"

"I'm glad to hear it."

"It's just that—having seen what the Plainfolk are capable of—it occurred to me that if they're going to learn anything at all, we should control the process—rather than someone else. Like the Iron Masters. If these mystery men are trading crossbows, you can be sure they've armed themselves with something better to give them the edge. They have Plainfolk working for them already, production facilities and water-borne transportation." He spread his palms. "Who knows what else they might have up their sleeves?"

Fran smiled. This young man was fast—and cute. "Don't worry about the Iron Masters, Steven. When the time is right, they'll be taken care of. And forget about improving the Mutes. Let them live out what remains of their grubby little lives. The overground is ours by right. It's been promised to us by the First Family. We don't have to share the blue-sky world with anybody."

FIVE

WHEN HE WOKE on the fourth day, Steve knew the
Assessors would turn their attention to his escape. This
was the moment that Steve had been worried about—and
with good reason—for the explanation he planned to offer
about the building of the hang-glider was a total fabrica-
tion. He had decided to tell the Board that, having recovered Naylor's knife and stolen certain tools, he had escaped
from the Mutes and made his way back to the spot where
the clan had left the wrecked Skyhawks. There, working
alone, he had salvaged enough parts to construct the
glider—a task that had taken him two weeks.

Thinking over this story on his way to the session, Steve
realised that it now sounded grotesquely implausible and
did not square with the other information he had given
about the Mutes. Like—for instance—if they were so good
at running, tracking and hunting, how had he escaped and
then managed to avoid discovery during the two weeks it
had taken to build the glider?

Omission of certain facts during this kind of examination was relatively easy provided you kept your story
consistent. If caught out you could, if blessed with a
nimble brain and agile tongue, blame it on a faulty memory or a misunderstanding of the question. But in offering
up a carefully woven tissue of lies you took a big risk.

92

Inevitably you needed more and more lies to support the first. It only needed one Assessor to become suspicious and that was it. Once someone started picking at the loose ends, the whole thing started to unravel.

Steve found himself in a real bind. Apart from his potentially fatal relationship with Clearwater, everything he had done had been to ensure his survival and provide the means and opportunity to escape. Even so, he was reluctant to reveal the full extent of his cooperation with the Mutes in case it was misinterpreted by the Assessors. Despite the assurances of their young President he didn't have much faith in the Board's impartiality. It was not the way Assessors functioned; under the Federation's system of justice anyone facing a full board was presumed to be guilty until he proved himself innocent.

As he entered the examination room and stood at attention, facing the Assessors, Steve suddenly decided to change his story. He would stay as close to the truth as possible. As the clouds of uncertainty were swept away, he was able to see several moves ahead and realised that it was the best decision he'd made all week.

When the Board was seated, the dark-haired President motioned Steve to follow suit then laid her hands on the table, linked her fingers together and cleared her throat. "Now, Steven—tell us about the events leading up to and surrounding your escape. In particular, how you managed to construct an aircraft in secret."

"I didn't, sir-ma'am. I got the Mutes to help me."

The shock wave generated by his reply practically lifted the Board out of their seats.

Fran Jefferson exchanged a look with the other Assessors then addressed Steve. "Would you care to explain that?"

"It's quite simple, ma'am. I discovered they had kept pieces of Naylor's and Fazetti's Skyhawks. They'd both crashed into the forest where the Mutes had their settlement. So I offered them a deal. I said if they would help me build an arrowhead—their name for our Skyhawks—I would teach 'em to fly."

The President's fingers dug deep into the back of her hands. "And did you?"

The lie came easily. "No, sir-ma'am." He grinned. "As soon as it was finished, I took the first flight out."

Much of the day was taken up with questions and answers about how he had designed and constructed the arrowhead and, in particular, the extent to which the Mutes had been involved.

Assessor 3, who had been working on a short fuse all week exploded again. "I can hardly credit what I'm hearing, boy! Are you telling us you taught these lumps how to build airplanes?!"

"No, sir," replied Steve. "I didn't *teach* them to do anything. I merely gave them the chance to demonstrate the skills they *already* possess. Skills which, up to now, we've either ignored—or have not even been aware of. If we're going to pursue our stated objective of winning back the overground, we should not underestimate the Mute's capabilities—"

Assessor 3 cut in. "Underestimate them?! Heck, boy— you just confessed to increasing their goddam capabilities! What you did is tantamount to treason!"

"No, sir," said Steve firmly. "You misunderstand the situation. I repeat—I did not *teach* them anything. Our current assessment of Mute skills is totally inaccurate. If I failed to tell this Board what I observed—if I remained silent in the hope of staying out of trouble—that *would* be treason. I'd deserve to have The Book thrown at me for betraying everything I believe in."

The dark-haired President looked at Assessor 3. "I agree." She smiled approvingly at Steve. "We applaud your courage and your honesty."

Damn right, thought Steve.

Assessor 2, a woman who had said little all day, leaned forward. "Steven, has it occurred to you that these 'skills' you speak of—and incidentally seem most impressed by— could be part of a vocabulary of instinctive behaviour? In the same way that other overground animals are born with the ability to hunt—and birds and reptiles know how to fly or swim, and build nests in which to rear their young?"

The President smiled. "I'm afraid Steven doesn't believe that Mutes are animals."

Steve knew he was being drawn back onto dangerous ground but felt obliged to reply. "With respect, ma'am, officially, the Federation does not describe Mutes as animals. They are categorised as sub-human."

"That's correct," replied Fran. "It means 'Less than human.' It means they can never be our equals—or are you challenging that definition too?"

"No, sir-ma'am."

"I'm glad to hear it. Go on with your story."

Editing the true sequence of events, Steve described the unsuccessful attempt to power the arrowhead with a motor from one of the wrecked Skyhawks and his decision to make do with an unpowered rig. And how, after completing the craft, he had overpowered two guards during the night, then fought and killed three more Mutes before making his dawn leap to freedom.

Steve told the story well. Fran, listening to her young golden-haired charge, was enthralled. "Do you mean to say that you leapt off the top of that cliff without even a test flight?"

Steve inclined his head with a modest smile. "It wasn't all that much of a risk, ma'am. Aerodynamics was one of my best subjects at the Academy."

Yes, I know, thought Fran. You scored 100 per cent. Just as you did in all the other exams . . .

On the fifth and final day, Steve stood to attention once again as the Board members filed in and the young President took her seat. While it was clear that many of his observations had been controversial, Steve was confident that he had struck the right balance between candour and servility. He was, after all, a wingman—a superbly trained, highly-disciplined lone-wolf capable of acting independently whereas others, like linemen for example—the ground troops of the Federation—could only function properly as part of a close-knit combat group. Wingmen were relatively unaffected by the morbid fear of the overground that assailed most Trackers. In a tightly controlled society such independence could be potentially dangerous. Not in the Federation. Wingmen were selected for their integrity and loyalty to the First Family. These were the guys who did everything by The Book. The guys whose zeal for the rules and regulations was only exceeded by Provos and Assessors.

Above all else, Steve knew how to radiate integrity. And he was pretty good on loyalty too. Endowed with a photographic memory, he could come up with an appropriate line from any of the First Family Inspirationals. The same went for the recorded wisdom of the President-Generals, and the Behavioural Codes from the Manual. No problem. Steve could quote chapter and verse. As he went to sit down, Steve was struck by the thought that, had he been a Mute, he might have been raised—like Cadillac—as a wordsmith.

Once again, the President of the Board of Assessors clasped her fingers together and fixed him squarely with her grey-brown eyes. "Steven, I've give much thought to your previous testimony—in particular, the account of your escape you gave us yesterday. I've also discussed it with my colleagues on this Board and we have been forced to the conclusion that you have not been completely truthful with us."

Steve fought down a sudden feeling of unease and scanned the Assessors with an air of slightly bewildered disappointment.

Fran's mouth showed a hint of amusement as his eyes swept round the table to meet hers. "The point that concerns us is the remarkable degree of cooperation shown by your captors. You say that you offered them a trade-off but that, in the final analysis, none took place. We find that difficult to believe—particularly in view of your earlier claim that we have underestimated the Mute's powers of reasoning. However, even if this clan was as dumb-assed as the Southern Mutes, they are led by two wordsmiths— both of whom you have rated as being of above-average intelligence—"

"Beg pardon, ma'am—may I qualify that?"

"Go ahead," said Fran.

"What I meant was—'Above-average intelligence for Mutes.'"

Fran swallowed a smile. "I take the point, Steven. I think the Board is aware of your, uh—position on that particular subject."

Steve cursed inwardly. His interruption had probably done him more harm than good.

Fran unlaced her fingers and placed her palms flat on the table. "But to return to what I was saying. We are puzzled by the fact no one seems to have thought that, once the arrowhead was ready, you might use it in an attempt to escape."

"But they did think of it, ma'am. They warned me that if I tired to make a break for it, they'd knock me out of the sky."

"And you believed them," said Assessor 4, the woman sitting on the President's right.

"I had every reason to, ma'am," replied Steve. "I'd already been shot down once by a crossbow bolt—and I'd seen most of my section aboard The Lady killed the same way."

"And yet that did not deter you," observed Fran. "You single-handedly overpowered two guards then killed three others who attempted to stop you taking off."

"I got high marks in close combat drills too, ma'am."

"Yes," said Fran. "We all know what you are capable of, Steven. But is it reasonable given the precautions that—on your own evidence—the Plainfolk take to guard their settlements, to ask us to believe that you were able to do all this, steal what they must have regarded as an extremely valuable object, and leave without a general alarm being raised, or any further attempt being made to stop you?"

Steve laid a hand on his heart and radiated an almost tangible aura of sincerity. "That's the way it happened, ma'am. On my oath to the President-General." The rest of the words spilled out before he could stop them. "I guess they didn't expect me to go at night."

The eight Assessors looked at one another then simultaneously flashed a request for a Supplementary onto Fran's video screen.

Fran asked the question they were all bursting to put to Steve. "Why not at night, Steven?"

Steve knew he dare not hesitate. "Because the Plainfolk don't really operate at night. In an emergency they'll move the settlement under cover of darkness but—from what I observed—they don't fight each other. When it get's dark everything shuts down—and most of the guards go to sleep."

Fran let Assessor 5—the man sitting on her left—put the question. "Let me get this straight. Are you suggesting that if we attacked these lumps at night we would have the drop on them?"

"Sir, it would be wrong for me to give the impression that it would be a walkover but I think it would be safe to say you would definitely achieve an element of surprise."

The eight Assessors reacted with varying degrees of excited astonishment. Assessor 5 turned to Fran. "Ma'am—do you realise what we've got here? This could be the breakthrough the Fed's been looking for. I think you ought to wire it through to AmEx straight away!"

Fran nodded amiably. "I share your excitement. But let's not go overboard. I know we have night-scopes and other infra-red weaponry but you seem to be overlooking the fact that a lot of our people are terrified of the dark too. However, I'm sure that's a problem we will be able to overcome." She turned to Steve. "I must thank you for revealing such a valuable piece of intelligence—even if it took you four days to get around to it."

Steve assumed a chastened look. "Ma'am, in my defence, I can only say it must have been because of what you've just said. Knowing how most of our people feel about the dark, I guess the real importance of it just didn't jump out at me. And with so many other things to tell you about . . ."

"Yes," said Fran. Yes, she thought. I can see why people get sucked in by the winning smile, the strong, honest face, the direct, unflinching gaze. It's the eyes, Brickman. You're clever. You do your best to hide behind them but I can still see *you* in there. They're right about you, Brickman.

You've got potential. But you need a lot more practice. Or maybe a few private lessons . . .

Locking her fingers together, she flexed them back and forth then sat back with her elbows on the arms of her chair and placed her forefingers under her chin. "Let's get back to the escape. I accept your explanation of why you were able to gain access to the arrowhead so easily but—when you took off—it was almost light. Did no one else witness your departure? Did none of these eagle-eyed warriors in the surrounding guard posts fire at you?"

"No, sir-ma'am. I was glad they didn't, of course but, like you, I found that kinda strange. Maybe it had something to do with the fact that both wordsmiths were away at the time. As I mentioned earlier, the clan always seemed to be a more cohesive unit—much more on the ball—when they were around." Steve paused, as if weighing up what to say next. In reality, he had it all worked out. So far—apart from the unintended revelation about the Mute's odd habit of shutting down for the night—everything had gone as planned. The start had been a trifle sticky but he had recovered brilliantly. Onwards and upwards, Brickman. "A posse of them trailed me but I stayed high and soon lost them in the mountains. Ever since then, and especially over these last few days, I've wondered why they gave up so easily—and why they let me build the arrowhead in the first place."

Fran raised an eyebrow. "And . . . ?"

"Ma'am, the only thing I can think of is that they wanted me to escape. That's why they didn't kill me right at the beginning when I crashed into the cropfield. They wanted me to bring back a message."

"And what message is that, Steven?"

"The Talis—"

Fran cut him short with a wave of her hand. "That's enough!" she exclaimed abruptly. She punched a button on the control panel of her video and spoke into her table mike. "Rewind the current tape and give me an edit facility on this station." Her voice was hard-edged, efficient. Her presence took on an extra dimension. A commanding arrogance that went way beyond the assured

manner with which she had controlled the proceedings of
the last few days. It was fascinating to see the mask slip.
Chilling, yet exciting at the same time.

Steve's eyes met hers. I was right, he thought. You *are*
Family!

Fran returned his gaze. Now he knows. NOW he knows!

Steve heard a high-pitched gibble-gabble of dialogue as
Fran backtracked over the tape then hit the Stop button
and went into Play.

". . . a posse of them trailed me but I stayed high and
soon lost them in the mountains. Ever since then, and
especially over these last few days, I've wondered why
they gave up so easily—"

Fran hit the Stop button again then went back into
Record and addressed Steve. "Thank you, Steven. We
have been most impressed by your detailed and extremely
interesting testimony. There being no other questions, I
pronounce this session closed. Your examination is terminated. The Board will now retire to consider your statement and your request to be reassigned to an overground
combat unit."

Steve leapt off his chair and stood to attention as the
eight Assessors followed Fran through the door. All of
them left without a backward glance. What the heck was
all that about, he wondered? He had been right about the
dark-haired lady. She *was* Family. In a way, it was a
compliment. From what good old Uncle Bart had said, it
was clear that his return was as welcome as a melt-down in
the main reactor. In the circumstances it was not surprising the First Family had put someone special on his case—
but why had she hit the panic button at the first mention
of the Talisman Prophecy?

Two Provos escorted him down to a nearby mess-deck
and left him sipping iced KornGold through a straw while
they chatted to another pair of meat-loaves at a nearby
table. Steve picked up his Beanburger and tried to summon up the enthusiasm to eat it. Before being captured by
the Mutes, Federation food had been his staple diet since
birth. Mute food had been vile in appearance and taste

but, after hunger had forced him to overcome his initial revulsion, he'd gotten used to it. So much so that now, his palate could not readjust to the bland taste of the food prepared on the mess-deck. It was tasteless, plasticised pap and about as appetising as a used butt-rag.

"Okay if I join you?"

Looking up, Steve saw Chisum standing over him. He was holding a mess tray. "Yeah, sure . . ."

Chisum put his tray on the table and glanced at his watch as he sat down opposite Steve. It was five after twelve. "You finished early today."

"Yeah," grunted Steve morosely. "Must have been something I said." He grimaced and straightened up a little. "The Board has now retired to consider its verdict."

"How'd it go?"

Steve shrugged. "All right." Except that it hadn't. He had planned to climax the account of his months in captivity with the revelation of the Talisman Prophecy. By exciting their curiosity about the content of the verses—which had predicted wagon-trains and wingmen centuries before the Federation had envisaged their use, he had hoped to make the Board receptive to his testimony about Mute magic. But the subject was obviously taboo. Why else would his mention of the Prophecy have been erased from the tape and his examination hurriedly terminated? It could only mean one thing; the First Family already knew about the Prophecy which, in turn, meant they not only knew about wordsmiths, but about summoners, seers and magic. Just as he had come to suspect. And not only did they know about it, they were taking it seriously.

But where did that leave him? Had he improved his chances of reinstatement and promotion by his knowledge of it? Or would he end up being shafted for knowing more than was good for him? Shit and triple shit . . . Steve hated to find himself in irretrievable binds like this. Most of the time, his nimble mind was able to do a critical path analysis of encounter situations, pinpointing the danger areas well in advance. If things looked tricky he always left himself an emergency escape hatch. It was

something he took pride in. This time, he had fallen
through a trapdoor he could not possibly have foreseen.

Chisum demolished his own Beanburger in two and a
half bites. Still chewing on the last mouthful, he pointed at
Steve's untouched portion. "You want that?"

Steve shook his head and pushed it towards him then
watched as Chisum set about it with obvious relish. "How
can you eat that shit?"

Chisum shrugged. "Don't know any better I guess. Can't
be worse than the stuff you've been eating over the last
few months."

"No . . ." mused Steve. "I guess not." He pulled his
eyes away from the four Provos seated nearby and spoke
in a low voice. "Listen. I've been thinking about what you
said about me getting a clean sheet healthwise—and about
not being the first."

Chisum nodded and kept chewing. "I was wondering
when you'd ask me about that."

Steve lowered his voice further. "This is serious, John.
You and I both know it doesn't make sense. In the five
months I was overground, I must have had more exposure
to air-sickness than my guard-father had in all his twelve
tours! Plus body contact with Mutes *and* a bellyful of
contaminated food! Yet *he's* the one who's dying, while I
never felt better! How come? Why him and not me?"

"Good question." Chisum pushed the last of Steve's
Beanburger into his mouth and chewed methodically until
it was all gone.

"Is that all you've got to say?"

"I'm not a doctor."

"You work with 'em, though. Don't you have any ideas?"

"Do you?"

"It's a pretty wild one." Steve glanced across at the
Provos, put a hand up to cover that side of his mouth and
dropped his voice to a whisper. "Over the last three
hundred years there's supposed to have been a reduction
in the level of air-sickness. Right? We know that because
of measurements taken by the Family. But who checks
those figures? They do. Who manufactures and controls
the measuring devices? They do. We have no way to

prove or disprove whatever they choose to tell us. We don't *know* what the present level of radiation is. Okay, it put my guard-father in a wheel chair—but it hasn't touched me." Steve leaned across the table and seized Chisum's wrist. "It may have dropped away to nothing! All of us could be free to move around up there. There may be no need for any of us to stay down here at all!"

Chisum grimaced and brushed a crumb from the corner of his mouth. "Interesting thought."

"You got a better one?"

Chisum shrugged. "I don't believe in conspiracy theories. They can be bad for your health."

"It was you who started me down this road."

"I said you were clean. I don't have any hard answers as to why that should be. I just thought you should know that you're not the first—that you're not some kind of a freak. And what happens? Before you can say Beanburger, your brain's gone into overdrive and you've got the First Family involved in some great secret plot against the Federation! What's the matter with you? You got some kinda persecution complex or somethin'?"

Steve grinned sheepishly. "Yeah, I suppose I've got a few things bugging me."

Chisum leaned across the table towards him. "Listen. I cee-bee a little now and then like most guys but I'm no renegade. When the chips are down you'll find me standing with the Family. Don't get me wrong. I'm not one of those freaks who tee-tee-eff-effs with every breath. Nobody's perfect, but I reckon they're doing the best they can."

"Nobody could ask for more," replied Steve drily.

"Listen," snapped Chisum. "If you're so hung-up on the goddam fucking overground, why the hell didn't you stay up there when you had the chance?!"

"Yeah . . ." agreed Steve. "Might have been better if I had . . ."

"Neeaaghh . . ." Chisum waved dismissively. His voice lost its hard edge. "Know what your *real* problem is? You're a wingman. One of the brightest and the best. Pick of the bunch. Top of the heap. Isn't that what they tell you? Tell us, too? Trouble is, you guys swallow all this shit and start thinking you're the smartest hats in town. Like you know the answer to everything. Well, it ain't so, good buddie. All you hot-shots from Lindbergh Field are just more meat to put through the grinder. Top grade meat maybe—but it all looks the same when it comes back in a body bag. The *really* smart hats are right here in town. And they stay here, well out of the line of fire. If you want to do yourself a favour, get that brain of yours working on something useful—like landing a desk job in the Black Tower. Forget about being a hero. The promotion prospects are lousy."

"I'll try and remember that," said Steve.

Chisum grinned. "Like hell you will. You're a front-runner. It's written all over you. Why should you pay any attention to a no-account shit-kicker like me? Go ahead. Do it the hard way."

"John," said Steve. "I hear what you say—but lay off with that shit-kicker stuff. I may not be as smart as I think I am, but I know one thing. You ain't as dumb as you're trying to make out."

Chisum smiled and spread his hands. "I like to keep a low profile. The smart hats who run things don't feel threatened by guys who clean out test-tubes. I live a quiet life but—I keep my eyes and ears open." He leaned towards Steve. "You asked me why you're not a basket case. I don't know why. Not for sure, anyway. What I *can* tell you is that most of the guys who are into double-time on way-stations and wagon-trains are still pulling tricks."

"Trick" was the conversational version of the medical acronym TRIC—meaning Terminal Radiation-Induced Cancer.

"So your idea about a big bad Family plot is way off beam," continued Chisum. "Some time back, I worked for a while at the Life Institute. That's where I first ran into Roz. She and some other Inter-Med students were touring the place. Anyway, a guy there told me that the Family have had a research team working on the development of an anti-radiation drug—some kind of serum—for over fifty years." He grinned. "Maybe they've been using you for field trials. Maybe you've been shooting Mute juice instead of Vitamin B at your quarterly MedEx. Maybe you and those other guys are proof that it works." Chisum shrugged. "That would explain everything—right?"

"Yeah, it would," conceded Steve. "Provided what that guy told you was true. I admit I've still got a long way to go but, over the years, I've come to realise that in this big, bright new world we're building, things are not always what they seem."

"Nothing ever is," replied Chisum cheerfully. He looked at his watch and drained the last drop of Java from his cup. "Gotta get back to the unit and finish off some tests. You gonna be around tonight?"

Steve shrugged. "Don't know. I have no idea what's happening to me."

"I'll check," said Chisum. He went over to the Provos' table, conversed with them briefly then returned. "You have to wait here. The DPs will wheel you back in when the Board is due to reassemble."

"Did they say how long that might be?"

"No," said Chisum. "But it's bound to be today sometime. Which means by 1900 at the latest."

Steve glanced at the time print-out on the nearest overhead screen. 1245. "Terrific . . ."

Chisum smiled down at him. "Relax. Buy yourself another KornGold. Browse through the Archives. Sharpen up with a few games of Shoot-A-Mute. You could do with the practice."

"I can't. I haven't been issued with a new ID. I can't do anything, I can't go anywhere!"

"Got it. That's a tough one. I'll see if I can find out what's happening on that." Chisum glanced around the room then leant his fists on the table and put his head close to Steve's. "D'you want to see Roz?"

Steve rubbed his neck and thought it over.

"She's willing to take a chance if you will. All you have to do is say the word."

Steve sighed. "I don't know. I don't want to get her into trouble."

"You won't." Chisum dropped his voice even further.

"I've got friends. I can fix it. Three, four hours. No problem."

"Where?"

"Never mind where. 'Yes,' or 'No?' "

"No. I can't—listen, uh—I'll think about it."

Chisum gripped Steve's shoulder. "Okay. But don't leave it too late. These things take time to set up."

Steve glanced across at his escort and the two off-duty Provos they were talking too. Once again his eyes were drawn to their shoulder insignia: two inverted white triangles standing corner to corner with a bright blue triangle nestling between them. The memory circuits finally clicked into place and he was able to recall the moment in his childhood when the self-same image had registered in his brain. He looked up at Chisum. "I've finally worked out where I am. This is the White House."

Chisum's face gave nothing away. "You could be right. Does it worry you?"

"Nahh . . ." replied Steve lightly. "I always knew I'd make it here some day."

Chisum gave a quick laugh and walked away.

Around 1730, just at the point when Steve had run through all the ways he knew of keeping calm, the two Provos pulled the card on their high scoring Mute Massacre game and marched him back in front of the Assessors. Once again Steve stood at attention in front the hot seat, staring at the wall behind the high-backed chair. The eight Assessors filed in, took up their positions around the semi-circular table and waited respectfully for their vermilion-robed President.

Fran entered, took her place and nodded to them to take their seats. She smoothed back her dark hair, clasped her hands together briefly under her chin then lowered them to the table.

"Sit down, Steven."

Of course! How could he have missed it? That gesture with the hands. He must have seen it a thousand times on inspirational videocasts delivered by the President-General.

Fran cleared her throat. "Steven. As I made clear on

the opening day of this examination, this Board has no judicial function. Our primary task has been to evaluate the nature and content of your testimony and to make certain observations and recommendations on the basis of what we heard. The record of these proceedings and our conclusions, together with your request for reassignment to an overground combat unit will be forwarded to a higher review body. They may choose to accept our recommendations, they may modify them, or reject them. You may even be re-examined. Whatever course of action they decide upon, the final decision affecting your future rests with them. It may be more, or less favourable than the one we are about to recommend but, in either case, once they have ruled on your case, no appeal can be lodged on your behalf. Is that clear?"

"Yes, sir-ma'am!"

"Good," said Fran. "Now, before you are informed of this Board's recommendations, we would like to place on the record our admiration for the tenacity and courage you displayed while a prisoner of the Mutes and for the outstanding initiative employed to secure your escape by air. This, in itself, was a brilliant feat and worthy of the highest commendation."

This is more like it, thought Steve. A happy glow spread through him as the dark-haired President continued her preamble.

"We have also been most impressed by the highly detailed nature of much of your testimony regarding the weapons, tactics and day-to-day activities of your captors. I am convinced that it will prove of immense value to the Federation. You are to be congratulated on your coolness under the constant threat of death, your unwavering loyalty to the Federation and your steadfastness in what must have been the most appalling conditions. Your conduct, in this respect, has been exemplary."

Damn right, said Steve to himself. This was all good stuff. It had to mean a set of gold wings and lieutenant's bars at the very least. Plus an up-rated ID-card—and he wouldn't say "No" to one of those units in that fancy tower he'd seen at San Jacinto Deep. Yeah, carry on, lady, you're doing fine . . .

"However," continued Fran, "we are cognisant of the fact that none of this has been achieved without cost. It would be unreasonable to expect any normal human being to emerge from a protracted period of forced co-existence with a totally alien species without exhibiting symptoms of culture shock."

Steve's new-found confidence began to wilt.

"We believe that we have detected clear signs of this mental damage in parts of your testimony. Your inability to categorise Mutes as sub-human in clear, unequivocal terms, and your ambivalent attitude towards them generally is, in our view, evidence of the traumatic experience you have undergone. We can only hope that this damage is not permanent. Only time will tell. But your present condition gives rise for concern. It is quite obvious, from many of your replies, that you now view certain of these individuals and your relationship with them in quasi-humanistic terms—"

"Sir-ma'am—"

Fran slammed both fists down on the table. "Don't interrupt! That view is directly contrary to the accepted teaching of the Federation—the truth of which has been long established. Mutes are *not* human beings. They are a degenerate species of anthropoid whose condition is irreversible and their continued existence is an affront to civilised humanity! This Board cannot allow your present opinions to contaminate the minds of others, and were it not for the singular circumstances in which those opinions were formed, we would be forced to regard their expression as a Code One offence and recommend the appropriate penalty.

"However, having considered your exemplary record, this Board does not believe—despite the offensive nature of many of your remarks—that your attitude is inspired by wilful disaffection or criminal intent. It is, we believe, evidence of a deep-seated mental malaise. You are sick, Steven. And it is our duty to help you recover. In the circumstances, we cannot support your request to be reassigned to an overground combat unit. This Board's recommendation is that you be regraded and transferred to Service Engineering and Maintenance for at least three years, with the right to an Annual Review Board thereafter."

Steve sat there, unable to breathe, his body paralysed with shock, his brain a frozen block of ice. For a wingman to lose coveted combat-status was humiliating enough but—Sweet Christopher—three years in the A-Levels! That was worse than a death sentence! It couldn't be happening! It had to be some kind of a grotesque joke!

The dark-haired President rose, her eyes fixed on Steve, her face a blank, expressionless mask. "As from tomorrow, you will be transferred to the A-Levels and assigned to general duties. You will remain there, on temporary detachment, until this Board's recommendations are confirmed or modified by the higher review body. Steps have been taken to issue you with a new ID-card, and the appropriate uniform. All other personal items will be furnished by your new unit. From this point on, it is up to you to demonstrate that this Board's confidence in your capacity to achieve complete rehabilitation was not misplaced. Do you understand?"

The question was a formal one. No protest was allowed. No clarification could be sought.

Steve somehow managed to get his tongue round the standard reply. "Yes, sir-ma'am. I thank the Board for its sympathetic consideration of my case. Long live the Federation!"

"Long live the First Family," said Fran.

"For ever and ever, Amen," chorussed Steve and the Assessors.

Fran gave Steve a curt nod then turned on her heel and walked out. The Assessors followed. This time, some of them favoured him with a backward glance, meeting his eyes with the same blank gaze that Fran had employed. Only Assessor 3 displayed the belligerent contempt which had characterised his outbursts during Steve's examination; the others looked right through him.

Steve felt a hand on his arm. Turning, he found it was his Provo escort. "This way, soldier . . ." Not for much longer would they call him that. From tomorrow, once he donned the chrome yellow and brown coveralls of a Seamster, he'd be a Zed-head, a greaseball, a scumbag. The lowest form of life in the Federation . . .

SIX

ESCORTED by the two Provos, Steve returned to the medical unit where, as on the days since his first examination, he was placed in the small, but otherwise unoccupied, four-berth ward. Chisum had told him it was part of an isolation unit. The staff on duty in the corridor outside were not unfriendly but they were not curious either and made no attempt to engage him in conversation.

As Steve sat dejectedly on his bed, he realised that Chisum was the only person who'd been willing to talk to him. Not only talk but to actually offer help. Steve couldn't figure Chisum out. At the back of his mind was the thought that there had to be an angle. Nobody helped out a complete stranger without a reason. So what was the trade-off? Steve concluded it must be his kin-sister. In his present situation there was nothing else he could deliver on. He certainly couldn't exert any leverage on powerful but nutty Uncle Bart. It could only be Roz. She and Chisum had met and she had told him about her hot-shot brother who had powered down over Wyoming. It would be a natural thing for her to do. And then, by sheer chance, Chisum had found himself working in the White House medical unit to which he, Steve, had been brought for examination.

Small world . . .

111

Chisum obviously hoped to deal himself a better hand in his game with Roz by being nice to big brother. But what was he after that he couldn't get by himself? Chisum didn't need his permission to jack his kin-sister. There was nothing to it. It was a simple how-about-it proposition; a Yes/No situation. And if Roz said "No," fresh jack-bait was not a problem in a place like Grand Central. John Wayne Plaza was full of wide-eyed Yippies—Young Pioneers—on their big trip to see the shrine of George Washington Jefferson the First; sometimes referred to by those who like to live dangerously as GWJ—the Great White Jabberwock.

But maybe it was something more. Maybe Chisum had the same kind of special feeling for Roz that he, Steve, had for Clearwater. Prior to being shot down, Steve had not known such feelings existed but if he could feel like that about somebody maybe Chisum could too. Or maybe it was something else. Maybe it wasn't Steve's permission Chisum needed but his approval. Maybe Roz wouldn't put out as long as she knew Steve was alive and especially now, when she knew he was back in town. Because of the way things had been. The special closeness no one else had shared.

It was odd. In the three years he'd been away at the Flight Academy—a period when he had rarely been in contact with home, Steve had never once considered the idea that Roz might have begun hanging out with other guys on the base. Like him, she'd always been a study-bug, nose glued to the video screen or, to use Tracker High School slang, a pixel—picking up an 825 line tan. In the short time they'd spent together between the graduation ceremony and his posting to the wagon-train depot at Fort Worth, it had not even occurred to him to ask Roz if she'd been with anybody else.

Thinking it over, Steve realised that his apparent disinterest in this aspect of Roz's life was part of a reluctance to probe too deeply into her thoughts and feelings—especially those concerning him. As children they'd been inseparable but, by the time Steve was fourteen, he had begun to withdraw into the steel cocoon he was building around himself. He had been determined to sever all emotional ties, even with Roz—then twelve years old. To his annoyance, he had not succeeded. Even now, after Clearwater, Roz remained an unpluggable gap in his defences. Just as, in a lesser way, he retained an affectionate regard for Annie, his guard-mother, and pride and respect for his guardian, poppa-Jack.

It was only natural that his thoughts should fly back towards Roz as he waged a silent battle against the rising tide of hopelessness that threatened to engulf him. The sentence the Board had handed out—for no matter how they dressed it up, that was what it was—had been totally unexpected. And coming at the end of such a laudatory preamble it was absolutely shattering. Steve simply could not accept the idea that the brilliant career he had mapped out for himself since the age of five was about to end with his transfer to the A-Levels.

Sitting there with his head in his hands, he consoled himself with the thought that his future had looked equally bleak as he'd lain trapped in the wreckage of his Skyhawk in the middle of a burning cropfield. And again when Motor-Head, the paramount warrior of the M'Calls, had confronted him on the bluff as he was preparing to escape. He *had* to believe it would all come right. It would somehow. Christo—it had to! *Three years* in the A-Levels before his first grading review. He couldn't bear the idea of being down there three *hours*!

Steve stood up and paced around the room, trying to figure a way out of the jam he was in. First there was the problem of the statement he'd made to the Assessors. Despite the President's opening assurances about maintaining a spirit of enquiry, the Board had not been prepared to listen to any opinions about the Mutes that did not accord with the official attitude on the subject. He could still not get over the way he had not been allowed to even *mention* the Talisman Prophecy. In view of the Board's blind prejudice, maybe that was just as well. The mere mention of earth magic, summoners and seers would have had them popping their rivets. Chisum might believe that the First Family was doing its best but what had happened was a prime example of their cynical suppression of the truth. By erasing all mention of the Prophecy from the record and allowing no discussion of it, the dark-haired President had proved what Steve had suspected for some time. The First Family believed in Mute magic—and yet any public discussion of even the *idea* was a Code One offence! The First Family *knew* it was true—and yet they were still sending guys to the wall! It was crazy . . .

Steve had seen proof of the Mutes' magical powers on at least two separate occasions, maybe more. He could have told the dark-haired lady in the high-backed chair if she'd been prepared to listen. Just as he could have told her of Mr. Snow's gloriously quirky character, Cadillac's almost superhuman intelligence, and Clearwater's flawless beauty. Not to mention the depth of her mind and the powers at her command.

These three were not only human, they possessed an extra dimension that the dark-haired President and the Board were quite incapable of recognising—an awareness of the world, and the mysterious forces at work within it, of the great destiny of the Plainfolk under the leadership of the mysterious Talisman; the Thrice-Gifted One who had not yet manifested his presence. These were things which Steve himself had only just begun, with great difficulty—and considerable reluctance—to accept and to attempt to understand. It was difficult because "awareness" as a word-concept did not feature in the Federation's dictionary—at least not at the level Steve had access to. It had sprung fully-formed into his mind while in captivity and had left him troubled and confused. His Tracker psyche had felt as if it was being torn in two.

Mutes, Steve had discovered, cherished some batty notions and lived by rules which they regarded as inviolate, but they were at least prepared to listen to new ideas. Most Trackers on the other hand—as the Board of Assessors had recently demonstrated—suffered from tunnel-vision. Maybe it came from living underground. But why should it be so? Everyone in the Federation, including Steve, had been raised to believe that the First Family was the source of all wisdom, all knowledge. They *knew* everything. How could they deny for centuries what Steve, in five short months, had discovered to be true? What did they hope to gain by sticking their heads in the sand?

Chisum walked into the ward just after 1900 hours.

Steve sat up and swung his feet down off the bed. "Hi. You through for the day?"

"Yeah," said Chisum. "How'd you make out?"

Steve told him.

Chisum listened sombrely, then sucked in his breath. "Sounds like you got a rough deal, good buddie." He patted Steve on the shoulder then walked over to a swivel chair. Apart from the beds and a small table, it was the only place to sit. Chisum thrust his hands in his pockets and slumped down in the chair, feet wide apart. "Yep . . . The only way to get through times like this is to believe it's all for your own good. You have to try and learn somethin' from it."

"John—do me a favour," said Steve. "Leave the inspirationals to the P-G. Okay?"

"Just trying to help."

"Yeah, well, I don't need any help." The anger faded from Steve's voice. "Anyway, there's nothing you can do, nothing anyone can do. This time, I've been well and truly shafted."

Chisum grimaced. "Not quite. Okay, sure, you've drawn a shitty detail, but you're alive, you're still in one piece."

"Yeah," agreed Steve bitterly. "And from where I'll be, the only way to go is up."

Chisum sat up and the took his hands out of his pockets. "What d'you want me to do? Find you a butt-rag to cry in?"

"No." Steve summoned up a smile. "I appreciate you being here. I guess I should have expected something like this would happen. I saw the New Mex State Provo on my way here—"

"Oh, yeah?"

"Yeah, Bart Bradlee. He's kin. He told me that, officially, I was dead—KIA over Wyoming—and that I was gonna have to stay that way. I didn't realise they also planned to bury me."

"Mutes don't take prisoners—right?"

"His words exactly."

Chisum nodded. "S"pose in a way it makes sense. If the word got around about the nice relaxing time you had, maybe Trail-Blazers wouldn't push so hard. Pretty soon you'd have guys pallying up with lumpheads and shit knows what else. A man could end up not knowing what's right and what's wrong. Is that what you want? For the whole world to fall apart?"

Steve felt confused. "No!" he hissed. "That's not what I'm saying. I know what we're fighting for." He waved a hand at the ceiling. "That's our world out there—and I'm prepared to do my bit to help win it back. But we can't blind ourselves to the truth! I've been out there. I've lived with these people—"

"People?" Chisum looked puzzled.

"Mutes! Christo! What are you—an Assessor?!" Steve stood up and began to pace up and down. "John—I'm not some dumb scumbag, and I'm not passing on rumours or spreading alarm and despondency. I *know* what I saw! The Southern Mutes I saw in our overground work-camps may have had all the fight knocked out of them but the Plainfolk are something else! All that stuff about faulty memories is garbage. These people are bright—and dangerous in ways you can't imagine! But nobody wants to know! No one will admit it!" Steve broke off and waved dismissively. "Arrghh, what's the use. I can see you think I'm crazy too."

"Not true," said Chisum. "But if you came on strong like this with the Assessors, I can see why they dumped you in the A-Levels."

Steve gave a harsh laugh and sat down on the end of the bed. "Like you said, I suppose I should consider myself lucky. Could have ended up taking a nose-dive down a main vent."

"Yeah . . . well, that's a risk we all run," agreed Chisum. He moved his chair closer to Steve and studied his face intently. "You smoke any shit while you were out there?"

"You mean rainbow grass?"

Chisum nodded.

Steve hesitated before replying. "A few times, yeah. They, uh—well, they kinda pressed it on me. First time round it practically tore my throat out."

"I hear Mutes are piped into it all the time."

"A lot of them are," murmured Steve. "How about you?"

Chisum shrugged. "Now and then. It's hard to find."

Steve shook his head in disbelief. "I can't figure you out, John. One minute you're a reel-to-reel man giving me the hardline news, the next minute you tell me you're smoking shit. You into blackjack as well?"

"Isn't everybody?"

"Are you crazy?! You wouldn't catch me within a mile of any of that junk! What happened with the Mutes was a different situation. I didn't want to rub them up the wrong way. But not down here."

"Didn't do you any harm, did it?"

"That's not the point!" hissed Steve. "That stuff's Code One! How can you even think about it? Columbus! I mean *here*, in the White House!"

Chisum grinned broadly. "Exactly. If you're gonna do anything wrong, this is the safest place to do it."

"Listen, just—don't let's talk about it. You're a crazy man, John."

"The whole world is crazy," replied Chisum. "Or hadn't you noticed?"

Steve didn't reply.

Chisum kept his voice low. "The reason I asked if you'd smoked grass is because it can blow your mind. It distorts things. Bends the real world out of shape—so you no longer know where the edges are."

"Maybe. I'm not an expert," admitted Steve. "But let me ask *you* something. We're both cold turkey now. So go ahead. Tell me where the edges are, John."

Chisum smiled evasively. "That's a good question."

"Here's another. What are you trying to tell me?"

Chisum tapped the tips of his fingers and thumbs together then spread his palms. "There're all kinds of grass,

Steve. I know, because one of the labs I worked in did some research on it—"

"You certainly get around."

"Yeah," replied Chisum affably. "That's what makes me such a useful guy to know. Anyway, what I'm trying to tell you is that it affects different people in different ways. I'm no expert either but I know what's going down the wire. Maybe a lot of what you saw while you were out there didn't really happen."

Steve eyed Chisum then shook his head. "John, I'm telling you. I've seen things you wouldn't believe."

Chisum nodded. "That's what I mean."

"I'm not talking about hitting the sky."

"Just for the record, reafers call it 'tunnelling out'."

"Reafers . . .?"

"Yeah, if you don't have a pipe, you use a rolled leaf. A reaf—get it?"

"Got it. What I'm trying to say is that I know the difference between 'tunnelling out' and hard-rock reality."

"Lucky man . . ."

"Don't kid around. I'm talking about the big one, John. Mute magic."

Chisum laughed and waved his hands in front of Steve's face. "Whoa! Hold it right there!"

Steve frowned. "What are you frightened about—somebody listening in? You already burned out the wires, John."

Chisum stood up and moved the chair back to its original position. "Look, you're a nice guy. A little mixed up, but okay. And you've got a great sister. Let's not spoil a beautiful friendship."

Steve stood up. "You disappoint me, John. You're quite happy to buck the system, but the moment somebody threatens you with a new idea you run for cover."

"Nobody's perfect," replied Chisum. "Let me give you some friendly advice. There ain't no such thing as magic—"

"John, it's true. I swear it."

Chisum shook his head. "Look. I'm a good eight years older than you. I haven't been topside but I've been around. Truth doesn't win wars, soldier-boy. Okay, I bend the rules a little, but I also know what's right. Just get one thing fixed in your mind. Mutes are the enemy. And no matter how tough they are, we are gonna pound 'em into the ground. Because there ain't room for both of us. If we in the Federation, in the generations to come, are ever going to be free to live in that great big blue-sky world up there then the Plainfolk and the last of the Southern Mutes will have to go. The big ones, the little ones, the ugly ones and the not-so-ugly ones. We've got to get rid of them all, Steve."

Chisum paused and stared hard at the young wingman. Yes, he thought, the pressure's building nicely. This guy is not going to be able to hold it down much longer. It was a shitty job he had to do but Chisum was honest enough to admit to himself that he enjoyed it even though, in his shadow world of half-truths and outright deception, he no longer knew—as Brickman had reminded him—where the edges were.

Chisum clapped his hands together and rubbed them vigorously. "Okay! Change the subject. And I'm only gonna ask you this one last time." He aimed a finger at Steve's chest. "Do you want to see Roz?"

Steve chewed the idea over.

"Once you hit the A-Levels, there's no knowing when you'll be back up."

"I know," said Steve. "The way things are I don't really care about what happens to me. It's just that none of my kin-folk are supposed to know I'm alive."

"Yeah, well she knows. And she'd like to see you."

Steve eyed Chisum squarely. "What's in it for you, John? Come on. Level with me."

"Well, I'm not after your kin-sister's ass, I can tell you that. Don't worry. She sits on it real tight."

Steve felt the colour flood to his cheeks. This guy really got under his skin. "So what's the angle?"

Chisum shrugged. "I like doing favours—okay?"

Steve laughed. "Don't give me that shit! You've been putting out for me since I walked through the door. Why? You don't know me and you don't owe me."

"Wrong," said Chisum. "I know a great deal about you.

Roz is really hung up on you—but then she doesn't know what a hard-assed sonofabitch you really are."

"Okay, okay, if it's not me, what does Roz have to deliver?"

"Nothing," replied Chisum. "It's the way I operate. I'm a fixer. A little favour here, a little favour there."

"John, she's fifteen. A first-year M D student. If it's not her ass, what the eff-eff are you after?"

"Nothing," repeated Chisum. "Not right now, anyway. I'm just making a small investment in her future. I told you. That kin-sister of yours is a bright kid. She's on her way to the top. It's good to have friends in high places. I've got markers out from here to Phoenix." Chisum paused and smiled. "You don't understand, do you? Never mind. What's it to be—'Yes' or 'No'?"

"You mean about Roz? I don't know. It's difficult. How are you gonna—?"

Chisum cut him off. "Look, don't worry about the details. If I couldn't fix it, I wouldn't have suggested it. You don't know me all that well but when I promise something I deliver."

Steve took a deep breath. "Okay, let's go for it."

Chisum grinned happily and clapped his hands against Steve's shoulders. "Attaboy, that's more like it! Stick around. I've gotta make a few calls."

Leaving the isolation ward, Chisum hurried to the nearest closed video-booth and carded himself through with the aid of a special code to the ST-Section of Records control. The code routed his call through to Fran without the intervention of an operator. Her head and shoulders, clad in the familiar silver jump-suit appeared on the screen.

"3552 has agreed to see his kin-sister."

"Well done, John. Will you be using the same accommodation unit?"

"Yes—Eight on Three-8 Santanna Deep. If you could place your people on standby . . ."

"They'll be waiting for your call. How is the subject?"

"Badly shaken. I assume that was your intention?"

"It was indeed, John."

"The subject will need an ID to effect this rendezvous."

Fran nodded. "His new card has already been delivered to the gate unit in readiness for his transfer tomorrow morning. If you ask for it I am sure there will be no problem. Call me at anytime if you need further assistance."

"Okay, thanks."

Fran's head was replaced by the Amtrak logo.

When Chisum reappeared, about an hour after he had left the ward, Steve was just stepping out of the shower.

"Nice timing." Chisum tossed a yellow bundle across the room.

Steve unrolled the yellow and brown Seamster jumpsuit and eyed it with evident distaste as he finished rubbing himself dry. "Do I have to wear this?"

"Yeah," said Chisum. "It goes with your new ID." He pulled the card out of his breast pocket and flipped it onto the bed. "You're not supposed to have that till tomorrow morning but the guy on the gate-house owes me."

Steve looked impressed. He slid the card out of its protective wallet and examined it carefully. "Incredible . . . are you sure this will give me access to transporation on this level?"

"It will tonight," said Chisum. That problem had already been taken care of. "Come on, get dressed. Roz is already on her way over from State U."

"Sure." Steve laughed quickly. "You know, I can't really believe it. I just hope, one day, I'll be able to pay you back." He began to dress with growing excitement.

Chisum sat against the edge of the table and watched silently. It's not fair, he thought. This young guy and the girl, who had been raised believing Annie Brickman was their natural mother, are both bright kids who really feel good things about one another. And we're going to screw them up and bust them apart. Here he was, once again, saying "Trust me" to people who, because of what was about to happen, would probably never trust each other again.

How many did that make now? Chisum had lost count. In the beginning the betrayals had worried him; had kept him awake at night. But not now. Anyone who did the kind of job he did was soon stripped of all feeling. At one time he had been concerned to cover his own ass but, having learned, through his work as an undercover agent, of the First Family's chilling disregard for the lives of individual Trackers, Chisum had begun to find it more and more difficult to place any value on his own.

Dressed in his new chrome yellow and brown coveralls, and matching hard-hat, Steve followed Chisum onto the shuttle that linked the White House to Grand Central. Chisum, who was carrying a square-sectioned emergency aid case, was wearing the green jumpsuit that marked him out as a paramedic orderly. The suit had broad red and white chevrons on the upper part of the sleeves, aligned with matching bands that went across the chest and back.

"Relax," said Chisum, as the shuttle moved off.

"I'm trying," replied Steve. He waved a hand over his coveralls. "You just can't imagine how it feels to have to wear this . . ."

"Listen," said Chisum. "There are thousands of guys who never get a chance to wear anything else. Don't knock it. They do a good job. If it wasn't for them—"

"Yeah, I know. Don't tell me," replied Steve with heavy sarcasm. "There'd be no air in the vents and the cans would back up."

Chisum shook his head. "You guys from Lindbergh Field are all the same. You really think you're ace. If you ask me, they ought to have you all shovelling shit for a spell before you go topside. Might do you good to find out how the other half lives."

"I've done my quota of PD. And I busted rocks for twelve months on the shuttleway to Phoenix."

Chisum laughed drily. "Yeah, I know. The Yippie's year. You spend six months on the dig, six months in the sick-bay and all twelve putting the horse between the shafts."

"Putting the horse between the shafts' was the Young Pioneer equivalent of the Flight Academy's "putting the bomb in the barrel."

"John," said Steve. "I already feel lousy. Don't keep knocking me—okay?"

Chisum grinned. "Know your trouble? You take yourself too seriously." He slapped Steve on the knee. "C'mon. This is where we get off. Stay close. Act natural." They stepped off the shuttle but instead of going up the escalator ramp to One-1—street level—Chisum walked past, going on towards the end of the platform.

Steve's heart missed a beat as he saw two Provos walking towards them. Both were armed with the usual heavy, three-barrelled air pistols, and had long white truncheons slung from their belts. It was the normal patrol you could expect to find doing spot checks on IDs on platforms and in station precincts. Most of the time they didn't stop you but there was always the chance that they might. It was their presence that exercised a deterrent effect on potential cee-bees.

"Look miserable," muttered Chisum. "You've just been pulled out of the clay to answer an emergency call. Leave the rest of the dialogue to me." Then, as they drew nearer, he said, "It's okay. I know one of them." He gave a cheery wave, and fisted the shoulder of the nearest meat-loaf as they walked past. "Hey, there! How you doin'—all right?"

"Not bad," said the meat-loaf. "How's it with you?"

"Great," said Chisum. He kept going but turned so that he was walking backwards, holding onto Steve's arm. "You guys on till 2400?"

The two Provos stopped. "Yeah!" said one of them.

Chisum raised his hand in acknowledgement. "Catch you on the way back! May have a little something for you!"

The meat-loaf raised a thumb in reply then continued on up the platform with his companion.

Steve saw Chisum's cheery smile fade as he spun on his heel and went into forward gear. "What an operator. I can see I've got a lot to learn."

Chisum eyed him. "What you've got to learn to do, my friend, is to like people. In this world, nobody can get by on their own."

Steve smiled, thinking of what Lundkwist had said to him on Graduation Day. "That's what people keep telling me."

"Then maybe it's time you started listening."

Steve followed Chisum off the platform and down a corridor. "What's this 'little something' you promised the meat-loaf?"

"Don't worry about it," said Chisum. "If I told you, you'd have heart-failure." He stopped at the end of the corridor, pulled out an ID-card and fed it into the controlled entry door. Just as the red voice-print prompt light came on, he pulled out a small pocket recorder and thumbed it on.

"31075593," said a voice. It didn't belong to Chisum. The green light came on, the door opened, then locked shut automatically as soon as they'd stepped through. Chisum pocketed the recorder and grinned as he saw Steve's curious look.

Steve found that they had entered a service tunnel that was twice as wide as it was high. Bands of pipes and electrical conduits ran along both walls, passing in and out of a variety of cut-off valves and junction boxes. Large fans, mounted at intervals along the walls, sucked air in through vents. There was a noticeable draught blowing through the tunnel, a constant background hum from the fans plus a low steady roaring noise from the air passing through. Parked near the door was a line of eight yellow wheelies—small open electric carts that could carry up to six passengers or haul a trailer.

Chisum jabbed a finger towards his feet. "We're in the A-Levels here. Ain't too bad, is it? Apart from the noise that is. But you get used to that. This is A-1. They're numbered from the top down to A-10, then B-1 and so on."

"How far do they go down?" asked Steve.

"No idea. I just hope no one ever asks me to count 'em." Chisum walked confidently to the wheelie at the head of the line, climbed into the front seat and laid his case on the slatted bench behind. He beckoned Steve to sit beside him. "Can you drive one of these things?"

"Yeah, sure. Where to?"

"Straight ahead, right at the Tee, then keep going till I tell you." Chisum pointed to a yellow toolbox lying on the floor between them. "Take that with you when we get off. Okay—" he slapped the bonnet twice, "—let's get this show on the road."

Steve looked along the spartan dash. "I can't find the ID-slot."

Chisum sighed heavily and thumbed the start button. The motor whined into life.

"I didn't know you could do that," said Steve lamely.

"That's right, up top, you can't. But in the A-Levels, things are a little more relaxed. After you've been here some time you'll find you can do all sorts of things." Chisum saw Steve's look of bewilderment and shook his head with mock resignation as they drove off. "Boy—you high-flyers . . . you really don't know from nothin'."

Following Chisum's directions, Steve parked the wheelie in a wide, pillared service bay, picked up the tool box and tailed his intrepid guide into a service elevator. Chisum hit the button for Level Three-8 and whistled tunelessly as they were carried swiftly upwards.

Steve looked at the level indicator and saw it went from A-5 to Four-10. "That service bay looked pretty clean. Are we in one of the new towers?"

"Yeah, Santanna Deep . . ."

"I can't figure it out," muttered Steve. "Nobody stopped us. We weren't challenged once. What happens when someone finds out that wheelie is missing from the ramp? All it needs is for someone to check the cards put through that door and they'll be on to us!"

Chisum shook his head and dropped his voice to a whisper. "On to you perhaps, good buddie, but not me. Didn't use my own card."

Steve eyed him cautiously. "I know that wasn't your voice on the recorder but how is it possible?" he whispered back. "ID-cards are non-transferable!"

Chisum grinned. He got a lot of innocent amusement from ribbing this serious young man. And much of the fun came from telling him the truth—like now—or getting as close to it as possible without giving the game away. "In theory, yes. That's what most people think. But, in practice, some cards are less 'non-transferable' than others." He winked at Steve and dropped his voice even further. "I'm gonna let you in on a big secret. I've discovered the system is not perfect. COLUMBUS makes mistakes. How about that?"

Steve took a step back. "No. I don't believe it."

"That's okay by me," said Chisum. "Just keep on thinking that way." He nudged Steve in the ribs. "Listen. If everybody broke into the card game, I'd be out of business."

They rode the rest of the way to Three-8 in silence.

The lobby on the thirty-eighth floor was covered in dark green rubber tiles that deadened the sound of their footsteps. The walls were covered with a woven fabric: broad alternate diagonal stripes of the same dark green and dark brown. Light panels running across the dark green ceiling linked up with the brown stripes on the walls. The doors to the eight accommodation units had a metallic silver-bronze finish, with an orange number on the wall by the top right hand corner. Soft, blue-sky ballad music oozed out of speaker grilles on the ceiling.

Chisum ushered Steve towards Unit 8, put one of his mysterious cards into the slot that primed the lock, punched the entry code and stood back as the door eased back on its hinges. "Go ahead. It's all yours."

Steve hesitated, suddenly wary about falling into a trap. "Are you sure it's okay?"

"Yeah, no problem. The guy it's allocated to is on detachment up the line. Friend of mine—a computer engineer. He's sorting out some problem in one of the relay centres that feeds data to COLUMBUS. He'll be away for at least another four weeks." Chisum began to back-pedal.

"Aren't you coming in?"

"Later. I've just got to, uh—check up on a few things first. Y'know—smooth out the guys on the desk."

"What about the other people on this floor?" whispered Steve.

"Christo! You're a real nail-nibbler!" muttered Chisum. "Listen, provided you don't start knocking holes in the walls, nobody's going to give a fart. Relax! I've used this place before. The only thing that makes the people here nervous is guys standing around whispering on the landing. Now git——!" He propelled Steve through the door.

Steve held on to the handle. "Where will you be?"

"Around!" hissed Chisum. "Don't worry! If there's any trouble, I'll be the first person you'll see." *And you don't know how true that is,* he thought. He pulled the door shut in Steve's face.

SEVEN

STEVE MOVED cautiously down the short hallway followed by the same soft background music. He peeked through the doors on either side. Some storage space, with shelves bearing various neatly folded articles of clothing. A large shower unit and then, behind the next door along, the can, a butt-bath and hand-basin. Yes, thought Steve. What a joy it had been, on his return to the Federation, to be able to sit on the can and crap comfortably instead of crouching bare-assed in the wild, wondering if some goddam bug was gonna leap up and take a bite out of your anus. Plus the sheer luxury of being able to clean off with a fresh, moist butt-rag instead of a leaf. Searching for something large enough, he had twice picked on poisonous nettles with a blistering delayed-action effect. Christo! It had been worth coming back to the Federation just for that . . .

Steve opened another door. It was some kind of work space. A counter, with a basin and water supply, storage units, what looked like a small micro-wave oven, a glazed ceramic panel with a four-ring design and one or two electric appliances. The kind of thing usually found in mess-deck galleys. Steve was surprised by the sudden realisation that people living in Santanna Deep had their own private food preparation facilities. What a strange

idea! He moved on through the open arch at the end of
the hallway into the main living space and was immediately struck by its huge size. It must have been at least
twenty to twenty-five feet square with a large bed space
running off on one side on a raised floor. And the floor was
not tiled. It was covered in a kind of thick, soft, stubby-
haired material that Steve had not encountered before but
reminded him of the thick hair on the shoulders of buffalo.

The living space contained three free-standing, deep-
padded seat units with wide backs and arms, and another
big enough to lie full-length along it. There was the usual
video setup, a table with six chairs and, on the wall behind, portraits of the current P-G and the Founding Father, but the most striking feature was the wide, floor-to-
ceiling window that opened out onto a semi-circular balcony and a breath-taking view.

Santanna Deep—the architectural twin of San Jacinto
Deep that Steve had seen prior to going overground—was
a free-standing six hundred foot high tower rising through
four levels and containing balconied accommodation units
on fifty floors. The surrounding shaft had been sculptured
to form a backdrop of rocky terraces on which small ever-
green trees, shrubs, grasses and moss had been planted.
Streams of water trickled constantly from top to bottom
through a series of cleverly linked pools, cascading over
rocky ledges to the terraces below to fill a small horseshoe
lake around the base of the tower.

Like its twin, Santanna was occupied almost exclusively
by gold-braided desk jockeys who worked in the Black
Tower—the headquarters of the Amtrack Executive—plus
top-grade technicians and other specialists who had worked
their way up the rockpile from the cinderblock warrens of
the Outer State bases to the marbled vistas of Grand
Central. To the less successful, the envious, or the disaf-
fected, the process was known as "riding the wire." "All
wired up" was Tracker slang for promotion to executive
rank—distinguished by the silver (junior) and gold (senior)
wire rank stripes worn on the sleeve and cap.

To someone born in Monroe/Wichita, or on a frontier
way-station like Pueblo, a visit to Houston/Grand Central

had the same impact as Imperial Rome must have had on your average Visi-Goth. No matter how many times a guy might have seen shots on tv, the sheer size and the glittering magnificence made his first visit a real jaw-dropper. One look at John Wayne Plaza and you *knew* you were on the winning side. That was the reason why it had been built, along with the new Deeps. They swept away any feeling of doubt; left room for only one conclusion: a nation led by people with the vision and energy to do this could do anything. Long live the First Family!

Steve glanced around the living area and the bed space and called out softly. "Roz—?" No reply. He saw that some of the glass panels that opened onto the balcony were shielded by broad vertical blinds. "C'mon, quit hiding—where are you?"

Steve slid open one of the window panels and was met by the sound of water in movement; trickling and gurgling over rocks and pebbled beds, cascading over tongue stones; long feathery plumes falling ten, fifteen metres then bursting into fans of spray as they hit rocks placed to break their fall and, in the background, the gentle drumming as the streams joined forces and emptied over the stepped wall around the base of the shaft into the lake.

Standing at the open window, Steve listened intently, memories and feelings about the overground reawakened by the sights and sounds, and the faintly scented breeze circulating round the shaft. The only difference with what he had seen topside was that here, as at San Jacinto Deep, the foliage on the trees, the shrubs and grasses were not red, but green. According to the Manual, before the Mutes had fouled the blue-sky world with their poisonous presence, the overground had also been green. And would be green again when the Federation triumphed.

Steve mulled over the middle lines of the last verse of the Talisman Prophecy ". . . Death shall be driven from the air and the blood shall be drained from the earth . . ." Was that also a promise that the deadly sickness that blanketed the world would disappear? Did the Mute victory under the leadership of the mysterious Talisman her-

ald the greening of America? If it did, it meant the First
Family had lied again: the atmospheric radiation could
not have been caused by the "poisonous presence" of
the Mutes. Likewise, they could not be blamed for the
red grass and trees. The charge that they were a degenerate species of anthropoid was also patently untrue; the
perfectly formed bodies of Cadillac and Clearwater were
proof of that. Mr. Snow had spoken the truth when he
claimed that Tracker and Mute shared a common ancestry.
The Heroes of the Old Time had also been the forefathers
of the Minutemen and Foragers, the first Trackers who,
under the leadership of George Washington Jefferson the
1st, had formed the Federation . . .

Two arms snaked around his waist, and a body pressed
hard against his as someone laid their head against his left
shoulder blade. Steve looked down and recognised his
soft-hearted assailant by the striped blue, white and green
sleeves. "Hello, worm . . ."

"Don't move," murmured Roz, her mouth against his
back.

"Since when did you give the orders?" said Steve. Lifting his right arm he twisted around, encircled her with his
arms and squeezed hard.

"Harder," said Roz. She laid her head against his neck,
hugged him fiercely then covered his face with exuberant
kisses. "Oh, you bastard! If you knew what I've been
through on account of you!" She kissed him hard on the
lips and locked her arms around his ribs. Steve pulled his
mouth away, sucking in his breath sharply.

"What's the matter?" whispered Roz. "Did I hurt
you?"

The jagged pain in Steve's chest faded. "It's okay . . .
just a little fragile. I keep forgetting that a couple of weeks
ago, I was still a prisoner of the Mutes."

As Roz looked up at him her eyes widened and her
hands flew to the cross-shaped scars on his cheeks. "How
did that happen?"

"Someone stuck an arrow through my face."

"Christopher Columbus . . .?"

"It was a test. One of the ways they have of sorting out the men from the boys."

"Did they, uh—beat up on you a lot?"

"Not too much." Steve grinned. "Most of the damage happened on the way here. Don't worry. Nothing's broken. Just, uh . . . bumped into a few things."

Roz caressed the two scars then slipped her arms around his neck and planted a soft-lipped kiss on his mouth. "You pleased to see me?"

"Of course I am. I just hate the idea of you risking everything on account of me."

"It's okay. Provided I don't say anything to Annie and Poppa-Jack, there's nothing to worry about. Chisum—"

"You've gotta watch that guy, Roz. He's crazy. And so's this."

"I don't care," said Roz. Her arms tightened around his neck.

"Did Chisum tell you where they're sending me?"

Roz placed a hand on his lips. "Don't talk about it. I don't want to think about it. Not tonight, anyway."

"You're right. I don't want to think about it either."

"Chisum says you're okay. Otherwise, I mean. No deterioration in your blood cells, no tissue or bone damage, or anything. Well, you can imagine my reaction. I was speechless. But then he explained he thought the reason you hadn't pulled a trick was on account of some new drug the First Family has been developing."

"Do you believe that?"

Roz frowned. "Are you asking me do I think he's lying, or do I think it's medically possible?"

"Both I guess. There's something about that guy that worries me."

"Yes," said Roz. "He's a nice, warm, happy human being—and that's something you still can't handle. Medically? Yes, I'd say it *was* possible. And you're the proof that it works. Isn't the First Family amazing?"

"Yeah," agreed Steve. "Lucky, aren't I?"

"Be serious." It was the doctor, not his kid sister who was looking at him now. "Can you imagine what this could mean for the rest of us?"

"I can, but I wouldn't get too excited about it until they make an official announcement." He dropped his hands, patted her butt then led her over to the long seating unit. "Let's sit down. I've been dying to try out one of these ever since I got here." He tested the upholstery with his hand then sprawled backwards into it, savouring its resilient softness. "Great—what do they call this?"

"A couch."

"And this stuff on the floor?"

"A carpet." Roz sat down close to Steve and took hold of his hand.

"You got any at Inner State U?"

"Yeah—in the dean's study."

"Fantastic . . ." Steve waved a hand around the living area. "All this space for one guy! Did you know that there were Trackers who lived like this?"

"Not until I ran into Chisum."

"Amazing . . . And this guy's just a computer specialist. Just think what Uncle Bart's unit at New Mex State must be like. It must be enormous! Did you know this unit's even got its own galley?!"

"Yes." Roz lifted his arm around her shoulder and snuggled up against him. "I've been here before."

"Who with?"

"Guys. Classmates from Inner State. Friends of Chisum." She reached up and tilted Steve's face towards her so that his cheek rested against her forehead.

"He certainly gets around," muttered Steve.

"Don't let's talk about him, or anybody else. Let's talk about you. Us."

"What d'you want to know?"

"Everything. What happened to you. What you saw, who you met, what you felt."

Steve gave a quick laugh. "How long have you got?"

Roz kissed his cheek. "Long enough. Let me start you off. I knew you were coming. I connected with you on the shuttle. Did you know that?"

"Yes," whispered Steve. "I heard your voice in my mind. You said 'they were watching'. What did you mean? Who are 'they'?"

"I'm not sure. It's just something I've felt ever since you were captured." Roz hesitated. "I knew you had crashed. I felt this terrible pain in my right arm and here—" Roz sat up and touched the right side of her head—the exact point where the bolt fired from Cadillac's crossbow had pinned Steve's arm to his helmet. "I was in class, working at a 'scope, when—all of a sudden—my arm flew up like this. I felt this terrible pain, the whole lab started to spin. I felt I was falling then—I fainted."

"That's just how it was with me," whispered Steve. "The bolt went right through my arm here—" He gripped his right bicep. "What happened then?"

Roz took hold of his hands. "When I came round, Kirkorian—the Chief Pathologist at Inner State—was checking me over. They must have given me a shot of something. I couldn't move and found it difficult to speak. Everything was kind of—muzzy. I couldn't quite work out what was going on but I'm pretty sure Kirk stuck something in my arm—a probe, I guess. He kept asking me if it hurt. It didn't but, at first, I couldn't figure out what he was saying and then, I couldn't get my mouth to work. It was like—y'know—when the dentist fills your jaw with novocaine."

"Might have been shock. I hit the ground hard. Messed me up pretty good."

"I bet . . ." Roz squeezed his hands. "Well, anyway, they kept me in hospital for a whole day. When whatever they'd given me wore off, I looked at my arm but there was nothing to see. Not a mark—or on my head either." She smiled. "Weird, huh?"

"Very . . ." mused Steve.

"You're not the only one to think that. A couple of guys from the Black Tower—one of them a woman—paid me a visit, asked me a lot of questions but—" her eyes locked onto Steve's "—there was nothing I could tell them." She brushed the scar on his left cheek. "I felt this too. It happened late at night, didn't it?"

"That's right . . ."

Roz nodded. "I was dreaming. I was surrounded by huge leaping flames, and there were drums beating, the noise was frightening. I woke up with my mouth full of blood. My face felt as if it was on fire. It was like having a shrieking toothache except the pain was in my cheeks not my gums. My jaw muscles were clenched and trembling."

"That figures. I had to bite on the arrow to break it."

"I washed my mouth out and took a quick look in the mirror. There was blood coming out of both sides of my face."

"Did anyone see you?"

"No, fortunately everyone was asleep. The bleeding stopped half-an-hour later."

"What about your face?"

"You mean next morning? Nothing. Both cheeks were clean. Like it never happened." She smiled. "All in the mind, I guess. Except there was blood all over my pillow. I told my room mates I'd had a nosebleed."

Steve nodded. "And you think someone from the Black Tower has been keeping an eye on you ever since."

"Yes. But I don't mean I'm being followed around night and day. I mean they've got my number. The high-wires don't like you to be, well — different."

Steve smiled and ran a hand over Roz's hair. "They'd like it even less if they knew how different we really are."

"Yes . . ." Roz took hold of Steve's hand as it rested on her neck and ran her lips over it. "For a while I thought they were going to throw me off the course. I really spooked the rest of the class. Kirk—Kirkorian—still hasn't got over it. I can tell by the way he looks at me."

"Did you, uh—tell anyone you knew I was alive?"

"You mean Annie—or d'you mean Chisum?"

Steve shrugged. "He says he's heard a lot about me."

"That's right," said Roz. "Your little sister is very proud of you. But I've never told him about us. Only you and me know about us." She bit the edge of his hand playfully. Their eyes met. "D'you remember how it was?"

"Sometimes, yes. Other times I try to forget."

"I'm not going to let you."

"Roz, I told you—right after Graduation—people change. Even you aren't the same person you were when I left."

Roz shrugged. "In some ways perhaps. But not deep

down. We'll always be part of one another. We belong together. I've known it since the moment Annie brought me back from the Life Institute."

Steve laughed, remembering. "Aww, c'mon—you couldn't see straight—you cross-eyed little runt!"

"And what about you? Even at two and a half you were already a pompous little fart, marching off to primary training with your nose in the air—"

"How could you remember that?"

"I remember everything!" exclaimed Roz. "And what I remember most is you running around going 'bzz-bzz-bzz' with that stupid little model plane—"

"It was more fun than having to play with you, *worm!*"

"Well, I hated it!" exclaimed Roz. She threw a punch at Steve's shoulder. He blocked her fist and caught hold of her left wrist as she tried to get through his guard. They rolled around on the couch, wrestling playfully. Roz was strong, with quick reflexes, but she was no match for Steve. They tumbled off the soft cushions and landed with Steve pinning her to the floor. Roz gave up the unequal struggle. Steve could feel her heart beating against his ribs. He pressed his nose down on hers. "I was crazy about that plane. Poppa-Jack gave it to me. It was a model of his Skyhawk."

"I know," said Roz. "Annie told me. That's why I hated it! Because of what flying the real thing did to him." She pulled her wrists from his relaxed grasp and slid her arms round his neck. "Because I knew that same goddam airplane was going to take you away from me."

"Yeah," muttered Steve. "Y'know, a few months ago, I thought I knew everything, but now . . ." He shook his head and sighed. "I feel like I'm right back at the beginning." He rolled over on his back alongside the couch.

Roz hung on round his neck and ended up on top. She kissed the tip of his nose. "You must have learned *something* out there. Everything must be so different."

"Yeah . . ." Steve smiled, remembering. "If I've learned anything at all, it's that life means being separated from those people you . . ." He lapsed into silence. In his mind's eye were a series of pictures of Clearwater; her face as he first saw it across the firelit circle; standing naked in front of her hut in the forest, stretching her lithe, supple body; the secret look she gave him when she passed by in the company of her clan-sisters; her body close to his in the darkness during their one night together, warm and vibrant, arched beneath him and over him, whispering sweet-sounding words in his ear; words he had never heard and did not know the meaning of, but which made his heart quicken.

" 'Those people you' . . . what?" asked Roz

"Those people you love," replied Steve. "Have you ever heard of that word?"

"Yes, I've heard it."

"Where?"

"In songs. On some of those tapes you don't like me listening to. What d'you think it means?"

"I'm not sure," said Steve. "This old Mute asked me if it was a word we used. I said 'No'. Later on he explained what it meant. Love is a word you use to describe a special kind of feeling you have about somebody. It's much more than just being friendly with a guy. It's to do with wanting to, uh—*be* with someone all the time. But it's more than that. It's stronger. It's like . . ." Steve searched for an appropriate description. ". . . wanting to be part *of* them. When you feel this way about someone, you can't think of anything else. Nothing else matters. And when they're close to you, y'know, it, uh—takes your breath away. You feel you're going to suffocate. Not in a bad way, but because you're so goddamn *happy*!" Steve ran his hands over Roz's shoulders and down onto the base of her spine. "Have you ever felt anything like that?"

"Yeah," murmured Roz. "It's the way I feel about you." She kissed him hungrily before he could reply, the tip of her tongue chasing his. She slid her trousered thighs outside his and pressed down hard with the point of her pelvis.

Steve felt the zing through the double layers of clothing; felt the heat building up between their sandwiched thighs. This is crazy, he thought. He took her face between his hands and lifted her mouth from his. "Tell me about you and Chisum."

Roz lifted her butt a few inches and brought the point of her pelvis down hard against Steve's crotch. "Fuck Chisum . . ."

"That hurt . . ."

"It was meant to. Never mind. I have a Grade One InterMed and I'm studying for my M.D. D'you want me to kiss it better?"

"Later." Steve wriggled free and sat down on the couch. Roz sat up, pushed her hair back into place, then curled her feet under her and leant against the couch at Steve's knee. "I'm waiting."

Roz shrugged. "There's nothing to tell. I first ran into him on a tour of the Life Institute when I was doing my InterMed. We met up again a few months ago. We've been together here a few times—usually with other people from Inner State. Not often. I don't get a lot of free time. We have classes six days a week. Sunday is supposed to be our day off but everybody spends it transferring class notes from their Memo Typers onto disk files, and doing extra revision. The pressure is," Roz grimaced, ". . . pretty horrendous."

"I can imagine . . ."

"You can't afford to let up for a minute. Sometimes I think if it hadn't been for Chisum, I'd have . . ." She let it hang there.

"And you've still got another two and a half years to go," observed Steve.

"Yeah . . ." Roz smiled wanly. "Don't worry, I'll make it. And, just for the record, he hasn't jacked your little sister."

"I'm not worried, Roz. You're a big girl now. I just want to know what the score is. What's his angle? What's he after?"

"I don't know, and I don't care. If Chisum wasn't around I'd pop my rivets. He's a nice, relaxing guy. He knows how to make you laugh. A few of us sneak over here for a few hours every couple of weeks or so. We sit around, swap ideas, talk about things—everything except medecine—

brew Java, plug into some blackjack and burn off some grass. It helps take the heat off."

Steve sat bolt upright and seized his kin-sister's wrist. "Sweet Christopher! I told you to lay off that blackjack junk before I left. And now you're smoking grass!"

Roz eyed him calmly. "So what? You were piped into it while you were out there."

"Is that what Chisum told you?"

"Yeah, tonight. When he was fixing up for me to come over to meet you. I asked him how he thought you might react if I lit up."

"And what did he say?"

Roz smiled. "He said you might hit the roof but probably wouldn't go through it. And that if I twisted your arm, you might loosen up and take a puff."

"The crazy sonofabitch!" hissed Steve angrily. "I told him! Roz! How could you get sucked into something like this?! Blackjack and grass are both Code One! If the Provos were to hit this place while you were all here—"

Roz cut him off. "Steve! Half the Provos in Grand Central are tunnelling out. How d'you think the stuff gets here? They're part of the network!"

"Is that what Chisum told you?"

"Of course. You don't think I walked up to some meat-loaf and asked him, do you?"

"And you believe it . . ."

Roz pulled free of his grip and held his hand between hers. "Why not? True, untrue, right, wrong. I don't know what those words mean anymore—do you?"

"I used to once. Now, well—I'm not so sure."

"Exactly. Anyway, what are you getting so upset about? You've done the same thing."

"That was different. I was a prisoner."

"Yes, of course. I forgot." Roz smiled. "Did you tell the Assessors the Mutes forced you to smoke grass?"

"No. They might not have understood."

"I bet. And what else didn't you tell them?"

Steve pulled his hand free. "Drop it, Roz. I've got enough problems."

"I know."

"What d'you mean?"

Roz rose to her feet abruptly and looked down at him. "You keep forgetting I can get inside your head, Steve. I was with you on your first overground solo, when you crashed, when you were on your way here aboard the shuttle."

Steve was filled with sudden foreboding. "I know. You already told me."

Roz nodded. "There were other times too, big brother."

"What 'other times'?"

Roz smiled ruefully. "Steve—I *know* there are things you don't want to tell me. That hurts but—okay, I know you've been trying for years to build a wall around yourself. Maybe you can shut out other people but I will always get through. We really *are* different. Sometimes I hate it, hate having to hide it, hate knowing that you—the other part of what I am—are trying to break the bond between us."

"I'm not," said Steve. "Not all the time. It—you have to understand, Roz—this thing we have . . . scares the heck out of me."

"It used to scare me—but not anymore. What frightens me now is knowing *why* you're trying to shut me out."

Steve's stomach felt like a ball of lead. "I don't know what you're talking about."

"I'm talking about Clearwater."

Steve caught his breath and tried to look puzzled. "Clearwater?"

"Yes, Clearwater!" cried Roz. "Did you really think you could keep it from me?! Her name is burned right through your fucking brain! Dark hair as long as my arm, blue eyes, brown skin! Are you trying to tell me you don't remember that stinking piece of lump-shit crawling all over you?!"

Steve stared at her, unable to speak, then made a grab for her as he started to get up.

Roz pushed him back down and stepped back out of reach. "Don't touch me!" She mimicked his fake innocence. "Clearwater . . .? Bastard! How could you lie to me?! You make me feel sick!" She beat the air with her fists then, skirting the couch, she strode across the living area space and went up the carpeted steps into the bed space.

Steve got up from the couch and went after her. His legs were trembling. When he reached the bed space, Roz was on her knees by the head of the bunk. It was a kind Steve hadn't seen before—wide enough for two people side by side. Roz had turned back a corner of the bedroll and was pulling a small flat metal box from a compartment hidden underneath.

"I was going to tell you, Roz."

She kept her back to him. "Yeah, sure," she sniffed, rubbing her eyes with the back of her hand. She dropped the bedroll back into place and sat down on the edge of the bunk with the small box on her lap.

Steve leant back against the doors of the storage unit that formed one wall of the sleeping area. "Roz—look at me."

Roz kept her head down. She fumbled open the lid of the box, pulled out a reaf and a hot-wire coil, tossed the box aside and plugged the coil into a socket set near the head of the bunk.

Steve watched with a sinking feeling. "How did you know?"

Roz bit her lip and kept her eyes averted.

Steve squatted down in front of her and waited patiently for her to restablish contact. She pulled the glowing coil from the socket, used it to light up the reaf then puffed on it rapidly and drew the smoke from the rainbow grass down into her lungs.

Steve felt a sudden desire to wrest the leaf from her fingers and slap some sense into her but his anger was overwhelmed by a feeling of utter helplessness. A feeling that everything was slipping out of control.

Roz raised her eyes to his and pulled down some more smoke. "How did I know?"

"Yeah."

Roz gave a lopsided grin. "After everything that's happened between us . . . you still have to ask me that?"

"I want to hear you say it."

"I was *there*, Steve. In you, with you. I could *feel* her

touching you. Touching *me!*" Roz bared her teeth, and shuddered violently. "I could feel her mind—the power inside it—trying to possess you! Uuugghh—it was revolting!"

Steve fell forward onto his knees and took hold of her free hand. "No! It wasn't like that. It isn't like that. She—"

"She's a Mute!" Roz spat out the words then swallowed some more smoke.

"Okay, okay!" he hissed. "Keep your voice down! *Yes*—she's a Mute! I couldn't tell anyone else but I'm not ashamed to tell you. Have you forgotten all those nice things you said about 'em before I left? About how maybe Mutes had a right to live just as we did?"

"Yes, I remember. But I didn't mean for you to go out there and jack the ass off them!"

Steve waved the smoke away from his face. The fragrant odour was getting to him, pulling him back. "Stop it, Roz. Junk that stuff—please!" He made a grab for the reaf.

Roz pulled her hand out of reach. "No! Let me alone. It helps deaden the pain." She balled her left fist and smashed it angrily against Steve's shoulder.

Steve fended off the second and third blow then grabbed her wrist and twisted it until her arm went limp. "Listen to me!" he hissed. "It wasn't the way you think! What happened between us that night was great. It was a *good* feeling. If you were there, like you say, you'd know that."

"I *was* there!" cried Roz. "It's always been the same. In a moment of crisis, great emotion, or danger, something inside me flies out to join you. I was in that hut. I could smell it—the animal skins, the wood, the earth. And I could smell *her*—the oil on her body, the flowers in her hair. I loathed every minute of it. She had taken you over. You were trying to *shut me out!*"

"Roz, it's not true!" exclaimed Steve. "I didn't shut you out—not deliberately, anyway. This wasn't something I could have shared with you. Nothing like this has ever happened to me before. I—I didn't even know the *word* for it!"

"You mean 'love'—the way I feel about you?" Roz laughed brokenly. "What do you think it was that brought us so close to each other? What do you think it was you felt when we——?"

Steve cut in. "It's not the same thing, Roz."

"It is!" she cried. "Can't you see? The only difference is you've always tried to deny the feeling *we* have for each other. I understood why. It hurt but it didn't worry me because I knew you could never destroy it. But——" She grabbed the collar of his coveralls, "——how, after all you've said, how can you say you love a Mute?! How could you even bear to *touch* one?!"

Steve dragged her hand away and held it tightly. "Roz! Listen! I didn't know about the Plainfolk then. They're not animals and they're not poisonous. If they were I wouldn't *be* here. They are *people*, Roz! Okay, most of them look pretty awful, but they're not dumb! And some of them—like Clearwater—are very special people. She's a Mute, yes, but she's not a lumphead like the others."

"What is she then—a yearling?"

"No. According to the Manual, the straights traded in as twelve-month old babies by the Southern Mutes are supposed to be straight-boned and smooth-skinned but they've always had multi-coloured bodies—right? I mean, that's how you're supposed to be able to tell the difference—between them and us."

Roz nodded.

"Well, Clearwater is something else again. She's a *super*-straight! Her body is absolutely perfect. Her skin is almost the same colour as yours. *All over*! She's been raised to think of herself as a Mute but there's nothing wrong with her brain. If she was dressed in a jump suit she'd look just like us!"

"Not like us," muttered Roz. "We're special, Steve."

"So is she, believe me." Steve put his hands on Roz's shoulders. "And that's not all. Cadillac—this other Mute who helped save me after I crashed—is the same. They've both got skins and bodies like Trackers, their minds are like our minds—maybe even better than ours! I tried to tell the Assessors about how intelligent the Mutes were but——" Steve broke off with a laugh, "——they wouldn't listen to me!" He ran a hand down his kin-sister's face.

"I'll tell you something else. There *is* such a thing as Mute magic. I saw 'em use it, Roz. It was fantastic . . ."

Roz puffed on the reaf then leaned forward and gently blew smoke into Steve's face. He held out for a brief moment then drew it in through his nostrils. Roz put her open lips on his and passed the rest of the smoke from her mouth into his.

Steve drew it down into his lungs. "Mm-mmm . . . that feels good. Forgive me?"

"Not yet," said Roz. She placed the reaf between Steve's lips. "Your turn."

Steve burned off a good half inch of grass, passed some of the smoke back into her mouth then swallowed the rest.

"Mmmmm . . . things are beginning to look a lot better." Roz took charge of the reaf, lay back on the bunk and wriggled across to the other side to make room for Steve. "You'll find another one in the box . . ."

Steve used the coil to light up and lay down beside his kin-sister. "Hope they haven't got some kind of shit detector fixed to the ventilation system."

Roz giggled. "If they have, I don't think it's working." She turned onto her side and lay against him, head up on one elbow. "Does this take you back?"

Steve exhaled slowly and watched the smoke drift to the ceiling. "Yeah . . . Funny isn't it? Five months ago, the idea that an intelligent human being would voluntarily inhale smoke from burning grass would have seemed absolutely insane. And yet—"

"You now find everybody's doing it."

"So you tell me."

"How was it out·there?"

"Good and bad. They're an amazing people. Totally different to what I would ever have imagined—and to what we've been raised to believe. Most of the stuff we've been fed by the First Family isn't true, Roz."

"So tell me about it."

"Okay . . . what d'you wanna know?"

"Everything. Even the boring bits."

"It's hard to know where to begin. How much time do we have?"

"Masses. Chisum'll tell us when we've got to go. If you haven't finished we'll fix up to come back here some other time . . ."

"Yeah, why not . . ." Steve began to feel agreeably light-headed.

"Right . . . you and me . . . we've got forever . . ." Roz opened the long front zip of her jumpsuit and began to wriggle out of it.

"Okay, I'll tell you about this old guy, Mr. Snow. He's a wordsmith—that's like a walking video-archive. Knows everything you want to know about, and about everything that's ever happened. And that's not all. He's a Storm-Bringer. D'you know what that is . . . ?" Steve tried to raise his head and only half-succeeded. "What're y'doing . . . ?"

"Trying to unzip this . . . fucking yellow thing you're wearing," mumbled Roz.

Steve was seized with a sudden desire to laugh. "Why…?"

"Cos I wanna . . . wanna get inside it, that's why."

He felt her hand slip under his T-shirt and slide down past his navel. "Hey . . . should you . . . should you . . . I'm trying to tell you about Mr. Snow. He's a summoner. He's got . . ." Roz began licking his left ear. "Hey, c'mon, give me a break! See . . . there are . . . these, uh . . . Rings of Power . . ."

"Yeah, I know, I got one," she giggled. "C'mon, Steve. Let's *do* it. Just one more time. Please! Oh, Sweet Christopher . . . it's . . . been so *long*!"

Steve felt the room start to spin. "Wait a minute . . . wait a minute . . . Don't you want to hear about Mr. Snow? How about Cadillac? Now he's, uh . . . really bright. A real friend of mine. Did you . . . did I, uh . . . tell you I taught him to fly. Clearwater now . . . she, uh . . . she's like Mr. Snow. She does, uh . . . magic too . . ."

"Yeah, I bet she does," whispered Roz. "Go on, tell me about it . . ." She moved on top of him. "Ohhhh . . . oh! Steeeee-ve!"

"No . . . listen . . . Christopher, what's happening? Roz . . ." He felt her naked body sliding over his. A softness . . . smothering him, swallowing him. The dim light around the bed space began to change colour, glowing and dimming in sync with the rhythmic movements of her body. "No, don't . . . wait! There's . . ." His voice seemed to come from a long way away. He could no longer feel Roz pressing down on his belly. The body of his kin-sister began to twist out of shape, grew bigger and bigger until it loomed over him like a huge, threatening storm cloud . . . blotting out the light . . . the bunk became a whirlpool, sucking him down into a dark, impenetrable void . . .

In Unit 7, on the same floor, Chisum sipped a cup of Java as he sat watching the video-screen linked to the camera recording the action in the bedspace next door. Roz, who was seated astride her kin-brother, swayed drunkenly then toppled sideways and slid gently off the bunk onto the floor. Steve lay on his back sprawled diagonally across the duvet with one arm outstretched, hand hanging over the edge. The half-smoked reaf lay where he had dropped it, on the low table by the bunkhead.

Chisum decided to wait another fifteen minutes before calling in Fran's Q-Squad. Yes . . . it had been a good move to suggest using the subject's kin-sister. Chisum had known she was a sensitive but hadn't realised her power. She would need to be handled carefully. Or eliminated. Right now, she was the key to Steve. She had cracked him wide open. And now she could be used to apply leverage. Yes, a good night's work— provided, of course, he hadn't heard too much for his own good. But then, that was a risk everybody ran—especially in his line of work. Dismissing the thought, Chisum sipped the rest of his Java in leisurely fashion and let the blackjack tape he had put on as background music run to the end of the reel.

The forbidden music track ended with a triumphant crescendo on brass and percussion instruments. Chisum put the small cassette player away then pulled the video-tape of Roz and Steve out of the recorder and put a call through to Fran's men. "Be right with you," promised the voice on the other end. Chisum picked up his emergency aid case and went into Unit 8.

Roz and Steve were still lying where they had keeled

over when the drugged grass took effect. Chisum put the half-burnt reafs back in the box and put the box in his case, then he injected Roz with a strong dose of barbiturates, dressed her quickly and expertly and laid her out alongside Steve. He then rearranged Steve's clothing and was in the process of zipping him up when the four-man Q-squad came through the door. All four were dressed in black and silver-blue jump-suits—the mark of men from the Black Tower: Amtrak Execs, one step below the First Family. And, as Chisum knew, any or all of them could *be* Family. It was one of their favourite disguises.

"Where you going to pump him?" asked Chisum.

"Here." The man who spoke had the kind of face and voice that said, 'I'm in charge'. "It'll save time. How long have we got?"

"As long as you want," replied Chisum diplomatically. "But ideally, I should have him back in the White House before 0600 hours."

"No problem," said the man. "Leave it with us. How about the girl?"

"She'll be out cold till 10 or 1100. I'll ship her back to Inner State later."

"Have you got the tape?"

Chisum took the video-recording of Steve and Roz from his emergency aid case and handed it over. "Interesting stuff."

The man nodded. "Yes. We were watching." He checked the time. "Come back at 0530."

"Wilco," said Chisum. He left the accommodation unit without a backward glance.

"Okay, let's get to work," said the man.

Two of his companions lifted Steve off the bunk and laid him out on the couch. The third man, who had brought a case similar to that carried by Chisum, bared Steve's forearm and injected him with a carefully measured dose of sodium pentothal. The other two pulled a tall camera tripod from another bag and connected up a portable video-camera to a monitor and the nearest power socket. With the aid of a counterbalanced extension arm, they set the camera pointing straight down at Steve, adjusting the focus so that his head and shoulders filled the screen on the monitor. One of them slotted the number 3552 into a clapper board that carried a digital time/date display and held it briefly in front of Steve's face. "Subject 3552, Operation Overlord, Q-squad 6 . . ."

His companion checked the picture balance and sound levels on the equipment and gave a satisfied nod. "Up and running . . ."

The Exec who had administered the "truth" drug went into the galley to make coffee, humming in tune to the endless music-track that drifted through the ceiling-mounted speakers.

The man in charge took a chair from the set around the table and placed it by the arm of the couch on which Steve's head lay. He sat down and placed a gentle hand on Steve's forehead. "Steven? Can you hear me? I want you to nod your head if you can hear my voice."

Eyes closed, face totally relaxed under the effects of the drug, Steve responded with a slight movement of the head.

"Good . . . very good," said the man. His voice was deep-pitched, the cadence measured, reassuring. "Now, I want you to help me. I want you to tell me who you are. First, tell me your full name."

Steve breathed deeply. His mouth moved soundlessly for a moment then he replied in a slurred, detached voice. "Steven Roosevelt Brickman . . ."

"Thank you. That's a great help. Now, tell me your number . . ."

EIGHT

WHEN STEVE opened his eyes, he found Chisum sitting beside him on the edge of the bunk, shaking him by the shoulder and gently slapping his face. "Hey, hey, c'mon! Wake up! Wake up!"

"Wassa . . . ?" Steve sat up woozily and was seized with a fit of coughing. The smell of burning rainbow grass filled his nostrils and the taste of it coated his tongue.

Chisum's nose wrinkled. "How much of that stuff did you smoke last night?"

"Don't remember . . ." said Steve hoarsely. His tongue felt stuck to the roof of his mouth. "Is there anything to—?"

"Yeah, here—drink this . . ." Chisum handed him a mug of water that fizzed noisily.

Steve inspected the contents suspiciously. "What is it?"

"Something that'll help get your ass off that bunk and your feet on the floor. C'mon! Get the lead out! It's 0545 and you're due to card-in on A-2 at 0630."

Steve drank the contents of the glass then swung his legs off the bunk and sat slumped over, hands hanging between his knees. "Think I'm gonna be sick . . ."

"No, you're not." Chisum rubbed him vigorously on the back. "Breathe in, c'mon—all the way."

Steve did so. It triggered another bout of coughing but

149

he began to feel better. His brain sharpened sufficiently to enable him to remember his kin-sister. He jerked his head up. An invisible lead weight dropped with a soundless thud against the base of his skull. "Roz! Where's Roz?!" he gasped.

"Right behind you."

Steve twisted round, almost slipping off the edge of the bunk in the process. Roz lay, fully dressed, stretched out on the far side, breathing deeply through her mouth. Her eyes were rolled up under half open lids. Her left arm was angled across her stomach, the other lay palm upwards, the butt end of a reaf resting between her fingers. The duvet underneath had been scorched brown where the reaf had extinguished itself—a little touch Chisum had arranged before rousing Steve with an injection designed to counteract the effects of the sodium pentothal.

"Columbus, she looks awful!"

"She'll be okay. Let her sleep it off. I'll take care of her later." Chisum took the butt from between Roz's fingers and picked up the other he had put back on the bunkhead table where Steve had dropped it before the arrival of the Q-squad. He sniffed them and grimaced disapprovingly. "Kentucky Blue . . . no wonder you got blocked out of your skulls. Strong but iffy. Know what I mean?"

"No. What *do* you mean?"

"The quality's variable. If it's good, you can tunnel out on three or four puffs but if you get a sour bag it can be bad news. Instead of your ears turning into wings, it's like getting punched between the eyes by a two-hundred-pound Provo. A real downer."

"Terrific." Steve stood up and leaned against the wall to steady himself. "How could you let her smoke that shit?"

Chisum assumed an air of injured innocence. "How could *I* let her? Why did *you* let her?"

"It was you who got her started!"

Chisum waved the butts under Steve's nose. "Not with *this* stuff. I only ship sweet grass. Okay, it was through me she maybe got to know it was around—but I didn't push it."

"I bet!"

Chisum remained calm. "Steve, I don't give a bucket of beaver piss what you think. But as it happens, I didn't make Roz do anything she didn't want to. If you ask me, she got into smoking shit on account of you. She never touched the stuff until the news came that you'd powered down." Chisum turned away with an angry laugh. "Columbus! You try and do a guy a favour . . ."

Steve grabbed his arm. "John! Look, uh—I'm sorry— okay? I didn't mean to get uptight. I'm just . . . Christo! I feel like a ton of rock just fell on me!"

It just did, thought Chisum. But you won't know that till later, flyboy. He turned on an understanding smile and patted Steve's arm. "Did you manage to talk?"

"Yeah, a bit." Steve felt better now that the floor had stopped moving under his feet. "I know we ended up arguing. But then that's not unusual." He threw a last anxious glance at Roz then stepped down into the living area. "This place is okay, isn't it?"

Chisum looked puzzled. "What're you getting at?"

"I mean there's no chance that, uh . . . well—that someone could have been listening in?"

Chisum laughed dismissively. "Why would anyone want to do that?" He handed Steve his yellow hard-hat and the borrowed toolbox.

Steve looked unconvinced. "It happens, doesn't it?"

Chisum grinned and ushered him down the hallway and out into the lobby. "If it does, the boys in the Black Tower are not going to tell me." He shut the entrance door to Unit Eight, led the way over to the freight elevator and thumbed the call button. "Relax. Listen—if that place wasn't safe, I'd have made my goodbye speech on tv a long time ago." Chisum was referring to the ritual confession of error made by Trackers following a death sentence for a Code One offence and prior to their televised execution by firing squad.

They entered the elevator and were carried downwards. A fearsome thought struck Steve. "Christo! What about those two guys on duty outside the ward?! Supposing they checked up during the night? They'll have reported me missing!"

Chisum waved him down. "They didn't and they haven't. What d'you think this is—amateur night? You're looking at a professional. If I offer to fix something, I fix it!"

"How?"

Chisum eyed him with a sly smile. "How? Huh! Do you think I'm going let you in on all my secrets? What're you aiming to do—muscle in on my operation?"

Steve managed a half-hearted grin. "Some chance. No. I'd just like to be able to square this with you one day but—where I'm going . . ." His voice trailed off.

The elevator reached the service bay. Chisum patted Steve on the back as they stepped out and walked towards the parked wheelie. "Don't worry. You'll be back up. Who knows? One day, you may find me asking you a favour."

The President-General, George Washington Jefferson the 31st, stepped out of the private elevator that linked his office in the White House with Cloudlands, and walked to his desk. Jefferson was a silver-haired solidly-built man in his mid-sixties. He was a few pounds heavier than his personal physician would have liked but he moved easily, with the kind of straight-backed assurance you would expect from the man at the top of an extremely competitive heap. His medium tan made his pale grey-blue eyes look even paler. People facing him always watched the eyes. They were the kind that could twinkle one minute and turn to ice the next. When the light went out it was bad news.

Though not an exact copy, Jefferson's office had been modelled on the Oval Office used by the presidents of pre-Holocaust America. Like his predecessors in the First Family, he liked to think he was keeping alive the link with the great and noble traditions of the past; all that was brightest and best in a once-great country that, one day, would be reborn; would rise to even greater heights than before . . .

Two flags hung draped from crossed poles behind his chair, surmounted by a large eagle carved from dark wood, its neck arched defiantly, its wings half extended. The flag to the right, when seated, was Old Glory; the other was based on what had once been known as the "rebel" flag, a diagonal blue cross outlined in white on a red field. The cross carried nine white stars—representing the Inner State of Texas at the centre, flanked by the eight Outer States and New Territories. Two tall windows with wooden frames were set in the curving wall on each side of the flags.

The President-General gazed for a moment through the windows at the autumnal tints gracing his favourite computer-generated image of pre-Holocaust New England countryside then, with a brief sigh of regret, he settled down in his comfortable high-backed chair and addressed his multi-screen video. "Nancy . . . ?"

The head and shoulders of the Presidential aide on duty in the outer office appeared on the big centre screen. "Good morning, Mr. President."

The P-G nodded in reply. "Is Fran there?" A needless question: no one was ever late for an audience with the President-General. The question was asked because the wielder of absolute power believed—again like his predecessors—in the maintainance of a courtly, old-world protocol.

"Yes, sir."

"Good. Ask her to come in. And Nancy?"

"Yes, sir?" said Nancy Reagan Jefferson. Like most of the P-G's personal staff, she was a close relative.

"Put Brickman's file summaries and any related material up on my screen." One of the luxuries of presiding over a push-button world was having other people to push the buttons. The P-G's video unit was activated by the sound of his own voice—as were the doors to his private elevator and the elevator itself.

Fran Delano Jefferson pressed the door buzzer. The action put her picture on another of the P-G's desk-mounted video screens.

"Enter . . ."

This time, the P-G's voice activated the revolving door linking his office with those beyond. As Fran entered the cylindrical compartment, it rotated, carrying her into the P-G's presence. Doors of similar design—known as turnstiles—which only allowed authorised personnel through one at a time, were now fitted to all high security areas. Turnstiles had been installed in the P-G's office complex some two hundred years ago following an attempted "palace coup" in which six first cousins of the then President-General—George Washington Jefferson the 22nd—had burst in and gunned him down before being apprehended.

"Pull up a chair," said the P-G.

Fran did so, adopting an upright, attentive pose, her hands linked together in her lap.

The P-G waved his hand at the display on the first of his screens which Fran could just see sideways on. "I think I'm going to have to hire someone to summarise the summaries," he said good-humouredly. "Give me the bottom line on this young man."

"Brickman was shot down over Wyoming. Instead of being killed he was befriended by some of his Mute captors who nursed him back to health. They seemed to practise a form of 'natural' medicine. A mixture of herbal remedies and the laying on of hands. It works. Brickman's left leg—which he claims was broken—was x-rayed in the unit downstairs. No sign of a break. It's completely whole. His two principal captors were wordsmiths—Mr. Snow and Cadillac, his heir-presumptive. You'll find them mentioned in his statement to the Board of Assessors. What he didn't mention was that Mr. Snow is also a summoner. Seventh Ring . . ."

"A Storm-Bringer?"

"Yes, sir. He came within an ace of wrecking The Lady from Louisiana. The incident is mentioned in the combat sit-rep filed by Commander Hartmann for June 12th. You may find that worth reading. Mr. Snow is definitely bad news. He and Cadillac are—according to Brickman—highly intelligent."

The P-G nodded. "It doesn't surprise me. COLUMBUS had predicted the possible evolution of 'smart Mutes'."

"Cadillac, the second wordsmith is young. Eighteen. He's not a summoner but he, too, has an ace up his sleeve. He's a seer. He claims to be able to read the stones. Brickman did not witness this but Cadillac's statement was corroborated by Mr. Snow."

The P-G studied Fran. "Do you think it's possible?"

"That Cadillac is a seer? Or do you mean the whole idea of being able to foretell the future with the aid of seeing stones?"

"Both . . ."

"Sir, I, uh—I'm not qualified to make a judgment in that area. But if you were to press me for a personal opinion I'd have to say I approach such matters with an open mind."

The P-G smiled. "You sound like a Supreme Councillor. Is there any more?"

"Indeed there is. Brickman didn't waste his time. He got the Mutes to help him build a hang-glider using bits from a couple of wrecked Skyhawks and in return, he taught Cadillac to fly. Within a week, the Mute was handling it like a graduate from the Academy."

"Go on . . ."

"Brickman also discovered that Cadillac's sleeping partner—a sixteen-year-old Mute female called Clearwater was a summoner of the Second Ring. She and Brickman had a brief physical liaison prior to his departure. It was, literally, a one-night stand but it appears to have left its mark. It's not clear from Brickman's 'confession' whether the young wordsmith is aware of this."

The P-G nodded. "I guess it depends which stones he's been sitting on."

Fran laughed. Her relationship to the P-G was close enough to permit a certain measure of informality. "Yes. But don't let me give you the wrong impression. It's not as bad as it sounds. Brickman may—as Trail-Blazers say—have 'bounced beaver' but he hasn't gone native. Mr. Snow is a true lumphead but both Cadillac and Clearwater are straights. More than that. They are—to use Brickman's own words—'superstraights'. Not only are they straight-boned and smooth-skinned—they are also *clear*-skinned, bright and *gifted*. Ideal candidates for the Talisman target-list."

"Incredible . . ." mused the P-G. "Did Brickman say anything while he was under the truth drug as to why he concealed all this from the Assessors?"

"Yes. A misplaced sense of loyalty. He felt he owed his life on more than once occasion to Mr. Snow. He gave the old man his word never to reveal the clan's biggest secret— that not only are Cadillac and Clearwater gifted but that, bodywise, they're indistinguisable from Trackers." Fran paused. "Add in this Mr. Snow and you're looking at a lot of power packed into one clan."

"Too much," said the President-General.

"There were two other reasons why Brickman kept quiet. He happens to be somewhat smitten with this . . . young lady. Given his background it's not surprising there was some reaction. And also, being a well-trained, ambitious young man, he didn't want to damage his career prospects by talking about magic."

The P-G nodded. "Why did they keep him alive? That's what really intrigues me. Did he throw any daylight on that?"

"Yes, sir, he did. The clan wanted to show him—and for him to tell us—what the Plainfolk were capable of. They also gave him something else to bring back. The Talisman Prophecy. It seems to have made a deep impression on him."

"It impressed me too, Fran. Still does . . . after all these years." The P-G swung his chair round to the right and gazed reflectively out of the windows for a moment then turned back to Fran. "Is that it?"

"Yes, sir—apart from a couple of footnotes. The M'Calls— the Plainfolk clan that held him captive—apparently told Brickman that he was linked to the Talisman."

The P-G's interest quickened. "You call that a footnote? What else did he say."

Fran spread her palms. "Q-6 did their best but there was no further clarification. The actual phrases Brickman used were 'linked to' and 'under his protection'. It appears that Cadillac and Clearwater also come into this category. That might be more interesting. As 'superstraights' they make an ideal breeding pair."

"Yes . . ." The P-G's eyes narrowed as he mulled over what Fran had said. "And there are also other permutations . . ."

Fran didn't understand what he was getting at but chose to remain silent. She saw the P-G look at her expectantly. "Uh—the, uh—second item is from Brickman's statement to the Board of Assessors. It concerns the people who supply the Plainfolk with their cross-bows—"

The P-G cut her short with a wave of his hand. "Yes, the Iron Masters. I know about them. At the moment, we have that particular problem on the back burner."

Fran inclined her head respectfully. "I understand, sir. The fine print of what we've discussed is in his statement to the Assessors and the Q-6 report. Both are attached to the summaries of his bio-file that you now have on-screen."

The P-G ignored the material displayed on his video. "I prefer to listen. In my experience I've found that, with an oral briefing, you not only acquire information, you also learn a great deal about the person who's presenting it." He paused briefly to let that sink in. "What do you think, Fran?"

"About Brickman?"

"You're his controller. You also presided over the board that questioned him for the last five days."

Fran pressed her lips together as she considered her answer. "He's got what it takes."

"Yes. That's what we all think."

"He also delivered some really high-grade intelligence."

"Is that why he came back?"

Fran smiled. "I'd like to think it was but our Mr. Brickman is not that straightforward. No . . . he came back for all sorts of reasons. Even so, I think Programming has done an amazing job—on both of them."

"Yes," agreed the P-G. He grimaced thoughtfully. "It's this possible link with Talisman that causes me some concern. I'd like to think it was all nonsense but—if this 'link' was activated—would the mind-blocks hold?"

"We must make sure they do," replied Fran.

It was the P-G's turn to smile. "Easier said than done. It was an unfair question. None of us can predict what will happen when the joker in the pack turns up—if he ever does. But there is no point in storing up more trouble for

ourselves. If there is any serious doubt about Brickman
. . ." He didn't need to say any more.

"That, of course, must be your decision," said Fran
respectfully. "If he's scratched then, obviously, any potential threat is eliminated. You have to balance that against
what we might gain by having him under our control."
She hesitated, choosing her words carefully. "If it turns
out he *is* one of the links in the chain—or becomes a
source of power that we can turn against the Mutes . . .
Isn't that the real reason why he and the others are on the
ST-list?"

The P-G nodded soberly. "It's one of them, yes . . ."

"Then it would be a pity to waste all the effort that's
been expended on getting him this far. He also happens to
be the only person that can lead us to Mr. Snow and those
two superstraights."

"Yes, that just occurred to me too," replied Jefferson.

Fran said nothing more on the subject of Brickman but,
inside her head, she was playing back the video-tape Chisum
had made of Brickman and his kin-sister. And she recalled
with an inward smile her feelings as she had watched Roz
strip off her uniform and climb on top of Steve. Fran had
been surprised to discover herself watching with less than
clinical detachment. In fact, she had found herself wishing—
albeit briefly—that she could have taken Roz's place. She
pushed the thought out of her head again. Ridiculous . . .

As the man who—in order to stay on top of the job—was
expected to have an encyclopaedic grasp of everything that
was going on at every level throughout the Federation,
the President-General was bombarded with a never-ending
stream of information twenty-four hours a day. And this
was despite a fifty-strong team of loyal, closely-related
aides whose job it was to sort out the dross from the gold.
The pre-Holocaust maxim, "Knowledge is power," still
held good but, since becoming Head of the First Family
some fifteen years ago, the P-G's appetite for glowing
green phosphor screenfuls of facts had become slightly
jaded. He was still a skilled manipulator—that was part of
the job profile—but he preferred to talk over ideas on a

one-to-one basis or with a small group of close relatives. Best of all, he liked to retire to Cloudlands, where he could be alone to think things over while he tended his roses.

This morning, however, Fran's presentation had aroused his interest. Brickman—or, rather, what Brickman had stumbled across—was too important to ignore. Jefferson the 31st had often tried to wish the problem of the Talisman away but he knew it was a real threat that would have to be faced sooner or later. It would be a betrayal of his sacred duty to neglect to do whatever could be done to protect the Federation. Summoning up his remarkable powers of concentration he scanned the file summaries covering Steve's background and development, then began to read the transcripts of his examination by the Assessors and his interrogation by one of the many truth-drug squads—Q-6.

At three o'clock in the afternoon, two days after his talk with Fran, the President-General walked from the Oval Office into an adjoining, windowless conference room. The nine Supreme Councillors who had answered his summons rose respectfully as he entered and remained standing until he had taken his seat at the head of the long table.

The P-G's pale grey eyes fixed upon each of the group in turn as he greeted them with a practised smile and a nod of the head. He knew them well, and they knew him. They were all members of the exclusive First Family—the perpetual holders of power within the Federation. Apart from their other Family duties, this particular group—Group Nine—was responsible for planning the overall strategy of the secret operation code-named OVERLORD—Amtrak's response to the threat contained in the Talisman Prophecy. The purpose of the present meeting was to take certain decisions concerning the "neutralisation" of the Plainfolk. The main item on the agenda was the clan M'Call, Steve's cooperative jailers.

"Have you all scanned the data on Brickman?"

They all nodded to show that they had.

The P-G looked at the print-out on the video set on the table in front of him. The others in the group all had similar screens to look at. "You have Ben's proposal in front of you. What is your verdict? Does it compute?"

Ben—who was sitting on the President-General's right— was Commander-General Karlstrom. His full name was Ben Karlstrom Jefferson but, amongst the Family, the historic surname was not used except on certain formal occasions. Karlstrom was the current head of AMEXICO— the AMtrak EXecutive Intelligence COmmando—a select, highly-trained group working under the direct orders of the President-General. Not only was it the most secret operational unit in the Federation, it was also a secret within the First Family. Less than a tenth of their number was aware of AMEXICO's existence and even fewer knew the details of its past history or the full extent of its present activities. Its operatives were, inevitably, referred to as "Mexicans"; the unit itself by the abbreviated initials "MX."

Abraham Lincoln, one of the President's first cousins and the director of Group Nine replied with an affirmative nod. "The boy has all the necessary qualifications. His survival as a captive of the Mutes and his escape flight shows he has the necessary courage and resourcefulness. The big question is—given his background—can we trust him?"

The President-General smiled benignly. "Abe—the reason why the First Family is still in control of the Federation is because we never *ever* put ourselves in the position of having to trust *anybody*. Of course we can't trust Brickman. Nevertheless he has all the qualities we need." He let his gaze rove round the table. "Behind that honest face lies a devious, calculating mind and a burning ambition to succeed—"

"The result of years of careful programming," said Quincy Adams. As Director of the Life Institute, he was anxious that his department's contribution should not be overlooked.

"Quite so, Quincy," said Jefferson the 31st, hiding his displeasure at being interrupted. "He will jump at the opportunity to return to his new-found friends but he will balk at what we are asking him to do. However, he will accept the assignment because, with his Tracker upbringing, it is his solemn duty to do so—and also because we intend to make him an offer he can't refuse. And he will do his utmost to come back with the goods because the Federation is the only place where young Mister Brickman's lust for power can be satisfied."

Warren Harding, one of theP-G's younger brothers, looked across the table at Commander-General Ben Karlstrom. "When do you plan to initiate SQUARE-DANCE?"

SQUARE-DANCE was the code-name given to the proposed MX field-operation in which Brickman was to be reunited with his Plainfolk captors.

"We have no firm date as yet," said Karlstrom.

Warren glanced around the table with a puzzled frown then came back to Karlstrom. "I don't understand. Shouldn't we be taking some positive action on something as important as this right now?"

"It's the end of November, Warren," said Karlstrom. "I know that doesn't mean much down here but the first reports of snow falls came in yesterday. The wagon-trains are all on their way back in and they'll stay in Nixon/Fort Worth for the usual winter over-haul and refit, and stateside patrols. All our MX field-teams will remain up and running as usual but with snow on the ground most of the Mutes won't put their noses out of doors. We will probably go for an insertion in the early spring." Karlstrom broke off and looked at the P-G. "Assuming, of course, that Brickman agrees—"

"He will," said the P-G.

Karlstrom turned back to Warren Harding. "He will have to go through an induction course and then the usual pre-op planning sessions. We still have a lot of work to do on various aspects of the operation before we get to that stage."

"And meanwhile?" said Warren.

Karlstrom passed the question on with his eyes to the P-G.

"Meanwhile?" The P-G smiled. "Young Mr. Brickman

will stay in the A-Levels—gaining what, I hope, will prove
to be valuable work-experience."

From 25 November 2989—the date of his transfer to the
A-Levels—to the end of February in the following year,
Steve worked with a pipe-laying battalion. Not in the
A-Levels, but on Level B-3, some two hundred feet below
the marble floor of John Wayne Plaza. Steve's unit was
under the command of Brad Maxey, a hard-driving Seamster line-boss with the compassion of a bulldozer blade and
the good humour of a man with an outbreak of boils on the
butt. Maxey, who had an obsession with performance quo-
tas, had divided the men under his command into A and B
teams and was running a three-shift round-the-clock operation, making a nine-shift, seventy-two hour, six-day week.
Deep in the bowels of the earth, with a constant level of
light, there was no night or day—just a continuous rhythmic ebb and flow of time; eight hours on, eight hours off
and then, just when everyone had been worked onto their
knees, a whole twenty-four hours that most people spent
horizontally, cancelled out in their bunks. Even if they
had been standing up, there weren't a lot of places they
could have gone to. Seamsters were only allowed up into
the Quad—Level One-1 to Four-10—during their periods
of furlough. At all other times, their ID-cards restricted
them to the A-Levels. COLUMBUS—the computer that
acted as the central nervous system of the Federation—
controlled access to the elevators. If your card did not
authorise you to change levels you could not get through
the turnstiles into the elevator lobbies; something Steve
had discovered since going "through the floor."
  Steve had also been surprised to discover that, under
the grime and grease, some of the guys he was working
with were girls. Broad-shouldered, wide-necked and hard-
handed. Real jack-hammers, with strong powerful thighs
that, had you been foolish enough to stick your head
between them, would have welded your ears together.
But girls just the same. Steve was offered a few chances to
crack the pot but couldn't raise either the steam or the
enthusiasm. After a straight eight hours hauling pipe he

couldn't even have pressed the buttons on one of the mess-deck electronic arcade games. He wasn't alone. When the whistle blew there was very little bunk-hopping. Most guys had but two thoughts—slop and shut-eye. Slop was Seamster slang for the food supplied by the A-Level mess decks. Guys would cancel out on the ride back from the site and would have stayed there until reveille if someone hadn't hauled them out of the trailer. Some mess-deck comedian had claimed that Maxey was not his name but stood, instead, for Maximum Effort. It was probably the same guy that had christened Maxey's battalion "The Walking Dead." Having joined them, Steve had to admit it was not far from the truth. After washing up, the majority would shuffle past the mess counter like a sullen, dull-eyed chain-gang of Mutes. Even the effort of choosing one of the three meal choices was too much. Most thrust their mess tray forward and mumbled "Gimme whatever's goin . . ." then they would prop their heads up with one hand while they ate their slop with the other. Once or twice, Steve didn't even get that far—he fell asleep in the shower.

Although Steve had been tagged for General Duties—the lowest grade of the lowest form of life—the engineering training he had undergone during his three years at the Flight Academy came to the attention of one of the supervisors who decided to put it to some use. For one whole week he was transferred to a squad welding clean new sections of pipe together. For six glorious days, in the brief moments of silence when he changed rods, he congratulated himself on the slight improvement in his fortunes. A skilled job was the first step up the ladder. It was only a matter of time, he told himself, before Maxey's staff recognised his leadership qualities and then . . . No such luck. After the twenty-four hour weekend break, he found himself back in his original squad, disconnecting old, corroded sections of pipe containing a thick, foul-smelling coating of effluent. It was with a distinct feeling of desperation that Steve learned that Maxey's assignment was to replace and expand the sewage system under the whole of Houston/Grand Central.

Like the overground, the world of the A-Levels left
within him its own set of vivid impressions. Huge, echoing, slab-sided tunnels lined with pipes and power lines,
valves, and vents belching steam. Pools of darkness and
light with brown-and-yellow-suited Seamsters illuminated
one minute, thrown into silhouette the next, then just as
suddenly swallowed up by the darkness. The white hard-
hats of supervisors and line-bosses. Snowdrops. One or
two sprinkled among the yellow hats was a sign that things
were okay; on schedule. One or two wheelies full of them
usually meant they'd come to kick ass. Down in the A-Levels
they didn't go in for handing out prizes.

Noise: the constant thrumming of the huge fans in the
main vents; the staccato clamour of compressed air drills
and rivet guns hammering at the eardrums, the shrill buzz
of metal edge-grinders cutting into the brain. Wave upon
wave of sound, pulsing through the air with tangible force,
reverberating off the tunnel walls, seeping through the
insulation lining the bunkhouse walls. During the first few
days, Steve thought he might crack up but, after a few
weeks, his body gradually built up a resistance to the
initially unbearable level of noise. His brain began to
blank off the raw nerve endings; began to build a wall
around itself.

Water: running in rivulets down the walls; dripping
from ceilings of service tunnels and galleries. Sometimes
Steve found himself working in it up to his knees. Pumps
worked constantly to drain areas where it threatened to
become a flood. During his travels he encountered huge
steel and concrete watertight doors that could seal off
whole sections, or one level from another. And he wondered how it would feel to find yourself on the wrong
side of the door when the water began to rise towards the
ceiling.

Heat: enervating, inescapable. Despite the geothermal
power-plants, heat-exchangers, refrigeration, air conditioning and the complex ventilation system that made life
bearable in the rest of the Federation, conditions in the
A-Levels varied enormously. The environment in the rest
and recreation areas was roughly equivalent to that in the

Quad but in some of the less-populated work-faces, such as the service tunnels on B-3—which were nearly seventeen hundred feet underground—it was hot, and it was humid. Great conditions for growing rice and bamboo shoots in narrow tanks as long as football pitches but liable to stunt your growth if you were unlucky enough to be working on Maxey's pipeline.

Think of it as a challenge, Steve told himself as he collapsed gratefully onto his bunk at the end of each shift. They're trying to break you. Don't let them win. Don't go under . . .

Two days before the end of February, at the end of yet another shift, Steve rolled out of his seat on the ten car trailer, arched his back to try and take some of the pain out of it and shuffled along to the showers. As was usual throughout the Federation, all the guys shared the same facilities. Uniforms, bunkhouses, washrooms, work assignments, P-D, military service, combat duty . . . no differentiation was made on the basis of sex. There were two major exceptions to the unisex principle; the female Trackers selected to be host mothers to the new generation, and the male members of the First Family who inherited the position of President-General. The only minor variation was in the haircuts. Not all the girls had crewcuts; some opted for the only permitted alternative—the short bob.

Steve spent a good twenty minutes under the shower letting the heat draw the tiredness from his body, then finished off with a needle sharp burst from the cold tap—a move which drew howls of rage from his immediate neighbours. He towelled himself dry in the crowded locker room, changed into his off-duty set of coveralls, headed over to the mess-deck and joined one of the lines at the food-counter. In the weeks he had been working down under, he had gotten to know the guys he bunked down and worked with. At first some of them had been a little hostile; had taken pleasure in the fact that a high-flyer from Lindbergh Field had landed in the A-Levels. Steve had been warned to say nothing about his period of captivity with the Mutes. As far as his Seamster bosses knew, he had been transferred to Service Engineering & Maintenance because of quote—"his negative operational performance." The official way of saying that he had crapped out of an overground firefight.

Such an entry on his records was supposed to remain confidential but the word had gotten around and Steve had been hassled by a few guys who took him for a soft target. He shrugged off as much of it as he could then had been obliged to fatten a few mouths. Some of his opponents had been hard to crack, but they were brawlers not fighters. They were mean, but Steve had a lot of cold anger stored up inside him—and he'd been trained to kill. After a while, when he had established that he wasn't a guy to mess with, things got a lot better.

Steve learned something too. It had been a terrible blow to his pride to be reduced to the rank of a Seamster but he discovered that the despised Zed-heads, the grease-balls, the scumbags he was now working alongside were not as hopeless, awful, or as pitiful as he had imagined when his elitist opinions on the subject had been formed in the rarified atmosphere of the Flight Academy. The Seamsters in his unit might not share his vaulting ambition or sense of destiny, but most of them were OK guys with a firm grasp of the realities of their situation and more modest, achievable goals. None of them were aiming to make it to the Black Tower and wouldn't have thanked you if you'd offered them a free ride up the wire. Alongside that it had to be admitted some of them were real Zed-heads with zero upstairs, and there were a number who, even on the most generous appraisal, were a genuine pain in the ass. But then, so was Gus White, a fellow-graduate from the Academy—and someone with whom Steve still had a score to settle. Yes, good old Gus, who had flown off promising to get help, leaving him trapped in the middle of a burning cropfield . . .

Steve laid his tray of food in front of an empty seat at one of the mess-tables, sat down and began to eat hungrily. His earlier reservations about Federation food had disappeared. Ever since he'd started work in the A-Levels, he had eaten anything and everything that was an offer and had gone back for more. He looked around at the other tables as he raised the first heaped spoonful and almost missed his mouth as he spotted John Chisum sitting at a table over on his left. Steve sat slack-jawed, unable to decide whether to go over at once, or stay put and clear his tray first. He stayed put but kept his eyes on Chisum while he ate, making only monosyllabic contributions to the conversation around the table. Chisum did not look his way. He sat with one arm over the back of his chair, talking to the guys seated opposite him. He wore the same green uniform Steve had seen him in before but now, a chrome yellow diamond patch had been inserted between the white and red chevron on his sleeve. And when he swivelled around to look at somebody one of his companions was pointing at, Steve saw he had another yellow patch on the back of his jumpsuit. Seamster yellow. Surely that couldn't mean . . .? Unable to bear the suspense any longer, Steve grabbed his tray and threaded his way through the seated diners towards Chisum.

As Steve approached, the two guys sitting opposite Chisum got up, shook hands with him and walked away. Chisum began speaking to the guy next to him as Steve put his tray down.

"Hey—John—remember me?"

Chisum broke off his conversation and glanced back over his shoulder. As their eyes connected, Steve saw the neutral expression on Chisum's face change to one of thinly disguised anger.

"What gives? You just visiting—or what?"

Chisum turned back to his neighbour and slapped him on the shoulder. "Must go. I'll check with you later." He stood up abruptly without looking at Steve and began to walk away.

Steve dodged round the table and grabbed Chisum's arm. "Hey, John—c'mon! What'd I do? What the heck's going on?!"

Chisum stopped and turned around, his arm stiff and unyielding in Steve's grasp. "Let go of my arm, scumbag." The harshness in his voice matched the expression on his face.

A couple of guys from Steve's work-squad sitting at the

next table looked at each other, pushed their chairs back, and ranged themselves alongside him. Dan Dover and Ty Morrison. Dover, the bigger of the two, aimed a finger at Chisum's nose. "You'd better watch your mouth, medic. Otherwise you'll find yourself in urgent need of life-support."

Chisum eyed his interlocutor contemptuously. "Go suck a bucket of lumpshit—"

The people at the surrounding tables stood up and moved out of the way as the two Seamsters made a grab for Chisum. Steve moved in between and wrestled them off. "Whoa! Hold it, guys! Hold it down! Listen, I really appreciate your help but, uh—I can handle it. Just, uh—leave it with me. Okay?"

"Okay," said Dover. "But get that jerk-off out of here. He's spoiling my digestion."

Steve hustled Chisum through the crowd that had gathered round them before he could reply. "Come on, move! Let's get out of here."

Chisum tried to wrestle free. "Hey! Get your fucking hands off me?! What the hell's the matter with you?!" he demanded angrily.

Steve managed to propel him into the corridor outside the main entrance doors and pinned him against the wall. "Calm down, will you? I just want to talk!"

Chisum stopped struggling. "Look, fly-boy. *I* don't want to talk to you. Can you understand that? Or have you swapped your brains for shit since you've been working down here? I'll give it to you one more time. I—don't—want—to—talk—to—you. I—don't—want—to—even—see—you. You got that? And if you're planning to fall sick, don't do it on A-1 to A-5. You may get the wrong prescription. Comprendo?"

Steve let go of Chisum and stood back totally perplexed. "I don't get it, John. Why? What did I do?"

Chisum gave a sniffy laugh. "Why? Because you're big trouble, that's why! What did you do? You tell me! Whatever it was you said to your goddam kin-sister left her so upset, she turned rat-fink and blabbed it all to some hot-wire in the Black Tower! Result? The lumpshit hit the fan, my friend! Your sweet little sister fingered me as the

guy that set up the meeting with you at Santanna Deep!
She spilled her guts! What the eff-eff did you tell her?!"

"Nothing," said Steve dully. "Well—not anything special."

"Lying sonofabitch!" hissed Chisum. He tried to push
past but Steve blocked the way. "AmEx had four guys
working on me for over a week! I'm lucky to be alive!
Christo!" He gave a bitter laugh. "The only thing she
didn't tell 'em about was you two smoking grass and me
shipping it. If they'd got onto that . . ."

Steve grabbed Chisum's arm. "John, you've got to believe me. I had no idea Roz would pull anything like this.
I can't think what made her do it!"

"Must have been something you said."

Steve waved his hands helplessly. "So . . . what happened to you?"

"Me? They sent me down here to serve out the rest of
my time. I'm twenty-eight now, so what's that—twelve,
fifteen years? And unlike you, I don't have the luxury of an
Annual Review." Chisum gave another bitter laugh. "Ah,
well, that's what happens when you try to do a guy a
favour. Nice one Stevie." He drew back. "Is it okay if I go
now?"

Steve felt confused and guilty. "John, listen. There's
was no way I could have known—"

"Sure of course. I understand that. Don't let's talk about
it. Okay? Just stay well away from me from now on. You
are a real disaster area, Brickman."

"Yeah, okay, okay. Just tell me one thing. What did
they do to Roz?"

Chisum laughed. "Well, they didn't pin a medal on her,
I'll tell you that! I don't know *what* happened. Not for
sure, anyway. I think I heard someone say she'd been
suspended."

"From Inner State U? Oh, sweet Christopher! I should
never have gone to see her!" He rounded on Chisum
angrily. "It was your idea! You—"

Chisum cut him short. "Look, I don't need any of this
shit!" I've got enough trouble! Just get out of my way!" He
pushed Steve aside.

Steve made no attempt to hold him. "What's going to happen to her!?" he shouted.

Chisum turned around and waved his arm dismissively. "Who gives a fuck? From here on in, you'd better start worrying about what's going to happen to you!" He turned the corner and was gone.

Dan Dover and Ty Morrison joined Steve in the corridor. "What gives with that guy?"

Steve shrugged. "He's someone I was involved with topside. He's just drawn twelve to fifteen down here on account of something he did for me."

Dover fisted Ty Morrison's shoulder. "You see? I told you our friend here was a bad hat!" He threw an arm across Steve's shoulder and gave him a friendly hug. "Welcome to the club."

As he walked along the corridor leading from the messdeck, Chisum quietly congratulated himself. It had all worked out much better than expected. He reached the end of the corridor, stepped out onto the main A-3 access road and hitched a wheelie ride back to the MedCare centre. Yes . . . another few days would see the end of this particular assignment and he would able to get back upstairs. He had done well—and might even have earned himself an invitation to spend a few weeks in Cloudlands.

NINE

IN the forty-eight hours following his surprise encounter
with Chisum, Steve's thoughts were centred round Roz
and what might happen to her—and also to him. He had
let Chisum go without asking him when Roz's 'confession'
and his demotion had taken place. In a way, the question
was irrelevant. Sooner or later, there was bound to be
further fallout. There was—and Steve didn't have long to
wait. On the 1st of March, 2990, as he was preparing to go
on the 0800 shift, his squad supervisor—a Tech-4 called
Mullins—came into the bunkhouse and yelled out his
name. "Brickman?!"

Steve snapped to attention. "Sirr!"

Mullins beckoned him over. "You won't be on this shift.
Get into your off-duty coveralls and get your ass down to
the main elevator deck. Pronto!"

"Yess-sirr!" Steve sidestepped Mullins and doubled
towards the locker room. Down in the A-Levels you only
saluted on ceremonial occasions—and there were very few
of those.

Mullins raise his voice again. "Dover?!"

Dan Dover straightened up by the end of his bunk.
"Sir?"

"Pack up Brickman's gear, strip his bunk, and hand
everything in to the Quartermaster."

171

"You mean *now*, sir?" asked Dover, already figuring that, if he spun it out, the time-wasting chore could mean missing up to half a shift.

"No, not now, Dover. When you come off at 1600, you asshole!"

"Yeah, and up yours," muttered Dover, as Mullins strode away. Turning, he saw his buddie Ty Morrison trying not to laugh. Dover aimed an angry punch at his solar plexus but Morrison danced out of reach.

Steve found three Provos waiting for him at the turnstile to the main elevator deck. The meat-loaf in charge asked for his ID-card, then he was hooded and chained and hustled through the turnstile. When the hood came off, he saw that his escort had changed. The two Provos now facing him sported the White House shoulder flash. He was back in the medical unit where he had first run into Chisum. The bigger of the two meat-loaves ordered him to stand with his legs apart and his hands by his side then moved behind him and unlocked the steel bands around his wrists and knees.

"Okay, strip off," said the other meat-loaf. He waved his truncheon towards the adjacent wash-room. "You've got five minutes to shower and get back into uniform. Move!"

Steve didn't stop to ask "What uniform"; meat-loaves didn't like being asked questions. He twirled on the shower tap, peeled off his clothes, washed himself thoroughly, then rubbed himself down with the aid of a disposable glove-towel in the warm air drier and emerged with a minute and a half to spare. The big meat-loaf had made himself comfortable on the only available chair; the other had hoisted his low-slung butt onto the edge of the table next to a neatly arranged pile of clothing: a flight-blue jumpsuit, field cap, underclothes and gleaming dark-blue parade boots.

The meat-loaf on the table pushed the pile of clothes towards Steve with the point of his truncheon. "Get this stuff on . . ."

Steve pulled on the pants, socks and T-shirt with a mixture of pleasure and surprise. He'd been given a wingman's uniform, and when he opened out the freshly-pressed jumpsuit he saw that it bore his name on the woven tag over the right breast pocket, and a pair of silver wings over the left. It even had the correct unit arm badges: one that identified him as coming from Roosevelt/Santa Fe; the other as serving aboard The Lady from Louisiana. They—someone—some mysterious benefactor—had given him back his identity! He donned the jumpsuit and tried to fight down a rising feeling of excitement. After all that had happened to him over the last few months it would be foolish to raise his hopes too high. He adjusted the field cap, straightened the long front zip of the suit and stood at ease waiting for the Provos' next order with seconds to spare.

The provo lounging in the chair checked his watch then got up and walked over to the door that opened onto the passageway beyond. His buddie followed. Steve heard footsteps. The two Provos took up position on either side of the doorway then jumped to attention and saluted as an Amtrack Exec entered. Steve followed suit.

The Exec wore the rank stripes of a JX-2. She eyed Steve then turned to the Provo-Corporal. "Is this the interviewee?"

"Yes, ma'am!" The Provo-Corporal had palmed Steve's ID-card in readiness for the hand-over.

The Exec lifted the flap of the protective wallet, glanced briefly at the card, put it in a thigh pocket then swept her hand towards the door. "Would you come this way please?"

The gesture and the courteous tone were so unexpected, they left Steve with his feet momentarily glued to the floor. The JX-2, whose name tag identified her as Pruett, J K, was a slim, brown-haired woman of around thirty. She had the kind of face you wouldn't look at twice unless you had to but, despite this, she radiated an air of cheerful efficiency.

Pruett led the way to an office unit on Level Four-2. En route, Steve noticed that the walls and floors of the corridors—which had high curved ceilings—were faced with almost pure white marble. Large portraits of Jefferson the 31st and the Founding Father were sited at strategic points along the way. The elevator that took them up from Level Two-1 was carpeted in pale cream throughout. The quality and finish of the decor in this section of the White House was even better than the much-vaunted John Wayne Plaza; the overall impression one of clean, luminous magnificence.

Pruett checked Steve in with a front office Exec then carded him through a turnstile door and left him standing in front of a large desk in a very large office with two curtained windows. Through them, Steve could see a view of a distant line of strange buildings with pale, ornate, coloured façades set against a blue, cloud-filled sky. The buildings looked as if they were sinking into the water that occupied the foreground. The view through the window was clear and extremely well detailed but there was something about it that was not quite real. Steve decided that it must have been created by COLUMBUS. He pulled his eyes away from the windows and took a closer look at the office interior. The floor was covered with carpet, the walls with long, flat strips of wood bearing the same wavy lines he had seen on bits of wood used by the Mutes. Even the desk and parts of the chairs were made of wood! How strange . . .

A door in the wall behind the desk slid open to reveal a man wearing a silver jumpsuit. He walked in and took his place behind the desk. Slim, medium height, with a high forehead, lean angular face, firm thin mouth and jaw, and dark deep-set eyes that gave every sign of being linked to a sharp, penetrating intelligence.

Steve sprang to attention with a slight chill of apprehension. He had been 90 per cent certain that the young President of the Board of Assessors was Family but this was the first time he had ever been physically face to face with someone dressed in the silver uniform with the blue and white stripes.

The man tapped out a single-stroke command on the keyboard of his desk video, eyed the result on the screen then looked at Steve. "So . . . you're 21028902 Brickman, S. R. . . .?"

"Yes sir!"

The man ran his eyes over Steve and gave the nod of someone who feels he's been landed with a difficult task. "I am Commander-General Karlstrom. It is not a rank you are familiar with as it applies solely to my position within the First Family. I shall not explain it further, other than to say it gives me direct access to the President-General and requires you, during this, and any subsequent interview, to address me as 'Commander'. Is that understood?"

"Yes, Commander."

"Good. Stand at ease." Karlstrom laid his well cared for hands on top of one another. "Let me put you in the picture. Following your transfer to the A-Levels, your kin-sister—" He glanced at the screen to refresh his memory, "—Rosalynn, contacted the Amtrak Executive on the first of December '89 and made . . ."

The date came as a surprise to Steve. It was just a few days after he had been sent down. Why had they waited three months before hauling him up before a highly-placed member of the First Family?

". . . a voluntary statement which indicated that you possessed information which, for reasons of your own, you had not revealed to the Board of Assessors. I am obliged to warn you that, as stated in the Manual, concealment of information vital to the security of the state is classified as a Code One offence. This interview is to decide whether further interrogation is necessary and what form it should take. There are, as I'm sure you must be aware, various forms of coercion that can be applied." Karlstrom sat back in his chair and became a little less forbidding. "That's the bad news. The good news is that the recommendation forwarded by the Board of Assessors has not yet been confirmed by the Adjudicating Council so—" Karlstrom smiled, "—it would be fair to say that it's all still to play for."

"I understand, Commander. May I have permission to speak?"

Karlstrom nodded. "Provided what you have to say forms part of a meaningful dialogue."

"What has happened to Roz—my kin-sister?"

Karlstrom's lips tightened. "Brickman, *I'm* the one who's

supposed to be asking the questions. However, if it will
help to clarify your thoughts I'll let that one through. The
answer is 'nothing'. So far, that is. Your sister is continuing
her studies but she is under technical suspension. That
means she has been informed that her involvement in this
matter is still under investigation and she may be removed
from Inner State U at any time. On the balance side, she
is to be commended on coming forward to report on the
conversation that took place during your illicit meeting."

"She played no part in arranging that, Commander. I
am entirely to blame for her being there."

Karlstrom responded with a thin smile. "Spare me the
noble gestures, Brickman. What your kin-sister has told us
is enough to indicate you possess information that could
affect not only the security of the Federation but its very
future. Having listened to her statement I can understand
your reluctance to speak openly about such things to the
Assessors but you must understand that, technically speaking, your silence was both criminal and indefensible. However, I am now going to give you a second chance. Your
last chance to set the record straight. You can either
choose to make a voluntary statement now—to me—or we
can extract the information by . . . other methods. You
will end up telling us everything, of that you can be certain.
But if we have to do it the hard way, you'll find yourself
up against the wall. On the other hand, if you cooperate—"
Karlstrom shrugged, "—who knows?"

Steve bit his lip. Columbus, what a situation! Any discussion of Mute magic was strictly forbidden. If he told
Karlstrom the whole truth he risked execution by firing
squad and if he refused he faced the same fate! If only he
could remember how much he had told Roz! He had been
trying to put the pieces together ever since running into
Chisum. Unfortunately, most of that fateful evening remained a smoke-filled blur. He remembered arguing with
Roz over Clearwater then lighting up a reaf and talking—
but about what . . . ? "Commander—if I, uh—tell you
everything I know, is there any chance that Roz—"

Karlstrom slammed his hands on the desk and jumped
out of his seat. "Christo! You've got some nerve, Brickman!

There are no 'ifs', no 'buts', and no deals except the ones *I* make! You have nothing to bargain with. We've got your balls in a vice! And as for your kin-sister, she's going to be extremely fortunate not to find herself laying pipe alongside you—and your friend Chisum! So pull up a chair and start talking!"

Steve picked up a moulded pedestal chair, put it down facing the desk and sat straight-backed. "Where would you like me to start, sir, uh—I mean, 'Commander'?"

"At the beginning," snapped Karlstrom."Where else?" He hit the Record button on his video deck.

Steve followed the same story line he had presented to the Assessors but this time he left nothing out. He didn't dare. With Roz's confession in their hands he was cornered. Karlstrom listened attentively, asking few questions. Occasionally he would say something that made it clear he knew everything of substance that Steve had previously concealed. Steve, who up to that moment had never experienced the slightest hesitation in selling someone down the river, felt totally wretched at having to break his solemn promises to Mr. Snow. To his surprise, Karlstrom—whose tone was hectoring one minute and conciliatory the next—appeared to understand the anguish he felt. "Don't worry," he urged. "I know they saved your life but don't let that confuse you. They are the enemy. Promises to Mutes don't count." The only consolation for Steve was the intelligent way in which Karlstrom conducted the interview. Where the Assessors minds had been closed, Karlstrom's was wide open.

As he listened to Steve unburden himself with an increasing sense of relief, Karlstrom wondered if he had any inkling of the real situation. Having studied the videotape made by Q-6, the Family already had most of the information it needed to come to a decision about Brickman. This second interrogation was just part of the elaborate setting-up process. Giving Brickman back his uniform was another move in the game. Once he had put it on, Karlstrom knew Brickman would do anything to avoid losing the right to wear it . . .

The interview lasted several hours during which time

Karlstrom ordered deliveries of Java and salted soya-beef rolls. Steve told his story with fluent economy but included one or two anecdotes to make it interesting. Karlstrom showed no sign of being upset by his more contentious observations about the educability of his captors but he became tight-lipped and shook his head resignedly when Steve told him about teaching Cadillac to fly. Eventually, they reached the moment of his escape.

"What I find hard to understand," said Karlstrom, "is why you stayed on when you'd built the rig. Once you were off the ground why the heck didn't you keep on going? Why go back?"

"If I'd gone then, in broad daylight, they would have knocked me out of the sky, Commander. There were two Mute lookout posts on the high ground to the south of the bluff. My only chance was to go under cover of darkness but it wasn't that easy. As I've explained, I shared a hut with Cadillac. I had to wait for the right opportunity. It was only when Mr. Snow and Cadillac left the settlement on a five-day trip that I finally got the break I needed."

Karlstrom responded with a thin smile. "Yes, with Cadillac's shack-mate. Don't treat me like an idiot, Brickman. You didn't come back here to tell us the Plainfolk's secrets. The only reason you left your lumphead friends was to save your own skin!"

Steve felt the colour flood to his cheeks. "That's not true, sir! They're not my friends! And to suggest that I would have preferred to stay out there does not, with respect, make sense. We all know that the atmospheric conditions make it impossible to survive overground without proper protection. It was my *duty* to escape but for the first couple of months I was unable to walk properly. And then, when I learned what the Mutes were capable of, it was clear that the only way I could escape was by air. To build the glider I needed their cooperation—and the only way I could obtain that was by getting them to trust me. It's true I taught Cadillac how to fly but without an aircraft that knowledge is useless. And even if, by chance, they were able to rebuild another crashed Skyhawk they would not be able to use it effectively. It doesn't fit in with their way of thinking—their concept of warriorhood."

"That remains to be seen," replied Karlstrom. "You have still given them that knowledge. And not to an ordinary lumphead who, with luck, might forget it all but to a wordsmith—whose role it is to teach others! Never mind . . . there may be some way you can repair the damage you've done."

Steve leapt eagerly off his chair. "How, sir?!"

"Calm down," said Karlstrom. "I'm not promising anything. To be frank, Brickman, I'm not totally convinced we can trust you. Your attitude towards the Mutes worries me. You talk about them as if they were people."

"Commander—the point I was trying to make to the Assessors is that we have underestimated their abilities. We can't afford to be complacent. Whether they are people, or not, is immaterial. I have never forgotten that they are the enemy. What I learnt out there is how dangerous they are. All I want is the chance to put that knowledge to some use—for the benefit of the Federation."

Karlstrom nodded. "That's what I thought you'd say. And you know something? I almost believe you."

"It's true, Commander. I swear it! Just give me the chance to get back into combat on board a wagon-train."

Karlstrom shook his head. "I don't know, Brickman." He waved a hand toward his desk video. "You've got a good record, you've got the right connections, and prior to going overground you did everything by The Book. Who would have figured you as a guy who jacks up Mutes?" He screwed up his face at the thought. "I think if I ever found myself that far downhill I'd rather cut my dong off."

Steve felt the need to defend himself. "Commander, if she'd been an ordinary lumphead I'd have probably felt like doing the same. But she wasn't. Clearwater has the brain and the body of a real human being!"

"Yes, so you say . . . But that doesn't make her one of us. She's still got the *mind* of a Mute. She thinks and acts like one. And so does Cadillac—the lump she shacks up with." Karlstrom's choice of words was deliberate. He saw them strike home. "You see? That's what I'm getting at.

You're involved, Brickman. The line between them and us has become blurred. What we now have to ask is—when the chips are down, when the good guys are up against the bad guys, whose side will *you* be on?"

Steve straightened his back. "Ours, Commander. I could make a big speech with all the right words but we both know there's a better way to prove my loyalty to the First Family. Put me in a Skyhawk, point me at the Plainfolk, and watch the feathers fly."

Karlstrom looked distinctly unimpressed. "Brave words, Brickman. I'll bear them in mind. Okay . . . now give me a brief outline of your trip from the Wind River Range to the way-station at Pueblo."

Steve described the last perilous stage of his journey in which the patched wing fabric of his glider constantly threatened to rip apart, and his arrival at the Tracker way-station on the Arkansas River. In the end, there were only two subjects that had not been broached. Mute magic and the Talisman Prophecy. Steve, who had been secretly dreading this moment, knew he would not be able to hold off much longer.

As if reading his thoughts, Karlstrom laid his empty cup on the desk, checked his watch and said, "Very good. Okay, we'll leave it there. Tomorrow, we'll talk about Mute magic."

"Uhh . . . Mute magic?"

"Yes," said Karlstrom. "About your friend Cadillac's ability to read the pictures in "seeing stones." About the magical powers that Mr. Snow and Clearwater were able to summon from, where—the earth?"

Never, in his wildest speculations, had Steve imagined he would ever hear a high-ranking member of the First Family talk so openly about Mute magic. So this was it! There *was* going to be a trade. He had something the Family wanted. Experience. Knowledge. Something. Steve knew it was not the time to hold back but his throat felt constricted. The taboos surrounding the subject were too firmly imprinted on his subconscious to allow him to speak unrestrainedly to someone like Karlstrom. His sixth sense told him that this was the time to play it by The Book. "I, uh—Commander, uh—you know the position as well as I do. The Manual is quite specific on this point. There is no such thing as Mute magic—and any public statement in defiance of that ruling is a Code One offence."

"That's right," replied Karlstrom amiably, "And so is smoking grass and plugging blackjack. Do you think we don't know what's been going on in Unit-8, Santanna Deep?" He laughed as he saw the expression on Steve's face. "Now perhaps you can understand how much your kin-sister's future career depends on your cooperation." He switched off his desk video and stood up. "Think it over."

Steve leapt to his feet and stood to attention. "Commander," he began, ". . . you have Roz's statement. There's, uh—nothing I can tell you that you don't know already."

"That's true," agreed Karlstrom. "But I'd like to hear it once again. This time from you." He acknowledged Steve's salute with a curt nod then stepped through the door in the wall behind the desk.

A few seconds later Pruett came in from the outer office and ushered Steve back to the empty four-bunk unit in the isolation ward where he had been kept the previous November. Only the medics on desk duty in the corridor outside had changed. Steve wondered what had happened to the guys who'd been on duty during his last stay. Had they gone down with Chisum? Steve smiled to himself remembering Chisum's boastful assurances about how he had friends in high places. Fixer . . . Some fixer *he* turned out to be . . .

"I'm afraid you'll have to spend the rest of the day by yourself," said Pruett. She pointed to one of the two overhead tv screens. "I can arrange to have these switched on if you like. Do you have a preference for any particular subject, or channel?"

Steve toyed with the idea of asking for a diet of First Family Inspirationals then decided that, since his stay with the more forthright Mutes, his insincerity might show through. "That's good of you, ma'am. I think I'd prefer to sit here and get my head straight for tomorrow."

Pruett gave an understanding nod. "Okay. If you change

your mind, the medics on the desk will put something through. A Provo will be along later to take you down to the mess-deck." She smiled and pointed towards the door. "Down the corridor you'll find a wall-store with a flat-iron and everything else you need. Put some work in on that jump-suit. I only want to see the regulation creases when I pick you up at 0830 hours."

Steve saluted. "Yes, *ma'am!*" After she had gone, he lay back on the bunk he'd used last time and mulled over his meeting with Commander-General Karlstrom. Interesting guy—and not someone you could feed the usual garbage to. Karlstrom was one of the dangerous kind. He didn't try and overpower you with his intelligence. He gave the impression of being a casual listener but he didn't miss a trick. His brain was razor sharp. Steve consoled himself with the thought that, so far, he had not fumbled too many passes. But he had to watch his step. To be ushered around courteously by an Amtrack Exec worried him. It was true that Pruett was only a JX-2 (the junior grades ran from 1 to 10, the senior high-wires (SX) from 1 to 5) but it was VIP treatment compared to being prodded along by a Provo truncheon. Despite the verbal bruising from Karlstrom his ego was being gently massaged. Something was going down. He didn't know what it was—not yet, anyway—but his sixth sense told him he was being set-up. It also told him he should go along with it; should make the most of this opportunity.

Yes . . . to be hauled out of the A-Levels, put back into uniform and then find yourself talking to one of the First Family—to someone working directly with the President-General—was, well . . . amazing, incredible. Steve sensed that this new situation was different from his appearance before the Assessors. Then, he had been overconfident, had allowed himself to be drawn out by the dark-haired young President of the Board into making provocative statements—and had been well and truly slapped down. That wouldn't happen this time. No, there was a deal in the air. He could smell it. The way Karlstrom held off talking about Mute magic until the very last moment, and had then mentioned it almost as an after-thought, confirmed Steve's suspicion about there being a conspiracy of silence on the subject. So be it. The Family was in a position to know what the score was. They wouldn't do anything without a good reason. It was important to let Karlstrom know that the loyal, stalwart and trustworthy Steven Roosevelt Brickman could also keep a secret.

Steve had not forgotten his earlier decision to hew his own path through the impenetrable forest of lies and deception that had sprung up around the First Family but now that he had gotten within spitting distance of a man who worked with the President-General this was not the moment to start wielding the axe.

When Pruett came to collect him next morning she found Steve standing at ease in an impeccably pressed jump-suit by the door to the ward. "Good morning, Mister Brickman."

"Good morning, ma'am," replied Steve. Again the smile —and now "mister!" Was this part of the softening-up process? Or was this how Junior Execs addressed each other? Steve had never met anyone from the Black Tower before. He'd come into contact with some of Uncle Bart's senior staff but they were Provos. And like Uncle Bart they were, well—a special brand of shit-head.

Steve and Pruett retraced the route that led to Karlstrom's office "The Commander-General will be with you in a moment." She left him standing facing the large, solid desk made of red-brown wood. Smooth and gleaming, with swirling black lines that reminded him of the pattern on Clearwater's oiled body . . .

Commander-General Karlstrom appeared through the door behind the desk and acknowledged Steve's salute with a curt nod. "You ready to talk?"

"Yes, Commander."

"Good. Step this way." Steve followed him back through the door and found they had entered a small elevator. The door slid shut as Karlstrom aimed his voice at a grille that occupied the place where the floor selector buttons were usually found. "Up four please . . ."

Steve assumed he meant four floors—which would bring them out on Level Four-6. In other parts of the Federa-

tion the level was displayed boldly on the wall facing the
elevator but he had noticed this was not the practice in the
White House. Steve concluded that it must be a security
measure designed to confuse intruders. But who, he asked
himself, would contemplate storming the White-House?

He followed Karlstrom out of the elevator into an enormous circular lobby with a domed thirty-foot-high ceiling.
Doors to other elevators were set at regular intervals
around the wall. Clustered together in the centre of the
lobby were four big tubes each about a yard in diameter.
The tubes came out of the floor and went up through the
ceiling. Set around the tubes was a circular wall of marble
about ten feet high divided into segments by turnstiles. A
bevelled, horizontal aperture set in each section of the
wall at counter height made the whole structure look like a
cross between a futuristic reception desk and a way-station
bunker. Trackers wearing uniforms Steve had never seen
before manned the counters. They wore parade caps with
red tops, white headbands and a dark blue peak that was
angled down sharply over their eyes and short, tri-colour
jackets over white straight-legged ducks. The jackets were
cut waist-high at the back and up in a V over the abdo-
men, the blue across the shoulders, upper chest and sleeves
being separated from the red by a broad white chest band
and matching chevron on the arm. Each guard carried an
extra-long-barrelled air pistol in a white leather holster
and all of them wore gold ensign rank bars on their high
collars.

The set-up, Steve decided, could only be designed to
guard one person. His knees became watery at the thought.
Karlstrom was recognised as he approached and a captain
appeared at the turnstile, saluting as the Commander-
General went through. He handed an ID-card to the
captain, who passed it on for verification. One of the
ensigns at the counter gave Steve the nod as his card
was returned to Karlstrom. "Okay, you're clear to go on
through."

Steve joined Karlstrom inside the marble wall as the
captain summoned a couple of elevators. The four tubes
each contained a capsule just large enough to accommo-

date one person at a time. Steve stepped inside as instructed and was carried upwards into a large office with dozens of desks and video consoles, staffed entirely by people wearing silver jumpsuits. The turnstile doors and elevators were guarded by more red, white and blues. Karlstrom led the way past a saluting ensign to one of the turnstiles, stepped inside, and was rotated through. The ensign indicated to Steve that he should step aboard. The 'stile rotated, carrying Steve into a large room with long windows set in a curved wall at the far end. The walls were white, the carpet deep blue. A high-backed rocking chair and two sets of facing armchairs were placed either side of a low framed alcove in which flames leapt from what looked like charred wooden logs. Karlstrom stood by the side of a large blue-topped wooden desk. Sitting behind the desk, framed by two draped flags and a magnificient carved wooden eagle, was a white-haired man dressed in a pale blue-grey military style jacket with a high collar, matching pants and shoes. As he sat with his elbows on the padded arms of his chair, looking at Steve over the joined tips of his fingers, his tanned face bore the same firm but benign expression that gazed down from countless walls throughout the Federation. George Washington Jefferson the 31st. The President-General, Father of the Federation, Giver of Life, Guardian of the Earthshield, Creator of the Light, the Work and the Way.

Steve had guessed where Karlstrom was taking him when he'd seen the marbled defences below but now that he was here, in the Oval office that had formed the backdrop to so many of the First Family Inspirationals, he found himself totally intimidated, rooted to the spot. Jefferson the 31st rose and beckoned to him. "Come on in, Steven."

Steve moved across the carpet unable to feel his feet touching the ground. The P-G came out from behind the desk and offered his right hand. Steve thrust his own forward but did not dare make contact until the P-G's fingers closed around his palm. Despite all his previous cynicism it was a moment that took his breath away.

Jefferson gave an understanding smile and patted Steve

on the shoulder. "Good to have you back with us, my boy.
Ben here's told me all about you. You're, uh—a remarkable young man . . ." The P-G used his grip on Steve's
shoulder to turn him around and steer him over to one of
the armchairs by the fire. "Sit down, make yourself
comfortable."

Steve waited until Jefferson and Karlstrom had seated
themselves opposite. The P-G in the rocking chair by the
fire; Karlstrom in the chair furthest away making it impossible for Steve to see both of them at once. The armchair
was deep and soft. Softer and more embracing than anything that Steve had ever sat upon in his whole life. He lay
back savouring the luxury for one brief moment then sat
up straight with his butt on the front half of the seat
cushion.

Jefferson stretched a hand towards the leaping flames.
"So . . . Steven, Ben here tells me you're thinking of
joining us."

"Uhh, sir—?"

Jefferson looked at Karlstrom.

"There are a few details still to be ironed out."

"A formality, I'm sure." Jefferson stopped roasting his
hand and waved at the framed alcove. "Bet you never saw
one of these before, eh, Steven? You know what they call
this? A fireplace. A long time ago, back in the days of the
blue-sky world, every house used to have one of these.
Yes . . . they used to call it the heart of the home. The
good ole boys would come in at the end of the day after
working on the ranch, the wells, in the mills and the
townships; the womenfolk would come in from the fields
and they'd sit together round the fire, share a meal made
with fresh food won from the good earth and they'd talk
about their dreams for an even better tomorrow." Jefferson gazed at the fire reflectively. "Yes . . . it was a great
country. Folks stuck together, believed in the same things.
People were honest, upright and true. With courage and
hard work there was no limit to what a man could do, or
how far he could go." He turned his gaze onto Steve.
"Those good ole boys built it up just fine. They blazed
trails, put down railroad tracks and highways, built cities

out there on the grass. Built 'em of brick and stone, pine and cedar, glass and steel. Look out of the window there—!"

Steve followed the P-G's outflung arm. Through the windows set in the curved wall behind the desk, he could see a great sweep of green grass, burgeoning willows, silver-trunked larches, and in the middle distance, a white timbered steep-roofed building with a pointed tower topped by a cross.

"You know what that is?" cried Jefferson. "A picture of part of this country as it used to be. New Hampshire . . . in the spring. All over America a man could look out of his window onto views as good as that! Green grass, green trees, green hills—just like it says in the song. And one day, it will be green again. Our forefathers fought wild beast and nature for every inch of it so as to be able to hand it on to future generations. It was worth fighting for then and it's worth fighting for now—to win it back again. The Mutes shattered those dreams, turned 'em into a nightmare, robbed our forefathers of that bright tomorrow. It's up to us—to me, and Ben here, to young, gifted men like you, and every able-bodied Tracker, to do what we can to put the Federation back where it belongs." The P-G pointed to the ornate, moulded ceiling. "Up there in the blue-sky world. What we've managed to do down here within the earthshield is nothing to what we'll accomplish when the overground is ours again!" He raised his right hand, made a fist and brought it down sharply on the arm of his rocker. "That's my one regret, Steven. The fact that I won't be around on that evening when there'll be fires again all over America. Not flames and smoke in the sky from the burning cities, but here—" The P-G gestured towards the blazing logs, "—in the hearth, in the homes of the brave. But you . . . you might see that day or, at the very least, join with us in helping to bring it nearer. My whole life has been spent working towards that one goal. So has Ben's, and the rest of the Family. Are you prepared to dedicate *your* life to making it happen, Steven?"

Steve squared his shoulders. "Mr. President, sir,—up to now I've always tried to do my duty as best as I know how. I'm ready to do whatever you ask of me, sir."

Jefferson gave a satisfied nod. "Good, good, that's what I like to hear." He looked across at Karlstrom. "I like this boy, Ben. He speaks my kind of language." The P-G turned back to Steve and fixed him with a penetrating gaze. "Do you trust me, Steven?"

"Absolutely, 100 per cent, Mr. President sir."

"Enough to talk to me about Mute magic?" Jefferson kept his eyes on Steve, studying his reaction. "You don't look surprised."

Steve caught the laugh in his throat and managed to turn it into a strangled cough. "Uh, Mr. President sir, after five months out there with the Mutes it's, well— kinda hard to be surprised at anything. When the President of the Board of Assessors cut me off as I began to tell her about the Talisman Prophecy it was obvious that I wasn't the only one who knew about it. But since the rest of the Board were being kept in the dark it could only mean that other people, in more senior positions, were taking it seriously. And if they felt that way about the Prophecy then it followed that they took the same view of Mute magic. The threat to the Federation contained in the Prophecy is so serious that one of those people had to be you, sir."

Jefferson chuckled and slapped the arm of his rocker. "I don't think you need worry. Ben. This boy's going to do just fine." He returned to Steve. "You're right, of course. But it has been necessary to deny the existence of Mute magic in order to maintain field discipline among wagon-train and way-station crews—and the morale of Trackers in general. From a study of the records I know that it was a hard decision for my predecessors to take but they believed that the only way to crush all doubt and rumour was to back that ruling with the force of law. And so any public discussion of Mute magic became a Code One offence."

"But . . . Mr. President sir, does that mean all those Trail-Blazers who have been court-martialled and shot for dereliction of duty were innocent?" It was a question Steve was unable to resist asking. The look he got from Karlstrom told him he was pushing his luck.

The P-G's eyes had also lost their sparkle. "You don't

seem to understand, Steven. Innocent or not, they still contravened the Code by claiming the use of magic by the Mutes. They died as the Foragers and Minutemen died. In order that others might live. It is a sacrifice that every Tracker worthy of the name has been prepared to make in the past—and may be required to make at any time."

Steve got the message.

"Including yourself, less than one hundred people in the whole of the Federation know of the existence of the Talisman Prophecy. The official view has been, and will continue to be, that there is no such thing as Mute magic. The truth is somewhat different. Over the past hundred years the First Family has accumulated enough evidence to prove beyond doubt that certain Mutes *do* possess the ability to manipulate natural phenomena. How and why they are able to do that is something we do not yet understand but we view it as a very real and a very serious threat." Jefferson paused to weigh up the effect of his words. "However, you will never hear me admit such a thing outside the Oval Office—just as you will never speak of what you have just heard or what we are about to discuss. This meeting never took place. Is that understood?"

"Yes, Mr. President sir."

"Good . . ." Jefferson's eyes and manner softened slightly. He clasped his hands together and placed his elbows on the arm of the rocker. "Who related the Prophecy to you—this Mr. Snow?"

"Yes, sir. I think he meant it to be some kind of message he hoped I would pass on. I must say it scared the hell out of me."

"Me too," said Jefferson. "But I was about half your age when I first heard it." The P-G grimaced wryly, "Way back before even your guard-father was born. Yes . . . I wonder if the version you heard is the same as the one I know?" He began the opening verse:

"When the great mountain in the West speaks
with a tongue of fire that burns the sky
and the earth drowns in its own tears,
then shall a new-born child of the Plainfolk

become the Thrice-Gifted One,
who shall be Wordsmith, Summoner and Seer."

Jefferson leaned forward. "Tell me the rest, Steven." Steve
began the second verse—

"Man-child or Woman-child the One may be.
Whosoever is chosen shall grow straight
and strong as the Heroes of the Old Time.
The morning dew shall be his eyes,
the blades of grass shall be his ears,
and the name of The One shall be Talisman.

The eagles shall be his golden arrows,
the stones of the earth his hammer,
and a nation shall be forged
from the fires of War.
The Plainfolk shall be as a bright sword
in the hands of Talisman, their Saviour.

Then shall the cloud-warriors fall like rain
and the iron snake devour its masters
The desert shall rise up and crush
the dark cities of the sand-burrowers
for heaven and earth have yielded
their secret powers to Talisman.

Thus shall perish the enemies of the Plainfolk
for the Thrice-Gifted One is master of all.
Death shall be driven from the air
and the blood shall be drained from the earth.
Soul-sister shall join hands with soul-brother
and the land shall sing of Talisman . . ."

The words transported Steve back to that magical moment when he had first heard them in Mr. Snow's hut,
squatting on the talking mats in the flickering firelight
opposite Cadillac and the wiry, white-bearded wordsmith.
He felt a sudden need for their good-humoured company,

a longing to look again into the eyes of Clearwater, an urgent desire to be close to her.

But there was something else. The first verse of the Prophecy as recited by Jefferson contained a variation that altered its meaning completely. After the line "and the earth drowns in its own tears" the Federation version ran—

"then shall a new-born child of the Plainfolk
become the Thrice-Gifted One . . ."

In the version of the Prophecy recited by Mr. Snow the line ran—

"then shall a child born *of* the Plainfolk
become the Thrice-Gifted One . . ."

From what had been said, Steve had little doubt that the First Family was already working on ways to deal with the Talisman but any plans they had appeared to hinge on the idea that, when the earth gave the sign, they would be looking for a *new-born child* who would grow up to be the promised saviour of the Plainfolk. But if Mr. Snow's version of the Prophecy was the correct one, it meant that someone born *years before* the predicted event could be the Talisman. A grown man or woman—like Cadillac or Clearwater in whom the powers that would make them the Talisman were lying dormant. Ready to burst forth at any moment . . .

The scenario based on the Federation version of the Prophecy appeared to include a fifteen year breathing space between the birth and the emergence of Talisman as the magical warrior chief of the Plainfolk; Mr. Snow's version allowed practically no reaction time at all. If the Federation hoped to confound the Prophecy and triumph over the Plainfolk it was extremely important to know which, of the two versions, was the correct one. Or was there a third—or a fourth version? And if so, would any of them come true? Or was the Talisman Prophecy the inevitable product of the endangered Mute psyche? The last, great, smoke-filled illusion; the dying dream of a race on the verge of total extinction.

And there were practical problems too. If Prophecy was truly possible, at what point in time would this "sign" be given? Where, for example, was the "great mountain in the West?"

Steve dragged his thoughts back to the Oval Office and to what the President-General was saying to Karlstrom. ". . . the amazing accuracy with which this stuff is transmitted orally. More than a hundred years separate the version I quoted and the one Steven here has just given us and yet they match word for word."

Karlstrom nodded thoughtfully. As he listened to Steve he had wondered if the young Tracker realised that, apart from being the only person on record to have survived capture by the Mutes, he was also the *only* person this century—that the First Family knew of—to have learnt of the Talisman Prophecy from an overground source. How interesting that he, of all people, should have been chosen by the Plainfolk as a messenger. As Karlstrom considered all the possible implications, it occurred to him that Q-6, knowing Steve had already revealed that he knew of the Prophecy, had not gotten him to repeat it line by line. It was a minor oversight and in all probability didn't matter but it was yet one more example of procedural sloppiness and it niggled him. "Tell me—does the first verse of the Prophecy as spoken by the President-General match what Mr. Snow told you?"

Steve faced him squarely. "Yes, Commander. To the best of my recollection I'd say it was a dead match."

"Okay. Did this, ah—Mr. Snow give you any background on the Prophecy? For example, where it first came from?"

"Yes, Commander. He told me it was first transmitted— that was the exact word he used—through a wordsmith called Cincinnati Red about four hundred years ago."

Jefferson and Karlstrom exchanged thoughtful glances. "Four hundred years," mused Jefferson. "I'd say that pretty well validates it, wouldn't you? It means that whoever composed it predicted the appearance of both wagon-trains and wingmen two centuries ahead of time."

"The wordsmith may have been lying," said Karlstrom. "The problem is we have no way of proving that—even if he was available for questioning. He may just be passing on what his predecessor told him. Not that it really matters. Our plans are based on the assumption that it may be true."

Steve caught Karlstrom's attention. "Uh, Commander—this 'great mountain in the West'—where this is all supposed to start. Do we know its precise location?"

"Yes, we do," replied Karlstrom drily. "Or at least we're 95 per cent certain we do. But we're not here to talk about that. Why don't you tell the President-General what you've learned about summoners and seers?"

Jefferson settled back in his rocker. "Yes, go ahead, Steven."

Steve took one look at the eyes and told him almost everything.

Everything except the claim made by Mr. Snow that he, Steven Roosevelt Brickman, was also under the protection of Talisman.

When Steve had finished, Jefferson aimed a questioning look at Karlstrom.

Karlstrom responded with a barely discernible nod. His face gave nothing away. "The earthquake you mentioned when you and I talked earlier. The one that split the bluff when you were about to escape. Do you think Clearwater could have been responsible for that?"

"It's possible, Commander. Without me going back and asking her I have no way of knowing for sure but if it hadn't happened when it did I wouldn't be here now. I know it seems unbelievable but compared to what she claimed Mr. Snow had done to try and wreck the wagon-train—"

"And almost succeeded," said Jefferson. "Ben, I think we can take a chance on this young man. I've got a good feeling about him." Clasping his hands together he placed his elbows on the arms of the rocker and leaned forward. "Steven, do you know what a quest is?"

"Yes, Mr. President sir."

The P-G nodded. "Good. How would you like to take part in the quest for the Talisman?"

Steve's heart leapt. He tried to hide his excitement. "I'd like that very much, uh—Mr. President."

"Okay." The P-G waved a hand towards Karlstrom. "Ben runs an outfit that carries out special assignments for the Family. As you can imagine, from time to time, there are things that I need done that can't be handled by existing units. Jobs that require people like you, with a high degree of resourcefulness, a brain that can function under pressure and a certain . . . originality. People who can operate with absolute discretion and—" Jefferson's eyes locked on to Steve's, "—on whom I can depend totally. Looking for the Talisman is just one of several top priority tasks. The Commander will tell you everything else you need to know." Jefferson stood up to signify that the interview was at an end.

Steve leapt out of the armchair and grasped the P-G's hand—this time without trepidation. He felt an electric shock run up his arm. One hundred volts of human warmth and sincerity. A sign he was dealing with a real pro.

"Your guard-father, Jack Brickman, I met him twice you know."

"Yes, sir, Poppa-Jack told me. He felt very proud, very, uh—honoured."

Jefferson walked with Steve and Karlstrom towards the 'stile door. "I was the one who felt honoured. There are not many of our wingmen who qualify for two trips to the White House." He patted Steve on the back. "Ben, here, seems to think that some of Jack's dedication may have rubbed off on you."

Steve faced both of them as they reached the 'stile. "Mr. President sir, I'd like nothing better than to be able to prove to you and the Commander that he was right."

"It will be dangerous, Steven. It's tough, lonely work."

Steve judged that this was a moment when he could laugh and get away with it. "Mr. President sir, it can't be worse than what I've just been through."

Jefferson chuckled and gripped Karlstrom's arm. "Make

sure you let me know how this boy shapes up." He gave Steve a goodbye nod. "We'll meet again. That's a promise."

Karlstrom pressed a button on the wall by the 'stile to alert the ensign guarding the door that someone was coming through. "Step aboard Brickman."

As Steve was rotated through to the outer office, the genial smile faded from Jefferson's face. "Watch him, Ben."

"You bet," replied Karlstrom. "Like a fucking hawk . . ."

TEN

THE DAY AFTER his visit to the Oval Office, Steve returned to the White House to be formally enrolled into the ranks of AMEXICO. The simple ceremony, which was conducted by Karlstrom, required Steve to swear a new oath of personal allegiance to the President-General followed by a vow to maintain absolute secrecy about the existence of AMEXICO and his membership of it. As he repeated the words of the oath and the vow, Steve and the President faced each other, laid their right hands on each other's heart and covered it with their left.

Once the formalities were completed, Jefferson, who had remained stony-faced throughout, treated Steve to a paternal smile, shook him warmly by the hand, wished him well and despatched him with a pat on the back. Karlstrom too, in his dry, faintly mocking way, welcomed him onto the team and explained that the act of enrolment meant automatic promotion to JX-1, the first rung on the executive ladder. He was to begin training immediately; his first mission was already being planned. Steve promised once again to do his best, saluted and left.

A stiff-necked ensign from the Presidential Honour Guard met Steve as he came back down into the fortress-like reception area and escorted him across the marble concourse to Karlstrom's private elevator. Maggie Pruett, the friendly JX-2, whose appearance had heralded his rehabilitation, was waiting in the office to take him on the next stage of his journey. Still glowing from the news of his unexpected promotion, Steve walked alongside her chatting casually. Just after he had learned she came from Arkansas, Pruett stopped in her tracks and pointed towards a turnstile. "This is as far as I go. Here—you'll need this." She handed him a blue ID wallet.

Steve took out the Sensor card marked with a silver "X" that signified his new rank and read off his name and number. He was back in business. He fingered it lovingly, wondering how far it had been upgraded, what new levels of information and services he now had access to. "Thanks a lot."

"Just doing my job," said Pruett. She turned abruptly and walked away.

Steve carded himself through the turnstile. The right-angled corridor led to the platform of a shuttle line where a two-car unit stood waiting. As Steve stepped onto the platform the illuminated panel above the card-key slot controlling the doors of the shuttle flashed an "Insert Card" instruction. Steve keyed himself on board the rear car, recovered his card from the slot on the inside of the door frame and sat down. He was the only passenger.

At the end of the one-stop line, a soft pleasant voice came through the shuttle system, inviting him to disembark. Steve stepped out onto an empty platform. A flashing red light drew his attention to an overhead tv screen carrying the image of a female Exec. Steve turned to face the screen and automatically came to attention before remembering he now had the same rank as the person he was looking at.

The pleasant voice addressed him again. "Good morning, Steven. Please stand at ease and listen carefully."

Steve stared up at the face framed by short, neatly combed hair. Its symmetry was perfect, its features with the firm chin and jawline and high cheekbones, the strong neck and wide shoulders, contained all the desirable elements of the ideal Tracker but the blue eyes had a curious glassy quality that left Steve with a vague feeling of unease.

"On behalf of the Reception Staff, I would like to welcome you to AMEXICO. My name is Lisa. This is the Rio Lobo training centre where you will be based for the next four weeks. There is no formal induction procedure, your presence here has been registered automatically. The issue of necessary clothing and equipment will take place this afternoon. Your first period of instruction will commence at 0800 hours tomorrow. I am required to explain to you that all instruction at this centre takes place on a one-to-one basis. Contact with other trainees is not permitted during this phase. Any attempt to contravene this rule during your stay here will result in immediate expulsion from the course and punitive sanctions as laid down for a Code One offence."

In other words death . . .

"Let me emphasise that this restriction is not a punishment but an integral part of AMEXICO's maximum security profile which you have sworn to maintain. Contact with other members of the Intelligence Commando is at the discretion of the Operational Director. You will find your quarters equipped with everything you need, including an inter-active tv channel on which you may seek assistance. I have been assigned to look after you during your stay with us and will be available on a twenty-four hour basis to answer your queries or process any problems you have. Follow the yellow arrows. They will guide you to your quarters where you will receive further instructions. Have a nice day."

Lisa's face was wiped from the screen to be replaced by an instruction. "Follow the yellow arrows." The words, which were in yellow, were underlined by a flashing arrow of the same colour. Whoever ran Rio Lobo clearly intended to leave no room for any misunderstanding.

The shuttle's electric motor thrummed into life. Steve turned and saw the two empty cars glide back into the tunnel that led to the White House. Steve left the platform, turned right as directed, and strode confidently down a long corridor lined on both sides with flush, anonymous doors. At the far end, he followed more arrows and finally reached his alloted accommodation unit. He carded himself through into the small hallway then, acting on an impulse, tried to reopen the door. It stayed shut. The indicator panel displayed an Off-Limits sign and buzzed angrily. Lisa hadn't been kidding.

Inspecting his new quarters, Steve found they were spacious but strictly functional. The unit had a separate bunk and study area, its own shower facilities, a small exercise room with workout equipment and video screens everywhere. Laid out on a shelf were the patched camouflage fatigues he had been wearing when he made his escape from the M'Calls. He had forgotten how worn and faded they were. A message on his videoscreen told him to change into them and put his blue wingman's uniform down the laundry chute.

Chastened by his experience with the door, Steve obediently dumped his new uniform and slipped into his old combat fatigues. His remote-control reception and the threat of virtual solitary confinement had struck him as slightly odd but it was nothing compared with what followed in the next four weeks. The training program and conditions he encountered at Rio Lobo were both strange and totally unexpected; a bizarre, and sometimes painful experience.

For the whole month he was there, Steve was not allowed to remove his clothes without permission—not even when he slept—and at no time was he allowed to take a shower. Nor was he able to. The supply to the shower head had been turned off. A limited amount of cold water dribbled through the faucets of the washbasin in the shower room but there was no liquid soap, the basin had no plug, and he soon discovered that the toilet flush only worked once a day. Worst of all, there was no cotton waste. He was obliged to wipe his ass with a handful of leaves from a pile in a bucket. Not one of them, on its own, was big enough for the desired purpose and the discomfort was compounded by the discovery that the supply was only replenished once a week. The bunk was fitted with the standard padded cotton mattress but instead of the usual cover sheet and quilt there were two layers of smelly animal furs. Meals were delivered twice a day via a small service elevator. They were a surprise too. It was Mute food. When the first dish of hot spicy stew arrived Steve understood what was happening. He was being conditioned. They were going to send him back to the overground.

Steve was not only required to become dirty and sweatstained, his body had to be tanned and weathered to the point where his skin peeled, then became raw and blistered and his lips cracked. With over two hundred years of experience behind it, MX had brought the process to a fine art.

It was hard to concentrate on anything beyond just staying alive when you were being blasted by driving salt spray in a wind chamber but, during the time he lay under the banks of UV lamps, Steve was required to continue with his video studies, committing to memory pictures of various locations so that when tested, he could recognise them instantly and describe the route from one point to another.

Apart from Lisa's screen image, Steve did not come face to face with anyone. The instructors he met during the live training sessions, or via the tv screen, all wore close-fitting helmets with tinted visors and on such occasions he was required to do the same. And he had been addressed not by name but as "Zero-Two," the number sewn on the front and back of a sleeveless cotton jacket he had been ordered to wear over his fatigues.

The three years of specialist training at the New Mexico Flight Academy had already furnished Steve with many of the skills required by a member of the Intelligence Commando and after a month of twelve-hour workdays and seven day weeks, his anonymous instructors judged him ready for "insertion"—an MX term for transfer to a specific field assignment on the overground, or within the earthshield. There were no parades or presentations, no back-slapping celebrations; one morning, towards the end of his stay, he was simply informed by Lisa that he had completed his period of instruction, and had been given the code-name HANG-FIRE.

Steve, who had never heard the word before, was un-

aware that it was a term used by the military before the
Holocaust to describe an artillery shell whose propellant
charge had not detonated. The procedure for dealing with
a hang-fire consisted of opening the breech of the gun, and
waiting for several minutes before attempting to remove
the faulty charge. Artillerymen traditionally regarded it as
a risky business for there was always the danger the charge
could explode when being removed from the gun—with
fatal effects for the person handling it. Given Steve's background, it had seemed an apt label and its choice had
given Commander-General Karlstrom a certain amount of
dry satisfaction.

As he rode back down the line to the White House to be
briefed on his first mission, Steve reflected on the weird
set-up he had just left. He'd been obliged to undergo
several kinds of hell to become a member of the Intelligence Commando but he had been unable to discover
anything about the unit's organisation, the scope of its
operations, the number of people involved or their identities. Apart from knowing it was linked directly to the
President-General and that Karlstrom was its Operational
Director, MX itself remained as secret and as impenetrable as ever.

The only person he could have picked out of a crowd
was Lisa, the member of the reception staff who had been
assigned to look after him. Considering AMEXICO's obsessive concern with security it seemed a curious omission
especially since Lisa and, presumably, her colleagues would
be in the position to identify everyone who passed through
Rio Lobo.

What he did not know was that Lisa only existed as a
pattern of pixels on the screen of a cathode ray tube. She
was a computer-generated image created by COLUMBUS—
like the view through the windows of the Oval Office. The
ability of COLUMBUS to create talking heads was one of
the many things Steve had yet to discover about the world
created by the First Family.

An hour after sunset on 1st April, 2990, Steve settled
into the passenger seat of an unmarked dark grey Skyrider

that was waiting on a special airstrip above Houston/G C and headed north.

As they rose into the sky Steve felt the same joyous feeling of release that had swept through him on his first overground solo but he had not yet escaped AMEXICO's obsession with security. For despite the fact that he was sitting in an enclosed cockpit beneath a darkening sky, he had been instructed to keep the tinted visor of his helmet closed. The pilot did the same and conversation throughout the eight hundred mile flight was minimal.

Steve's initial sense of frustration faded before the wonder of his first night flight. There was no moon but, for the first part of the journey, the sky above was clear of clouds and full of stars, the "eyes in Mo-Town's dark cloak" that watched over the Plainfolk while they slept.

Gazing up through the canopy at the shimmering points of light, Steve wondered, yet again, who had put them there and why. What did it all mean? Only a handful of the Trackers destined to spend their lives within the "dark cities" of the Federation knew that such marvels existed— and many of the wagon-train crews studiously ignored them. Trackers were trained to obey orders, not ask questions—especially about subjects not covered by the Manual. Overground operations were always terminated when the light began to fade. Trail-Blazers headed back to the safety of their wagons, battened down the hatches, turned their backs on the video pictures of the great outdoors and went to sleep with the lights on.

As they crossed the state line between Oklahoma and Kansas, the clouds began to build up. The MX pilot flew on steadily into the gathering darkness. Steve looked down over the side. There was no sign of the ground below. "You happy about this?" he asked with a hint of anxiety.

The pilot nodded. "No problem." He pointed to a glowing panel in front of him. "Terrain radar. It'll take us all the way there and get us down in one piece."

Steve decided there was no point in asking him to explain further. He had to believe that MX knew what it was doing. If it didn't, he would be in big trouble. Not that it mattered overmuch. He was in big trouble right now, whether he failed or succeeded, and he was not even halfway there. The totally unexpected interview with the President-General had been an awe-inspiring moment and his promotion to JX-1 had been a welcome surprise but neither event had caused him to lose sight of his own objectives.

Faced with at least three years in the A-Levels, Steve had grabbed at the opportunity to regain his former status and had leapt at the chance of going overground. He would have agreed to almost any proposition that offered the prospect of seeing Clearwater again. But even he, a past master in duplicity, had been quietly appalled as Karlstrom had calmly briefed him on his first mission. Questions were allowed, objections were not; there had been no choice but to accept. As a result Steve was now between a rock and a hard place. Karlstrom had spelt it out quite clearly. If he didn't go through with it, if he betrayed the organisation and his oath to the President-General, his own life would be forfeit and his gifted kin-sister's chosen career would also come to an abrupt end.

And the threat didn't end there. Steve knew that Roz and Annie, his guard-mother, could be transferred to the A-Levels, or sent to the wall; Poppa-Jack, the dying hero who had been his guard-father could be stripped of his combat badges and publicly dishonoured. Steve nurtured no deep feelings towards his guard-parents beyond the normal ties of kinship but he still found the prospect disturbing. The danger to Roz upset him even more. Despite his deliberate neglect of their extraordinary mental relationship he knew, deep down, that their lives were interlinked in ways and for reasons he did not care to dwell on. If she was threatened, so was he. He was obliged to do all he could to protect her for his own sake. The unwelcome sense of responsibility he felt ran counter to his highly-developed instinct for self-preservation but he could not shake it off. It was a burden that was impossible to ignore.

Steve sat back, willed himself to relax and dozed fitfully until the Skyrider banked steeply and headed down to-wards the rendezvous point near a watercourse once known as Medicine Creek, some thirty miles north of the pre-Holocaust site of Cambridge, Nebraska. At two thousand feet the pilot cut the motor and wound down the flaps. The sky was no longer pitch black but it was still dark and there was a heavy ground mist that cut the visibility to under ten yards. Steve glanced at the altimeter and held his breath. He could hear the wind swishing through the wing struts. The masked pilot hummed the opening bars of a blue-sky ballad, made a few adjustments to the glide path, and put the aircraft down without a bump.

"Neat," said Steve, as they rolled smoothly to a stop.

The pilot grunted. "All part of the service . . ."

Steve dropped to the ground, opened the cargo hatch behind the cockpit, grabbed the two nearest carrying loops of the body bag and tipped it out onto the ground. Taking hold of it again, he dragged it clear then returned to the Skyrider and took out a weather-scarred air rifle, the fur bedding roll he had slept in at Rio Lobo, and the wicker-work basket that held the animal who had shared his quarters during training. He left the hatch open and slapped the side of the cockpit. "Okay. See you around."

"Maybe," said the pilot. He turned his masked face towards Steve and gave a brief, casual salute. "Buena suerte, amigo."

"Thanks. I have a feeling I'm gonna need it." Steve shouldered his load and strode away from the plane towards the fuzzy orange glow he could just make out through the leaden murk.

The glow was coming from inside a primitive dug-out built into the side of a slope. The entrance was partially concealed by stones and branches. As he drew nearer he saw an unkempt bearded figure carrying an air rifle. Like Steve, he was dressed in worn combat fatigues plus a long, sleeveless fur coat made up of the skins of different animals.

Steve identified himself through the special device all MX operatives carried; the bearded figure—the first real Mexican he had met face to face—did the same then thrust out a welcoming hand. "Snake-Eyes . . ."

"Hang-Fire," replied Steve.

"Good trip?"

"Quiet."

Snake-Eyes grinned, displaying a set of stained, yellow teeth. "They usually are. You must be new to this outfit."

Steve nodded.

"It's okay to take off your helmet now. I'm gonna need it for the trip back."

Steve passed over the helmet and glanced through the doorway of the dug-out. A short flight of steps led down to the messy interior. After living with the M'Calls, Steve's nostrils knew what to expect but the first whiff of the pungent aroma made him catch his breath.

"You'll find everything you need." Snake-Eyes smoothed back the long hair and pulled on the helmet leaving the greasy tangle of whiskers sticking out from under the chin guard. "Just think," he said, as he tried to fasten the neck strap, "Ten hours from now I'll be able to razor this fuzz from my face and lather up under a hot shower. And best of all, I'll be able to take a crap without freezing my balls off, or worrying if some crawlie's gonna latch on to my ring."

"I know the feeling," said Steve. "Anything happen in the last twenty-four hours I should know about?"

"D'you read the weather reports before leaving Rio?"

"Yes."

"Then you're up to date." Snake-Eyes picked up his fur bedding roll and slung his rifle. "Okay, dump your stuff. Let's get it over with."

They walked over to where Steve had dropped the body bag. Snake-Eyes unzipped it and helped him pull out the Skyrider's third passenger; a bearded, unkempt Tracker with a tanned hide, dressed like renegade. Except this wasn't a renegade or an undercover Fed and he wasn't dead. It was a cee-bee, a code-breaker who, while awaiting execution had been conditioned like Steve then been given a hearty breakfast laced with a tranquilising drug.

"How d'ya want him, face up or face down?"

"Doesn't matter." Steve put his rifle on single shot.

Snake-Eyes stepped back and began to hum "South of the Border," the tune that Mexicans used to alert other operatives to their presence. He picked up the body bag

and folded it with neat practised movements. Steve aimed
down at the unconscious cee-bee, took a deep breath then
calmly put two rounds through the forehead and a third
through the left eye.

Snake-Eyes stopped humming, picked up his gear and
slapped Steve on the shoulder. "Hope it stays fine for you,
good buddy. Hasta la vista."

Steve watched as Snake-Eyes was swallowed up by the
clammy greyness. The outline of the plane was barely
discernible but the pilot had switched on the small red
navigation light mounted under the fat fuselage pod. The
light winked out. Steve heard the cargo hatch slam shut
then a brief snarling burst of sound as the pilot gunned the
motor to turn the plane around and start it rolling. The
snarl became a smooth disembodied hum that faded rapidly as the Skyrider became airborne leaving him marooned
in the middle of a dark and hostile landscape. The only
sounds were the plaintive whimpering of the caged animal
at his feet and the faint crackle from the wood that Snake-
Eyes had thrown on the fire before leaving. Steve squared
his shoulders, made a mental resolution to face whatever
lay ahead with his customary courage and persistence,
then carried his gear inside.

The interior of the dug-out was more or less identical to
the mock-up in which Steve had spent the last week of his
training. Snake-Eyes had moved a few items around and
had hung the Mute crossbow by the door instead of on the
wall to the left of the primitive fireplace but otherwise,
Steve felt completely at home. The only thing missing was
the video through which he had been taught and tested
right up to the last minute. It was all part of the careful
preparation for his return to the overground. His mind
had been required to soak up information the way his
body had soaked up the ultra-violet radiation. He had
committed to memory the salient details of the weather for
every week of the past winter in Southern Nebraska,
together with the movements of herd animals and general
wildlife activity. He had even memorised several hunting
anecdotes relating to the acquisition of the furs that hung
from the walls.

Steve pulled the buffalo skin curtain across the doorway then unrolled his sleeping furs and took out Fazetti's helmet. The scabbard containing Naylor's knife was already strapped to his right leg. He spread the furs over the thick bed of dry fern, hung the helmet on the end of a branch buried in one of the walls, threw some more wood on the fire then let Baz out of his basket.

Baz was a young wolfcub. He leapt up happily at Steve then padded nervously around the dug-out, snuffling at everything within reach. Steve pulled a coiled piece of rigging wire from the cage, fixed it around Baz's neck, tied him up outside the door of the hide and gave him a strip of raw meat to chew on. Baz subsided happily.

With that vital chore completed, Steve ducked back inside, tossed the wickerwork cage on the fire then sat down on the bunk and watched it burn. He took off his boots and surveyed the holes in his threadbare socks. The grimy nail of his big left toe stuck through one of them. There was no doubt about it, the masked make-up technicians at Rio Lobo had done a great job. Pulling the furs over his body, he lay back with a yawn and watched the play of the firelight on the woven pattern of thick branches that made up the ceiling. He wondered briefly if anyone had found the wreckage of Blue-Bird that an MX field team had carefully hidden in a tangle of undergrowth a hundred and ten miles northwest of his present position, then he fell asleep.

A few hours later, Steve was woken by the yapping bark of the wolfcub. Pulling his boots on, he grabbed the crossbow, loaded it and stepped outside cautiously. There was no sign of any movement. The sun, rising above the trees into a clear sky, had begun to melt the heavy overnight frost. Crystal-clear droplets, filled with trapped sunlight, hung from the curving blades of grass, sparkling like diamonds scattered by a mad millionaire. Buds were straining to burst through the smooth bark on the leafless branches of the trees and new shoots of bright orange grass were already pushing up between the yellowing seed stalks that had somehow weathered the White Death.

Steve drank in the cool sweet-tasting air, felt it cut deep

into his lungs, felt his heart quicken. Once again he felt
the same sense of belonging, a sense of unity and, with it,
the realisation that he was now truly alive. And, once
again, he did not dare ask himself why. His reverie was
broken by Baz, the wolf cub leaping up at his legs, barking
and whining alternately. Steve untied him and let him into
the hide where Baz cajoled him into handing over part of
his own breakfast of freshly grilled buffalo meat.

As he watched the cub eat, Steve reflected on his relationship with the animal he had acquired at Rio Lobo. In
the beginning, it had seemed a strange idea to live in close
proximity to a smelly beast that, when it grew bigger,
might revert to its savage state and attack without warning. The instructor had emphasized the importance of
regular physical contact and, once he had overcome his
initial revulsion, Steve's curiosity and interest had been
aroused. Gradually, he had become used to handling it
and now, as it finished its share of the meat and came to
him for more, he rubbed its head and let it wrestle with
his hand.

According to his instructor, some renegades had developed a rapport with certain overground animals. The two
main types were wolves and falcons, of which young wolves
were the most common. Then trained, the wolves provided companionship and a source of warmth during the
winter and could be harnessed to pull loads through the
snow. They acted as sentinels, and in skilled hands they
could be trained to hunt down game. And when their
keeper was faced with starvation, they could always be
killed and eaten.

Baz gave up trying to bite Steve's hand off and rolled
over onto his back and begged to have his belly stroked.
Steve laid a hand on the cub's chest and shook him playfully. "Okay, that's enough." He reached for a piece of
wood and tossed it towards the door of the dugout. Baz
leapt after it, pinned it down with his paws and began to
gnaw one end.

As he watched, Steve wondered why Mutes, who were
formidable hunters, had not developed a similar relationship with animals. He concluded that the Plainfolk, who

he judged to be totally in tune with their environment, probably related to animals in a way that he did not yet fully understand. He had, after all, only spent a little under six months among the Mutes and his knowledge of them was based entirely on the M'Calls, who were She-Kargo Mutes. The customs of other clans, such as those belonging to the D'Troit, the San'Paul, the C'Natti and M'Waukee might be quite different.

Steve had been ordered to live in the dug-out for a week before setting out to find the M'Calls. Those seven days would allow him to put his mark on the place and give him time to explore his immediate surroundings. It would also enable him to improve his control over Baz. The videotapes he had watched at Rio Lobo had already given him a working knowledge of the area; now he had to physically cover the ground to get the feel of it. To check the fish trap where the stream ran deep under the big leaning rock, to renew the blaze marks on the trees beyond the river to mark the way back to the hide where he was supposed to have spent the winter. But first, he had to bury the body.

Steve fetched a small entrenching tool from the dug-out and went over to where the dead cee-bee lay. The four dark birds that had been pecking their way into the skull scattered then returned to perch on nearby branches. Steve dragged the body over to a patch of softer ground, dug a shallow grave then covered the infill with a layer of rocks, the dead cee-bee was part of his cover story. He wanted the evidence to stay there until it was needed—not dug up and dragged away by some scavenging animal.

When the task was completed, Steve headed for the other grave whose location he had memorised while under training at Rio Lobo. The cee-bee in this one had lain buried since last November. Grass and moss had already taken root amongst the stones. Beneath them lay the remains of the other dead man in Steve's cover story. He did not relish the task of having to dig up the body and hoped he wouldn't have to.

*　　*　　*

As the end of the week drew near, Steve spent several
hours studying the creased and grimy AirNav map that
Snake-Eyes had left behind. The dug-out in which he had
been living was located to the south side of the Platte
River which ran east to join the Missouri at the NavRef
point called Omaha. To the west, the Platte divided into
two smaller tributaries known as the North and South
Platte. If he followed the North Platte as it snaked westwards around the Laramie Mountains, it would take him
into Wyoming, the scene of last year's battle between the
M'Calls and The Lady.

According to the latest information Karlstrom had received, the clan were expected to pass through this area
sometime in the next three months. All Steve had to do
was to position himself along their general line of advance
and make contact.

Nothing to it—or so MX appeared to think.

His insertion had been planned down to the smallest
detail but the hardest part had been left to him. Just how,
wondered Steve, was he make contact without getting
himself killed? And even if he managed that, how long
would he survive? The shadowy cabal within the clan that
had resented his presence before would be bound to try
and avenge the death of Motor Head and his two companions, Cannon-Ball and Freeway. More importantly, how
would Clearwater react—and could he ever win back the
trust of Cadillac and Mr. Snow? Without it, he would
never be able to carry out his mission. That left the
biggest question mark of all: even if all went as planned,
when it came to the crunch, would he be able to find
enough iron in his soul to do what had been asked of him?

ELEVEN

ON THE DAY he was due to leave the dug-out, Steve packed the essentials he would need for the trip onto a wooden back-frame that his fellow Mexican had put together during the winter. Baz prowled around restlessly, sensing that they were about to embark on some new adventure. Steve hoisted the bulky load onto his back, locked his thigh muscles to stop himself buckling at the knees and adjusted the shoulder straps.

Satisfied the harness was as comfortable as he could make it, Steve set the pack down and considered whether or not to take the crossbow. Since he was supposed to have spent the winter on the overground, the three compressed air bottles he had were all less than a third full, and he only had a limited supply of bullets. All of them showed signs of having been fired at least once and bore traces of blood. Like any other renegade Steve would have been forced to recover the rounds from the carcasses of the animals he had shot for food, and whose furs now adorned the interior of the hide.

If he ran out of compressed air, the bow would afford useful protection. He had been taught how to use it at Rio Lobo and turned in a high score. It was accurate and lethal—and it was also a liability. Steve knew that if he ran into a bunch of Mutes whose clan mark was on the bowstock he could end up being killed before getting a chance to explain. Crossbows weren't things you just "found." A warrior would rather lose his life than surrender such a highly-prized object. For Steve to have one could only mean he had killed one or more of their clan brothers to get it.

During his briefing, Karlstrom had revealed that killing Mutes was something that Tracker renegades avoided whenever possible. During the last several decades, the small groups of scavengers who roamed the overground had gradually gained a measure of acceptance among the clans whose turf bordered the New Territories.

As enemies of the Federation, their presence was tolerated but not actively encouraged. A limited amount of trading went on, mainly abandoned items of equipment, but no other kind of social interaction was sought or offered by either side. They might be on the run but most renegades were still Trackers at heart. None of them were looking to share their bedrolls with lumpheads. The result was a fragile and rather precarious kind of co-existence which AMEXICO supported wholeheartedly when it suited their devious purpose and also, with equal dedication, did its best to undermine.

Steve decided to leave the crossbow in the bolthole—a small escape tunnel Snake-Eyes had excavated during the winter, and which was just big enough to crawl through. The exit, which was at some distance from the dug-out, was concealed by stones and undergrowth; the entrance by an earth and wickerwork plug that the escapee pulled in behind him. Everything of value that he did not need on the trip had already been stowed inside.

Having closed up the bolthole, Steve then remembered he had forgotten to pull the fish trap out of the stream. With a muttered curse he picked up his rifle and went up the steps of the dug-out. Baz scampered past him then stopped a few yards away with one front paw raised and snffed the air cautiously. Steve dropped down behind the rocks and branches shielding the entrance to the dugout and surveyed the surrounding area with the aid of a battered pair of binoculars.

Once again he could discern no sign of danger. The

landscape was as empty of humans as it had been all week. Still one could never be sure. Any renegade planning to evade the Trail-Blazer hit squads had to master the art of concealment—something that was second nature to Mutes. Steve had taken a crash course on the theory but was still short on practical experience.

Whispering to Baz to come to heel, Steve moved out from cover and headed down the gentle slope towards the stream, holding his rifle at the ready, finger cocked around the trigger. The fur on Baz's shoulders bristled as they entered the trees. He stopped again and his muzzle shortened as he bared his teeth in a silent snarl.

Steve crouched down against the trunk of the nearest tree and listened carefully. All he could hear was the rippling murmur of the stream that marked the curving line of the valley floor. He checked the ground behind him, on both sides of the dug-out, then made a crouching run down the slope, zig-zagging from one tree to another until he reached a large redwood.

Peering round the trunk, he saw what had made Baz's hackles rise. Over to his left, by the leaning rock, a large furry animal was crouched at the water's edge. Probably a bear. Steve had learned that some bears made a habit of raiding fish traps in search of an easy meal. The trouble was they usually wrecked the trap getting at whatever was inside.

Steve closed in on the intruder. If he could save the fish *and* nail the bear it would add variety to the menu. With a limited supply of ammunition he had to try and bring the bear down with one triple burst. These bears were tough customers. Three rounds in the rump would only annoy it. He needed a head shot or, if he could get the creature to rear up on its hind legs, three in the heart.

Reaching the bank about fifty yards downstream of the trap, Steve found a spot which gave him an unobstructed view of his target. The bear lifted the trap out of the water and rose obligingly on its hind legs. It was only when he pulled the rifle firmly into his shoulder and took aim that he saw that this particular bear had already been turned into somebody's winter overcoat. He lowered the rifle and moved forward, finger still on the trigger. The owner of the bearskin turned towards him, still holding the trap. A rifle and a homemade backpack lay nearby in the grass at the base of the rock. The rag-taggle appearance of his visitor matched his own. It was a renegade. The bulky furs concealed the finer points of build and gender but he, or she, was on the short side, with a weathered oval face and grey deep-set eyes that were vaguely familiar.

Steve drew closer, keeping his rifle pointed at the middle of the bearskin coat. He called to Baz. The wolf cub came to heel but continued to defy the intruder with a low, continuous growl. The left side of the renegade's face including the neck right down to the collarbone had been badly burned. The lumpy scar tissue was a raw, ugly pink.

Bearskin hefted the empty fish-trap. "This belong to you?"

Steve nodded. "You almost got youreslf killed."

Bearskin responded with a twisted smile. "So did you."

Steve threw a quick glance over both shoulders and saw several more renegades step from behind cover. One of them wore a yellow command cap. They all had three-barrelled air rifles—and they had him surrounded. It was no time to appear unsociable. Steve set the butt of his rifle on the ground. "If you and your friends here are hungry, you are welcome to share what I've got in the hide."

"That's right friendly of you, soldier." Bearskin tossed the woven fish trap towards Steve. "You'd better let me have that rifle of yours until we get better acquainted. My friends here are very nervous people."

Steve exchanged the rifle for the fish-trap which he stuck casually under his arm. Baz had already started to make friends. Steve looked long and hard at Bearskin as they started back up the slope. "Don't I know you from somewhere?"

"Funny you should say that. I was thinking the same thing. What train did you fall off?"

"The Lady from Louisiana. I powered down last June."

"Sonofabitch!" exclaimed the renegade. "I thought it was you! Brickman, right?!"

Steve stopped and turned towards Bearskin. "Don't tell me *you're* from The Lady too!"

"Yeah. Don't you recognise me?" The renegade pulled back the hood of the fur coat and brushed the tangled fringe of dark hair away from his forehead. "Try the right side. The left don't look too good."

Steve's mouth sagged open as recognition dawned. Bearskin was not a he but a she, his section leader who had been swept off the flight deck in a flaming shroud of napalm during their first major battle with the Mutes. "Jodi . . .? Jodi Kazan?!"

"Right first time."

Steve tried to master his confusion. "But . . . I—I was there on the flight deck when you got killed!"

"Correction. *Almost* got killed. And believe me, until these guys found me, there were moments I wished I had been."

Steve gazed at her, his brain still refusing to believe the evidence of his own eyes. "This is incredible. I just don't understand how . . ."

Jodi nodded. "Luck I guess. Must have made quite a spectacular exit."

"You can say that again." Steve eyed the scarred side of her face. "Looks like you had a rough ride."

"I did but—" Kazan shrugged, "—here I am. Large as life and twice as ugly."

The other renegades who had been with Jodi closed in on both sides. Steve counted eight of them. They made a real rag-taggle collection. All of them wore a patchwork of animal skins over threadbare combat fatigues, and sported a variety of non-regulation headgear. Hand-sewn bandoliers stuffed with air bottles and spare magazines were slung across their chests, and most carried machetes or combat knives. Their weathered faces were unshaven, and their eyes were those of hunters and fugitives who had learned how to survive the hard way.

"This is Brickman," explained Jodi. "He's okay. We shipped out together last April aboard The Lady. He powered down in June."

"Same day as she went overboard," added Steve.

"Where's Malone?"

"He's checking out the hide," said Yellow-Cap.

"Okay, let's go join him," replied Jodi. "Our friend here has kindly offered to share what's in the larder."

As they made their way back to the hide, Steve counted a dozen more armed renegades standing guard with varying degrees of watchfulness. One of them went down the dirt steps to fetch Malone, the boss of the outfit. Jodi pointed him out as he emerged. The five guys with him fanned out on either side, cradled their rifles and gave Steve the once-over. Yellow-Cap joined them. The other guys closed in to form a half circle behind Steve.

Malone was a lean, mean-looking sonofabitch with pale piercing eyes like the Assessors who had given Steve such a hard time. Unlike most of the renegades, Malone was relatively clean-shaven. His long brown hair was tied together on the nape of his neck with a strip of camouflaged fabric and he wore a sweatband of the same material around his high forehead. Somewhere along the line someone had tried to kick his nose through the back of his head and, from the expression on his square, deeply lined face, he was still sore about it.

Malone sat on a rock and listened in silence while Jodi said her piece then waved her aside and switched his attention on Steve. "Okay, friend, what's your story?"

Steve launched into an account of his capture and escape from the Mutes, omitting all mention of Clearwater and the fact that he had taught Cadillac to fly. He described how the patched fabric of the home-made hang-glider had started to unravel, forcing him to abandon his original plan to return to the Federation.

Malone listened to his adventures with an expressionless face that made it hard for Steve to guage how well he was doing. He hesitated, hoping to trigger some reaction but Malone merely nodded and gestured to him to continue.

Steve went on with the story he had carefully rehearsed at Rio Lobo. How he had hidden the glider then headed south on foot until sighting a posse of Mutes. Deciding to work his way round their turf, he had struck out eastwards, eventually reaching the junction of the North and

South Platte rivers. Once again he encountered Mute warriors from the same clan and managed to escape, floating downstream past their encampment during the night on a small raft of logs. Gaining the southern shore he had set off south again determined to reach the Federation—his only hope of survival. It was at this point, close to collapse from exhaustion and hunger, he had had the good fortune to stumble across this hide—where he had spent the winter.

Malone glanced over his shoulder and signalled to one of his side-kicks—a guy with a straggly blond beard. The renegade produced a portable radio set and put it down between Steve and Malone. Steve had learned how to use one like it at Rio Lobo. It was one of several highly-sophisticated pieces of communications equipment manufactured exclusively for AMEXICO.

Steve looked down at the radio then up at Malone.

"You want to tell me what this is doing here?"

"It belongs to the guy I found living here. Joe Tyson." Malone nodded. "Where is he?"

"I, uh—shot him." Steve paused but there was no reaction so he continued as per the script. "I thought he was okay. He offered to share his food, let me rest up, then taught me to hunt and set traps. We were getting along fine then, one day, towards the end of December he sent me out hunting. I came back early 'cos my gun had iced up. That's when I heard him talking. So I snuck up real quiet and found him working that thing. The sonofabitch was giving somebody my name and number!"

Malone didn't look impressed. "So what? Wasn't that what you wanted—to get back to the Federation?"

"Yes, sir. That's what I set out to do but this Tyson had me figured for a renegade and—"

"Aren't you?"

Steve gave it the old down home touch. "No, sir! Leastways I wasn't then. I'd escaped because I wanted to get back to my outfit. I didn't know any other way to function—ask Jodi. And here was this guy marking my card."

"How d'you mean?"

"Well—he said how he'd caught me roaming around
and how he had a hunch I'd been cosying up to the
Mutes."

"And had you?"

"No!" cried Steve. He pointed to the scars on his cheeks.
"Look! They even stuck a goddam arrow through my face!
That's how cosy we got!"

"But Tyson didn't believe you."

"No. But don't ask me why. I didn't want to find out
what his job was or who he was talking to. None of what
he said about me was really true but the damage was
done. You know what the rules are. As far as the Federation was concerned I was finished. So I gave him three in
the head." Steve spread his hands. "Only thing I could
do."

"And you stayed here . . ."

"Had nowhere else to go."

Malone nodded in agreement and fingered the radio
set. "Ever see one like this before?"

"Nope. It's new to me."

Malone appeared to accept this. He inspected the fin-
gernails on his right hand then fixed his pale eyes on
Steve. "Did you catch the name of the person he was
calling?"

"It was a code-name. 'Mike-X-Ray-One'." Steve saw
Malone exchange a sideways glance with Yellow-Cap. "Tyson
called himself 'Snake-Eyes'."

"What did you do with him?"

Steve pointed in the direction of the first grave. "He's
under that pile of rocks over there."

Malone turned to Yellow-Cap. "Check it out."

The renegade tapped three guys for the grave-digging
detail.

Steve called to them as they walked away. "He ain't
gonna look too pretty!" He turned back to Malone.

"So . . . Mr. Brickman. You spent the winter here
alone . . ."

"That's right. Didn't see another human being until a
week ago." Steve hunkered down and stroked the wolf
cub. "Good old Baz here woke me up in the middle of the

night. Before I had time to get my boots on some joker steps off a plane and away it goes."

"Who was he—a friend of Tyson's?"

"I didn't ask." Steve pointed to the newly-dug grave. "But if you want to check *him* out, he's under that other pile of rocks over there." The newly-dead cee-bee was Steve's alibi in case any stray renegades had seen or heard the Skyrider passing overhead. If they were in the vicinity, it would be only natural for them to mount a precautionary search of the area.

Malone looked in the direction of the grave then sent someone to break the news to Yellow-Cap. "Is that why you decided to leave?"

"Yeah. I'd figured that, what with the snow and the bad weather an all, they probably wouldn't come looking for Tyson until the spring. And sure enough everything was fine until a week ago—when the guy that's under those rocks dropped in out of the blue. I decided that if Tyson's replacement didn't report in things might start to get a little hot around here."

"That's right, they could." Malone kept his eyes glued on Steve. "What do you think Tyson was doing out here?"

"You tell me. All I know is he wasn't out to improve my career prospects."

Malone's mouth twisted into the semblance of a smile. "You certainly didn't do much for his."

"Survival's the name of the game. I learned that while I was with the M'Calls."

"So where were you heading? Back to your Mute friends?"

Steve shook his head. "Just away from here. And let's get one thing straight. Those lumps ain't no friends of mine."

Malone nodded. "Where did you get the fur coat?"

"Same place I got the bedding roll. Tyson. All I own is that rifle and what I'm standing up in."

"And the cub . . ."

"Baz, yeah, well . . it got kinda lonely. I needed someone to talk to."

Malone favoured him with another twisted smile. "I've got to hand it to you, Brickman. Aren't many people

around able to survive on their own the way you have.
Handling animals too. You learn fast."

"I always have."

"I bet . . ." Malone called Baz to him. The wolf cub
ambled forward wagging his tail playfully. Malone pulled a
dried meat twist from the tucker-bag slung from his waist,
snapped a piece off and held it up so that Baz had to leap
for it. "Tyson teach you to hunt grizz?"

"Yes," said Steve.

Malone's voice suddenly hardened. "Hold him!"

Two renegades grabbed Steve and put him in a double
arm lock. Malone grabbed the wolf cub by the neck as it
turned back towards Steve and pulled out his air pistol.

"No!" shouted Steve. But it was too late. As the cry left
his lips, Malone placed the muzzle against the back of the
cub's head and put a bullet through its skull.

"Okay, let him go," snapped Malone. He lobbed the
limp body of Baz towards him. "Skin it."

Steve stood there trembling with rage, the dead wolf
cub clutched to his chest. "You sonofabitch . . ."

"Save your breath, Brickman. And please, no heroic
gestures. You're in enough trouble already."

Steve drew Naylor's combat knife from the scabbard
strapped to his right calf, threw a murderous look at
Malone, then set to work. The razor sharp blade had been
specially worn down to look as if it had been hand-sharpened
on primitive grinding stones. Steve skinned the cub with a
judicious mixture of skill and clumsiness. His instructors at
Rio Lobo had spent hours coaching him on how to act
naturally, and they did not relent until he could perform
the whole range of mundane tasks connected with basic
survival with the unaffected ease one would expect from
somebody who had spent more than nine months marooned
on the overground. He peeled the fur from the bloody
carcass and threw it down at Malone's feet.

"Now butcher it," said Malone imperturbably. "And
when you've done that, light a fire and cook it for me."

Steve exchanged a look with Jodi Kazan. It was clear he
had her sympathy but she made no move to intercede on
his behalf. Given the real facts of the situation, Malone

and the other renegades had every reason to be suspicious but, by the same token, it meant that AMEXICO's overground operations were not as secret as Karlstrom might have wished them to be.

Inserting his knife between the rear legs, Steve slit open the carcass up to the rib cage and set about removing the intestines, heart and lungs, wishing, as he did so, that he could ram the whole stinking mess down Malone's throat. The threat of any revenge attack by Steve appeared to be the least of Malone's concerns. He and his men returned to the task of ransacking the hide. Malone got the pick of what was found, the rest was distributed to the members of the group according to need.

Yellow-Cap returned with the grave-digging detail and confirmed the presence of two corpses. Steve busied himself with lighting a fire. Malone left Steve under guard and went to inspect the bodies.

While he was gone, Jodi gathered up some kindling and brought it over to Steve. "Listen, don't do anything stupid. Just hang in there. It'll all work out."

"Were they this way with you?"

"No, but . . . the circumstances were a little different. I wasn't in any shape to argue."

"Okay, okay," muttered Steve. "So he's the honcho. He wants to prove he's a hard man. Point taken. But you told him what the score was. Why's he giving me such a hard time?"

"I don't know. Could be that radio set."

"It's not mine, Jodi. I swear it. Come on—you know there isn't any stuff like that aboard the wagon-trains."

"That's true. But since I've been free-basing with these guys I've discovered there's a lot of things I didn't know about."

"Such as?"

Jodi glanced over his shoulder and saw Malone and Yellow-Cap heading towards them. She started to back off. "Later . . ."

Steve grabbed her wrist. "Hey, Jodi—try and put in a good word for me, huh?"

"Sure . . ." She pulled free and hurried away.

Malone and Yellow-Cap came over and watched as Steve threaded the wolf cub's carcass on a stick and suspended it over the fire; a technique he had learned from the Mutes. He stood up as the renegade leader surveyed his handiwork. "Satisfied?"

Malone replied with a lightning-fast, left-hand punch to the solar plexus. As Steve staggered under the unexpected blow, Malone followed up with an equally hard right to the jaw that put him on his back. Stunned, and bleeding from the mouth, Steve rolled over and tried to haul himself up onto his hands and knees. Malone waited until his body was off the ground then sank a boot into his groin. Steve went down in a heap.

Malone stood over him as he lay doubled up in agony. "Lemme give you a word of friendly advice, Brickman. I don't like wise guys. Comprendo?"

Steve gritted his teeth in an effort to block the pain flooding through his body and nodded mutely.

Malone turned to the nearest of the renegades who had gathered round them. "Pick him up. He makes the place look untidy."

Two guy hauled Steve to his feet and held on tight to his arms as he swayed unsteadily. Malone stepped forward and thrust his face in close. "I'm going to tell you something else too. I don't believe a word you've said. Y'know what I think? I think you're an undercover Fed. A fuggin rat-fink sent out here by the Family to shaft us breakers."

"If you think that, you must be off your trolley," said Steve, barely able to move his lower jaw. "You've been out here so long your brain's been deep-fried."

Malone nodded soberly then stepped back and delivered a left hook that nearly took Steve's head off. "You've got a big mouth," he said amiably.

Steve felt the right hand side of his face stiffening and swelling to match the left. His mouth felt as if it was full of pebbles—pieces of chipped tooth enamel whose size and shape had been misread by his swollen tongue. He tried to summon up the necessary coordination to spit in Malone's face but only succeeded in dribbling blood and saliva down his own chin. "Listen," he said thickly, "if you're going to kill me, go ahead and get it over with. What difference does it make? After being out here for nine months I'm finished anyway."

"That's right," replied Malone. "But we don't waste bullets on rat-finks." He turned to Yellow-Cap. "Post him."

"Oh, no!" cried Jodi. She pushed her way through and tried to grab Malone's arm. "Listen—"

Malone brushed her away and levelled a warning finger. "Shut your mouth and stay in line!"

Jodi stood her ground. "Malone, please! I shipped out with this guy. He's okay, I promise you! I'll stake my life on it!"

Several of Malone's lieutenants cocked their weapons and covered Jodi to forestall any rash move. Malone drew his air pistol and with a slow, deliberate movement extended his arm, bringing the muzzle within an inch of Jodi's forehead. "Not another word . . ."

Jodi bit her lip and backed slowly away.

Using standard-issue axes, two renegades cut and sharpened a five inch thick stake then set about planting it firmly in the ground. Unable to tell whether he was about to be killed or merely suffer another round of punishment, Steve watched dull-eyed, mentally berating himself for obeying his instructions so precisely. If he had left the hide a day earlier he might have avoided meeting Malone's rag-taggle gang of cut-throats. On the other hand, he would not have encountered Jodi Kazan. It was obvious she had been reduced to subservience but she had, nevertheless, stuck her neck out as far as she dared and might still be able to provide some assistance—always assuming he survived Malone's next party trick.

Admittedly he had not improved the situation by mouthing off. Ever since he had soared off the ramp at Lindbergh Field and had come face to face with the overground, had felt its presence pierce the core of his being, Steve had found it increasingly difficult to hold his tongue. He had even pushed his luck with the President-General. Well, his luck had finally run out. Karlstrom had warned him that renegade groups had become extremely cautious about picking up stray Trackers. They had good reason to be. Like all graduates from Rio Lobo, Steve had been well-prepared for such an encounter. His knowledge of the area was encyclopaedic, his appearance could not be faulted, his cover story was watertight, and the two carefully-planted corpses were conclusive evidence that every word of it was true. Even the radio had been part of the care-fully rehearsed scenario.

Running into Jodi Kazan had been an unexpected bo-nus. Her word alone should have been enough to allay any doubts about his story. But, for some reason, her compan-ions seemed reluctant to believe her. Indeed, in Malone's case, his suspicions bordered on paranoia. The only way to satisfy him would be to admit the truth of his accusation. Not a good move. Given the renegade leader's simmering hatred of the Federation, it would be a graveside confes-sion. He just had to hang tough and take whatever nasti-ness Malone was preparing to hand out.

When the earth had been stamped flat leaving four feet of post sticking in the air, Steve was hustled over and forced to kneel with his back to it and with a leg on either side. He was then pulled tight against the post by ropes that went around his waist, chest and neck. Steve won-dered why his hands had been left free. The full horror of what lay in store soon became apparent. The week-old corpse of the cee-bee that Steve had shot and buried was dragged over and man-handled into a kneeling position facing Steve. Two renegades grabbed Steve's wrists, pulled his arms around the corpse and bound his wrists tightly together.

Steve pulled his head away from the grey, dirt-streaked face of the dead cee-bee and tried to avoid looking into the gaping eye sockets. "Hey, guys," he croaked through swollen jaws. "What is this? Come on, give me a break."

Yellow-Cap leaned towards him. "Friend, if you want to do yourself a favour, tell the man what he wants to hear."

"I already told you! I been out here since I powered down over Wyoming! It's Tyson and this guy who are the Feds!"

"You may be right," admitted Yellow-Cap.

"So why are you doing this to me?"

"We're just trying to get to the bottom line, Brickman. You claim you shot this guy—"

"That's right—"

"Yeah . . . but which one of you got off the plane?"

"He did!"

"So you say—but can you prove it?"

"Christo! What d'you want—a videogram from the P-G?! I know this area like the back of my hand. I got traps out everywhere. I can take you back to where I stashed what was left of Blue-Bird—"

Yellow-Cap cut him short. "If you wanted to get back home why didn't you use Tyson's radio?"

"I thought it was broken. I didn't know how to fix it."

Yellow-Cap responded with a sardonic smile. "Come on, you can do better than that. You're a wingman. You people are supposed to be sharp."

"We are. That's why I didn't try to call anybody. There was no point. Tyson had already screwed my chances of getting back home."

"Yeah, well, we only have your word for that."

"What was I supposed to do? Work my ass off keeping both of 'em alive until you guys decided to drop by?"

Yellow-Cap nodded. "Good point. Maybe you *are* a genuine drop-out. You just can't tell these days. For all you know we might be undercover Feds ourselves." He grinned. "That would be a real joke, wouldn't it?"

"Yeah, terrific," said Steve sourly. "I always wanted to meet one."

The two renegades who were securing the ropes pulled the corpse's arms over Steve's shoulders and tied them around the post. Yellow-Cap checked the bindings to make sure Steve could not wriggle out of the grisly embrace then undid the straps holding the combat knife to Steve's calf. "Guess you won't be needing this . . ."

Steve watched them all walk away with a mixture of despair and disbelief. Over by the dug-out, the other renegades were hitching up their backpacks and getting ready to depart. Jodi came over to Steve with a waterbottle. She knelt down on one knee and put it to his lips. "Compliments of Malone."

Steve responded with a harsh laugh. "What's this supposed to do—make me feel better, or prolong the agony?"

"Drink . . ." She let the water trickle into his mouth.

Steve swallowed thirstily but did not overdo it. "Thanks."

"Listen, I'm really sorry about this but—you didn't exactly help by mouthing off. We may look a raggedy-assed bunch but Malone runs a tight ship—the way Big D did aboard The Lady. You made it through the winter but only because you found this place and the guy who was living here showed you how. A breaker can't make it on his own. If you want to survive you have to run with the pack. And that means toeing the line the honcho lays down."

"I'll try and remember that. Mind how you go."

Jodi glanced over her shoulder then slipped a knife into the ground between Steve's knees where it could not be seen. "Hang on in there, good buddy," she whispered. "I'm still on your case." She stood up and screwed back the cap of the water bottle. "When we've gone, try working that post loose."

Steve nodded. Jodi rejoined the waiting renegades. Malone's party had already left. The remainder split up into several small groups, each of which took a different path towards the west.

Nobody looked back. It was as if he had ceased to exist.

Steve glanced up at the sky. It would not be long before he attracted the attention of the flying flesh-eaters. The burden of the dead cee-bee was already becoming intolerable. He shuffled his knees around in an effort to get rid of the cramps that were starting to build up in his legs. The ropes allowed him very little movement but by shifting his weight from one knee to the other he was able to ease the discomfort. Steve knew the relief was only temporary. The pain would get steadily worse and, in a matter of hours, would be continuous and unbearable.

The head of the cee-bee lolled forward onto his left shoulder. Steve pulled his face away and glanced down out of the corner of his eye. The corpse's mouth hung half open. A fly alighted by the side of it and went inside to explore.

Oh, Talisman, thought Steve. If it is true that I was born in your shadow, now is the time to prove it. If you can get me out of this, I swear I'll never doubt anything that Mr. Snow says about you ever again . . .

TWELVE

WHEN the last renegade had disappeared from view, Steve shuffled his knees forward as far as he could then pushed back hard against the post and tried to rock it from side to side. For a long time he seemed to be getting nowhere then, after a frantic bout of rocking in the arms of his dead partner, he managed to produce a small sideways movement. In fact, it was so small it was barely detectable. It didn't matter. It meant he was in with a chance. It was going to work, he told himself. You are going to get out of this, Brickman. He rested a while to catch his breath and ease his cramped muscles then returned to the attack, straining backwards and forwards to produce an all-round widening of the post hole.

The hours passed, each one bringing miniscule increments in the degree of movement. By nightfall, Steve had secured what he judged to be a couple of inches of movement in the top of the post and was able to rotate it by moving the upper part of his body.

Darkness brought respite from another problem. As the day had gone by, Steve had noticed his bonds had gotten tighter, making it difficult for him to breathe. It took him a while to work out what was happening. The disinterred corpse had started to swell up in the warm spring sunshine. It would get even bigger tomorrow. If he did not break free soon, he would end up crushed against the post suffocated by the ballooning body.

And then there were the dark, broad-winged birds with long hooked beaks. Several had gathered on the branches of the nearby trees and the bolder ones had fluttered down to take a closer look at the strange half-dead beast that had fallen to its knees in the middle of the clearing. Steve had driven them away with harsh animal-like screams—a product of his fear and his stiff, swollen jaw. The birds had turned their attention to the remains of the other, older corpse that had been unceremoniously dumped back in its shallow grave but left uncovered. Steve knew that when it had been picked clean, they would wait patiently for his voice and his body to weaken. And then. . .

The horrific images of what would happen if he did not escape released new reserves of strength. His initial panic had subsided. What he had to do now was to make the maximum use of his remaining energy. Throughout the night, with dogged determination, he worked his body back and forth and from side to side. The pain in his legs had expanded to fill his whole body and was now so intense his brain had become semi-anaesthetised. He had reached the point at which the overloaded nervous system translates suffering into a kind of perverse pleasure.

While Steve fought for his life, Commander-General Karlstrom lay back in a well-upholstered armchair in a small viewing room. Around him were other high-ranking members of the First Family. The film that was being shown that night was one of Karlstrom's favourites—a thousand year-old gem called "Sands of Iwo-Jima" starring the legendary John Wayne.

Wayne, who had died several decades before the Holocaust, had been the guiding light of the Founding Father— George Washington Jefferson the 1st. Ordinary Trackers knew nothing of actors or the pre-Holocaust film industry. The Federation neither possessed nor produced any art, drama or literature. There were no musicians or instru-

mentalists. All music was produced electronically; the only
singers, blue-sky balladeers fronting vocal ensembles from
the various bases. The video network provided by CO-
LUMBUS was the sole source of information and entertainment which, in the Federation, consisted of inspirationals and video-games. The First Family, however—like
all elites—had access to a veritable treasure house of pre-
Holocaust material stored in the air-conditioned vaults at
Cloudlands. The most highly prized items were the videotapes of Wayne's feature films and there was a large team
of expert technicians whose sole task was to maintain them
in a perfect state of preservation. In the best of his films,
Wayne enshrined all the noblest qualities of Trackerdom
and it was from this body of work that succeeding generations of Family leaders had drawn their strength and
inspiration.

Karlstrom watched Wayne die as he had countless times
before, the letter in his breast pocket was discovered and
read out, the Stars and Stripes was raised on the summit
of Mount Surabachi. For Karlstrom, the letter sequence
was embarrassingly sentimental but the overall message of
the film rang true, the defeat of the now-vanished nation
of Japan was a direct parallel to the present struggle for
control of the overground. When the final battle had been
won, Old Glory would fly side by side with the flag of the
Federation on all the peaks of North America. The blue-
sky world would have been regained through the sacrifices
of men and women with the same indomitable courage
and dedication.

When the film ended, Karlstrom took leave of the others and retired to his personal quarters. The video-screen
by his bed displayed a flashing logo indicating that two
messages were waiting in his electronic mail-box. Karlstrom
tapped out the command which brought the first message
up on the screen. It was a coded signal consisting of
several alphanumeric sequences. Inserting his private key-
card he entered a five-digit personal ID number then
pressed the "DECODE" button. The jumble of letters
and numbers rearranged themselves into words. It was a
signal from an MX field operative called High Sierra.

Karlstrom didn't need to check their identity. He had been waiting for them to make contact.

The message read: "HANG-FIRE TAKEN AND PUT TO THE TEST."

Karlstrom erased the signal from the circuit's memory, and screened the second message. It was from an MX operative at Inter-State U and it was about Brickman's kin-sister. During the evening study period Roz had developed severe breathing difficulties and on admission to the first aid section it was noted that red weals had appeared on her neck and wrists. She was being kept in under observation. Karlstrom acknowledged receipt of the message and asked to be kept informed of her progress. The uncanny relationship between Brickman and his kin-sister was proving an invaluable guide to his general state of health. As he undressed, Karlstrom mused on the prospect of what might happen if one of these "psychic-twins" had the misfortune to meet with a fatal accident. He took a leisurely shower then lay down in his clean, comfortable bed. The thought that AMEXICO's most promising new recruit would be spending a somewhat less comfortable night brought a faint smile to his lips. The experience Brickman was currently undergoing was deeply harrowing and painful but he was not in mortal danger. High Sierra would see to that.

As day dawned, the base of the post was still firmly rooted but there was an encouraging amount of play in the top. Pushing his body hard over to the right, Steve managed to extend his left leg straight out to the side then lift his knee. Once he had his foot on the ground he was able to apply more leverage to the post. After a while, he switched over to the right foot, pushing the post over and upwards to the left.

When the sun was well up into the morning sky, Steve detected a slight vertical movement in the post. Leaning sideways and then backwards, he tried to get both feet on the ground but it proved impossible. He was pinned too closely between the post and the body of the dead cee-bee. The continuing process of fermentation and decay

had inflated the corpse even further, causing the ropes
that bound them together to cut into Steve's body. Fortunately the cord around his throat was only attached to the
post behind him. He had avoided slow strangulation but
his neck was torn and bleeding from his efforts to loosen it
and he was now attracting the attention of the flies that
had been swarming over the dead cee-bee. Steve knew he
had to break free by sunset. Another day without water,
trapped under the suffocating weight of a rotting corpse
would weaken him to the point where he would be at the
mercy of the birds who had returned to feed on the
remnants of "Tyson." He began another bout of pulling
and pushing, shuffling slowly round in a circle, dragging
his dead partner with him.

The sun went down with Steve still pinned to the same
spot but just before darkness fell, he finally manoeuvred a
knee between the cee-bee's thighs and got both feet on
the ground at the same time. Rocking backwards and
forwards, and then around in a circle, he slowly straightened up and, with one last gut-busting heave, managed to
pull the post clear of the hole. It was then he found that
the post was longer than his legs making it impossible for
him to stand upright. He toppled sideways, his fall partly
cushioned by the swollen corpse, and lay there in the
gathering darkness without attempting to move, content to
enjoy the luxury of being able to stretch both legs.

When the cramps had eased to a dull ache, he took stock
of his situation. The knife. He had to find the knife. Jodi
had stuck it into the ground between his knees but he had
knocked it over as he had shuffled round and round in his
efforts to work the post loose. Where was it now?

Steve peered over the dead cee-bee's shoulders and saw
that the knife now lay across the widened post-hole. As he
had thrashed blindly around in his efforts to free himself,
he had inadvertently kicked the knife towards the hole. It
now lay with the blade tipped up at an angle and the
handle lodged precariously against the opposite side of the
hole, some six inches below the rim.

With painful slowness, Steve humped his double burden towards the knife. His two-day struggle against the

combined weight of the dead cee-bee and the post had sapped his strength to the point where he could barely move. But there was also another problem. He had a clear view over the cee-bee's shoulder but he could not see his own hands which were tied around the dead man's waist. He could manoeuvre himself into approximately the right position but from there on it would be pure guesswork. And he could not afford to make a mistake. One false move on his part might cause the handle to slip. If the knife dropped down to the bottom of the hole he was finished.

Reaching what he judged to be the best position, Steve probed the air delicately with his fingers. He felt the tip of his right middle finger brush the edge of the tilted blade. He took a deep breath and with infinite care, he nudged the dead body forward and tried again. This time he managed to slide the flat of the blade between the two middle fingers of his right hand. Gripping it as tightly as he could, he pressed down firmly on the tip of the blade with the first two fingers of his left hand and see-sawed the knife out of the hole. Dragging it clear, he laid it down carefully then slid it under his right hand and got a firm grip on the handle.

Well done, Brickman. Now for the next step. He had to free his hands but there was now no play in the rope that bound Steve's wrists together behind his victim's back. As the body became more and more distended, it had forced his palms apart making it impossible to grip the knife handle with both hands. There was only one thing to do. He had to vent the gases that had built up in the stomach and the abdominal cavity.

Guiding the blade between his fingers, Steve lodged it in the small of the back between the rib cage and the pelvis, wedged the butt of the handle in a small depression in the ground and drove the blade home by rolling their combined weight on top of it. The body emptied with a slow, gurgling hiss. A foul stench assailed Steve's nostrils and made his bile rise. He lay there coughing and retching then, a short while later, he noticed that the ropes had slackened off a little. He was still bound securely but the cords no longer bit deeply into his flesh.

Clawing at the handle of the knife, he succeeded in pulling it partway out. With the last quarter of the cutting edge exposed Steve began to saw through the cords around his wrists. A great surge of relief flooded through him as the last strands fell away. He was going to make it!

Cutting the other ropes took hardly any time at all. Steve stood up, stretched his aching limbs then stumbled down through the trees towards the stream, rubbing his chafed wrists to get the blood flowing again. He drank greedily. He had survived yet again—but for how long? Apart from the knife Jodi had provided and the clothes on his back he had nothing. The renegades had stripped the dug-out down to the dirt walls. They had taken every scrap of food, the fishtraps and snares, the firepot, his backpack, weapons, helmet, and the items of clothing removed from the dead cee-bees prior to their burial. Worst of all, they had taken his boots.

Steve started back up the slope, his initial feeling of euphoria fading rapidly as he considered the formidable problems that now confronted him. The object whose loss he felt most keenly was Naylor's combat knife. During his stay at Rio Lobo, a tiny but powerful radio transceiver had been cleverly concealed in the handle. Steve had been given the hidden device to allow him to make contact with an MX field-team. The task of the team was to keep track of his whereabouts and relay any messages to and from Karlstrom. They were, in theory, also there to provide back-up in an emergency—such as the jam he now found himself in. The loss of his radio-knife meant he was now unable to summon assistance. Once again he was on his own.

So be it. He preferred it that way.

Even so, Steve felt frustrated and vaguely disgruntled. MX should have foreseen the possibility that he might be relieved of all his kit and should have come up with a second device to cover such a situation. Quite where he could have concealed it he did not know. The only secure place was up his ass. And even that had its dangers. If, through some freak accident, the radio in the knife handle was discovered he could always disclaim knowledge of it on the grounds that it was not his knife. But if someone discovered a similar device stuffed up his rectum he could hardly claim to have sat on it by accident.

The sweat that had poured from Steve's body during his exertions started to congeal, causing him to shiver violently. It was a cold night, and would get even colder before dawn. Steve stared up at the heavens. The whole sky was covered by a dark, formless layer of cloud that blotted out the stars. How did the Mutes explain away a night like this, when the ten thousand thousand watchful eyes in Mo-Town's shimmering cloak no longer looked down upon them? Mr. Snow would have an answer. He had an answer for everything.

Steve laid the dead cee-bee face down in the shallow grave, kicked a layer of dirt over it and put back the stones then, fighting down a wave of nausea, he did the same for the eviscerated remains of "Tyson." The act of reburial was not inspired by any feelings of deference towards the two murdered men. Back in the Federation, once you were dead, that was it. Your body was disposed of with the same lack of ceremony with which one would throw out a heap of garbage. No, it was the birds. The broad-winged flesh-eaters that roamed the overground had a habit of circling high in the sky above a dead or dying animal before alighting to feed. The column of wheeling predators could be seen miles away, attracting the attention, not only of other birds but also Mutes, renegades and other, four-footed scavengers. Now that he was virtually defenceless Steve had no wish to give away his position. He dropped the last stone into place, gathered up the severed lengths of rope and went down into the hide with the sickly smell of death on his hands.

In pitch darkness, Steve felt his way over to the bunk, a rectangle of beaten earth raised a couple of feet above the rest of the floor. The covering of furs had gone. No matter. He threw himself down thankfully on the thick layer of dried fern. Bliss. Sheer luxury. Three words that did not feature in the Tracker vocabulary. A fact which did not prevent Steve from enjoying the sensation in the same

way he had experienced love without being able to put a
name to it.

Steve knew that resting up was the wrong thing to do.
He should have begun his trek towards the last reported
position of the clan M'Call immediately, but his exhausted
body simply would not respond. He ached from head to
toe. His skin was raw and bleeding where it had been torn
by the ropes, every layer of flesh and muscle fibre seemed
to be pierced by red-hot needles, a slow fire burned inside
his bones. Death, he thought, would be a welcome
deliverance.

He thought of Clearwater and the night they had spent
in each other's arms, the warmth of her embrace, the
supple responsiveness of her oiled and perfumed body.
The tumultuous emotions that had been released by their
conjoining and the pangs of bitterness at their forced sepa-
ration had haunted him ever since. He drifted off to sleep
but instead of the longed-for nothingness, he was plunged
into a confused dream state in which he found himself on
an endless journey through an alien landscape, menaced
by shadowy pursuers and beset by problems of mind-
blowing complexity and importance whose solutions he
knew but could not articulate. As a consequence, he woke
feeling as drained and exhausted as before.

Raising his head he saw daylight filtering down the
angled stairway. Christo! Time to get going. Easier said
than done. His back was still one solid slab of pain. With
slow, jerky movements he levered himself into a sitting
position on the edge of the bunk, and slumped forward,
head down. If he had not taken the precaution of resting
his elbows on his knees he would have hit the floor nose
first. Come on, Brickman, you can do better than this.
Move it!

Responding to the resident drill instructor that lurked
within the inner recesses of his brain Steve straightened
up and put himself through a short aerobic routine to
loosen his arm and leg joints. He would go down to the
stream, drink and freshen up, then try and find some way
to protect his feet. The Mutes used buffalo hide. Any skin

would do at a pinch but Malone's renegades had taken everything. He picked up a length of cord and, after considering various possibilities, wound it into a sausage-shaped coil. If the strands could somehow be stitched together it would form the sole of a primitive shoe. He could break down one of the cords into finer threads but what could he use for a needle?

As he wrestled with the problem he heard a faint muffled shout. Then other voices, indistinct but getting louder. Going to the bottom of the steps, Steve heard more shouts mixed with the fainter whooping cries of Mutes in hot pursuit. Then came what sounded like several bodies crashing through the surrounding undergrowth. He shrank back into the darkest corner. What the heck was he going to do? He was trapped! And then he remembered. Of course! The bolt-hole! The fur coverings had been stripped away but the earth and wickerwork plug was still in place. And the Mute crossbow with its bagful of bolts was in the small storage space behind it!

Before Steve could move, a flash of daylight pierced the gloom as the doorflap was thrust aside. Grabbing the knife, Steve darted into a corner where he could not be seen from the steps that led down into the hide and crouched down, ready to spring at the throat of his unwelcome visitor. The person that stumbled into view was someone he hadn't expected to see again. Yellow-Cap, weighed down by his back pack and air rifle, and very short of breath.

But not slow to react.

Sensing a hostile presence, Yellow-Cap spun around with his rifle aimed at Steve's chest and backed away from the raised knife. "Freeze, soldier!"

Steve froze but held on to the knife.

"I'm not looking for trouble," said Yellow-Cap. "So ease off, set the blade down, and everything'll be just dandy."

Jodi Kazan came crashing down the steps. She, too, was short of breath. When she glimpsed Steve she sagged against the wall and let the butt of her rifle fall to the floor. "Christo! There you are!" Her words were punctuated by a racking laugh. "At least it wasn't a—a totally—wasted journey—" She broke off again to gulp down more air and turned to Yellow-Cap. "Have you told him?"

"Gimme a chance. Your pal here was about stick it to me."

Jodi eyed Steve. "Not surprising, considering what you guys did to him."

"Just following orders, Kaz. Call him off."

"Okay, okay." she waved them both down. "Cool it, Brickman. This is no time to start fighting amongst ourselves." Jodi held out her hand for the knife. "Trust me."

Steve gave her the knife.

"Cover the stairs," said Yellow-Cap. He laid his rifle across his forearm and jerked a thumb towards Jodi as she moved into position. "This guy here's a real good friend of yours. I don't know what it was she said to the boss-man but he decided to give you a second chance. Guess he didn't figure on you getting away on your own." He gave Steve an admiring nod. "Ain't never heard anyone ever do that before. Yep . . . you are one real slippery sonofabitch." He offered Steve his hand. "Kelso's the name. Dave Kelso. Welcome aboard."

"Sounds like an offer I can't refuse," said Steve. Kelso's vice-like grip made him aware just how painfully stiff his hands were.

"Ungrateful bastard, ain't he?" said Kelso. "We risk our necks so as he can join the best bunch of breakers this side of the Rockies and he comes on like someone who's been handed a plate of lumpshit."

"Give him a chance, Kelso. He needs time to get adjusted." Jodi turned to Steve. "Malone agreed to let you join us provided I was willing to come and fetch you," she explained. "Kelso and a couple of other guys offered to backtrack with me in case I needed some help."

"Worse decision I ever made," grumbled Kelso.

"Why?" asked Steve.

"Because we're up to our asses in trouble, good buddy! Didn't you hear 'em? We got a big posse of Mutes on our tail!"

Before Steve could reply, the door flap was pushed roughly aside for a third time. Kelso and Jodi whirled

round to cover the stairway, then lowered their rifles as
two more renegades leapt down the steps and promptly
sank to their knees. The younger of the two looked a few
years older than Steve, the other had a weathered face
framed by a short, iron-grey beard and was wearing a
green command cap with a red cross on the front. The
white circle, framing the cross had been darkened down
with mud.

Jodi introduced the elder renegade first. "This is
Medicine-Hat, and that's Jankowski—Jinx for short. Steve
Brickman."

Both renegades answered with a nod.

"How does it look?" asked Kelso.

"Not too good," said Medicine-Hat. He paused to catch
his breath. "They're coming along both sides of the valley."

"They see you come in here?"

"Can't say," gasped Jinx. "Nearest one I saw was down
by the stream."

"Well, it's not gonna take 'em long to work out where
we are," grunted Kelso. He turned to Steve. "This is your
neck of the woods. You got any bright ideas?"

"We could always try the back way out." Steve scraped
the dirt from the centre of the plug to expose the piece of
wood that served as a handle and opened up the bolt-hole.

Kelso hunkered down and peered inside. He gave a low
whistle. "How far does this go?"

"It runs about eighty yards into the ridge. Comes up
amongst a pile of rocks in the middle of some thick scrub.
The other end is covered by a rock slab laid on a log
frame. You just lever it up."

Kelso looked at the others. "What d'you think?"

Medicine-Hat turned to Steve. "Have you used this?"

"No, but I have checked the exit. I was planning to
climb inside when I heard you guys coming—only I didn't
have time."

Medicine-Hat exchanged glances with Kelso then said.
"Let's do it."

"Okay, on your way, Brickman."

"I need a torch."

Medicine-Hat handed one over. Kelso produced a ball

of twine and tossed it to Jodi. "Go with him. Tie that on you. I'll reel it out as you go. When you get there, give two tugs. I'll acknowledge with one. If the route is clear, reply with another three then tie the torch on the end so that we can pull it back down. Mutes, or no Mutes, I ain't goin' in there without a light."

Steve paused by the entrance. "Anybody have a spare pair of boots?"

"You can have your own," said Jodi. "I brought 'em with me."

"Later," said Kelso. "We ain't got time to frig around with that now. He's caused enough trouble. Oh, and Brickman—"

"Yeah?"

"I'll take care of that crossbow . . ."

Steve showed Kelso how the last person through could close the bolt-hole behind him, then began to work his way along the tunnel. It was just high and wide enough for an average size person to move forward in a ground-hugging tiger crawl. The place was swarming with bug-uglies and the air inside felt stale and clammy on the tongue. The tunnel came up at an angle into the side of a small pit some four feet wide and six feet deep covered with logs and woven branches onto which earth and boulders had been laid.

Packed around the edges were smaller, supporting stones with narrow, sometimes hairline, apertures between them. These let in a glimmer of daylight and afforded a valuable glimpse of the surrounding terrain. Anybody escaping via the tunnel could thus hear, and to some extent see, what was going on outside and chose the most opportune moment to emerge.

Pushing her back-pack ahead of her, Jodi hauled herself halfway out of the access tunnel and turned her dirt-streaked face towards Steve. "Christo!" she whispered hoarsely. "I never want to do that again. See anything?"

"Not so far." Steve passed the torch down to her. "Get back inside the tunnel. I'm going to open up."

He crawled into a small recess cut into the side of the shallow pit, pushed up the flat-bottomed cover-stone and

poked his head out cautiously. A few shrill, bird-like cries—
which he recognised as signals between M'Call warriors—
reached his ears but they came from a long way off. He
clambered out, took a quick look round then stuck his
head back inside. "Jodi!"

Her head slid into view.

"There's nobody up here but the birds," he whispered.
"But I'm gonna take another look round to make absolutely sure. Stay there. When I rap three-two-three on
this cover stone, bring the others through."

"Okay!"

Steve lowered the rock slab back into place then rose to
his feet, turned and stopped dead in his tracks. Mr. Snow,
the white-haired wordsmith, sat cross-legged on a nearby
boulder, flanked by two M'Call Bears—Doctor-Hook and
Kid-Creole—two warriors who had attended Steve's quarterstaff classes.

Steve was momentarily speechless. The wily old Mute
must have been hiding close by all the time but the way
he had appeared made it look as if he had stepped out of
thin air. "Wha-what are you doing here?" he stammered.

Mr. Snow replied with an enigmatic smile. "Cadillac
said we'd meet again. He saw it in the stones. Aren't you
glad to see me?"

Steve felt the blood rush to his cheeks. "Yes—of course—
but . . ." His voice faltered again. Why did he feel so
uneasy whenever Mr. Snow's piercing glance fell upon
him? He wanted to ask for news of Clearwater but suddenly found himself tongue-tied, unable to speak her name.

Mr. Snow, as if sensing this, said, "I know. So many
questions. We'll have plenty of time to talk later. Why
don't you ask your friends to come out."

"There is just me, Old One. I don't have any friends."

Mr. Snow sighed. "Oh, Brickman, Brickman . . . I
thought we always told each other the truth."

Steve said nothing.

Mr. Snow threw up his hands. "Look, we know there
are at least four other people in there. No one is going to
harm them, so please—don't let's have any unpleasantness."

Steve didn't move.

Mr. Snow turned to Kid-Creole. "Pile some brushwood in front of the door. We'll try smoking them out."

The others didn't take long to come through.

THIRTEEN

JODI'S DESIRE to rescue Steve may have contributed to
their capture but they were not alone in their misfortune.
The clan had spread its net wide. As they marched towards
the north-west, other groups of M'Call Bears and She-
Wolves joined them, each with its own haul of renegades.
The final count, including Steve, was thirty-three. Malone
and his closest lieutenants had, apparently, evaded capture but, from the snippets of conversation he managed to
overhear, Steve got the impression that Malone had lost
about a third of his force.

From the way the M'Call warriors strutted around, Steve
could see they were delighted to have captured so many.
Steve guessed he owed his life—yet again—to Mr. Snow
but he could not understand why the renegades had been
spared. It also surprised him to learn that no one, on
either side, had been killed during the chase.

To prevent their escape, the renegades were split into
pairs and tied, side by side, by the wrists and throat, to a
length of sapling placed across their shoulders. Only Steve,
on Mr. Snow's orders, was allowed to walk unbound. The
preferential treatment did nothing to increase his popular-
ity with the other captives. Most of them, following Malone's initial reaction, still harboured lingering suspicions
about him and now that he was seen to be on familiar

terms with their captors they responded to his approaches
with sullen hostility, calling him a "beaver-lickin' bastard"
and "a lumpsucker"—the two most insulting epithets in
the Trail-Blazer vocabulary, reserved for those who con-
sorted with Mutes.

Following Mr. Snow's lead, the warriors treated him
with polite reserve. Steve saw many familiar faces among
the Bears and She-Wolves but they showed no sign of
recognising him. As far as they were concerned, he was
just another renegade. Which was fine with Steve. He had
viewed his run-in with Malone as an extremely unwelcome hiccup in his game-plan but his capture, along with
Jodi and her three companions had provided him with a
new cover story that was even better than the one he
started out with. The mysterious entity known as Talisman
had got him off the hook yet again. Whatever fate was in
store for the grim-faced bunch of breakers, Steven Roosevelt Brickman, would be okay. Mr. Snow had not said as
much, in so many words, but he had let Steve know, with
a nod and a wink, that their previous relationship still held
good.

As if to confirm this, the old wordsmith had allowed him
to recover his boots from Jodi's back-pack and had even
handed over Naylor's doctored combat knife that had been
found amongst Kelso's possessions during a general share-
out of the spoils. Kelso also lost his prized yellow command cap to one of the She-Wolves. Medicine-Hat, on the
other hand, still had his. For some reason, Mutes did not
appear to find green a desirable colour.

On the long journey back to the M'Call settlement,
Steve was given the task of tending to the captive renegades. Distributing water, flat bread and dried meat twists
was not a problem but some of the renegades had been
injured and their wounds needed expert attention. Steve
pleaded with Mr. Snow and secured the release of Jodi
and Medicine-Hat to help look after the others.

Despite being fed and watered, Kelso continued to eye
Steve with simmering resentment and made it clear on
several occasions that he viewed his capture as being
entirely Steve's fault and something for which, if he ever

had the opportunity, he would make him (Steve) pay dearly.

During a brief rest period, whilst sipping his ration of water from a flask held by Steve, Kelso spied the She-Wolf wearing his prized cap. He gave her a hate-filled glance as she walked past. "Friggin dick-eater," he snarled.

"Hey, hey, hey, keep it down!" muttered Steve. "What're you trying to do—get yourself killed?"

"Some chance," growled the renegade who sat cross-legged beside Kelso, his wrists and neck tied to the same pole. "If they was goin' to do that none of us'd be sittin' here."

"Right," said Kelso. He raised his voice and addressed a nearby group of Bears. "Look at 'em! D'ya ever see a bigger bunch of dumb-assed shit-heads?!"

"Christo!" hissed Steve. "What the eff-eff's got into you?!"

Kelso eyed him and laughed harshly. "Don't worry, lumpsucker. These friends of yours may bend us a little but we ain't about to go into the meat business."

"You mean because they didn't kill me when I powered down last year? Listen—these are the guys that almost took The Lady apart."

"That's different," said the other renegade.

"They won't kill us because we're too valuable." Kelso noted Steve's puzzled reaction. "I forgot. You're a new boy. April and May are open season for breakers. That's why we were heading west. Malone was aiming to get clear before the head-hunting season started. We didn't expect these lumps to be so quick off the mark."

"I still don't understand," said Steve. "I thought the Mutes and you guys left each other alone."

"That's right. Most of the time they do. But not when the wheel-boats come."

"The wheel-boats?" Steve's interest quickened. He tried to keep his tone casual. "Oh, yeah, I heard about them last year. Something to do with the Iron Masters—whoever *they* are. All I know is the Mutes trade food, skins and stuff in return for their crossbows. What they call "long sharp iron'."

Kelso nodded. "They also trade us."

"To the Iron Masters? What for?"

Kelso exploded. "I don't know what for! They're your friends—why don't you ask 'em?! Dick-head . . ."

Steve ignored Kelso's abusive language and looked at them both with evident concern. "Columbus . . . the Fire-Pits of BethLem . . ."

It was Kelso's turn to look puzzled.

"That's what the Mutes call the place where the Iron Masters come from."

"Terrific. Sounds great. I can't wait to get there."

"Listen," said Steve, "I know you guys don't trust me but if there is anyway to help you I will."

Kelso responded with a sneering laugh.

"You can help me right now," said his companion. "Unzip my pants. I'm dying for a leak."

Steve recognised him as one of the two renegades who had tied him to the post. He stood up and stepped back. "You left me zipped up for two days, compadre. Call me the day after tomorrow."

Medicine-Hat, who had done such a good salvage job on Jodi was a skilful doctor who, like many of the captured renegades, had gone adrift during a Trail-Blazer operation. In his case, it had been three years ago, during the last fire-sweeps that had culminated in the "pacification" of the pre-Holocaust state of Oklahoma—one of the three New Territories.

Sent out from The Fighting Kentuckian with a combat-squad to effect the rescue of some badly-wounded Trackers, Medicine-Hat and his companions had found their line of retreat cut off. The terrain had prevented the wagon-train from reaching them, bad weather had denied them air support and their radio had malfunctioned. When he and the surviving Trackers had finally reached the original rendezvous point the wagon-train had left the area, having posted them as "missing, believe killed in action."

As was usually the case, several of the survivors had become disoriented, sinking into a catatonic state from which they had not recovered. Medicine-Hat was one of three who, despite their lineman grading, had managed to live through that first critical two-week period. He could not explain why he had been spared but there was, apparently, a simple rule. If your group numbered four or less and you were still on your feet and moving after three days of being out of contact with the wagon-train it meant you probably wouldn't go "ground-sick." Whether or not you regarded this discovery as good news was another matter entirely.

As the trek continued, Steve had an opportunity to talk with Medicine-Hat and Jodi about what it was like to live as renegades, or breakers, as they preferred to call themselves. Medicine-Hat explained that not every breaker had gone adrift. Some were straight-forward deserters—mainly from way-stations. Usually they were cee-bees seeking to avoid punishment. Sometimes it was a low-level code violation but there were other, more serious cases of indiscipline, assault on an Exec, blackjacking, smoking grass, or, worse still, cowardice in the face of the enemy. There was also the catch-all charge of "operational failure." Rather than face a Board of Assessors and possible execution for dereliction of duty, many otherwise loyal and competent Trail-Blazers had chosen to go over the side.

To hold such unruly and disparate elements together demanded an iron fist allied to a keen intelligence. Unfortunately, said Medicine-Hat, there weren't enough honchos with Malone's mixture of toughness and vision. As a consequence, many groups of breakers perished through fratricidal disputes over leadership and the consequent failure to agree on a coherent strategy that would ensure their survival. When pressed by Steve to say whether the renegades were numbered in hundreds or thousands, all Medicine-Hat would say was—"Ask the First Family."

In a subsequent conversation, Medicine-Hat revealed there was a third group of breakers. Small groups who had succeeded in escaping from the Federation's underground bases, usually through illegally constructed tunnels. The phrase "tunnelling-out" had quickly entered the unofficial Tracker vocabulary as a synonym for any emotional high but was now used almost exclusively by reafers to describe the extended moment of euphoria that came from smoking rainbow grass.

In the short and somewhat imprecise history of renegade existence it was these fugitives from the Federation who were the original breakers and it was they who had coined that name for themselves. Medicine-Hat was of the opinion that it was probably derived from the historic event known as "The Break-Out." The moment in 2464 when, according to the Manual of the Federation, the first permanent interface between the earthshield and the overground was finally established, allowing the battle for the blue-sky world to begin in earnest.

Steve shook his head in disbelief. "I had no idea there were ways to escape from inside the Federation. What kind of people are involved? Where's it happening—and how?"

Medicine-Hat smiled. "I imagine it's people who don't agree with the way the First Family runs things. I'm told that, if you look hard enough, you'll find them all over the Federation. As to how . . ." He shrugged. "Best not to ask. The less you know about things like that the less there is to tell the folks back home."

"You mean if I get picked up?"

"If your Mute friends don't trade you with the rest of us, you may soon have a bunch of Trail-Blazers' breathing down your neck." Medicine-Hat checked through the contents of his first aid bag. "You've done time on a wagontrain. It's not just Mutes they're looking to kill. Breakers are a high priority target too."

"True," admitted Steve. "But what do you expect when you jump the rails? Even so, I've never understood why the Family spends so much time and energy trying to wipe you guys out. I mean, with conditions the way they are out here none of us are going to be around for very long."

Medicine-Hat treated him to another faint smile. "When did you power down?"

"June 12th, last year."

"And how do you feel? You been sick? Noticed any skin lesions? Your gums been bleeding?"

"No, not yet," replied Steve. "But I had my quarterly MedEx aboard The Lady. I got a shot of anti-radiation serum a few days before I powered down. And I got another one from Tyson—the guy I found living in that dug-out."

"Oh, yes . . . the undercover Fed."

"Right."

"I know about vitamin shots but . . . anti-radiation serum . . ." Medicine-Hat eyed Steve derisively. "Who gave you that story?"

"Tyson. He was worried about running out of the stuff. Said he was down to his last three capsules."

"You told Malone that Tyson was planning to hand you over to the Feds. If he was running out of this 'serum,' why would he share it with you?"

"He didn't," replied Steve glibly. "I injected myself after I shot him."

"And you think this is what has stopped you falling sick."

"Isn't it what you guys have been using?"

Medicine-Hat responded with a wry laugh. "Wake up, Brickman. Every item in this bag has come from the pockets of dead Trail-Blazers. Okay. Malone was tough on you. He had reason to be. You know what those undercover Federal sons of bitches have been doing? Like Tyson and that other guy you killed? Booby-trapping the goddam bodies! When you move 'em, or pick up their equipment— BLAM!" He threw up his hands and sighed. "Lost three good men that way. You wanna know something? It's over a year since I broke open my last wound dressing. And as for morphine . . . getting hold of that is harder than getting your hands on the President-General's dong. I haven't, personally, taken a pill or a shot of anything for the last three years."

Steve shrugged. "Maybe you're immune."

"Maybe . . ." Medicine-Hat eyed Steve. "I can see you've got a lot to learn."

"It could happen, couldn't it?" insisted Steve.

"Yehh . . ." said Medicine-Hat with a laugh. "Once you been out here for a while you discover all kinds of things are possible." He slipped his head through the strap of his first aid bag and stood up. "Better go check on my patients."

Seven days after their capture, Steve and his fellow captives came in sight of the M'Call's spring settlement. On the way in, Steve noticed several patches of ground that had been dug up to form new crop-fields. The Mutes tending the soil abandoned their tools and rushed to join the happy crowd that flocked out to meet the returning warriors.

When the triumphal procession reached the outlying huts, Mr. Snow drew Steve to one side and handed him over to Kid-Creole and Doctor-Hook. "I want you to go to my hut and wait till I come for you. May I take it that you won't do anything to cause me further embarrassment?"

Steve held up his right hand, Tracker-style. "I promise."

"So you said before."

"I can explain all that."

"I'm sure you can. But it'll have to wait. I have to attend a little celebration."

Steve laid a hand on Mr. Snow's arm as the old word-smith went to turn away. "Listen—I just want you to know that I regret what I did. I shouldn't have run away."

Mr. Snow tried not to smile. Having managed to catch Brickman off balance he now had to try and keep the advantage. "In the circumstances it was probably the wisest thing to do."

Steve wondered what lay behind that remark. How much did the crafty old coot know? "That may be so," he replied, "but when I left, part of me remained here . . ."

How true, thought Mr. Snow.

". . . and my one wish," continued Steve, "has been to return."

Mr. Snow accepted this avowal with a gracious nod. "Your wish has been granted." He indicated their surroundings with a sweep of his hand. "Enjoy it while you can."

Steve watched uneasily as the old wordsmith rejoined the long column and saw that Jodi and Medicine-Hat had been tied side-by-side to a sapling. He caught their eye as they were driven past with the other renegades into the settlement and gave them what he hoped was a reassuring look.

Drums started an incessant beat, developing and repeating increasingly elaborate rhythmic sequences. As Steve knelt to enter the wordsmith's hut the drums were joined by stick instruments, reed pipes and voices; separate melodic threads subtly woven together to form a vibrant tapestry of sound.

To the assembled renegades, hearing it for the first time, it must have been an awesomely frightening experience. A savage, alien symphony that awakened their worst fears, those deep-rooted primal terrors that lurked in the blood and which had been reinforced during childhood. For the ordinary Tracker, this was something that years of living on the overground could never totally dispel.

Steve understood but remained untouched. He lay back on the woven grass mats and let the waves of sound wash over him. His body seemed to resonate to the music, bringing him into harmony with the world around him. It felt . . . it felt as if he . . .

Had come home.

Home. Steve knew the word was to be found in the Federation's video-dictionary but he was suddenly aware that the word held some special, deeper meaning for him. And he heard voices again. Distant echoing whispers that he could not quite decipher. Like the voice he had heard on catching his first glimpse of the overground. The magic moment of awakening he had shared with Roz.

Was it the music, or was it the familiar odours of herbs and dried fruits draped in bunches around the walls of the hut that had triggered this reaction? Or was it his total response to the overground? He was, after all, entering his third week of . . .

Freedom.

The Federation, the First Family, Karlstrom and his secret war games suddenly seemed a long way off and strangely irrelevant. It was as if a door had unlocked in the recesses of his mind, opening up new avenues, new vistas of consciousness. He was being invited to begin another stage in the journey towards deeper knowledge and understanding. He would go, but reluctantly, for beyond these fresh horizons lay the hidden secrets about his true nature that he both coveted and feared. Mr. Snow had likened the search for Truth to climbing a mountain. But what he had omitted to say was that the unwary, or the misguided, could lose their footing on the way to the summit and be plunged into the abyss.

Darkness fell; the celebrations continued. Steve fuelled the fire-stone to light the interior of the hut then lifted the door flap and saw that a large bonfire had been lit on one edge of the settlement.

Some time later, Mr. Snow thrust his head into the hut and beckoned to Steve. "Okay, let's get it over with."

Kid-Creole and Doctor-Hook were waiting outside. On a signal from Mr. Snow, they draped a long, hooded cloak over Steve's shoulders then retired out of earshot. The cloak was made up of an irregular patchwork of small skins, dyed in a variety of dark colours. It also smelt. But that was something Steve was rapidly readjusting to.

"What's this in aid of?" he asked.

Mr. Snow pulled the hood forward so that Steve's face was completely shadowed. "You're about to be resurrected. Apart from Cadillac and Clearwater, no one knows you escaped. Everyone thinks you were killed in that landslide."

"With Motor-Head . . ."

"And his two friends. Yes. Their bodies were recovered, of course."

"And Blue-Bird?"

Mr. Snow shrugged. "It was buried along with you."

"What about Motor-Head's other friends—the ones who didn't want me around?"

Mr. Snow laughed dryly. "Let me worry about that. You're past history, Brickman. All these people have forgotten what happened last year. As their wordsmith, it's my job to remind them."

"Which also means you can choose what they remember."

Mr. Snow responded with a mischievous smile. "Exactly. It's a great responsibility." He patted Steve's shoulder. "Come on, let's go." As they walked towards the waiting warriors he said, "Oh, by the way—can you do an aerial somersault?"

Steve hesitated. "Well, I haven't done one in a long time but I imagine so—at a pinch. Why?"

"Everybody's high. If I hit 'em now, I should be able to paint you back into the picture without too much trouble. But I need your help to create a little excitement. A little razzmatazz."

"Razzmatazz . . . ?"

"Forget it." Mr. Snow handed him over to Kid-Creole and Doctor-Hook. "They'll tell you what to do."

"Wait a minute! What do I have to say?" hissed Steve, as he was led away into the darkness.

"Nothing! *I'll* do the talking. Just make sure you don't blow your entrance by falling in the fire!"

The assembled clan-elders squatted in a semi-circle facing a large bonfire that had been lit near the edge of the surrounding forest. The entire clan, apart from those on guard, was ranged behind them. Rolling-Stone, the wiry chief elder who had survived yet another White Death, sat in the middle of the front row; the drummers and the players of wind and stick instruments were grouped on either flank. All of them listened spell-bound to Mr. Snow, who strode up and down the front row pausing every now and then to fling his arms up into the sky.

Walking shoulder to shoulder, Kid-Creole and Doctor-Hook circled round through the trees with Steve tucked in close behind them. They stopped just beyond the leaping circle of orange light, their broad-shouldered bodies masking the cloaked figure of Steve from the view of those seated on the other side of the flames. Flurries of sparks spiralled upwards into the starry sky. The heat was tremendous. Steve remembered Good-Year's dreadful death and felt suddenly uneasy. If these guys didn't do it right . . . He tried to concentrate on what Mr. Snow was saying but the drums and the equally thunderous reponses from the clan drowned his words.

"Heyy-YAHH!! Heyy-YAHH!!" they roared, fists punching the air above their heads.

Mr. Snow held up his arms then swept them round towards the fire in a gesture of supplication. Steve saw something leave his hand and fall into the flames. There was a dull "whoo-oompf." A dazzlingly bright light flared briefly in the heart of the fire and was quickly swallowed up by billowing clouds of dense white smoke. Now completely hidden from the audience, Kid-Creole and Doctor-Hook moved closer to the bonfire and offered Steve a cupped hand.

Come on, Brickman. Nothing to it . . .

Steve placed a boot on each palm and laid his hand on their heads to steady himself. In one swift movement, they raised him level with their shoulders then straightened their arms like well-oiled pistons, punching him high into the air. Looking down, Steve saw tongues of orange fire shooting up towards him through the swirling clouds of smoke. A rising blast of heat slammed into him, searing his throat and lungs. For one brief moment, Steve's nerved failed then, an instant later, he snapped back into action. He jack-knifed his body, turned head over heels then threw his arms out sideways, spreading the dark cloak like the wings of a giant bird of prey as he curved down to earth, landing on the balls of his feet by the side of Mr. Snow.

The old wordsmith grabbed Steve's wrist as he bounced back up and raised it above his head like an old-time boxing referee. "Well done," he muttered. He turned to address his wide-eyed audience. "You see how my words echo the will of the Thrice-Gifted One?!" he cried. "First Talisman gives us a great victory and now the cloud-warrior he sent from the sky and took back through the earth is returned to us to perform a mighty deed in his name!"

The ground shook as the clan leapt to its feet and roared approvingly; the drums thundered. "HEYY-yahh! Heyy-yahh, heyy-yahh, HEYY-YAAHHH!!"

Steve was filled with sudden foreboding. "What do they expect me to do?"

"Don't worry," said Mr. Snow. "I'll think of something."

"What about Kid-Creole and Doctor-Hook? If they talk, won't it ruin everything?"

Mr. Snow shook his head. "I put their minds to sleep and told them to forget what happened."

Before Steve could react to the news that he had been given the heave-ho by two zombies he found himself surrounded by Mutes, laughing and shouting and leaping up and down. As they made their way back to Mr. Snow's hut, the clan formed two jostling lines on either side, those at the rear running round to the front to catch another glimpse of the newly-returned cloud-warrior. Men, women and children called out to him excitedly as he passed between the rows of bright-eyed, eager faces. Hands reached out to touch him. Steve could only presume that their owners hoped some of Talisman's powers he was thought to possess would flow into them. Kid-Creole and Doctor-Hook, Mr. Snow's, strong but silent bodyguards, thrust aside those who got in the way.

Steve tried to adjust to the new situation. The rapid changes in his fortunes has left him momentarily bewildered. How stupid. He, more than anyone, should have realised that the Mutes, with their faulty memory banks, might not remember him. But not even he, in his wildest dreams, could have imagined making such a triumphant return. As they entered Mr. Snow's hut, a small, still nagging voice warned him to be on his guard.

Something was wrong. Things were going far too well. Brickman had always considered himself to be lucky but he was not prone to self-deception. He had achieved his first objective but it should not have been this easy.

When the last group of celebrants had drifted away and some semblance of normality had returned, Night-Fever, the She-Wolf with the fearsome bucket-jaw, appeared with two clan-sisters and laid small dishes containing a variety of hot and cold food before them. Steve thanked them profusely. The three She-Wolves retreated on their knees—a sign of submissive devotion. As she lowered the door-flap, Night-Fever treated Steve to a hot-eyed glance. The mes-

sage, which transcended the need for language, was unequivocal. Night-Fever may have ranked zero on a scale of
one to ten in terms of attractiveness but she certainly
deserved full marks for persistence.

Steve turned to Mr. Snow and saw his amused smile.
"I thought you said no one remembered me."

Mr. Snow began to eat. "Some people's memories are
better than others."

Steve wondered if this was another allusion to Clearwater. He had a strong suspicion that Mr. Snow was playing
one of his devous games. They would have to talk about
her sooner or later. Indeed, Steve had lost count of the
times he had mentally rehearsed the conversation but now
that they were face to face he did not know how to begin.
He had been hoping to catch sight of Clearwater but so
far, he had been disappointed. Cadillac should have been
at Mr. Snow's side during the ceremony but he too had
failed to appear. Perhaps the young wordsmith had discovered what had happened with Clearwater and was reluctant to meet him. Best not to rush it. Let everything
happen in its own time. Let them do the talking. Steve
selected one of the small dishes. Thin slivers of meat in a
thick, spicy sauce. Memories flooded back as the aroma
entered his nostrils. He ate hungrily.

Mr. Snow sat cross-legged on the other end of the talking-
mat and studied the cloud-warrior. Brickman was also
making a great effort to appear relaxed but, in his case, it
wasn't working. His inner turmoil was reflected in his
eyes; his perplexity was almost palpable. Mr. Snow had
spoken the truth when he has said that Cadillac had seen
the cloud-warrior's return in the stones. But he had not
expected him to appear during the hunt for the red-skins;
the sandworms who had fled their underground burrows.
Fortunately, Mr. Snow had managed to hide his surprise.
As a result, Brickman was under the impression that they
were there to meet him. Since this enhanced Mr. Snow's
reputation for omniscience, and put Brickman at a temporary disadvantage, why disillusion him? He would soon
recover his natural guile.

Brickman was a born deceiver but then, that was only to be expected. He had been fashioned by others to live a lie. His true self could be reclaimed but not through the actions of someone on the outside. The layers of deception had to be stripped away by Brickman himself, from within. The process of self-discovery, in which Clearwater had such an important part to play, had begun. Mr. Snow could sense the cloud-warrior's mind was opening but, in many respects, he was still burdened by the blindness that afflicted all sand-burrowers.

One day, that darkness would lift from his inner eye and on that day, the powers that now lay dormant within the cloud-warrior would be awakened. This much, Mr. Snow had learned from the Sky Voices; what they had not made clear was whether these powers were a gift from the Beings of Light or the Creatures of the Abyss. Cadillac had predicted that Brickman would return with death hiding in his shadow and would carry Clearwater away on a river of blood. So be it. The Wheel turned. The Great Dying had been foreseen long ago. In the wider destiny of the Plainfolk the fate of the clan M'Call was unimportant; his own demise—now only months away—of no account. If this was the will of Talisman these things would come to pass. His spirit and those of the clan would return. The struggle would continue.

For Mr. Snow only one question remained and he prayed that it would be answered before he went to the High Ground. The Sky Voices had said that the cloud-warrior was destined to be a leader of his people. But whose side was he on? Which people would he choose to lead? Was he the Talisman—or was he his dark twin, the Death-Bringer—sired by Pent-Agon, Lord of Chaos, whose hideous strength might, once again, be unleashed against the Plainfolk in the final battle for the blue-sky world?

When they had finished eating, Mr. Snow reached for his pouch of rainbow grass, filled the bowl of his pipe and lit it with a grass taper from the fire-stone. Steve watched him draw the smoke into his lungs then took the pipe from his outstretched hands.

"So . . . what happened?"

Good question. Steve had originally intended to feed Mr. Snow the same story he had given Malone, then following his capture with Jodi and Kelso, he had hurriedly adapted it to suit his new circumstances. Now that he was here, and had been accepted back with some ceremony he realised that any attempt to lie would totally destroy whatever was left of their original relationship. There were still things that didn't add up. For that reason alone he had to remain on his guard but it was vital he appeared to withhold nothing. If he hoped to regain some measure of trust, nothing less than the truth would do.

Or a reasonable facsimile of it.

Steve drew deep on the pipe and prepared to unburden himself. His decision had lightened him considerably. He hated the mental turmoil, the feeling of powerlessness that came in the dark moments of indecisiveness. He liked things clear, clean cut; the rainbow grass made it all seem simpler still. "I have failed you, Old One."

Mr. Snow took another turn on the pipe. "Tell me about it."

Steve launched into his confession. How he had been consumed by an overpowering desire to possess Clearwater since first catching sight of her during the ceremony of Biting the Arrow. The furtive looks they had exchanged as she had been escorted about the camp, the fatal night when she had come to his hut while Mr. Snow and Cadillac were absent. Powerless to resist and unmindful of the dangers, he had broken his promise to Mr. Snow, betrayed the trust of the clan and his friendship with Cadillac. Unable to face the consequences of his actions and in a desperate bid to save Clearwater from sharing in his disgrace, he had decided to run away.

Mr. Snow listened silently, with the occasional solemn nod, as Steve recounted his fight with Motor-Head, Black-Top and Steel-Eye, his perilous flight south aboard Blue-Bird, which had ended at the Pueblo way-station, his arrest and return to the Federation in chains, his trial before the Assessors, his banishment to the A-Levels, and how Roz, his kin-sister had been used as a hostage to wrest the final secret from him. Secrets he had sworn to keep.

It had, Steve confessed, been a crushing, double betrayal, first by succumbing to his desires for Clearwater, then by breaking under interrogation. It was . . . unforgivable.

"You're right," muttered Mr. Snow, his eyes twinkling. "I'm surprised you had the nerve to come back."

"I had no choice, Old One. I learned many things from your lips last year. My destiny is bound up with the Plainfolk. My life or death is in your hands."

"Perhaps . . ."

Steve went on to describe how he had been unexpectedly lifted out of the A-Levels and offered a chance to win back his former status by becoming a secret agent of the Federation.

"And you accepted . . ."

"It was my only chance to escape," replied Steve. "To get back here. To see Clearwater again."

"Even though your journey could have ended in death. . ."

Steve responded with a fatalistic gesture. "I'm a Tracker. The overground kills us with every breath we take. If I'd turned down Karlstrom's offer I'd have been sent to the wall. This way, at least, I can die looking up at the sky."

"What did your masters ask you to do?"

After a moment's hesitation Steve said, "They wanted me to find you, win back your trust, then lead you, Cadillac and Clearwater into a trap. The plan was to bring you back alive to the Federation."

"Why?"

"After what you did to The Lady, they fear your magic. The three of you represent an unwelcome concentration of power. They are worried that the M'Calls might join forces with other clans under your leadership."

"But it is not I who lead this clan. Our chief is Rolling-Stone."

"In name only," replied Steve. "You're the brains of the outfit. I've watched Cadillac. I know how it works. And so

does the First Family. They know all about wordsmiths
and summoners and rings of power. And they know about
the Talisman Prophecy too."

Mr. Snow smiled. "But do they believe it?"

"Oh, yes. They heard about it a long time ago."

"Why did they choose you?"

Steve shrugged. "I was the only one that could identify
you. And the only person with any chance of getting near
you."

"Of course, yes . . . and if the plan to kidnap us failed?"

"I was told to kill you."

Karlstrom had called it "removing them from the
equation."

Mr. Snow accepted his reply with a brief nod. "I see.
Thanks for letting me know. Tell me—were you supposed
to do all this single-handed?"

"No." Steve unsheathed the doctored combat knife and
laid it on the mat between them with the handle towards
the old wordsmith. "Somewhere out there is an eight-man
team waiting to hear from me. Inside the handle of that
knife is a device which allows me to speak to them."

Mr. Snow picked up the knife, inspected it closely and
shook his head in wonderment. "It is said your people are
masters of the High Craft." He handed the knife back to
Steve. "Whatever will they think of next?"

"Don't you want to know how it works?"

"Do you intend to use it?" countered Mr. Snow.

"Not unless you want me to." Steve slipped the knife
back into the sheath strapped to his leg.

The old wordsmith eyed him carefully. "So—does this
mean you are prepared to betray your masters?"

"Have I not told you everything, Old One?"

"You have told me many things," replied Mr. Snow.
"But words are not deeds. Are you also prepared to kill
your own kind? And what about your kin-sister?"

"Don't worry. I haven't forgotten. She's the one big
problem. It's a risk I have to take. I think she'll be okay. If
they kill her, they no longer have any leverage." Steve
shrugged. "There comes a time when you have to choose
whose side you are on."

"Fortunately I don't have that problem," said Mr. Snow. "But for someone like you it, uh . . . must be a difficult decision."

Steve shrugged. "Something happened to me out here. Don't ask me what it was. All I know is that when I went back underground I felt as if I was being buried alive. Since the day I was born I've been taught to think of you people as the enemy. As sub-human creatures who must be wiped off the face of the earth. You and Cadillac taught me to see things differently, to understand that there was another way. When I got back I tried to tell them but no one would listen. They told me I was sick in the head. That's why they sent me to the A-Levels, as punishment for daring to suggest there was room for both Tracker and Mute in the blue-sky world."

The old wordsmith closed his eyes as he inhaled more smoke. "You were brave to speak such words but you were wrong. It will never be possible for the Plainfolk to breathe the same air as the sand-burrowers. We spoke of this before. Your masters are the slave of Pent-Agon. Their forefathers unleashed the War of a Thousand Suns that drenched the world in blood and put an end to the Old Time. As punishment, they were buried beneath the earth and there they must remain until the River of Time runs dry."

"But that's crazy," protested Steve blurrily. "You're being as blind and as unyielding as they are. There must be some way we can do a deal."

"Compromise" was the word he ought to have used but it was not part of the Tracker vocabulary.

Mr. Snow shook his head. "No way, Brickman." For the Mutes, too, the word had perished along with the Old Time.

"But you're prepared to give me a chance. What about the other people who feel the same way? Like these renegades you've captured, for instance."

The old wordsmith smiled distantly, his eyes half closed. "Why should you care about what happens to them? They tied you up to a corpse and left you to die."

Steve lowered the pipe and placed a hand on top of his head in an effort to hold his brain in place while he grappled with this totally unexpected remark. "Wait a minute, wait a minute . . . are you telling me you saw what they were doing and did nothing about it—that you left me tied up for two whole days while you sat around picking your nose? Christopher Columbus! How could you—?"

"Whoa! Hold it!" Mr. Snow made a soothing gesture. "Slow down. I was miles away." He took the pipe back. "Someone told me what happened. Anyway, what are you complaining about? The girl left you a knife. By the time I arrived on the scene you were up and running with your new friends. You certainly don't waste time, Brickman. What story did you tell them?"

Steve tried to collect his thoughts. Before his last-minute decision to opt for a full confession he had been about to tell Mr. Snow he had become a fully-fledged breaker, running with the pack. Close! "Uh . . . they changed their mind about killing me. Going along with them was the only chance I had of staying alive. I planned to break away at the first good opportunity." He smiled. "I had no idea you were going to find me first."

It was Mr. Snow's turn to shrug. "Like I said, Cadillac saw it in the stones."

Steve took another turn on the pipe. "What else did he see?"

"Ohh . . . lots of things."

"Like what for instance?"

"Like the fact you would come back for Clearwater. However . . ." Mr. Snow took the offered pipe and drew deep. ". . . I'm afraid you're in for a disappointment."

Steve blinked rapidly in an effort to overcome a sudden wave of drowsiness. "How do you mean?"

"Clearwater isn't here. Neither is Cadillac. They flew to Beth Lem."

Steve felt his stomach turn to stone. "Flew . . . ?"

"Yes. Flew. After you took off with Blue-Bird, Cadillac built another craft from the pieces we kept hidden from you."

"B-but how?"

"How?" Mr. Snow laughed. "You *showed* him how! And in so doing, you allowed him to pick your brains. Some wordsmiths—and I regret to say I am not one of them—have special gifts when it comes to absorbing and transmitting knowledge. When you gave him the chance to make the connection he just added the totality of your knowledge to his."

"I don't believe it," said Steve. His voice seemed to come from outside himself. He tried to shake off the pleasantly numbing effect of the grass.

"It's true nevertheless," continued Mr. Snow. "Pity you didn't see it. It had a motor, seats for both of them. I must say, I was very impressed. And I'm sure the Iron Masters were too."

This isn't really happening, Steve told himself. It's the grass. I'm imagining all this. It can't be true. It can't be . . . "But why go to the Iron Masters?" he heard himself say.

Mr. Snow spread his hands. "It was part of the deal. We agreed to deliver an arrowhead and the secrets of flight and, in return, the Iron Masters promised to give us new long sharp iron. Something that will stop a wagon-train dead in its tracks." He leaned forward and patted Steve on the knee. "And it's all thanks to you."

Steve started to come down rapidly. He thought about what Karlstrom had said about teaching Cadillac to fly. If the First Family ever discovered that Cadillac had passed on the whole goddam technology of flight to the Iron Masters then he, Brickman, would be well and truly shafted.

"Wha—when did this happen? When did they, uh—go?"

"Last year. Before the White Death."

Steve swallowed hard. He could see that Mr. Snow was enjoying himself hugely. Bastard . . . Six months . . . "Are they coming back?"

"Yes. When the wheel-boats ride up the great river."

"When will that be?"

"In one and a half moons."

Six weeks. Time for all kinds of things to happen . . .

Mr. Snow smiled mischievously. "Do you think you can wait that long?"

"I can wait forever, if necessary," said Steve. "Is she, uh—are they well?"

"I believe so, yes." Mr. Snow didn't actually know for sure but he felt Brickman was in need of a little reassurance.

"Thank for telling me," muttered Steve. His mind was still reeling from the news of Clearwater's absence and the countless ramifications that proceeded from the manner of her departure.

"You shared your secrets with me."

"I wanted to. I needed to."

Mr. Snow reponded with a slight bow of the head. "I appreciate your honesty. In return, there are things I must tell you. The Sky Voices—in which you do not yet believe—grant me knowledge of many things. Wisdom, however, does not cure our natural weaknesses; it only illuminates the path to perfection." He shrugged. "I still have a long way to go. There are times when I fall prey to foolish conceits but . . . I am not easily deceived—"

"I am not trying to de—"

Mr. Snow held up his hand. "Hear me out. I already knew about the relationship between you and Clearwater. I could see you both felt the same way, and wanted the same thing—in fact you could think of nothing else—but it was *I* who made it happen."

Steve's eyed widened. "You—?"

"Yes, I know. I warned you to stay away." He threw up his hands. "Situations change. I just do as I'm told. All any of us can do is play it as written. But if it's any help—and this is strictly off the record—I once went through something similar myself. Loving someone you can't be with is like having a red-hot knife twisted round in your guts. I understand, believe me. But there are still dangers. Be cautious, but do not feel ashamed. Treasure the moment. They don't come that good that often. It was meant to be. You are both guided by the will of Talisman."

The next question was a long time coming. "Does, uh—Cadillac know what happened?"

"Yes."

"Does *he* understand?"

Mr. Snow grimaced ruefully. "He will eventually."

Steve placed his palms together and bowed low over them. "I treasure your words. Old One."

Mr. Snow replied with a similar gesture. "You are wise to do so. Where I'm concerned, advice, like wisdom, is a gift that is rarely bestowed twice." He passed the pipe to Steve. "We're talked enough. Let's hit the sky."

Steve closed his eyes and inhaled deeply several times.

Mr. Snow saw the cloud-warrior's body relax visibly as his mind floated free. That's right, Brickman. Make the most of it. And hang onto your hat. Because when you come down I've got a feeling you're in for a bumpy ride . . .

High in the night sky above the southern horizon, two Sky-riders from Karlstrom's private air force flew back and forth along cloud-stacked corridors in a pattern that kept the planes fifty miles apart. Other pilots had been doing the same during the hours of darkness since High Sierra had told Karlstrom that Hang-Fire had been captured along with thirty-two other renegades. Their patience was finally rewarded when their radio equipment picked up the transmission they had been waiting for. The signal was made up of two code groups repeated several times in accelerated bursts. Seconds later, the on-board computer gave each pilot a bearing on the signal, enabling them to get an accurate fix on its location.

When he had replaced the knife in its health, Steve had put the blade in back to front, engaging a pressure pad that activated the concealed transmitter. As he sat there talking with Mr. Snow it was automatically broadcasting his call-sign and a codeword which would tell Karlstrom he had made contact with the clan M'Call.

Steve felt no sense of betrayal. He had told Mr. Snow of his mission, and he had meant everything he had said. He did feel detached from the Federation. He longed to see

Clearwater and felt drawn back into his previous relationship with Mr. Snow. But the old wordsmith had been right. His kin-sister *was* a problem. He could not abandon her. He had to send the message that Karlstrom was waiting for. It was the only way to make sure Roz stayed alive. He was obliged to play a double game until he could figure out the best thing to do for all concerned.

FOURTEEN

THE NEXT MORNING, when Steve returned from washing in a nearby stream, he found Night-Fever squatting outside Mr. Snow's hut. As he approached, she hurriedly assumed a kneeling position and unwrapped his breakfast—a meal of flat-bread and sliced rings of dried fruit.

Steve thanked her politely then proceeded to eat without paying her the slightest attention. He didn't object to the food parcels but he was definitely not interested in the fun and frolic she clearly had in mind. Not with Night-Fever anyway.

As if sensing his disinterest, the She-Wolf waited patiently with eyes averted. When he had finished the meal, she took away the straw mat then got to her feet and went to fetch something behind Mr. Snow's hut. A moment later she returned carrying Steve's quarterstaff. Kneeling down, she laid it reverently before him. The last time Steve had held it in his hands was on the edge of the bluff when he had faced the triple menace of Motor-Head, Black-Top and Steel-Eye. And here it was—except now, a gleaming blade, fashioned from a Tracker machete, had been fixed to one end by means of a metal collar. Below it, two spikes made from crossbow bolts had been threaded through the shaft at right-angles to each other to deflect

267

downwards blows from an opposing blade. At the other
end, the staff had been balanced by a second metal collar.

Steve drew the quarterstaff out of its leather sling and
ran his hands along it, caressing the scarred wood. It felt
good. A tingle of excitement ran up his arms as if, in
holding it, he had released a store of hidden energy in the
shaft. He thanked Night-Fever, using the elliptical syntax
that characterised Mute fire-speech; the language of formal encounters. "My tongue cannot speak the words that
fill my heart. You honour me with a great gift."

Night-Fever raised her eyes to meet his. "It is you that
honour me, Cloud-Warrior. After the earth-thunder I
searched for your body among the stones. This was all I
could find to mark your passing. I gave it to our clan-sister
Clearwater. When she left us she gave it back to me to
guard until she or you returned. I kept it when I could no
longer remember why. Yesterday, when Mr. Snow summoned you from the fire, I understood. His words swept
away the dark mists that cloud my mind."

Steve laid the quarterstaff down between them in the
hope that it would bring Night-Fever's hazy memory into
focus. "Did Clearwater speak to you of me? Did she leave
a message?"

The struggle to remember brought tears to her eyes.
She wiped them away and shook her head. "The words
have gone. I was to give you the staff."

Steve responded by bowing his head. "Thank you for
bringing it to me. May the great Sky-Mother watch over
you."

It was one of the polite ways to say goodbye, but Night-
Fever stayed put. She bent forward until her nose was
almost touching the ground. "Let me walk in your shadow,
Cloud-Warrior. If you have need of anything let my hands
and body provide it."

"My needs are few," replied Steve, anxious not to upset
her.

Night-Fever met his eyes again, this time with a faint,
mocking smile. "I ask only to serve you. I do not seek the
reward of your bed-favours."

Uncertain whether she was referring to his previous rejection of her, Steve said, "I am not of your people, Night-Fever. Only when I have done that which Talisman has sent me to do will I be of the Plainfolk. Until then, the pleasures you speak of are not mine to enjoy. If, knowing this, you still wish to walk in my shadow during the day, then so be it. Let's give it a whirl."

Night-Fever seized his hands and kissed them rapturously. Steve shooed her away and went in search of Jodi.

After being paraded in triumph in front of the assembled clan, the renegades had been dispersed throughout the settlement. Each breaker was made the responsibility of a small group of Mutes who fed him and made sure he, or she, was securely guarded at all times. They were kept barefoot, usually tethered to a post, and isolated from each other. This prevented any concerted plan of escape and, as a further disincentive, each breaker was clamped into heavy wooden leg restraints. Medicine-Hat and Jodi were no longer allowed to tend to the wounded. It was clear that the M'Calls had no intention of allowing them to be a conduit for whispered messages. Mr. Snow, already the clan's medicine-man, promptly identified those in need of treatment and began applying his mashed concoctions to the wounds that still remained to be healed. Having satisfied himself that Jodi was being as well looked after as the circumstances allowed, Steve proceeded to keep his distance. In their different ways they were both prisoners, and there was nothing he could do to change the situation.

For the first few days, after his unexpected elevation to the role of potential folk hero, Steve found it difficult to relax but, by the end of the first week it was as if he had never been away. Having already given proof of his courage by biting the arrow, Steve asked Mr. Snow if he could be allowed to dress as a Mute. The question was referred to Rolling-Stone and the council of elders. They, in turn, consulted Blue-Thunder. The new paramount warrior agreed to allow Steve to run with the Bears. He would not, however, be considered a fully-fledged warrior until he had chewed bone.

Steve called upon Night-Fever and her two blood-sisters
to help provide him with a set of "walking skins." His
request for aid met with an enthusiastic response and by
the end of the second week he had acquired a complete
outfit, including a stone-decorated helmet, body-plates
and a head-to-toe paint job. The last time Steve's hair had
been cut had been prior to his appearance before the
Board of Assessors some four and a half months back.
While at Rio Lobo it had been expertly "conditioned" to
look as if it had been clumsily trimmed with a knife. As a
result, the characteristic crew-cut shape had almost completely disappeared. Steve had been given back the strips
of blue, solar cell fabric he had been wearing on arrival at
Pueblo and he now asked Night-Fever to plait these back
into his hair.

Mr. Snow stopped by to survey the She-Wolves' handiwork.

"What do you think?" asked Steve as the final touches
were completed.

Mr. Snow answered with an admiring nod. "You could
fool me . . ."

Steve surveyed his patterned arms. "You sure this stuff'll
come off?"

"It was your idea. Would you be worried if it didn't?"

"I guess I could learn to live with it," replied Steve
diplomatically.

Mr. Snow chuckled. "Well, now's your big chance." He
gave him a friendly slap on the arm. "Listen, since Cadillac is away, why don't you take over his hut? You don't
want me breathing down your neck all the time."

Steve eyed him, wondering what lay behind this remark. "Will he mind?"

Mr. Snow shrugged. "It's where you slept before. It
should help make you feel at home."

The hut was erected a short distance from Mr. Snow's.
The flexible side poles were driven into the ground between the eight sections of the base frame then bent over
and tied into the smoke ring with tough strands of woven
grass. The cover, made of stitched panels of buffalo hide,

was pointless to speculate on what her response might
have been. He could say nothing to anyone. He had to
remain silent and take it on the chin. In the circumstances, her reaction was perfectly understandable but it
still riled him. It didn't matter. His anger would pass. He
still intended to save her from the Iron Masters if he
could.

As the month of May began, so did the clan's preparation for the journey to meet the Iron Masters. The warrior's long knives were finely honed and burnished until
they shone like mirrors; crossbows were cleaned and oiled,
the wooden stocks rubbed until they gleamed. The shaped
leather body armor and helmets were refurbished, cracked
stones and bones were replaced along with fresh arrays of
feathers and other, more gruesome relics attesting to a
warrior's prowess in mortal combat. Turf marker poles,
with their clusters of carved and coloured wooden plaques
were brightened up and adorned with ceremonial motifs.

The captured renegades also figured in these preparations. They were taken singly, under close guard, to the
stream running past the settlement and told to strip and
wash. Their patched fatigues and undergarments were
laundered and repaired, they were even given extra help-
ings of food, and each day they were groomed and exercised like prize show cattle.

Hunting trips and turf patrols continued alongside these
assiduous preparations and Steve—who had avoided all
contact with the captive breakers since his run-in with
Jodi—joined the posses whenever he was allowed to do so.

Four days before the renegades were due to begin their
journey to meet the wheel-boats, Steve joined a posse of
sixty Bears on an extended patrol of the southern section
of the M'Call's turf. On the second day, one of the flank
scouts found the butchered carcass of a fast-foot. The
head, ribcage and entrails of the deer had been buried,
but the grave had been too shallow and had not been
secured with rocks. As a result, it had been dug up by a
passing family of coyotes. Mutes did not bury carcasses of
animals killed on hunting trips. They were gutted and

carried back to the settlement on poles. For it to have been hidden in this way was a sure sign of intruders.

A careful search of the area turned up further clues. A broad leaf, crushed underfoot, bore a tell-tale pattern of dried blood—the bar tread sole of a Tracker boot—left by someone who had helped slaughter the deer. In a nearby cluster of rocks, a fire had been lit under an overhang where the flames would not be directly visible from the surrounding terrain. The ashes had been carefully dispersed and the site swept clean of footprints but the rock cleft bore traces of fresh soot and the Mutes, with their keen sense of smell, could detect the lingering odour in the larger pieces of charred wood. This fire had been alight the day before.

Observing the way the Bears prowled around looking for clues and the excited way they evaluated each discovery, Steve decided they got as much pleasure from the deductive process as from the subsequent chase and kill. Blue-Thunder, the leader of the posse, showed Steve a misshapen, hollow-point round that had been dug out of the fast-foot's skull. "Your people . . ."

Steve frowned. "This far north already?" Wagon-trains normally emerged from the Fort Worth depot at the beginning of April but the first month was spent on re-supply runs to way-stations. It was too soon for them to appear— and besides, Karlstrom had said that the Trail-Blazers units would be diverted elsewhere.

Blue-Thunder shook his head. "Not sand-burrowers. Red-skins."

The Mute name for renegades—who called themselves breakers. The Federation saw them as criminals, they saw themselves in a more heroic light, rebels who had beaten the system. The Mutes made no value-judgement, the red-skins were just another of the many life-forms inhabiting the overground.

"Are you going after them?"

"You bet. The dead-faces make good trade with us."

"Dead-faces . . . ?"

"Iron Masters. They take our clan-brothers and sisters and give us sharp iron. But one red-skin is worth twenty

Plainfolk. Better to trade them than send our people down the river."

"What happens to them?" asked Steve.

"Wheel-boats take them away."

"I know that. I mean when they get to the Fire-Pits of Beth-Lem."

Blue-Thunder shrugged. "No one has ever spoken of this."

One of the posse hurried over to where they sat and placed something in Blue-Thunder's palm. He looked at it then pulled it out between his fingertips until both arms were fully extended. It was a hair-thin metal thread, a filament aerial similar to the one inside Steve's knife—except that this one had become detached from its spool. "This too was made by sand-burrowers. What can you say of it?"

Steve chose his words carefully. He was 99 per cent certain that Blue-Thunder didn't have a clue about what he was holding but he couldn't be sure. "It is a thing fashioned by those of the High Craft. By itself it is nothing but when fixed to another device it sends words through the air—like birds flying over the mountains to places we cannot see."

Blue-Thunder ran his eyes slowly along the wire then wound it carefully into a small coil. "So . . . there are those who speak and those who listen." The Mute warrior rose to his feet. "And they tread on our turf . . ." He handed the wire to Steve. "Give me your thoughts, Cloud-Warrior. Do they talk of us?"

Steve had a sudden premonition that things were about to go horribly wrong. He shrugged. "If it worries you, let's go find them and ask."

As he spoke, they heard a shrill, bird-like call. A signal that Mutes used to communicate with each other when hunting. Steve remembered the first time he had heard it—when he had been chased through the woods after discovering Clearwater.

More footprints had been found. The last marcher had swept a branch across the trail behind him but not carefully enough. Blue-Thunder beckoned Steve to stay on his

heels then cupped his hands around his mouth to shape
the high-pitched bark of the coyote. The sound echoed
back and forth between the surrounding hills as the Bears
began running towards the south.

Steve's dilemma increased. The filament aerial was proof
that the group they were pursuing were not the red-skins.
Blue Thunder hoped to find. The Mutes were hot on the
trail of the MX back-up squad sent to aid Steve and act as
the channel for his reports to Karlstrom. Their capture
could wreck the whole operation and ruin his own byzan-
tine schemes. But there was no way he could throw the
M'Call Bears off the scent. The trail might run dry but the
Mutes were no amateurs. Hunting was in their blood. He
thought back to his last transmission. He had passed on
the date on which the clan was due to rendezvous with the
wheel-boats. If their quarry *was* the back-up squad, they
must have decided that the M'Calls and their neighbours
would be totally preoccupied with the preparations for the
big event. As a consequence they had gotten careless. A
bad move. The overground was an unforgiving place.

There were only two things he could do to impede the
chase. He could try and slow down the pace by generally
dragging his heels but this was bound to look suspicious.
He had already run a great deal farther without experienc-
ing any difficulty and Blue-Thunder had been with him on
both occasions. The alternative was to find some way to
alert the Trackers, breakers, or whoever they were, to the
fact that they were being hunted. But how? He didn't
have a rifle, or a crossbow that could be accidentally
discharged. All he had was his quarterstaff and his . . . and
his knife. Of course! What a dummy! He was becoming as
forgetful as his hosts! All he had to do was key in a
message to warn the back-up squad that a Mute posse
might be on their tail. If they *weren't* mexicans then it
would be tough shit on whoever was out there. Steve felt a
lot better. Yeah . . . that was it. Simple. But he couldn't
do it while everybody was looking. He would have to try
and unstick himself from Blue-Thunder, or wait until after
dark.

By nightfall, Steve had not managed to distance himself

from the posse despite fact that he had lagged behind complaining of a sudden, painful stitch, and had later developed a twisted ankle. Blue-Thunder had slowed down until he felt better then, when he simply dropped out, he ordered two pairs of warriors to take turns in carrying him along with his arms draped over their shoulders. Realising his ruse had failed, Steve made a dramatic recovery and carried on unaided.

When they finally stopped, Steve did not have to feign exhaustion and, to add the final touch to a day when everything had seemed to go wrong, it started to rain steadily. No fires were lit, there was moon, and a dense blanket of cloud obscured the stars. The M'Call warriors sat huddled together in groups, morosely chewing on dried meat twists or fruit rings. They didn't mind the rain but they preferred it during the day. It was the combination of no fire and no stars that was the real dampener.

For journeys that took them away from home for several days, the M'Calls carried light closely-woven mats which, when unrolled, measured approximately nine feet by six. The mat was folded down its length and the two edges of one the short ends had been sewn together to form a large hood that could be worn over the head and shoulders while using the bottom third of the mat to sit on, alternatively, you could lie stretched out inside it with your feet in the closed end. Used in combination with their travelling furs, it provided a reasonably waterproof shelter.

Despite the temporary gloom caused by the absence of a starry sky, Blue-Thunder was quietly confident that they would catch up with the red-skins by the middle of the following day. Steve realized that this was his last chance. He rolled himself into his furskin, wriggled inside the folded straw mat and lay there listening to the raindrops plopping noisily and endlessly onto the leaves of the surrounding trees. The cold and the damp began to seep into his bones. Rain—something that generations of Trackers had never encountered—had lost all its novelty value during his previous stay with the M'Calls. It was one feature of the overground he could do without.

By the time everybody was asleep, the darkness was so

complete Steve could barely see his hand in front of his face. It didn't matter. The keyboard, function switches and the liquid crystal display were illuminated automatically by means of a sensor which measured the surrounding level of light when the hidden transceiver was exposed.

Sliding carefully out of his furskin, Steve picked his way around the sleeping bodies then dropped his pants and squatted down in the middle of a waist-high patch of undergrowth. If anyone came looking for him his reason for being there would be immediately obvious. He couldn't be sure but he was fairly confident that there were no Mutes laws or customs that forbade nocturnal defecation.

Pulling the knife from its shealth, Steve searched with his fingers for the two hidden catches and pressed down simultaneously. Once, twice, three times. Nothing happened. The wooden hand-grip covering the transceiver remained stubbornly in place. Steve turned the handle over in the darkness and tried again. Nope . . . the catches weren't there. He had been holding it correctly the first time. He turned it back over and tried again. The triple-action pressure lock stayed shut.

What the fuck was going on? It was virtually impossible for it to jam. A sudden chill thought struck him. Rapidly locating the place where Lou Kennedy Naylor's initials had been stamped into the wood, Steve traced the letters with his thumbnail. What he thought was an 'N' turned out to be an 'R'. The initials were not LKN but SRB. Uhh, Christopher . . . Someone had done a quick switch. The knife he now held in his hand was his own—which had been taken from him after being captured the previous year.

Steve checked the initials once again just to make sure then put the knife away and cursed silently. Apart from the small initials—which only wingmen were officially permitted to apply—there was nothing to distinguish one knife from another. It was just a standard-issue item. He tried to figure out when the substitution could have taken place and the most likely person to have done it. Night-Fever would have had the most opportunity—while he was bathing, dressing, or lying asleep. In the end he decided the question of "who" and "when" was irrelevant. The important thing was *"why."* He had told Mr. Snow that he had been given a communication device—had even offered to show him how it worked. Did they suspect him of using it? Worse, had they observed him doing so? If not, what chance did he stand of getting it back? Three questions that were impossible to answer. Shit, shit and triple shit. Steve hitched up his pants and went back to bed.

Blue-Thunder was sitting up waiting for him. "Does something trouble you, Cloud-Warrior?"

"No, everything's fine." Steve rolled himself into his fur and straw cocoon and got his head down. Couldn't be better . . .

Manhattan-Transfer, the forward scout wriggled back through the grass to a point where he could be seen by the main party and raised eight fingers.

Steve's heart sank. There was no doubt in his mind now. It *was* the back-up squad. He mentally steeled himself for the coming encounter. It was too late to switch sides now. He glanced back over his shoulder at the horizon. The band of deep orange along the horizon had already turned yellow along its bottom edge but the sun had not yet stepped through the eastern door. In the eagerness to resume the chase, the Mutes had started out at first light and had caught up with their quarry sooner than expected.

Turning back, he saw Blue-Thunder confer with his four packleaders. From his gestures it was clear he was ordering them to encircle the "red-skins" position. Steve was attached as a supernumerary to Blue-Thunder's pack. Thirteenth man. The number held no special significance for Mutes but for Trackers the connotation with bad luck had been carried over from the pre-Holocaust even though the basic concept of luck—good *or* bad was frowned on by the First Family.

The pack-leaders stole away with their respective warriors. Around him, Blue Thunder's Bears drew their long knives and armed their crossbows. Steve drew his bladed quarterstaff. He had been practising daily with what was, effectively, a new and quite deadly weapon and was confident he could swiftly dispose of anyone armed with a knife, or knife-stick and that he would even be able to fight off a simultaneous attack by two or three assailants.

The quarterstaff classes he had given the previous year had gained him quite a following but he had seen disappointed to find that the M'Calls had not continued to develop their skills in his absence. He had seen some of the older Cubs using staves in mock combat but he had not seen a single Bear carrying a quarterstaff on turf patrol and nobody apart from Clearwater had been attracted by the idea of fixing a blade to one end.

For the Plainfolk, the Way of the Warrior was through one-to-one combat with the knife. The deadly accurate crossbow was used for hunting and against sand-burrowers but never against rival Mutes. To shoot down another member of the Plainfolk at long-range would have been absolutely unthinkable. Death itself was unimportant. If Mo-Town thirsted for the spirit of her people, she drank. Courage and honour were the essential qualities. Courage to face the point of an opponent's knife in the sure and certain knowledge that one of you must die. Courage to give your life to defend the honour of the clan and the name of the Plainfolk. Steve knew that if he was ever to gain their trust, he had to tread the same deadly path. What was about to happen was a small step along the way.

Crouched in the grass next to Blue-Thunder, Steve watched as a Mute warrior inserted a pointed rod into a hole bored in a small block of wood and set it spinning with his fire-bow. Moments later, the wisps of dry grass laid around the point of the rod began to smoulder. The fire-maker paused every now and then to blow gently until the blackened strands gave birth to tiny points of orange fire. More tinder, more coaxing from the fire-maker, his lips pursed as if he was blowing kisses then finally a tiny flame that he hastened to keep alive.

While this was in progress, Blue-Thunder produced a shank of long-bladed red grass from one of his trail bags and proceeded to bind it to a cross-bow bolt. He then

held out the bolt so that the fire-maker could apply the
nascent flame. The shank of grass began to burn giving off
a dense white smoke. Blue-Thunder laid the bolt into the
firing groove of a primed crossbow and aimed at the sky.
The bolt soared almost vertically into the air trailing a long
thin plume of smoke, seemed to hang there for a moment
on reaching its apogee, then plunged downwards in the
direction of the red-skins.

Steve took this to be the signal for a general attack but
nobody moved. "What's happening?"

"There are eight red-skins camped by big water. White
arrow tells them we want to have peace-talk, not kill. We
smoke grass, make trade."

"But I thought the idea was to capture them."

"Yes. But we always let some go. Red-skins run away
from sand burrowers. If they have nowhere to run to, they
not come anymore. Why leave bad place when the other
places are no better? This is why we make trade. If we
take everyone, red-skins will fight us. Everybody die." He
shrugged philosophically. "They don't want this. Nor do
we. A red-skin with no head is bad for trade. The dead-
faces want their brains in working order."

"Let me get this straight," said Steve. "Both of you fight
Trackers but the renegades—uhh, red-skins—don't attack
Mutes. Because if they did they'd have two enemies in-
stead of one. You'd wipe 'em out. And you don't kill the
red-skins because you need live bodies to trade with the
Iron Masters."

"You got it."

"But you don't take them all . . . so by not resisting,
some of them stay free. How many? A half, third, quarter
. . . ?"

"It depends," replied Blue-Thunder. "Most times we
make two way split." He smiled. "Unless it's a bad year."

Steve gazed in the direction in which the smoking bolt
had been fired. "Supposing they don't know what the
white smoke signal means?"

Blue-Thunder raised his heavy eyebrows. "We might
have some explaining to do."

"I see . . ." Although this was all news to him, Steve

imagined the AMEXICO must know about "white arrows." It seemed to know about everything else. "So—assuming they got the message, they are now busy deciding what to do. I mean who goes and who stays, right?"

"Right," said Blue-Thunder.

"What happens to those who stay?"

"They find other wanderers. Red-skin all alone get sick and die. Much safer to be all together. If we find small hand after wheel-boats have gone, we put them on trail of big clan."

A "hand" in Mute meant six. A "small hand" meant any number less than six—but usually four or five.

Blue-Thunder smiled again. "We like to make everybody happy. Good for trade."

I bet, thought Steve. The logic could not be faulted. The renegades were like buffalo. You kept track of where the herds were and when it was time you went in and cut out the animals you needed. No more, or less. You left the rest on the hoof to fend for themselves until the new hunting trip. Crafty four-eyed bastards. "What happens if none of them want to go?"

Blue-Thunder got to his feet. "If they fight, we kill."

The sun edged up over the horizon. Its rays flared around the paramount warrior, filling the side feathers on his helmet with golden fire and throwing the rest of his body into silhouette.

"Come, Cloud-Warrior. Before the day is out, maybe you will have chewed bone."

FIFTEEN

THE BREAKERS had camped overnight in a steep-sided, U-shaped depression that opened onto the edge of a large lake. In the middle of the lake were a cluster of small wooded islands. A dried-up water course cut a ragged line through the surrounding terrain into the bottom of the U. Steve followed Blue-Thunder along its northern edge. Half of his pack had crossed over to the other side. The floor of the depression—which was about one hundred yards deep and eighty yards wide—was strewn with rocks and pebbles. At some time in the past, presumably when water had flowed down the draw, it had been part of the lake. At the top left-hand corner of the U where the shoreline consisted of a precipitous twenty-foot-high cliff, erosion of the soil had loosened several huge boulders which had collapsed into an untidy heap at the water's edge. A few smaller ones lay half submerged just beyond.

Ranged around the rim of the U were the four other packs that made up Blue-Thunder's posse, standing like statues, their weapons glinting in the morning sun. The breakers, who had evidently been caught totally unawares, were backing slowly towards the rocks of the water's edge. Only half appeared to be armed and these held air rifles clutched to their chests. Two sloping-roofed shelters, made of skins laid on a frame of tied saplings, were ranged on either side of a stone-lined cooking pit about twenty or so yards from the water. The "white arrow," its point embedded with uncanny accuracy near the centre of the depression and in one of the few patches of bare sand, continued to put out a thin, drifting plume of smoke.

"Come," said Blue-Thunder.

Steve joined him as he started down the slope followed by the Bears. Everybody else stayed where they were around the rim of the draw.

Seeing the on-coming deputation, two of the armed breakers halted. Grasping the blade of his knife, Blue-Thunder held it above his head then sheathed it and raised his bare hand. The two breakers began to edge forward. The rest—four men and two women—continued to back off, shuffling sideways towards the cluster of boulders. One of the men ducked out of sight, the others froze awkwardly at the water's edge.

Steve was too far away to see their expressions but they all gave the impression of being absolutely terrified. And who wouldn't be, thought Steve, to wake up and find that sixty Mutes had dropped in for breakfast? One of the women looked to be pregnant. Instead of trousers, she wore a wraparound hide skirt similar to the kind some Mute women wore. Until he had been taken prisoner by the M'Calls, Steve had never seen a pregnant woman. In the Federation, guard-mothers stayed at the Life Institute from conception to delivery. The process of fertilisation and the development of the embryo were secrets to which only the First Family had access but through Roz's medical studies and then through first-hand experience with the Mutes he knew what the swollen belly signified. But what was a mother-to-be doing out here?

Steve placed himself to the right of Blue-Thunder as they stopped a few paces short of the smoking arrow; the six Bears spread out in a line behind them. The two breakers, who were about twenty yards away suddenly changed pace. Dropping their rifles to the trail, they leapt over an irregularly spaced band of small rocks and jogged towards the waiting Mutes with their right hands raised, palm open.

Why the sudden eagerness? wondered Steve. He tightened his grip on the quarterstaff and planted his feet firmly on the ground. The two breakers stopped an equal distance from the arrow, cradled their rifles and ran their eyes over the Mutes, according Steve the same cautious appraisal they gave the others. If they were ordinary breakers there was no reason to think he was anything other than a straight Mute.

Both men looked to be in their mid-twenties. They were dressed in a mixture of skins and the remnants of standard-issue red, brown and black combat fatigues. Both were unshaven; one had a long, straggly moustache. If they *were* mexicans then their disguise was perfect. They were ragged, gaunt and weather-beaten, and their eyes were filled with weary defiance. The kind of look you'd expect to get from someone who's gone through seven kinds of hell to stay alive yet won't give up—even though he knows he's losing.

The breaker with the moustache faced up to Blue-Thunder. "What can I do for you, sky-brother?"

The paramount warrior squared his shoulders and folded his arms. He was big but nowhere near as ugly or as fearsome as his predecessor, Motor-Head. "I am Blue-Thunder, of the Clan M'Call, from the bloodline of the She-Kargo, greatest among the Plainfolk."

Mustachio exchanged a glance with his companion, then inclined his head courteously. "I have heard of the M'Call and know the truth of your words. It is also said that your people are friends to the red-skins."

"We are friends to those who wish us well but not to strangers who take meat from our turf." Blue-Thunder snapped his fingers. One of the six Bears stepped forward and tossed the severed head of the fast-foot down by the smoking arrow. Blue-Thunder held up the tell-tale hollow-point round. "Can you say in truth that this was not thrown by your long sharp iron?"

The two breakers eyed one another, then the second—who was relatively clean shaven, with long corn-coloured hair held down by a camouflage sweat-band continued the exchange. "It is said that the M'Calls are mighty hunters and that their turf is heavy with meat. Can not the greatest among the Plainfolk share these riches with their sky-brothers who have nothing? Would you let us die with empty stomachs while the death-birds eat their fill?"

Blue-Thunder paused, momentarily lost for words and visibly perplexed by this robust and cogent response. Finally he said, "The M'Calls are as generous as they are brave. But a gift should not be taken before it is given. This is the way of the coyote and the long-tails who come like thieves in the night."

Corn-Hair turned the insult aside. "The greatest of the Plainfolk speaks with the tongue of truth. We are less then the coyote and the long-tails. We have no turf, we have no clan. We drift, like cloud-shadows, outcasts who know only shame and hunger. Yet we breathe, we are of the world and would be brothers with all those who live under the sky. But we are not afraid to die. And it is because of this we have the courage to seek justice from the strong."

Top that, thought Steve, momentarily forgetting which side he was supposed to be on.

Blue-Thunder gestured impatiently. Mutes loved these formal exchanges but this one was not leading in the desired direction. Worse, he was in danger of losing the argument. "You seek food and you seek justice. The M'Calls have the power to grant both these things but you are many."

Mustachio swept his eyes over the warriors spaced around the rim of the draw. "Not as many as you."

"These things must be spoken of," insisted Blue-Thunder. "Gather your people. Let us pass the pipe and make trade." He reached into one of his waist pouches and produced one of the slim compressed air bottles that powered the Tracker air rifle. He offered it to Corn-Hair. "Take it. We have more. And also many iron pebbles."

Corn-Hair weighed the bottle in his palm. An experienced Tracker could tell by the feel of it roughly how much it contained. He passed it to his colleague. "Half-full . . ."

"Yeah, I'd say that was about right." Mustachio looked up at Blue-Thunder. "What d'you want in exchange?"

The big Mute smiled and spread his palms. "Why don't we sit down and talk about it?"

The breakers got the message. "We'll get the others," said Corn-Hair.

Blue-Thunder gripped Steve's arm and pushed him forward. "Go with them."

The two breakers started back towards the lake with Steve close behind them. When they'd gone about five yards, he began to whistle softly the opening bars of the tune he'd learnt at Rio Lobo: "South of the Border . . . down Mexico Way . . ."

The breakers stopped briefly to glance up at the surrounding Mutes. Corn-Hair waved reassuringly to the breakers on the shore then, taking care not to look at Steve, he issued a muttered warning. "Watch your step, amigo . . ."

The two men broke into a jog, cleared the rock-strewn section with one bound and continued at the same pace. Steve followed, taking care to match his steps to theirs. Reaching the other five breakers, Steve and Corn-Hair quickly exchanged the secret signal by which mexicans could make themselves known to each other.

"Deep-Six," said Corn-Hair. It was the code-name of the leader of the back-up squad with whom Steve had been in regular radio contact.

"Hang-Fire," said Steve, identifying himself.

Deep-Six responded with a snake-like hiss. "What the fuck are you doing with this bunch?"

"I don't have time to explain. But if you don't move fast, you're headed down river—or worse. D'you have a way out of here?"

"Yeah," muttered Deep-Six. He turned to the other members of the back-up squad, gesturing to them and towards the Mutes to make Blue-Thunder think he was selling them on the idea they should sit down and talk. "We've got a powered inflatable. It's stashed in the rocks behind us."

Steve looked past him and saw the breaker who had ducked out at the beginning of the proceedings pop back into view and give them the thumbs-up. He ran his eyes over the rest of the group. The scruffy blonde girl with the swollen belly was kneeling on the sand gathering up some of their gear that had spilled out of a broken back-pack. Their eyes met briefly then she went on with what she was doing. Steve had a feeling he'd seen her somewhere before. "Where are you planning to go?"

"That big island out there," said Mustachio. "These shit-kickers can't swim, they don't have boats and they don't like deep water. They won't be able to touch us."

Steve gauged the distance to the islands. It was about a mile. "You'll never make it. These guys are hot-shots. They'll fill you so full of iron you'll be on the bottom before you've gone fifty yards."

Mustachio shrugged. "Better than staying here and getting a stiff neck."

"We got a couple of things going for us," said Deep-Six. "There are AP mines sewn around the camp—"

"Mines?"

"Yeah, you jumped over them. Nothing big but, if you stand on one, they don't leave too much below the knee."

"Shit . . ." Steve glanced over his shoulder. "In that ring of stones?"

"Yeah. And we can also put out smoke from the skimmer."

Steve's brain and belly went ice-cold as he realised what he had to do. He tried to swallow the lump in his throat. "Okay," he rasped. Good luck fellas. You'd better get going."

The five breakers behind Deep-Six and Mustachio started to melt away towards the rocks where they would be shielded from the crossbow-men on both sides of the draw. The engine of the hidden skimmer started with a powerful roar. A cloud of blue-grey smoke billowed out from behind the rocks.

"Make it look good," said Steve, raising his voice. "But don't put too many holes in me. I'm still on the case!"

Deep-Six's arms blurred as he swept his rifle shoulder high and rammed the hard rubber butt at Steve's head. Fast as he was he was still too late. Steve had already stepped back out of reach. His quarterstaff was also a moving blur, drawing in its wake a brief, brilliant arc of light as the rays of the sun glanced off the razor-sharp blade. A split-second later, it sliced across Deep-Six's body in a straight line that passed through his navel with the precision of a surgical laser. The mexican's long, straw-coloured hair lifted at the shock of the blow. His pale blue eyes ballooned out of their sockets, and turned downwards with an indescribable expression of horror as his guts spilled out. He tried to hold himself together but it was like trying to stuff live eels back through a gaping slit in the bottom of a full sack.

Mustachio, who had already begun his turn towards the hidden skimmer spun round pulling the butt of his rifle into his hip. For a split second, Steve found himself looking down the barrel-cluster with Mustachio's finger tightening on the trigger. But he was already into the reverse parry. Side-stepping Deep-Six as he staggered forward and tripped over his intestines, Steve advanced his left foot and swung the weighted base of the quarterstaff upwards and to the right, knocking the rifle across Mustachio's body. He was just in time. The triple volley tore past his right ear. Mustachio pulled his head back into his right shoulder to avoid getting hit in the face by the barrel-cluster and staggered as he lost balance. Before he could recover, Steve followed through with the bloodless coup de grāce—a battering ram blow to the left side of the head that tore Mustachio's brains loose and broke his neck at the same time.

"They died so that other's might live . . ." Hadn't the President-General himself reminded him of the fundamental precept that gave meaning—was, in fact, the *sole* reason for a Tracker's existence? Deep-six and Mustachio had made the ultimate sacrifice—and had paid the price for being in the wrong place at the wrong time.

As Steve came under attack, the Mutes spaced around the rim and those with Blue-Thunder behind the smoking arrow leapt into action. Steve, who had his hands full, had no time to warn them about the ring of AP mines and had there been time they would not have understood. Blue-Thunder and one of the Mutes with him cleared the rock-laden strip with one fortuitous bound but two others, running a few yards behind, landed squarely in the danger zone. The resulting detonations also took out three of their companions. The mines, an MX speciality, were double action. The primary charge, detonated on impact, sent a secondary charge upwards out of the ground spinning like an airborne top. This exploded at a height of three feet, spraying out a deadly disc of shrapnel that cut through flesh like a circular saw.

More mines blew, creating more carnage, as the warriors on the rim, realising they could not prevent the breakers from escaping if they stayed where they were, came leaping down the surrounding slopes onto the rock-strewn floor.

Steve, at the water's edge, was out of range of the disabling blasts, but as the first wave of explosions erupted he threw himself instinctively into the lake. The bottom fell away at a steep angle. He kicked out strongly in the direction of the big boulders. Breaking the surface, he found a footing in a waist-deep water and half-waded, half-swam into the drifting cloud of blue-grey smoke. From the shore came a confusion of screams and angry shouts, punctuated by more staccato explosions.

Closing in, Steve caught a glimpse of the skimmer. The engine had stalled unexpectedly; the helmsman and his five passengers were clustered in the stern, coughing and choking as they tried feverishly to restart it. The smoke that was supposed to mask their dash to freedom was rapidly threatening to become a funeral shroud.

The engine burst into life. Dragging his quarterstaff along the surface of the lake, Steve threw himself forward, left hand raised, the top of his thighs now clear of the water. "Wait! Wait for me!"

His cry came as the five passengers turned and threw themselves down on the slatted floor between the inflated rubber sides of the skimmer and the helmsman pushed the throttle wide open. The roar of the engine drowned out his voice. Only one of the mexicans was fast enough to react. Rising to his knees, he swung his rifle up over the side towards Steve as the boat leapt forward, pumping out smoke from bow and stern. The sudden acceleration threw the mex onto his back. He disappeared leaving his rifle waving in the air. The helmsman, alerted by his colleague's shout, turned the skimmer towards Steve—no doubt intending to run him down. It was then he realised there was a two-foot high chunk of rock sticking out of the water behind him. He veered away sharply to port but it was too late. He had made the fatal mistake of coming within range of Steve's quarterstaff. As the skimmer raced past, the blade sliced through his neck, sending his head rolling down his chest onto the slatted floor between his knees. The headless trunk, driven backwards by the force of the blow, fell across the tiller tightening the turn even more.

Now under full power and full left rudder, the skimmer became locked into a series of tight, skidding circles that kept it close to the shore, enclosed in a choking whirlpool of smoke. The surviving occupants tried to regain control but two of them were tumbled overboard by the dizzying spin. Steve headed towards them but before he could get there, several Bears ran in and seized the one closest to the shore, dragging him back into the shallows where he was savagely hacked to death with knives. The other, attempted to swim towards the islands but was stopped short in the water by a crossbow bolt that pinned the collar of her flotation jacket to the top of her spine and came out under her chin. The mexican turned over onto her back and floated gently with one limp-handed arm raised in a bizarre gesture of farewell.

The skimmer zig-zagged away from the shore, its outlines and occupants hidden by the continuous output of smoke. Steve stood waist-deep in the water and watched the blue-grey cloud move away towards the centre of the lake leaving the headless corpse of the helmsman floating chest up in a soft-edged pool of crimson. The Mute crossbow-men had fired several volleys into the heart of the smoke cloud. Of the three mexicans still on board one, at least, had been in sufficiently good shape to steer the skimmer out of trouble. But what about the other two? He knew that Blue-Thunder would not rest until this question had been resolved. Too many clan-brothers had died. This particularly bloody encounter and Steve's troubles were far from over.

He sought out Blue-Thunder. The warrior's broad back ran with blood from several shrapnel wounds. They were not large, or dangerously deep but they were not flea-bites either. Blue-Thunder simply ignored them. That was one of the Mutes' strengths. For some reason, either because of their genetic make-up or, possibly, through a special mental attitude linked to their strange beliefs they had an incredibly high threshold of pain.

Crushed by the realisation that he was partly responsible for the death and destruction that surrounded him, Steve followed the paramount warrior as he completed the doleful task of despatching the badly mutilated Bears. Warriors whose feet and lower limbs had been blown away or shredded to the bone, or whose bodies had been torn beyond repair by the murderous shrapnel blasts.

"Mo-Town thirsts, Mo-Town drinks . . ." One swift knife thrust to the heart and the light in their eyes flickered and died. Mr. Snow had told him that the light was a reflection of the spirit within. The soul-being which, on the death of the earth-body, was drawn upwards to merge with the loving presence of the Great Sky-Mother. The Mutes thought of this mysterious spirit-soul as being like a stream of crystal clear water, filled with shimmering light like the myriad starry eyes in the dark, seamless and infinitely beautiful cloak that Mo-Town drew over the sleeping world at the end of each day. It was a comforting thought, reflected Steve, to think that one might live again. To have a chance to get things right, to do things differently. Not just once, but over and over and over again as the world, and the star-filled space around it, were carried slowly down the River of Time towards the infinite horizons of the Sea of Eternity.

When Blue-Thunder finally kissed and cleaned his knife, eighteen Bears lay dead. Some twenty more were wounded but could walk and would recover with the help of Mr. Snow. The warriors began to gather wood to make a large funeral pyre whose rising flames would carry the departing spirits up beyond the clouds to where Mo-Town waited with the Cup of Life held in her outstretched hands.

While the pyre was being built, Steve waded out until he was neck deep then swam some twenty yards to retrieve the female mex. He dumped her slim body on the beach. That left the pregnant woman and two males to be accounted for. As he turned away, a passing Bear straddled the corpse, turned it face down, took hold of its arms and pulled it up into a kneeling position. A second unsheathed his machete, seized the wet hair on the crown of the head to extend the neck and cut through it with two swift blows.

The eighteen Bears were piled in three layers interleaved with lengths of wood; leafy branches were stacked around the sides. As the flames took a firm hold, the warriors circled the pyre singing a defiant chant that reflected the valour of the dead who had gone to join the past heroes of the clan M'Call.

Blue-Thunder turned to Steve, his lumpy features heavy with grief. He gestured towards the bodies of Deep-Six and Mustachio. "You fight well, Cloud-Warrior."

"Not as well as my sky-brother, Blue-Thunder."

The Mute shook his head and sighed heavily. "This is a bad day. I cannot fight men who wrap themselves in smoke. Where is the honour in that?"

"There is none," replied Steve. "We were misled. You offered the pipe to those with false faces. These were not true red-skins. They were sand-burrowers. They do not respect the ways of the Plainfolk."

"The sand-burrowers have powerful sharp iron. Did you know of these things that speak like earth-thunder?"

"I have heard talk," admitted Steve. "Today the truth was written in the blood of the Bears."

Blue-Thunder growled angrily. "The sand-burrowers tread with poison feet. They sow death in the earth. They send fire from the sky and now they turn the land against us. These are bad things. The wind that bears you aloft is the breath of Talisman, the earth his body, the sun and moon his eyes, the thunder his voice, the rivers his blood. The crimes that those without courage commit against the world violate his sacred being. This insult must be avenged."

Steve acknowledged this with a grave nod. "I also would be avenged. The sand-burrowers bring me dishonour in your eyes. Let me bring you their heads."

As he mulled over the proposition, Blue-Thunder looked past Steve towards the cluster of small islands. "How can you cross the big water? Will you not sink like a stone?"

"No, I shall wriggle through it like a snake."

"When will you go?"

"When night comes."

The Mute looked impressed. "You have true power."

Steve was not about to disillusion him. Like all Trackers, he had been taught to swim in underground pools as part of the daily programme of physical training. He was about to become one of the very few to put the skill to practical use. How odd, he reflected, that the Mutes hadn't bothered to learn how to swim. But then, in the same thousand years, they hadn't built boats either, despite their contact with the Iron Masters. And they had other odd ideas—like preferring to sleep out in the open rather than under the trees of a forest, and there was the whole business of Talisman, Mo-Town and the Sky Voices. A year ago he had been openly contemptuous of such things. But now . . . who could say they were wrong?

Some time back, there must have been a good reason behind all these ideas. Rational explanations that, despite the formidable memories of wordsmiths like Mr. Snow, had gotten lost along the way. There was no doubt that some Mutes possessed extraordinary powers. Whether or not they were "magic" was not important. "Magic," Steve had decided, was just a word that was applied to things, or events, which could not be immediately explained with the present knowledge that was available. Ahh, yes, but available to whom? That was the *real* question. Steve had already discovered there were different levels of access to information within the Federation, and he had heard from the lips of the President-General himself that the First Family believed in the power of Mute magic. But maybe the Family knew even more. Knew all there was to know.

Had they not created, and did they not control COLUM-
BUS, the guiding intelligence of the Federation? It was
not for nothing that, in the thrice-daily prayer of allegiance
through which Trackers collectively rededicated themselves,
the First Family were described as "Keepers of all Knowledge, Wisdom and Truth."

The sun sank through the western door, draining the
golden warmth from the sky. The clouds that had been
fired with glowing pinks and yellows faded to pale mauve
and violet then turned a cold, ash grey as the pale, lingering after-light was swallowed by the on-coming dark. To
the east, the hills merged with the sky as evening drew its
veil over the land. Colours, shapes and dimensions blurred
and coalesced to create a new world without depth or
form. The islands, now shadowy silhouettes set in a sea of
tarnished silver, appeared, at one instant, to be tantalisingly
near and, in the next, impossibly far away.

Runners, sent back by the Bears that had been despatched around the lake, came in to report that there had
been no attempt by the sand-burrowers to reach another
part of the shore. They were still holed up on the islands.

It was time to get started.

The surface of the lake had become ominously still. But
not quite still enough. Every now and then, something
would rise from the depths and nose the air for a fleeting
instant, sending concentric rings rippling outwards across
the mirror-like surface.

Steve had already begun to have second thoughts about
the whole enterprise but it was too late to back out. The
angry Mutes would not leave until the remaining mexicans
had been accounted for. They would wait days or weeks if
necessary, bringing to the task the patience and total
dedication with which the primitive hunter stalks an elu-
sive prey. The affront to Talisman had to be avenged. The
how and why of small anti-personnel mines did not concern them; the techniques by which they could be detected and de-activated were of not the slightest interest.
This is why they will never win, thought Steve sadly. But
like it or not, this was the side he was currently committed

to defend. The trading party was due to start its trek towards the wheel-boats at dawn the day after tomorrow. He had to bring this episode to a quick, bloody conclusion before Karlstrom got the wrong message and before the survivors called up a rapid assist. If AMEXICO sent in air support or mounted a rescue operation the whole situation could rapidly get out of control.

There was another equally pressing reason for wrapping this disastrous mess up as quickly and cleanly as possible. Steve wanted to be there waiting to welcome Clearwater and Cadillac when they stepped ashore. After what he had been through to get this far he did not intend to let her slip through his fingers again.

The funeral pyre, which had burned fiercely throughout the day, was now a ragged square slab of glowing embers some two or three feet thick at the centre. The heat it gave off was tremendous and now that it was dark, the rocky floor and sides of the draw were bathed in its bright orange glow. Conscious that the three mexicans would probably be watching—possibly through binoculars—Steve stepped out of the circle of light into the enveloping dark and walked halfway around the lake escorted by Blue-Thunder and three of his Bears.

Steve had swum long distances but only within the comforting confines of a sanitised, sparkling-blue pool— and within easy reach of the edge. He was confident he had the strength to reach the islands but he was not overjoyed at the prospect of having to traverse such a huge stretch of open, and possibly hostile, water.

As a precaution, Steve had prepared buoyancy bags using four large deerskin pouches borrowed from members of the posse. The inflated bags were primarily to support a light frame-work of branches on which he had tied a fully-loaded air rifle, a machete, and his combat knife. He had debated whether to take his quarterstaff and decided to leave it behind. It was a lethal weapon but it would be of no use if he could not get within range. If the three remaining mexicans were on the ball, they could drop him with a single volley at seventy-five yards—and more than twice that distance if their rifles were fitted with infra-red night scopes.

Finding a satisfactory spot, he stripped down to his underpants—the only item of Tracker clothing he had retained—and donned the sleeveless flotation jacket that the helmsman had been wearing. He exchanged the traditional hand slap with his escort then slipped quietly into the water, pushing the bag-raft ahead of him. To break up its outline, he had covered it with leafy twigs. The water was cold, but not unbearably so. He tried not to think about the dreadful nameless things that might be lurking beneath the surface. A couple of hundred yards out from the shore, when something slimy brushed across his belly, he began to think that the Mute's decision to stay on dry land wasn't so stupid after all.

At the halfway point, after several brushes with the unseen denizens of the lake, Steve was relieved to find he was still in one piece. Having overcome the wave of panic generated by the first unwelcome contacts and the inevitable nightmare visions of needlesharp teeth gnawing at his dong, he proceeded with growing confidence, his mind now concentrated on the task that awaited him once he reached dry ground.

The second half-mile seemed shorter than the first. As he drew closer, the broken clouds drifted further apart, uncovering more of the star-studded sky. The islands—of which there were five—were no more than rocky islets on which stunted trees and scrub had gained a tenacious toe-hold. The two nearest Steve were giant, steep-sided chunks of stone with virtually no cover and, of the others, only one measured more than fifty yards across.

In the distant past, even before what the Mutes called the Old Time, subterranean earth movements had forced the rocky bed of the lake to bulge upwards and peak above the present water level. Subsequent faulting had exposed striated layers of rock, like a pack of ice cream wafers that had been snapped in two, and several thousand years of wind and rain had smothered off the rough edges.

Steve paddled silently towards the largest islet. No lights

pierced the dark. Everything was deathly still; the only sounds his own breathing and the light slip-slap of water rippling against the flank of the rocks ahead which rose sheer out of the water to a height of four or five feet. Towing the bag-raft behind him, Steve used his free hand to haul himself sideways around the islet, looking for a suitable place to come ashore.

Given the fact that the Mutes could not swim and would not cross deep water, the islet made an ideal refuge. Steve found it hard to understand why the mexicans had chosen to camp overnight on the shore instead of crossing directly to the islet. The only explanation he could think of was that they had reached the lake during the evening and had been reluctant to make the boat trip at night. He himself, had adapted with remarkable ease to overground conditions; a fact which led him to forget that the majority of Trackers were extremely nervous of the dark—and that included most wingmen and mexicans. And very few would have dared swim the lake—even in daylight.

Treading water, Steve felt his toes brush against a ridged shelf of rock that enabled him to stand chest deep under the overhanging branches of a tree. The snarled roots snaked over the cracked slabs of stone like the sclerotic veins on the back of an old man's hand. Steve transferred his armoury from the bag-raft to a cleft in the rock then climbed ashore himself. His first act was to fix the sheathed combat knife around his right calf and strap on the belt carrying the machete. He left the raft floating in the water. It would not drift far and, with its covering of branches, would be less likely to arouse suspicion.

Squatting down against the trunk of a tree with the rifle laid across his knees, Steve relaxed his body and opened his mind to the earth, the silence and the darkness. After several minutes of total absorption, he became imbued with a mental impression of the islet and was able to decipher the broader details of the terrain.

A rising half-moon joined the uncovered stars, casting its pale glow on the lake and turning the trees ahead of him into dim silhouettes. Here and there, thin moon-beams found a path through the terraced maze of leaves to create ragged rock-pools of light. Somewhere ahead lay his quarry. The odds were three to one in their favour and they were probably on familiar ground but he had the advantage of surprise.

Drawing his knife, Steve slid the blade into a patch of earth until it met the underlying rock. The layer was barely two inches thick. Not deep enough to bury anti-personnel mines and besides the island too small and lacked proper cover. Any explosion would risk killing as many defenders as attackers. He was being over-cautious. The islet, which was about two hundred yards long by eighty wide, did not need to be defended. The lake made it impregnable, for who, apart from other mexicans—could be expected to reach it?

Steve decided to explore the centre of the islet first. By keeping in the middle, where the darkness was almost total and the ground higher, he could rest concealed while everything between him and the encircling shore stood out against the moon-struck surface of the lake. His stealthy text-book tactics masked his presence but served no other useful purpose. There were no trip wires, no pits with collapsing roofs and sharpened stake-floors to fall into, no strangling sky-nooses tied to sprung saplings, no deadly porcupine rock-ball poised to swing down like giant pendulums to crush and spear the unwary; not one of the horrors which grizzled 'Blazers like Bad News Logan used to describe in gory detail to each new batch of wet-feet.

Steve moved forward, his bare feet making no sound on the hard rock he had chosen in preference to the softer but potentially treacherous layer of pine needles and dead twigs. At the opposite end of the island he saw the squat outlines of the skimmer. It lay on a wide flat slab of rock that sloped down into the water making a natural slipway up which it had been driven. Crawling closer to the skimmer, Steve saw what had not been visible before: a camouflaged sleeve draped over the side near the bow. A sleeve that contained a lifeless arm ending in a half-closed hand with stiff, contorted fingers and an arm that belonged to someone lying face down on the slatted floor inside. The Bears who had shot blindly into the whirling smoke screen had

not wasted their precious metal bolts. One down, two to
go . . .

A few yards further inland, Steve spotted an air rifle and
a back pack. The way they were lying told him they had
been jettisoned by someone who was not planning to use
them again in a hurry. The two remaining mexicans could
not be far away—might even have him in their sights . . .

Steve retraced his steps cutting across the middle of the
islet to approach the sloping rock beach from the other
side. Once again he picked his way over the bare patches
of stone, skirting round the pools of moonlight. Now that
he was almost naked, the Mute body markings he had
adopted made an ideal camouflage and it was possibly this
that saved his life as the triple volley, fired at close range,
ripped through the air.

Chu-witt, chu-witt, chu-witt!

Steve threw himself to the right as he felt the scorching
blow on his left side and scrambled behind a tree. Gritting
his teeth against the pain, he held his breath, listening for
any sound that might betray the position of his attacker.
Nothing moved and the only thing he could hear was the
thunderous beat of his own heart. Reaching across with his
right hand he made a quick assessment of the damage.
Blood seeped through his fingers but he had been lucky.
One round had gouged through the skin as it glanced off
the fourth rib, a second had blazed a diagonal stripe across
the underside of his raised forearm and the third had
nicked the outside of his left arm just above the elbow. He
flexed his arm experimentally. It hurt like hell but still
functioned.

From the angle and direction of the shots Steve was
able to deduce roughly where the rifleman was and that he
had fired from a prone position. He sat there without
moving and reviewed the situation. He had been hit by
one volley from a single rifle and he had not fired back. As
far as his attacker knew he might be lying dead but even
now, half-an-hour later, there had been no follow-up. Interesting. He had clearly lost the element of surprise but
he still retained one big advantage—mobility. Steve was
now convinced that the two mexicans were both badly

wounded. Neither of them was going anywhere, but they were still dangerous. Steve was in no hurry to get himself killed. He would wait till first light.

Keeping close to the wide trunk of the tree behind which he had been sheltering, Steve rose slowly to his feet and studied the layout of the branches. Once again his luck held. The vestigial stump of a limb lost some time before the tree acquired its middle-aged spread offered a foothold from which he could reach up to grasp the lowest branch. Slinging his rifle across his back, he stepped up onto the trunk and kept going. Steve had never climbed a tree before but he approached it with the same confidence with which he had first scaled the tower frame designed to test the nerves of wingmen on the Academy's underground assault course. Some thirty feet in the air, he found a wide, three-limbed fork on which he could lie without danger of falling. He hung the rifle from the shattered stump of a smaller branch then made himself as comfortable as he could and dozed fitfully.

When he woke, it was not yet dawn but it was light enough for Steve to take stock of his surroundings. The world was wrapped in white. A thick, eerie blanket of mist now covered the surface of the lake, washing up over the ground below to swirl about the trunks of the trees like the ghost of some prehistoric sea. By moving to higher or lower branches on the far side of the trunk, Steve was able to peer down through the leaves. He glimpsed the veiled prow of the beached skimmer. His quarry was still on the island. The fact that both mexicans now knew they had a visitor but had passed up the ideal moment to escape was proof that Steve's original hunch had been correct. They were still here because they didn't have the strength to haul the boat back in the water.

The cold dead feeling that had formed in the pit of his stomach when facing Deep-Six welled up again. He had watched Blue-Thunder despatch the badly-injured Mute warriors. Now he was going to have to do the same thing to his own kind. But for his victims, and for him, it would be nothing more than a cold-blooded act of butchery. How could it be otherwise? Trackers only comprehended the functional, finite world of the living. The notion of some kind of an after-life simply did not enter their heads. You were given life by the First Family. The sole reason for being alive was to help secure the future of the Federation. Your on-line performance was the only thing that counted. Death was simply the cessation of all brain and body functions, the end of the work cycle; the moment when the Man Upstairs pulled the plug. When the bagmen came to carry you away that was it. Terminada. The last emotion registered by the fast-fading consciousness of the two beleagured mexicans would be an overwhelming sense of betrayal. It was a fitting epitaph on the brave new world created by the First Family.

Steve waited until the mist cleared then climbed down to one of the lower branches where he could see the mexican with the rifle. He was lying slumped against a rock with the barbed tip of a crossbow bolt sticking up out of the inside of his left thigh just below his crotch. His pants and the ground between his splayed legs were soaked in blood. With his right hand he was keeping the tension on the tourniquet made with a webbing belt and the handle of his combat knife but every now and then the blood would spurt from the severed main artery. His left hand was curled around the trigger guard of the rifle, but to fire it with any accuracy he was obliged to rest it awkwardly on his right leg or forearm without looking through the sights—a limiting factor which had probably saves Steve's life the previous night.

Steve aimed at the mexican's chest and put a volley through his heart. The impact slammed the mex back against the rock, arms spread wide. The rifle flew from his hand then his limp body toppled sideways onto the ground, the left arm still outstretched in a dying effort to reach it.

Steve dropped cautiously to the ground, using the tree as cover while he scanned the ground ahead. He spotted the pregnant female mex over to his right, lying propped up against a tree with her back to him, her arm lying limply by her side, hand empty, palm upwards. He retreated and came up on the other side. Same story, no movement. Steve took another careful look around then edged closer, rifle at the ready. Okay, this is it. He stepped out in front of her, the barrel-cluster aimed at her chest. She looked up at him, her pale eyes still ablaze in her exhausted face. He was right. She *had* looked familiar. It was Donna Marie Lundkwist.

"Christopher Columbus! Don . . . ? What the eff-eff are you doing here?"

Donna stared at him, aware that she also knew him but unable to reconcile that knowledge with the way he looked now. "I don't believe it. Brickman? Steve Brickman . . . ?" The words came out with a husky, whispering laugh.

"Yeah." Steve laid aside his rifle and knelt down. The right side of her patched, camouflaged tunic was stained with fresh blood. He lifted her right arm gently and saw the entry wound. The tail vanes of the ten-inch long bolt were just visible. "That must hurt . . ."

Lundkwist's sweat-stained face puckered up in a rueful grin. "Well, I ain't about to dance Turkey in the Middle."

"Can you move at all?"

"Only from the neck up. I was able to crawl this far yesterday with Tom helping me but—" she caught her breath, "—don't think I did myself much good. Bolt must've, uhh . . . lodged in my spine."

Steve laid a hand on her swollen belly. "This is crazy. How come they sent you out like this?"

"Relax. I'm not about to be a guard-mother. It's a UHF radio pack. Foam rubber with . . . water ballast . . . colour-matched to my skin. You gotta get real close to spot the joins."

"Certainly fooled me. But what happens if—"

"Lump-heads never manhandle or maltreat pregnant women—no matter where they come from. Didn't you know that?"

"I know they believe the unborn child is something special. Unfortunately for you it seems they forgot."

"Yesterday they couldn't see who they were shooting at."

"And yet they still hit every one of you."

"Don't remind me . . ."

Steve hesitated, uncertain how to frame the question he needed to ask. "Have you, uhh—sent a May-Day out on that thing?"

"Not yet. There's a concealed zipper but I haven't been able to reach it with my teeth."

"Does that mean . . . ?"

"Yeah. You're gonna have to tell them what's happened."

"I don't know the call-codes you've been using."

"It's S.O.P., Brickman. Feed in your own, and ask for help. Once you've identified yourself, the set will tell you whatever you need to know."

"Oh, yeah, of course." He cursed under his breath. "This is a real bitch. I wish I'd known you were part of this operation."

"Would it have changed things if you had?"

Steve spread his hands. "If I could've stopped this happening I would've. You guys blew the whole deal by leaving a trail a mile wide. Getting caught was not supposed to be part of the plan."

"Yeah . . . kind of a mess, huh?"

"The worst . . ."

A spasm of pain creased her forehead. "Guess . . . guess I'm lucky you came along. Tom couldn't have held out for long . . . bleeding too bad . . . was worried in case he . . . he didn't take me with him." Her eyes held his. "But you I can count on, eh, compadre?"

Steve grimaced. "Absolutely, but . . . are you sure this is what you want? Maybe there's—"

"Listen, the way things are, you're doing me a favour, right?"

"Right . . ."

"Is Tom, uhh . . . ?"

"He's dead," said Steve quietly, realising that Lundkwist could not even turn her neck. Great Sky-Mother, what a way to go. He stroked Lundkwist's forehead as he eased the combat knife from the sheath on his leg. "Tell me something. How long have you been with AMEXICO?"

"You're not supposed to ask things like that. But seeing how things are . . . I passed out of Rio Lobo the year before I went to the Academy. And guess what? I filed a

report recommending you for selection." Lundkwist bit
back a jagged shaft of pain and managed a lop-sided smile.
"Some joke, huh?" Her breathing became laboured. "Listen, promise me one thing. Don't let 'em . . . y'know—eat
me . . ."

"I promise."

She closed her eyes. "Thanks. It was the one thing I
. . . dreaded."

Steve ran his fingers over Lundkwist's unkempt hair and
down onto the nape of her neck, tilting her head back and
towards him. He laid his lips gently on her eyelids and on
her half-open mouth.

"Lips are dry," she whispered. "D'you have any water?"

"Yeah, sure, here—lemme help you . . ." He grasped
her hair firmly, pulled her head as far back as it would go,
placed the tip of her knife blade against the curve of her
throat and drove it up into her brain.

Drink, sweet Mother . . .

SIXTEEN

THE TRADING PARTY, led by Mr. Snow and Blue-Thunder, included nearly three hundred Bears, a hundred She-Wolves and a hundred and fifty camp followers and baggage handlers. The thirty-two captive renegades, once again bound side-by-side in pairs like yoked oxen, were dispersed throughout the column.

Leaving Southern Wyoming, the procession wound its way northeastwards across territory once held by the Da-Kota and the Minne-Sota, ancient bloodlines that had been swept away as the She-Kargo grew strong and moved westwards from its birthplace by the sacred waters of Me-Sheegun.

Although they were now crossing land occupied by rival clans there was no challenge to their progress. The turf marker poles carried aloft from head to tail of the column, and decorated with fluttering pennants and garlands of leaves or spring flowers, announced their peaceful intentions. This was the time known to the Mutes as "Walking on the Water"—a brief period when ancient rivalries were suspended while the Plainfolk clans gathered to trade with the Iron Masters.

The M'Call party proceeded at what they regarded as a leisurely pace but which, for their captives, resembled a forced march. Posses, usually four-hands strong, ran ahead bearing raised turf poles, circling wide on each flank before returning to the column to report what they had seen. There was no hunting; to take meat on someone else's "patch" would have been a violation of the truce. Unless gifts of food were offered, clans ate only what they had brought with them. At sunset each day, the decorated poles were planted to form a large square. A bonfire was lit in the centre from which smaller cooking fires were kindled. The breakers were fed and watered then shackled securely for the night. Fire songs were sung, a little rainbow grass got passed around then everybody settled down for the night in their travelling furs.

As a mark of their friendship, Steve was allowed to travel alongside Mr. Snow. He did not mention the reappearance of his own knife and the loss of Naylor's, or seek to discover who might have made the switch. With the unfortunate demise of the back-up team, the problem had become irrelevant. There was now no one to contact. When he had brought the skimmer back to the waiting Mutes and had stepped ashore bearing Lundkwist's severed head and those of her two companions, he had been acclaimed as a brother Bear. Night-Fever, who had moved into his hut during his absence, was now the proud guardian of six heads mounted on poles on either side of the door. Steve was glad he had to leave with the trading party before the fire-hardened stakes had been hammered through the skulls. He found the custom quite repellent but he had no plans to interfere. For a Tracker to be allowed to run with the Bears was an extraordinary accomplishment. It had cost him dearly to get this far and he did not intend to do or say anything that would destroy the tenuous trust he had managed to establish. What the Mutes did by brute force, the Federation achieved with the aid of technology—and on a much wider scale. Their hands were clean but their methods were equally barbarous.

At Rio Lobo, Steve had been given access to detailed relief maps of almost all the continental United States. These had been projected as a huge screen covering one end of a briefing room where he had met with Karlstrom on six separate occasions. For the Operational Director to

take such a personal interest could only mean that MX
regarded Operation SQUAREDANCE as being of the utmost importance. Cadillac had spoken of the wheel-boats
riding up the "Yellow-Stone, the Miz-Hurry and the Miz-
Hippy." From his study of the maps, and the direction in
which the column was heading, Steve had confidently
expected the meeting with the Iron Masters to take place
on the banks of the Missouri. When they crossed this
below a vast expanse of water, he fully expected them to
halt at the Mississippi. He was wrong again. Either Cadillac had been mistaken or he had not been telling the
truth. Probably the latter, Steve decided. When pressed
for more information about the Iron Masters, the young
wordsmith had become noticeably evasive. He had be-
haved in much the same way when Steve had first questioned him about Talisman.

The M'Call delegation continued on towards an absolutely gigantic stretch of water, reaching its shore near the
overgrown ruins of a pre-Holocaust site that had borne the
name of Duluth. Lake Superior, in the poetic imagery of
the Mute wordsmiths was truly a "great river."

Reflecting on the choice of rendezvous, Steve realised
that it made sense. When looking at the maps, he had
assumed the Iron Masters would travel south-west down
the Ohio River then turn north up the Mississippi finally
branching left along the Missouri into the heart of Plainfolk
territory. But this would have brought them dangerously
close to the eastern flank of the Federation's overground
estate—the New Territory of Kansas. Instead, they had
chosen a circuitous northern route, via Lake Erie, Lake
Huron and across Lake Superior. A big spread of water.
Any Mute making the return trip would be everlastingly
grateful to see dry land again.

When the M'Calls arrived at the trading post, several
other clans were already setting up camp nearby. The site
was marked by a carved and painted pole three to four feet
wide and some fifty feet high standing on a flat stretch of
ground near the shore. The traditional hosts were the
clans of the bloodline San'Paul whose turf bordered the
"great river." The camp site was octagonal, with the clans

of the She-Kargo and D'Troit occupying opposite sides. As
they were the most numerous, they were each allocated
two sections; the remaining four were allotted to the lesser
bloodlines—the San'Paul, the San'Louis, the M'Waukee,
and the C'Natti. Although they were all "of the Plainfolk,"
they were resolutely dedicated to fighting each other for
forty-seven weeks of the year. The other five encompassed
the present truce; seven hectic days of trading plus fourteen days on either side to cover the journey to and from
the trading post.

If, through the spirit of Talisman, this brief harmony could
have been prolonged, then the San'Paul and M'Waukee
would probably have aligned themselves with the She-
Kargo; the San'Louis and the C'Natti with the D'Troit. It
was the clans of the D'Troit which posed the biggest threat
to the She-Kargo's primacy amongst the Plainfolk. For
these two groups, "Walking on the Water" was like bal-
ancing on a knife edge because they were—literally—at
daggers drawn.

In the past hundred years the truce had been broken
twenty-three times with the D'Troit leading fourteen to
nine. Disputes resulting in minor injuries were not regarded as an infringement. Blackmarks—or points of
honour, depending on your point of view—marked a more
serious incident ending in one or more fatality as a result
of knives being drawn. According to Mr. Snow, the D'Troit
had always been mean mothers and were evidently quite
content to do whatever was necessary to maintain this
"bad guy" image, leaving the field of honour to the She-
Kargo. To Steve, they sounded like the team to watch.

Over the next forty-eight hours, the rest of the trading
parties arrived and set up camp alongside others of the
same blood-line. The carved trading post which was situated near the beach where the Iron Masters' boats would
run ashore, towered over an open square of ground delin-
eated by stones in which the bargaining would take place.
In the unoccupied centre of the nearby octagonal camp-
site was a smaller eight-sided area known as the "bull-
ring." At each corner was a stack of wood some six feet
high. Mr. Snow explained that these stacks would be

ignited when the wheel-boats arrived and would be kept
burning till they left. The "bull-ring" was where formal
meetings between representatives of the various clans were
held, and where the wordsmiths congregated to exchange
information. They also took turns recounting the history of
the Plainsfolk to spellbound audiences and it was here,
when darkness fell, that the fire-songs were performed,
the singers vying with each other in extolling the bravery
and feats of arms of their clan-brothers and sisters.

By tradition, no one was permitted to carry weapons
inside the area enclosed by the octagon or outside the
limits of their alloted camp site. It was also the custom for
groups of extravagantly decorated warriors to parade around
the perimeter of the camp, eye-balling the opposition and
generally being provocative. Any group engaged in this
activity was said to be "strutting their stuff." The verbal
exchanges—usually mocking remarks and thinly-veiled
insults delivered via the elliptical syntax of "fire-speech"
was the main cause of the sporadic outbreaks of violence.
Line capos, working in groups containing a representative
from each bloodline and empowered to break heads if
necessary, were usually successful in quelling any distur-
bance before it got out of hand.

Mr. Snow was concerned that there could be trouble this
time too. When the clans had all pitched camp around the
lines, it became apparent that the M'Calls had snagged a
record number of renegades. To make matters worse, they
had caught more than the whole of the D'Troit camp put
together. Their best haul—by the clan D'Vine, an old
enemy of the M'Calls, was a paltry seven. The D'Troit
were clearly discountenanced by their rivals good fortune
and things were not helped by exuberant groups of M'Call
Bears strutting their stuff and boasting about their encounter with one of the dreaded iron snakes.

Steve who, at eighteen, felt he had already seen enough
trouble to last him a lifetime stayed well back from the
action. This gathering of representative groups from every
clan was an amazing sight and he was acutely aware that
he was probably the first Tracker not only to witness but
to participate in such an event. Renegades taken over the

past few years had witnessed some of what he was seeing now but they had not returned to tell that story. He would. This was a unique opportunity to observe the Plainfolk and he intended to make the most of it.

Decked out in his feathered helmet and body plates that had been lovingly adorned by Night-Fever, Steve wandered around noting everything he saw and heard. It was fascinating to watch the inter-action of the various groups. Karlstrom had said that the Mutes had no sense of nationhood and no coherent command structure. Yet here they were, sharing the same patch of ground, a common cause and engaging in a dialogue of sorts. The way the camp was organised, the existence of the peace-keeping groups of line capos and the fact that similar gatherings had taken place over the last hundred years was proof that cooperation between the various clans and bloodlines *was* possible. But the sad fact was, in spite of this annual beanfeast, there was no inter-breeding or trade between clans, no pooling of resources. It all fell apart the moment everybody got back home.

It was hard to figure out why this should be so but it seemed to confirm the theme that was hammered home in the inspirational videos put out by the First Family: that only strong, inspired leadership could create an ordered and disciplined society where people could live and work together in harmony. The Mutes were able to achieve this sense of togetherness at clan level but could not, or would not, take it further. The idea of living at peace with their neighbours seemed to them as absurd as their ideas about life and death had first seemed to Steve. The reasons that lay behind their present attitude must have been burned deep into the Mute psyche by The War of a Thousand Suns, or its painful aftermath—the period Mr. Snow had called The Great Ice-Dark when it seemed that no living thing remained on the surface of the earth.

Darkness was the operative word. The Manual of the Federation only contained a few bald paragraphs about the first two hundred years of its existence. There were, of course, screenfuls of patriotic guff about the legendary wisdom and foresight of the Founding Father, George

Washington Jefferson the 1st and the sacrificial valour of
the Minutemen and Foragers. But there was no hard data,
no explanation for the Holocaust apart from attributing the
entire blame to the Mutes, no details as to exactly where
the First Family came from or how they rose to power, or
any hint that—as Mr. Snow had claimed—that Mutes and
Trackers had once shared a common heritage.

Steve knew, deep down, that he would never rest until
he had uncovered the last secret. Sooner or later, he
would have to go back in order to find a way into the
electronic bowels of COLUMBUS. The desire to *know*
had become an obsession, stronger even than his desire
for Clearwater, but he could not understand *why* it should
be so. He had not consciously chosen this path. Once
again, as so often in the past, Steve had the clear impression that the choice had not been his to make, that despite
all his cleverness and cunning he was nothing more than a
pawn in a game he had not even begun to comprehend.

Although much given over to moments of introspection,
Steve did not allow himself to dwell overlong on such
questions. This latest fog of incertitude was quickly swept
away by the surge of excitement generated by the sighting
of the wheel-boats.

They appeared on the horizon at the same time as the
rising sun, a conjunction whose significance Steve was not
able to appreciate until much later. Three specks which
slowly grew into dark, squat blobs. As they drew nearer
still, the outlines became clearer. Smoke curled from two
tall, thin funnels set on either side of the square superstructure. Apart from the inflatable skimmer—one of the
special devices used only by AMEXICO—Steve had never
seen pictures of boats or ships before. The video-archives
that could be accessed via the Public Service Channels
contained no reference to such things. The First Family
had obviously decided that, as far as ordinary Trackers
were concerned, waterborne vehicles fell into the category
of extraneous information—along with the Iron Masters,
Mute magic and, well—only COLUMBUS knew what else.

Some two-thirds of the Mutes left the lines—the name
given to the octagonal camp area—and trooped down to

the shore where they milled about in excited anticipation as the wheel-boats continued to advance steadily towards them in arrowhead formation. A cloud of white smoke billowed up from the lead boat then, a few seconds later, a deep steam-powered "vroooommm" drifted across the water. The Mutes replied with a whooping cheer, followed by a frenetic burst of drumming.

Now that the boats were closer, Steve—who was standing on the far left of the huge crowd—was able to see that they were propelled by large paddle wheels mounted at the stern and driven by two huge pistons that came out of angled housings on either side of the deck. The superstructure was made up of three ornate galleried decks with an extra housing fore and aft which, he guessed, served as a command centre like the saddle on a wagon-train. This massive pile rested on a wide, shallow-draught hull with low sides and a sloping, blunt-nosed foredeck.

The overall colour of the boats was black, relieved with dark stained wood and red, gold or silver trim. Pennants, bearing strange markings fluttered from masts spaced around the sides of the top decks. Steve glimpsed crewmen moving along the galleries and wondered which of the three ships Clearwater was on. At this very moment she might be scanning the shore, looking right at him without suspecting for one moment he was there.

"Excited?"

Steve turned to find Mr. Snow standing beside him with two of the M'Call clan elders, Boston-Bruin, and Awesome-Wells. "What do *you* think?"

Mr. Snow looked amused. "This is the twenty-eighth time I've made this trip and they *still* send shivers down my spine."

"I can understand how you feel. I mean, we've got some pretty spectacular stuff back in the Federation, but . . ." Steve gestured towards the wheel-boats, ". . . whichever way you slice it, these guys are in the big league."

The boats responded, as if on cue, sending wave upon wave of multi-coloured rockets soaring skywards. Steve watched openmouthed as they exploded, throwing out cascades of stars which burst apart as they fell, filling the sky with dazzling showers of rainbow-coloured light.

A rumbling "Heyy-yahhhhh" rose from throats of five thousand Mutes.

"Never fails to impress the natives," said Mr. Snow drily.

"We have rockets too," riposted Steve. "But they create a different kind of impact."

"I bet . . ."

Steve let it pass. "Tell me—the markings on those banners—do they mean anything?"

"The shapes—like that flower pattern for instance—are the marks of the various houses to which the wheel-boats belong. The Iron Masters are a warrior people like us but instead of clans they have families. They even have a first family."

"But not a President-General."

"No. Their great chieftain is called the Shogun."

"What about the other markings? The ones that look like animals tracks—or dead spiders."

Mr. Snow smiled. "That's a good description of them. I have no idea what they mean but in the Old Time they were known as ideograms. They are the signs for words which speak silently to the eye."

So . . . the Iron Masters could read and type. "I've never seen anything like them," remarked Steve.

"It is a strange tongue," admitted the old wordsmith. "Totally incomprehensible to the ear *and* the eye. Fortunately they can also speak as we do but in a curious way—as if they had the tongue of a snake."

"Why do you call them dead-faces?"

"You will see for yourself soon enough." Mr. Snow took hold of Steve's arm and led him aside. "A word of advice. I look upon you with feelings of friendship and high regard but you are a headstrong young man who sometimes speaks rashly. I, who am older and wiser, know this rashness springs from your undoubted courage and—more regrettably—from an inflated sense of self-importance. As the years pass, your manner may become more circumspect but in the meantime—"

"I think I get the message—"

"—watch your lip. These people you're about to meet have absolutely no sense of humour. Their idea of a joke is to watch some poor paisano get a red hot spike shoved up his ass an inch at a time."

"They sound like nice people to do business with."

"They may not be much fun to work with but they offer better terms than the Federation."

Steve grimaced ruefully. "I guess I asked for that."

Mr. Snow patted his arm. "You know something? You're too sensitive to be a Tracker." He saw Steve's eyes return to the approaching wheel-boats. "Listen—you want to watch? Go ahead. My advice is to keep back but if you do run into any of these dinks, or one of them speaks to you, act simple and—this may come hard—try a little servility. Avoid too much eye contact and bow a lot from the waist. They like that. They do it all the time."

"Anything else?"

"No, that's it."

The huge rear paddles of the wheel-boats slowed then went into reverse, turning the waters under the stern into a bubbling carpet of white foam. The lead boat dropped rapidly astern and, having arrested its forward movement, proceeded to turn in its own length. Foam boiled up from under the bows indicating the presence of an additional propulsion unit or units—presumably to aid just such a manoeuvre. Having presented its port beam to shore the boat dropped anchor in deep water while its two companions continued their stately advance.

Now that they were closer, Steve was better able to appreciate their impressive bulk. The Federation wagon—trains were longer, sleeker and technically more sophisticated but they suddenly seemed quite puny compared to these huge floating fortresses. There was an earsplitting crunch of iron-shod timber on gravel as the two boats ran their flat bow sections up onto the shelving beach, coming to rest about one hundred yards apart. A murmur of anticipation greeted the appearance of the first Iron Masters, short, stocky, dark-complexioned individuals with a broad white stripe running down the centre of their faces

from forehead to chin. Dividing into two teams, the Iron
Masters wound latticed wooden walkways out from both
sides of the bow decks of the flank boats; one for boarding
and one for coming ashore. Parties of Mutes waded into
the shallows to seize the ends as they angled down, carrying them onto the beach where they were firmly bedded
in the pebbles. With this task accomplished, the Mutes
formed two densely packed lines that began at the water's
edge by the bows of the vessels and converged on the
square of ground which lay behind the trading post.

It was here that Mr. Snow now stood with the two
senior M'Call elders and the leaders of the other clans.
Steve, who had elbowed his way through to the front row
of spectators thought the old wordsmith had rarely looked
so impressive as he did now. He had certainly never been
as well turned out, his walking skins freshly dyed and patterned with relief stitching, clusters of feathers and stones,
his brilliant white hair plaited, ribboned and boned.

Some two dozen "white stripes" swarmed down the
walkways of each boat, carrying lengths of timber and
blocks of wood, folding screens and rolls of cloth. The
"whites" wore loose, geometrically-patterned tunics over
wide trousers which ended several inches above the ankle,
and strange open shoes made up of a sole and straps—a
type Steve had never seen before. But it was their faces
which were the most arresting feature. The Iron Masters
all wore close-fitting masks moulded in the shape of a
savage, snarling face. As they scuttled past, Steve spotted
several variations in the basic design, all equally ferocious,
some quite alarming. All wore wide headbands made of
white cloth tied at the nape of the neck and bearing a large
solid red circle at the front flanked by two of the strange
word-signs.

With practised movements, the "whites" quickly turned
the material they were carrying into a raised, cloth-covered
platform facing the assembled Mute elders. The folding
screens were opened out and placed along the rear edge,
almost touching the fifty-foot high trading post. Their task
accomplished, the "whites" scurried back to the wheel-
boats. Seconds later, the heavies appeared. More masked,

stocky individuals but dressed in full armour and bearing a long and a short curved sword in elaborately decorated scabbards thrust through a sash tied around their waist. The contorted features of their black face masks were picked out in gold, silver and red, their gleaming metal helmets had wide, swept-down brims and they wore layered and jointed body armour that covered them front and back from head to toe.

"Samurai," muttered the Mute at Steve's shoulder.

To Steve, they looked like oversized bug-uglies. He watched them file down the ramp past the rows of armed Mute warriors who outnumbered them several hundred to one. Yet despite this vast numerical superiority, it was the Mutes who bowed low while the Iron Masters swaggered past as if they owned the place. Mindful of Mr. Snow's advice, Steve followed suit. Each samurai was accompanied by two armed "red stripes"—presumably a higher grade of flunkey. One carried a square banner hung on a spacer from the end of a long thin pole; the other a folding, highly polished stool. The twenty-four samurai, twelve from each boat, formed two lines from the water's edge to the trading post then turned inwards to face each other. The "reds" formed up in pairs immediately behind them.

As they took up position, a small slab-sided craft with a curving fore and aft deck line and slim central cabin set out from the wheel-boat moored offshore. It was propelled by four standing oarsmen and steered by a helmsman with the aid of a huge paddle. Six more masked samurai, stood guard in front and behind the cabin, their arms folded, legs planted firmly astride. When the boat reached the shore, the brawny rowers stowed their oars, threaded matching carrying shafts through each side of the red and gold cabin, got their shoulders underneath and lifted it clear of the deck. Preceded by the six swordsmen, they carried the ornately decorated box towards the trading post. This time, even the Iron Masters bowed, each one joining the procession as it went past.

The mine of information next to Steve whispered, "Yama-Shita."

"What's that?" hissed Steve.

"Name of big Iron Master. He controls boats which make trade with Plainfolk."

When the procession reached the square, the Mutes left the beach and reformed behind and on each side of the welcoming elders. The palanquin—for that is what the cabin had now become—was lifted gingerly onto the platform and placed in front of the trading post. The shafts were withdrawn and the sides and front were folded open to reveal the chief Iron Master reposing majestically in a lavishly decorated chair. At the sight of him all the Plainfolk fell to their knees and put their noses on the ground. Steve, taken by surprise, was the last one down.

Yama-Shita's mask, armour and general appearance was even more impressive than the samurai who now took their seats on either side of him. The "reds" having made sure their masters were seated comfortably, planted their banners along the back of the platform and spaced themselves out at ground level, around the front and sides of the platform, one hand on hip, the other poised ostentatiously on the hilts of their long curved swords.

Steve edged his way to the rear of the crowd as the formal welcoming speeches were exchanged. Mr. Snow had explained that the real business began on Day Two; on the first day, the Iron Masters compiled a list of all the clans now present and the heads of each delegation drew lots to decide the order in which they would be called into the square to "make a trade." Beside the captured renegades and the Mute journey-men, there were woven baskets of grain, dried meat, small pouches of precious Dream Cap, sacks of rainbow grass, skins and furs to be exchanged for new sharp iron. All items had to be inspected, quantities had to be checked, their barter value agreed. The merchandise had to be listed, tallied and loaded; the weapons that the Iron Masters had shipped from the east had to be brought ashore. But the dead-faces were not just merchants of death; they traded woven mats and cloth, thread, needles, knives and various tools and farming implements to which handles could be fixed—shovels, rakes and a host of other items Steve could not put a name to.

Once the formalities had been dispensed with, the samurai summoned their administrators, officials of subordinate rank able to translate the spoken word into silent-speech. The elders from each clan lined up patiently in front of a team of masked scribes equipped with brushes and rolls of a kind of plasfilm that Mr. Snow called paper. Using a brush and a jet black liquid called ink, the scribes noted down details of the clan's present numbers—how many male and female warriors, elders, den mothers, children, et cetera. The speed at which they composed the various symbols was amazing and Steve was forced to marvel at their dexterity.

The stated purpose of this "trading register" which was updated every year was to enable the Iron Masters to estimate the future needs of the Plainfolk. It occurred to Steve that Karlstrom would probably give his right arm for such information. The problem was it appeared to be completely inaccessible. It was compiled by hand in such a primitive way it was virtually impossible to process. Each scrap of data was recorded in symbols that only an Iron Master could understand and the sheer bulk of the complete register would make its theft a major operation.

Steve left them to it. Making his way down to the shore, he sauntered up and down in front of the beached wheelboats in the hope of catching a glimpse of Clearwater. It was a wasted journey. He scanned the decks and galleried superstructure for over an hour, willing her to appear, but only caught a glimpse of more Iron Masters. Steve consoled himself with the thought that, if the Shogun, the big boss back in Beth-Lem, regarded the delivery of an arrowhead and the secrets of powered flight as something special, then perhaps Cadillac and Clearwater had been treated as something special too. If so, they could be on the third wheel-boat, moored off-shore; the lavishly-decorated vessel that housed Yama-Shita.

From what Steve had seen so far, the dead-faces appeared to be a highly disciplined bunch who knew how to put on a good show and were clearly able to look after themselves. A Tracker could relate to people like that. In addition to their long and short curved swords, some of the samurai carried bows—not the crossbow with the rifle-type butt and stock prized by the Mutes, but a completely different design—a light, elegant, double curved bow that they carried on their backs in a flat woven basket containing a clutch of extra long arrows, flighted with cut feathers. Their ships, armour and weapons were proof of their superb craftsmanship but it was all low level stuff. There was no sign of them possessing what the Mutes called the "High Craft"—the technological marvels of the electronic age.

The Iron Masters' society seemed to be pitched halfway between the Trackers and the Mutes, taking something from each but totally different from both. They had taken a third way. But where had they come from? And how had they survived the Holocaust? Were they immune to the sickness that had been spread through the air by the poisonous presence of the Mutes? Or were they merely another species of lump-head, a breakaway bloodline that had come up in the world, and was now hiding their common ancestry beneath the masks and armour and a coded nonsense-language? More questions to which he would probably never find the answers. But . . . if the Iron Masters *were* a different race that had survived the Holocaust and had somehow sprung up later, then there could be others. There might even be other lands beyond the eastern and western seas—with *different* people with *different* ways of doing things. People who might never even have *heard* of the First Family.

Despite his rebellious nature Steve had been so thoroughly indoctrinated he found that hard to visualise. But in the Federation everything had been so simple. The world was divided into "us and them," Trackers and Mutes. There were no ifs and buts, no uncertainties. The way ahead was clear. Everyone knew who they were and what they had to do. But now . . .

Steve's thoughts returned to Clearwater. He toyed with the idea of swimming out to Yama-Shita's wheel-boat then decided to heed Mr. Snow's advice. At this point, there was too many unknowns. Better to wait and see what happened.

At the end of the day, the Iron Masters retired to their ships and backed them offshore to anchor in deep water for the night. Steve listened to the shouted commands as the Iron Masters prepared to get underway and could make no sense of the language at all. It sounded as if they were speaking Basic backwards with their tongue stuck halfway down their throats.

He returned to the lines where dozens of cooking fires sent up thin columns of smoke. Around the bull-ring, the eight bonfires were already well alight and a stick and drum group had swung into action. And round the lines, there were Mutes chanting, singly or in groups, accompanied by wind-pipes or percussion blocks, playing a game with coloured pebbles on a piece of buffalo skin marked out in squares, rapping in groups and generally having a good time. One of the prime aims of the week-long festivities was to ensure that the journey-men—the Mutes who had been tapped to go down river—had the time of their lives. As a result, the air was so thick with pipe smoke you got high just by breathing in, and it was difficult to walk more than ten yards in any direction without having to step over some heavy traffic.

The only group not participating in the festivities were the captured renegades. Steve had taken care to steer clear of Dave Kelso and his friends but he had continued to keep a friendly, if distant, eye on Jodi Kazen. The breakers were still kept separated from each other, and guarded twenty-four hours a day. Escape was not the only danger; there had been occasions, in the past, when captured renegades had been stolen by other clans—not always from rival bloodlines. And once they had been spirited away they were almost impossible to get back without a major blood-bath. The M'Calls had no intention of losing valuable trading points.

Steve had not spoken to Jodi since being venomously rebuffed but he bore her no malice. He wandered through the area where Malone's breakers were being held and eventually found her. She didn't look overjoyed to see him but, on the other hand, she didn't spit in his face when he hunkered down beside her.

"You getting enough to eat?"

"Would it matter if I wasn't?"

"Steve sighed. "Jodi, come on—give me a break. We were on the trail together. That still means something to me. D'you think I don't care about what's happening to you and these other guys?"

"Yeah, well, you won't have to care much longer. I hear we'll be shipping out in a couple of days."

"Listen—it may not be so bad. These wheeler-dealers look to be pretty sharp guys. I mean, they're clean, they cut their hair—and they look as if they run a tight ship. I've got a feeling we could relate to them a whole lot better than with the Mutes."

Jodi didn't look convinced.

"In fact," continued Steve, "in some ways I wish I was going with you. I'd like to find out more about their set-up." He paused. "Aren't you curious?"

Jodi eyed him dismissively. "I prefer to stay with my own kind."

"Jodi, listen. As you say, you're due to ship out in two, maybe three days. You're right—why should I care what you think about me? The fact is I do. If Kelso and Medicine-Hat and the other guys have got me pegged for a lump-sucker, okay, let 'em think that. But I want things to be straight between me and you. Like I said before, there are things you don't know about. Don't be fooled by the way I look. I'm here because I've got a job to do."

Her eyes held his as she ran her tongue slowly around her lips. "Why are you telling me this?"

"All kinds of reasons. When you went over the side, I asked for permission to take a search party down river—"

"Yeah, I know, you told me."

"Big D said 'no,' " continued Steve. "But you came back from the dead and helped save *my* life. Who knows? Maybe we might meet up again some day. If we do, I want you to know you can count on me to do what's right. Last time we spoke, you wanted to take the quick way out.

But you're too good a soldier to waste on the end of a knife. Oh, I admit that right now things don't look so hot. You guys may be in for a rough time but it can't be worse than what you've been through."

"True . . ."

"You gotta hang in there, Jodi. As long as you're alive, you've got to keep fighting. You owe it to yourself and the Federation."

Jodi responded with a harsh laugh. "The Federation . . . ?"

"Yes," said Steve. "I was on that flight-deck when the storm hit. I was one of the people who tried to haul you down out of the sky. I saw the shape you were in. Most guys would have given up and gone in nose first. But not you. If you could have, you'd have dragged yourself back upstream by your fingertips. You're not a breaker, Jodi—anymore than I'm a lump-sucker."

Jodi eyed him then laughed dismissively. "The person you're talking about died when I went into that river."

Steve responded with a searching look. "I find that hard to believe. Heck, I mean, you were so, well . . . gung-ho."

"I know. This change of heart came as quite a surprise to me too. Like you, being a wingman was all I ever thought about. The day I stepped aboard The Lady was the proudest moment of my life. I served under Hartmann and Big D for five years. Five *good* years. If I'd come through this one I'd have earned a Lucky Six and a trip to the White House." She smiled. "I used to lie in my bunk working out what I'd say to the P-G, wondering how I would feel when I actually met him face to face. My one big worry was that my knees would give way."

Steve nodded sympathetically but said nothing.

"When you're on the trains, or in the Federation, the pressure is on you all the time. You accept everything because you've been raised to believe that's the way it is. The *only* way. And it makes sense. It's only when you make the break, when you start free-basing, that you get time to think things out for yourself . . . to ask questions. Being a breaker gives you a whole new perspective on things. It didn't come easy. Took me a while to shake

loose from the system. I've still got a long way to go." She
grimaced. "The Family did a good job on us."

" 'Only people fail,' " said Steve, quoting Uncle Bart.
" 'Not the system.' "

"You still believe that?"

Steve shrugged. "Six months with the Mutes gave me
time to think about things too."

"And . . . ?"

"It, uhh . . . changes you . . . makes it hard to go
back."

"But you still want to."

Steve weighed his reply carefully. "Like it or not, that's
where the future is, Jodi. The Mutes can't win. And when
they're gone how long do you think you guys'll be able to
hold out?"

"It's a big country . . ."

"Sure it is. But even if you and the other guys had
gotten away from the M'Calls you'd still be living like
hunted animals from one year to the next."

"Not necessarily. Once we'd built up our numbers Malone was planning to cross over the Rockies. He told us
there was some good country on the other side. A place
close to the sea where it never snowed and where there
were so many food-trees nobody ever went hungry."

"Oh, yeah?"

"Yeah. A place called California."

"Pipe-dreams, Jodi. Even if this place existed why bother
to make the trip? It's a dead end. Who is there to come after
you? Only the First Family can create new life. It doesn't
matter how clever Malone is, or how many there are like
him. You guys are never going to amount to anything."

"You're probably right," she admitted. "But it's a dead
end either way. Even if you and I were lucky enough to
get back home in one piece the Federation would never
put us back into circulation."

Steve bit his lip. "Why?"

"Because we've been out too long. We know too much."

"Like what?"

The undamaged side of her face was creased by a dry
smile. "Isn't it obvious? You were captured last June and

you've been breathing unfiltered air ever since. How do you feel?"

"Okay, but—"

"Have you asked yourself why?"

"Yeah, but—"

She waved his reply aside. "There is no magic bullet, Brickman. The stuff they give you at your MedEx is either a vitamin shot or a placebo. I don't know who fed you this idea about an anti-radiation serum but there ain't no such thing. It's not necessary. There's no more sickness in the air."

Steve thought back to what the President-General had said about the need to deny the existence of Mute magic. If they could do that and make any claims to the contrary a Code One offence then they were capable—as he already suspected—of even greater deceptions. But he could not tell Jodi that. He had to appear a reluctant convert in order to draw out everything she knew—or now believed. He eyed her cautiously. "How did you figure that out?"

"Medicine-Hat has been free-basing for three years. He knows of breakers who haven't been near a hypodermic needle for more than five and they're still in good shape." She saw his look of disbelief. "The guy is absolutely straight—why would he make up a story like that?"

"Why not? He's a breaker. You didn't have any choice, and maybe he didn't either, but most of these guys are bad hats. Drop-outs, cee-bees, deserters. It's only natural for them to bad-mouth the Family and the Federation. They want to make themselves look good."

"Okay—what's your explanation?"

"Jodi, I don't have one. All I know is my guard-father put in a double six up the line and he's dying because of it—may even be dead for all I know. If there's no more sickness in the air how did he—and all the others—pull a trick?"

She gave a sour laugh. "Brace yourself, Brickman. I'm gonna let you in on the big joke. The radiation that's killing Trail-Blazers is not *in* the atmosphere. It's *inside* the wagon trains!"

Steve tried to come to terms with what she was saying.

"But . . . what about the geiger counters? When you take them outside—"

Jodi cut him off. "They're wired up to give a reverse reading. Everything's been riggedfrom start to finish. Everything we've been told is a pack of lies!"

It was too much. Steve was no stranger to conspiracy theories but the enormity and the ruthlessness of this alleged crime against generations of unsuspecting Trackers left him stunned, floundering. "This can't be right. There has to be some other explanation."

"That's what you keep saying."

"But where's the proof?"

"You and I are proof!" she cried. She swept a hand towards the nearest renegades "Look around you! If what the Family says is true, all these guys would be basket cases by now!"

Steve shook his head. "No . . . it doesn't make sense. Poppa-Jack was a hero. Why would they kill someone who was doing such a great job?"

"To keep us under control," replied Jodi. "To stop people escaping."

Steve frowned. "But why would anyone want to escape from the Federation? The First Family has sworn to lead us back to the blue sky world. That's what all the effort and the sacrifice has been for. What happened, Jodi? When you and I were together aboard The Lady, you were proud of being a Trail-Blazer. You said so yourself. Are you trying to tell me none of that means anything anymore?"

"Of course not. The way you're dressed up you've got a nerve even asking! I'm still a Tracker and always will be. All I'm trying to get into your skull is that the First Family has been lying to us. The overground's been safe for the last fifty years—maybe even longer!"

"Pure renegade talk, Jodi. Can't you see that? Malone and the others have fed you this shit to turn you against the Federation. But it's just a sick fantasy. They've piped too much rainbow grass. You want to know what I think? I think there are people who get sick and people like you and me who don't. Roz told me the Life Institute has been conducting clinical research on straight Mutes for several decades trying to isolate the genetic mechanism that makes them immune. Who's to say they haven't found the answer? All of us are created in the Life Institute. Maybe you and I—and these other guys were born with that "magic bullet" inside us."

Jodi responded with a deadpan look. "It's an interesting theory . . ."

"It's no more outrageous than the one you just came out with."

"No, I guess not."

"Like I said before, I've had time to think about things . . . ask a few awkward questions. But listening to you sound off makes me feel that maybe there are times when a little knowledge is a dangerous thing. You and I just don't know enough to be able to understand the whole picture. Maybe things aren't as straightforward as we would like them to be and maybe the set-up inside the Federation isn't as perfect as it should be but . . . that's the way the world is. I think it's important to believe that the people at the top are doing the best job they can. If we keep faith, and do the same, we'll win through."

She reflected a while, then said, "Level with me, Brickman. Are you Family?"

Steve frowned then laughed. "What a strange question. Do you really think I'd be here if I was?"

"I wasn't born yesterday. Last year was my sixth trip up the line. A guy gets to hear things. The Family is everywhere."

"You may be right. But I'm not one of them—and that's the truth. Although, if I was, I imagine I'd have to say that anyway." He smiled. "You can't be serious, surely. I mean, if you really thought I was Family would we be having this kind of conversation?"

"Why not? There's nothing they can do to me now." She eyed him evenly. "You worry me, Brickman. I thought I had you figured but now . . . I just don't know what the hell you're up to. Maybe Malone was right. Maybe you *are* an undercover Fed."

Steve reached out and gripped her hands firmly. "Lis-

ten to me, and listen good. I'm not Family and I'm not a
Fed—whatever that's supposed to be. I'm just a guy who's
trying to do his best to fight for what he believes in. And
that includes you."

Jodi appeared to take this last remark seriously—albeit
with some reluctance. "Well . . . I guess it's always good
to know who your friends are."

"Listen—no matter what the circumstances, if we meet
up again, all I'm asking for is a fair shake."

"Okay, I'll, uhh . . . bear it in mind."

"Thanks. And if I don't manage to see you again before
you leave—good luck and . . ."

She gripped his outstretched hand firmly. "Good hunting . . ."

SEVENTEEN

STEVE spent the next day in similar fashion, wandering around the lines making a mental note of everything he saw and heard until called upon to help carry bundles of furs and produce from the M'Call camp-site to the trading post for examination. It was during one of these delivery runs that he was tapped by Mr. Snow.

"Just the man I'm looking for . . ." He led Steve over to where a large group of M'Call Bears were clustered around Blue-Thunder. They stood aside as the wordsmith approached. Steve saw that Blue-Thunder was holding what looked like a rifle. "What d'you think of that?"

Steve accepted the weapon from the paramount warrior with a respectful nod and examined it from end to end, testing some of the working parts. He had never seen such a strange object before. It was a well-finished weapon, made of steel and brass with a polished stock made of dark, close-grained wood. But it had no optical sights, just a small blade at the front and a notched block that could be moved along a calibrated scale mounted on the rear end of a single barrel with a bore like a waterpipe. The magazine was a curious revolving metal cylinder with ten holes drilled through it. Two domed pieces of steel covered the back and front of the cylinder where it protruded on each side of the rifle stock. At the rear end of the barrel, behind and above the cylinder, was a flat, spiked metal hammer that could be pulled back with the thumb and which clicked forward when the trigger was pulled. This action caused the cylinder to revolve to the right, bringing another of the holes under the hammer.

"These holes must be for the bullets . . ."

"That's right. Iron plugs. You put them in from the back. Just press that catch."

Steve did so. The barrel, forestock and cylinder broke open, pivoting foward around a pin located just ahead of the trigger guard. He clicked the barrel back into place then looked inside the brass butt plate and examined the underside of the stock. "Where do they keep the compressed air bottle?"

"It doesn't used compressed air. Each bullet is filled with a powder that drives it out of the barrel."

"What kind of powder?"

"They call it gunpowder. You saw the fireworks. It's similar to whatever makes those rockets fly into the air." Mr. Snow released a catch on the stock just above and behind the trigger guard and swung aside a small cover plate. Inside was a recessed compartment with a central spigot and a primitive escapement mechanism. "A coiled ribbon made of paper fits on that spike and passes up under the hammer. The ribbon contains a string of small flat beads of the same special powder. When you pull the trigger the hammer hits one of the beads. It catches fire and lights the back of the bullet. Bang! Away it goes. When you release the trigger, a new piece of ribbon moves under the hammer."

Steve smiled. "Interesting idea. What's the range?"

"Half a bolt. You measure things differently. Yama-Shita said it was the equal of your rifle. Better in some ways."

Steve eased back the hammer and pulled the trigger to release it. "If you have to do this every time you fire, then our guns are faster—they fire three bullets at a time and hold many more."

"True. But as Yama-Shita pointed out, your rifles are no good to us. Once the wind has escaped from the bottles, they are a heap of junk. Your masters are not stupid.

They've made sure that those who see the light and run from your dark cities have nothing to fight with."

"You're right. I never thought of it like that before." Even so, thought Steve, it was no contest. An iron plug against 0.225 calibre steelpoints. Ten rounds against a sixty shot magazine with an option of single shot, triple volley or full auto. Exploding powder, fire, flame, noise. Stone-age stuff. Trackers would be able to locate the rifleman's position immediately. And with only a clumsy blade and sighting and ranging system how could they guarantee to hit anything? "Is everybody getting these?"

"No. This is a special bonus for delivering the arrowhead. We get the first hundred. If we are able to use them to beat back the sand-burrowers, Yama-Shita will bring more next year and the other clans will get the chance to make a trade."

"Hmmmm, well . . . I know it's none of my business but I have to tell you I'm not impressed. In fact, if you want my honest opinion, it's not worth a crow's fart."

Mr. Snow remained unfazed. "Yama-Shita says that, in the Old Time, all killing guns followed this principle."

"If they did it must have been a long time ago. We've moved on a little since then."

"Go ahead, laugh. You people think you know it all."

"I wasn't laughing, Old One. It is you who has taught me what little I know of the blue-sky world and of the time before it came into being. I still have much to learn."

"You also have much to *un*-learn. This thing doesn't send up lots of little coloured stars." Mr. Snow extended his little finger and pointed to the second joint. "It throws out a piece of iron this long and this thick that'll stop a buffalo in its tracks."

"Really?"

"Yes. And if it does that, it's going to blow your friends right out of their socks."

"Do you have any of these bullets?"

"No. But I have seen one. Yama-Shita has promised to give us a demonstration of their power."

"When?"

"Now. You're just in time."

Steve glimpsed a flurry of activity on the fore-deck of the nearest flank-boat. A group of Iron Masters—samurai and reds—appeared at the head of the walkway and descended in single file. In their midst were three bare-foot individuals whose arms were tightly bound behind their backs. They were clad only in red baggy trousers. A placard, bearing several of the strange word-signs, hung around their necks and down over their hairless, yellow-tinted chests. They walked with their heads bowed and instead of the usual masks, their faces were covered with a piece of straw matting, with holes cut out for the eyes and nostrils.

Defaulters, thought Steve. So the Iron Masters had their law breakers too.

More M'Calls joined those already on the beach and within minutes their numbers were swelled by She-Kargo Mutes from other clans. The leading samurai approached Mr. Snow. Everybody bowed.

"We will now demonstrate potential of new weapon." He indicated a second samurai. "Now you give rifle."

Mr. Snow bowed from the waist and handed it over to the second samurai who responded in a similar manner. Steve, Blue-Thunder and those closest to them watched carefully as the samurai marksman loaded the rifle. One of his red-stripes held open a small wooden casket. In it was a row of slots containing the ribbon detonators, and four rings of holes, each containing ten bullets. With deft fingers, the samurai inserted the reel of paper ribbon containing the beads of powder, advanced the first section under the hammer and tore off the excess. Then breaking the rifle open, he fitted ten rounds into the holes in the cylinder. Compared to the steelpoint rounds made by the Federation they looked enormous. A total waste of energy and metal. A clear case of overkill.

While this was going on, the three luckless dinks destined to be on the receiving end of this demonstration were marched northwards up the beach. Three stout posts had been planted one behind the other in the shingle, the first about one hundred yards from where Steve stood alongside the samurai with the rifle, the last a considerable distance away. The first defaulter was placed to the right of the first post, his head coming more or less level with the top. The execution party went on down the beach with the other "targets." As each victim was placed in position, the placard round his neck was reversed, presenting a blank white square for the rifleman to aim at. The red-stripes escorting each man then withdrew to the water's edge. Groups of Mutes, responding to waves from the chief Iron Master, ran along the grassy fringe of the beach and stood opposite each of the execution sites.

The stage was set. Steve could only make a guesstimate of the range but, by comparison with the first post, the second appeared to be some two hundred and fifty yards away, the third around five hundred. The guy standing alongside was little more than a dot on the landscape. Without an optical sight the samurai would need assistance from someone like Talisman to have a hope of hitting him.

The chief samurai barked out an order. The marksman raised the rifle, pulled it hard into his shoulder, took aim and fired. There was a loud bang. A tongue of flame leapt briefly out of the barrel followed by a cloud of white smoke. The noise made by the gun was followed almost immediately by a sharp explosive crack as the bullet smashed into the post by the side of the first victim's head, sending a shower of cream-coloured wood splinters into the air. The M'Calls standing nearby saw the dead-face raise his head and square his shoulders. The second shot pierced the straw mask, slamming him backwards as it blew his skull apart.

"Heyyy-yahhh," murmured the watching Mutes.

The rifleman adjusted the back sight, took aim, blew a hole through the second post then felled the victim with a chest shot, the heavy bullet passing through the centre of the placard. The small crowd responded with another cry of approbation.

Steve turned to Mr. Snow. "I take back what I said. It's got real knock-down capability but it's not the answer. Too much noise and smoke. It'll give away your position every time you fire."

"True. But first your people have to get into range."

"I wouldn't get too excited. Let's see how well he does with the next one."

Taking careful aim, the rifleman fired at the third post. The red-stripes standing opposite, by the water's edge, signalled a hit. The samurai eased the rifle off his shoulder, breathed deeply then cradled it again, drew a bead on the third dead-face and squeezed the trigger. Ba-boommm!

The man didn't go down.

There was a moment's silence then there was a curious breathy cry from the watching Iron Masters. "Hhhhawwww!"

Lowering the butt of the rifle to the ground, the marksman turned to the chief samurai and bowed his head. His shoulders drooped in mortification as his superior launched into a high-speed burst of abuse. When it was over, the marksman bowed lower still, passed the rifle to a waiting red-stripe, handed over his two swords to another, bowed again, then ran off down the beach. Reaching the third post, he positioned himself to the left, opposite the last defaulter.

Taking possession of the rifle, the chief assured himself that everything was in order, took aim and fired. The first warm-up shot split the post, the second took out the defaulter, the third blew a hole in the unfortunate samurai.

"Heyyy-yahhh . . ."

The samurai offered the rifle to Mr. Snow, acknowledged his deep bow and swaggered away with his red-stripes, leaving the other, lesser Iron Master to coach the M'Calls in the loading and firing of the weapon.

"Do you want to try it?" asked Mr. Snow.

"Later."

They walked along the beach to inspect the splintered posts and the inert bodies that lay beside them. To Steve, the demonstration was both sobering and highly instructive. Despite his dismissive evaluation, the primitive rifle packed a heavyweight punch and, in the right hands, could be fired with great accuracy. It still had, in his opinion, many limitations but its introduction in any appreciable numbers would totally upset the present tactical advantage enjoyed by Trackers in overground operations against the Plainfolk.

The Iron Masters had performed as impressively as the rifle. The disciplined way in which the individuals concerned had observed their own rigid codes of behaviour confirmed Mr. Snow's earlier remarks about their cruelty and ruthlessness. As in the Federation, "operational failure" was not tolerated, especially when the circumstances involved a loss of what the Iron Masters called "face."

He caught Mr. Snow's eye. "Amazing people. Did you see how those guys just stood there, chin up, waiting for the hit? Didn't move a muscle. That takes real dedication."

Mr. Snow answered with a grim smile. "When you think of the alternatives, I'd say that standing still and getting shot at was about the best these poor paisanos could have hoped for."

From time to time, during the afternoon, and throughout the following day, Steve wandered down to the shore and hung around expectantly. He waited in vain. By sunset, when the boats again withdrew to anchor off-shore, Clearwater and Cadillac had still not appeared.

He went in search of Mr. Snow and found him divesting himself of some of his finery. "Can't bear these jamborees," he grumbled.

Steve took in the happy bustle of activity going on around them. "What an odd thing to say. You're not a man of violence and I know, from what you've said, that its consequences sicken you. When you think of what is happening here, people from every clan coming together as one great big happy family—apart from a few little upsets here and there—the thing I ask *myself* is—'Why can't it be like this all the time?' "

"A very reasonable question," grumped Mr. Snow. "Things have certainly been very quiet so far. Don't worry. It'll hot up soon. It's bound to."

"But *why*? Why can't you take this opportunity to get together and iron out your differences? Instead of being constantly at each others' throats why don't you join forces and fight the Federation? If all the summoners came together and—"

Mr. Snow waved his suggestion aside. "Yes, yes, yes,

we know all that. Look—nobody's perfect, least of all *us*. You've decided to cast us in the role of the hard-pressed but noble savage—I suppose because of Clearwater, and the fact that we didn't turn you into dried meat twists. Dangerous, romantic notions, Brickman. There *are* mysteries, and there *is* magic, but this is a hard, cruel world. It's true that for a brief moment every year the Plainfolk gather to 'Walk upon the Water.' And yes, for a while it works, in spite of the bad blood between the She-Kargo and the D'Troit. But the sad truth is that four or five days of fellowship is about as much as most of us can stand. I mean—can you imagine what it would be like *always* having to be nice to such a bunch of shitheads? Mo-Town! Their clans would be wandering all over our turf, taking the meat from our knives. We wouldn't have a place to call our own! Next thing, they'd be chasing our womenfolk and, if that didn't start a fight, everyone would just lie around getting fat and making babies. Pretty soon you wouldn't be able to move for people. You call that living? We *need* the action, the excitement, the danger to get the, uhh—," he snapped his fingers, "what d'you call it . . . ?"

"Adrenalin—"

"Right. To get the adrenalin going. Surely someone with your background can understand that?"

"Yes, sure, but what about the Talis—?"

Mr. Snow cut him short again. "Look—don't start beating me over the head with the Talisman Prophecy! I was the one that told you about it—remember? 'A nation shall be forged from the fires of war, and the Plainfolk shall be like a sword in the hands of Talisman their Saviour.'"

"Do you believe it?"

"Of course I do! It's a great idea. I can't think of anything I'd like more," said Mr. Snow with less than total conviction.

"Okay, if it's possible, why can't it happen now?"

"Because *we* have to change first!" cried Mr. Snow. He banged his fists against his chest then threw his hands in the air. "And for that to happen we need Talisman. *He's* the only one who can work miracles."

"What's a miracle?"

Mr. Snow loosed a long-suffering sigh. "A miracle is a divinely-inspired event that transcends the known physical laws thought to govern the universe—" He broke off. "But then you don't know about 'divine' either. You don't accept any of that stuff."

"You mean like Mo-Town, the Sky Voices and Talisman? That's not quite true. I've escaped death so many times I'm beginning to think that perhaps some power *is* watching over me." He saw the look of cynical disbelief. "I mean that."

"Wonders never cease."

"Okay, you've told me you don't like the D'Troit but you still haven't really explained *why* the Plainfolk is so divided. Night-Fever told me that even the She-Kargo clans fight each other."

"It's a long story, Brickman. And it all happened a long, long time ago. If we're both round this winter, stop by the hut one night. We'll share a mat and a pipe and I'll tell you about it."

"Why not now?" insisted Steve.

"I've got other things on my mind."

"Like what?"

"Rifles . . ."

"What's the problem?"

Mr. Snow gestured wearily. "The clan elders don't think we should take them." He proceeded to give Steve an account of the debate—at times heated—that had been taking place between the senior members of the M'Call delegation who formed the trade council. It was they who were the final arbiters on the various deals struck with the Iron Masters. They also attempted to agree on standard rates of exchange with the trade councils from the other clans—no easy task when each sought to out-bargain the others.

The most vociferous opposition had come from those who saw acceptance of the rifle as a further erosion of the Plainfolk tradition of bravery. Mr. Snow saw the merit in this argument but believed that change was inevitable. The Old Ways must go. If not, the Plainfolk would perish. The traditionalists had replied that if the Old Ways were

abandoned, if valour became worthless, then the great
tree that was the Plainfolk would wither and die from
shame. Clan-brother would be parted from clan-sister like
yellowing leaves before the wind, scattered across the face
of the earth and ground into dust. If they did not adhere
to the Great Truths, argued the die-hards, the essential
values by which a man measured himself and by which
their society was defined, then they would deserve to be
swept into oblivion.

The trade council was also reluctant to accept the new
weapons for a more practical reason. To do so would
further increase their dependence on the Iron Masters.
The bolts that came with the crossbows were, to a large
extent, recoverable, the stock remaining more or less constant. But this would not be the case with the new "long
sharp iron." Once it had passed through the barrel, the
"iron finger" could not be used again. Only the Iron
Masters were able to fill it with sky-fire and supply the
ribbons containing the beads of flame. If the rifle was
allowed to become an essential part of the Plainfolks's
armoury they would be forever in the grip of the Iron
Masters, forced to trade whatever the price. With the
numbers of red-skins falling rapidly, it would mean sending more and more clan-brothers and sisters down river.
Having suffered heavy losses last year against The Lady
from Louisiana, this was something the M'Calls were reluctant to do. It was an almost insoluble dilemma, for if
the Plainfolk did not acquire more powerful weapons, they
would be faced with even more disastrous losses when the
iron snakes returned in greater numbers.

"So how do things stand now?" asked Steve.

"They're still arguing. I left them to it. I went through
all this nonsense twelve years ago when Yama-Shita turned
up with the first crossbows. Everyone predicted that the
sky would fall in but, as you can see, we're still here."

"This may come as a surprise but I understand how they
feel. Only warriors who have chewed bone are allowed to
use crossbows in combat—and then only against sand-
burrowers. And you have to be physically strong just to be
able to arm the damn thing. But with a rifle . . . all it

takes is one finger. A child of seven or eight could be taught how to use one—to kill grown men. You've seen the range it has. If he was a good shot, you wouldn't see him and you'd never know what hit you."

"Exactly. That's how the Old Time ended. Those who unleashed the War of a Thousand Suns had never drawn blood or had their courage tested in the face of death, had never conquered the smell of fear or scented victory. Buried beneath the earth, in a phantom world created by the High Craft, they lost touch with the Truth. Scornful of living creatures, ignorant of the wonders of the natural world and untouched by its beauty, they fell prey to false dreams of power, loving nothing but the giant iron birds of death whose lairs they shared. It was the weakling fingers of these white worms that turned the sky to ashes and plunged the world into the Great Ice-Dark."

"And you think it might happen again . . ."

"Some fear we have already taken the first steps down the same path." Mr. Snow shrugged. "But how else can we resist the sand-burrowers and their iron snakes?"

"You're a summoner. Why can't you use magic?"

Mr. Snow smiled ruefully. "When you pull the trigger of a loaded rifle, you can be pretty sure what's going to happen next. Magic, on the other hand, is . . . unpredictable."

"But you're a Storm-Bringer. Clearwater told me you hold the powers of the Seventh Ring and that only Talisman was stronger. That makes you a top gun."

"I don't *hold* the powers, Brickman. I'm only the *channel* for them. The power is Talisman's. He releases it through me. As a channel I can, to a certain degree, direct them—as a river bed directs the flow of rushing water. But to do this the banks of the river must be strong, otherwise they will burst when there is a flood. A summoner faces the same problem. His mind and body must be strong in order to direct the earth forces. But each time they pass through him he is weakened, worn away—as the banks of the river are worn away."

"And so . . . if the power that is unleashed is too strong for him to contain, he dies . . ."

"In a nutshell, yes."

"Which is why *you* would like the rifles."

Mr. Snow spread his palms. "I can only do so much. The clan has to learn to stand on its own feet instead of always looking to me to get them out of a jam. Let's face it, I may be a wiz when it comes to magic, but I'm not going to be around for ever."

"None of us are," replied Steve. "But what about Cadillac and Clearwater—aren't they going to be able to replace you?"

"That was the plan, yes."

"What d'you mean—*was* the plan'? Aren't they on Yama-Shita's boat?"

"That's what I'm hoping. But so far, I haven't been able to find out. You've seen how things work. These dinks handle all transactions in a very formal way. None of us is allowed to address Yama-Shita directly—"

"Maybe he doesn't speak Basic," interjected Steve.

"Perhaps . . . anyway, whatever the reason, you can only speak to samurai number one, he passes the message on in gobbledy-gook to Golden Nose and the answer comes back through his number two samurai. I asked twice but . . . no joy."

"He must have said *something*."

"Yes. He said: 'It is not yet time to speak of such things.'"

"What was the original arrangement?"

"About their return? There wasn't one. When the wheel-boats came last year, Yama-Shita let us know of his interest in arrowheads and cloud-warriors and promised that any clan able to deliver one of each in working order would receive a shipment of new, powerful sharp iron. Of course, at that time only a few of us, who'd been on trips to the south, had ever seen one of these things in the air. Having heard that the iron snakes were coming our way, and knowing what they'd done to the Southern Mutes, it seemed like a good deal. The idea was to hand the craft and the pilot over at the next trade-off."

"You mean here, now . . ."

"Yes. But that meant Cadillac would have to stay out

east until this time next year—or maybe the year after.
We couldn't afford to wait that long."

"Why not?"

"Because I'm due to die before the Yellowing." He saw
the look of shocked surprise on Steve's face. "I'm not
kidding. I was with Cadillac when he read it in the stone—
right where it's going to happen."

"And . . . do you believe it?"

Mr. Snow shrugged. "He also said you'd be back in the
time of the New Earth—and here you are. Sure, I believe
in prophecy but who wants to listen to bad news? You
keep telling yourself—'He's a beginner. Maybe he got the
name wrong, or the date.' To be honest I didn't take it
seriously. If I had, he'd be here and *you'd* be about to take
a boat trip."

"So you sent him last year—with Clearwater to protect
him."

"Yes. They were going to hand over the arrowhead, do
whatever had to be done then hitch a ride back on one of
Yama-Shita's wheelboats."

It was getting worse by the minute. "Do you have any
way of communicating with the Iron Masters in between
these boat trips?"

"Not directly, no. But I *am* in touch with the Sky
Voices."

"Yes, of course," said Steve. Terrific. "But apart from
that, you've received no actual message saying they had
arrived safely."

Mr. Snow threw up his hands. "We *have* the confirma-
tion. Yama-Shita brought us the rifles. He is a man of
honour whose word can be relied on. The same is true for
all the Iron Masters. They have never reneged on a deal."

"But—as I understand it—the deal was to deliver a
plane and its crew in exchange for rifles. They didn't
promise to return the pilot and passenger."

"True." A mischievous gleam crept into Mr. Snow's
eyes. "You're sharp, Brickman. A real shyster."

Steve had never heard the word before but it didn't
sound like a compliment—in spite of the tone of admiration.

Mr. Snow's frown returned as he picked up the main

thread of their conversation. "Cadillac and Clearwater were
aware of the situation. I left it to them to explain things.
The Iron Masters are intelligent people." He paused to
tug at his beard. "I really didn't think there'd be a problem."

Steve's heart sank as his master plan, already in tatters,
was finally torn to shreds. "You're insane, you know that?!
I mean . . . how could you be so . . . *irresponsible?!* The
whole future of the clan is at stake and you . . . ! Nobody
ever comes back from Beth-Lem! Isn't that what they
say?!"

"Not in the ordinary way, no but—"

"Christopher Columbus! What a mess!"

Mr. Snow motioned him to stay calm. "Look, let's not
get too overwrought about this. We've got three more
days before the boats leave. We'll be talking to Yama-
Shita again. They're on board his ship—I'm sure of it."

"Then why hasn't he brought them ashore?"

"Good question. You know what I think? I think he's
holding them back. You see, he knows we're unhappy
about the rifles so he's . . . trying to pressure us into
accepting them."

"It's possible," mused Steve. "I hope you're right."

"Well, there's nothing we can do about it. We'll just
have to wait and see what happens." Mr. Snow settled
down wearily, wrapping his travelling fur around him.
"Mother Mo-Town! This noise is terrible, isn't it? And so
many people! This is what it was like in the Old Time.
Wherever you turned there were human beings jammed
shoulder to shoulder from horizon to horizon and living on
top of each other in stone trees that reached all the way up
to the sky! No wonder the world went mad . . ."

Steve squatted on his own furs close by. "What's going
to happen if Cadillac and Clearwater are not on Yama-
Shita's boat and you die at the end of the summer as
predicted?"

Mr. Snow uncovered his head. "I'd say the M'Calls are
in for a rough time. Still . . . they'll always have you." He
lay back, then added. "Maybe that's what Talisman had in
mind when he sent you back to us."

Maybe . . .

Away from the fires, the night air was chill. Steve rolled himself into his furs and tried to shut out the confused murmur of voices around him, the chanting and drumming from the more distant bull-ring. He managed to create a mental oasis of silence but the void was soon filled with a dark cloud of conflicting doubts and suspicions to which were added the burden of past and present betrayals, the secrets he shared with others and those known only to himself. He closed his eyes but sleep did not come. The kaleidoscopic images of love, death and jeopardy continue to swirl through his fevered brain till the first light of dawn.

The trading between the Plainfolk clans and the Iron Masters continued, the deals were struck. The dried meat, grain, furs and skins were carried aboard by the Mute journey-men—those destined to go down river; the weapons, cloth, knives, tools, pots, pans and all manner of useful objects were brought ashore. But no one, apart from Yama-Shita and his escort, appeared from the third wheel-boat.

Later in the afternoon of the fourth day of trading, Steve made his way to the post and joined a group of M'Call Bears sitting watching the proceedings from the edge of the square. After a long wait in line, the M'Call trade-council was wheeled in front of the platform and Mr. Snow finally got to speak to Yama-Shita through his two interpreters. Steve didn't need to hear to know what was said. The bad news was written all over the old wordsmith's face. He bowed respectfully along with the rest of the trade-council and backed out of the square. Steve hurried round to meet them as they came out through the ranks of spectators. The ten-man council looked like they'd been hit by the Trans-Am Express.

"They're not on the boat . . ."

Mr. Snow shook his head. "It's worse than that. Cadillac does not wish to return."

Steve's bowels turned to frozen spaghetti. "What about Clearwater?"

"Yama-Shita assured me that neither is being held against

their wishes. Both are in good health and have been
rewarded with many favours—"

"But she ain't coming back either . . ."

Mr. Snow gestured helplessly. "Be reasonable. She just
can't leave him there."

Steve threw a dark look towards the dais. "Do you
believe this guy?"

"I don't have much choice. Like I said, they've never
crossed us up yet."

"In other words you're going to let them get away with
it."

Mr. Snow gasped irritably. "Look, young man, just slow
down. If Cadillac has, for whatever reason, decided to stay
there, *he* is the one who's crossed us up, not the Iron
Masters. *They* are not getting away with anything."

"*If* they're telling the truth. Why don't we grab one of
these boats then tell Yama-Shita to go back and fetch Cadillac and Clearwater so as we can have a word with them?"

The suggestion caused the trade-council to catch their
breath.

Mr. Snow eyed him dismissively. "And to think you
accuse *me* of being irresponsible. Just supposing we were
mad enough to try and, by some miracle, we actually did
manage to capture a boat—do you seriously think the
other clans would just stand by and do nothing? They'd
tear us apart!" He gestured towards the platform where
Yama-Shita and his samurai were concluding the last business of the day. "These trade-offs are their lifeline!"

"Okay, okay, maybe it wasn't such a good idea. So what
are you going to do?"

Mr. Snow popped his cork. "Great Sky-Mother! I don't
know what I'm going to do, Brickman! She-ehh! Questions, questions, always questions! For the last fifty years
it's been the same, day after day after day! I'm sick and
tired of coming up with answers—" He rounded on the
hapless trade-council. "—And being trailed by a sorry-assed
bunch of meat-heads who keep asking for my advice and
who never *listen*!" He turned to the west and threw his
arms out towards the setting sun. "Oh, Talisman! Why
did you have to make me a wordsmith when you could

have made me deaf *and* dumb!" He pushed past Steve and stomped away.

The council watched him disappear with expressions of pained surprise. "What's eating him?" asked Flying-Tiger. "It was *his* idea to send Cadillac and Clearwater to the Iron Masters. None of us wanted to make a trade for the rifles. He pushed us into it."

"What have you decided?"

Flying-Tiger responded with a helpless gesture. "We're taking them, of course. What else can we do?" He rolled his eyes heavenwards. "That's the trouble with wordsmiths. If you don't do what they say, you never hear the last of it."

The trade-council murmured approvingly.

Steve laid a hand on the Mute's shoulder. "Leave it with me." He went in search of Mr. Snow and eventually found him sitting on a rock by the shore about a quarter of a mile down the beach to the left of the wheel-boats.

The old wordsmith ignored his arrival and continued to stare moodily out to sea.

"I think I know the answer to my question, Old One . . ."

Mr. Snow glanced at him briefly but said nothing.

"You're sending eighteen clan brothers and sisters down river. Let me take the place of one of them."

"You must be out of your mind . . ."

"On the contrary. I've never been more serious in my life. I will go to Beth-Lem, find Cadillac and Clearwater, and bring them back to you—safe and sound."

Mr. Snow's eyes remained on the horizon while he weighed up the proposition then turned to Steve. "Did your masters tell you anything about Beth-Lem? Do you have *any* idea of what you're getting into?"

"Nope, I haven't a clue. I'm just going to have to play it by ear." He laid a reassuring hand on the old man's shoulder. "Look, don't worry, we'll make it. You want 'em back, don't you?"

"Of course I do."

"So do I. For all kinds of reasons."

Mr. Snow still looked doubtful. "Well, obviously I appreciate the gesture. I just hope you don't live to regret it."

Steve smiled. "You've got it wrong. If I live, why on earth should I have any regrets? Listen, there's just one thing. I think they've made up the loading manifest for the journey-men and handed out the tallies. Will you be able to get me on board?"

It was Mr. Snow's turn to smile. "No problem. To these dinks, one Mute looks pretty much like another. But we might need to dye your hair."

"Then we'd better get started."

The life seemed to flow back into the old Mute's face. He slid down from the rocky perch and gripped Steve's shoulders. "This is the last time I'll ask—are you sure you want to go through with this?"

Steve grimaced. "I don't have any choice. Probably never did. 'The Wheel turns'—isn't that what the Plainfolk say? In fact, I have a feeling that when you told the clan I had returned to perform a mighty deed in the name of Talisman you probably knew this was going to happen."

Mr. Snow shrugged. "You've built up such a flattering picture of my powers, I'd hate to disillusion you. Especially now." They began to walk toward the lines.

"There's something I need to know."

"Fire away . . ."

"Is there any chance of smuggling a blade, or this quarterstaff aboard?"

"Absolutely none. And to try could endanger others besides yourself."

Steve grimaced. "How about if you were to use a little magic?"

Mr. Snow rolled his eyes heavenwards. "I'm a summoner, not a conjuror. At the risk of rupturing myself I can move bits of heaven and earth around but I can't make things disappear, or produce eggs from under people's armpits."

"Okay, okay, I get the picture."

"There's something else I think you ought to know." Mr. Snow grimaced reluctantly like someone about to impart bad news. "When Cadillac left he was unskinned and dressed as a wingman. Clearwater, who was posing as his escort, kept her normal body markings."

Steve frowned. "Why was Cadillac dressed up as a Tracker?"

"I would have thought that was obvious."

"Come on. Don't play games. This is important."

"He went as a Tracker because we didn't want to upset the present relationship. The Iron Masters think of us as not being too bright—which most of us aren't. If they found out we also had some very *clever* Mutes who know, for instance, as much as you do, they might behave quite differently towards us."

"But what about his name? Doesn't that give the game away?"

Mr. Snow couldn't quite swallow his smile. "He's using yours."

"I see . . . couldn't he have used someone else's—like Lou Kennedy or Fazetti?"

"Well, he used Fazetti's uniform but he cut the name tag off your fatigues. You probably remember it was missing when you first woke up."

"I thought someone had taken it as a souvenir," said Steve.

"They had. It never occurred to us to build an arrowhead until you suggested it. We agreed, naturally. It was a heaven-sent opportunity."

"Yeah, I can imagine . . ." said Steve ruefully. "But you know something? You've outsmarted yourself. As I understand it, they've never let anybody else go but they just might have made an exception in his case—because of the deal you struck with Yama-Shita. *If* he had gone as a Mute. But there's no way they're going to send back a Tracker—especially one possessing knowledge they can make use of. What would be the point? His knowledge is no good to you. As far as they're concerned the only thing you can do with his brain is eat it."

Mr. Snow tugged at his beard. "You're right . . . I just didn't think of that. Full marks, Brickman."

Steve savoured the moment of triumph. "So . . . I'm looking for Clearwater, and a dark-haired Tracker who answers to the name of Steve Brickman."

"You can't miss him. He's got a crew-cut." Mr. Snow

recovered his aplomb and put an arm round Steve's shoulder. "There was no malice involved I can assure you. Look upon it as a mark of respect. After all, it was you who taught him almost everything he knows."

"Don't remind me," said Steve.

EIGHTEEN

HAVING impulsively volunteered to go to Beth-Lem, Steve began to have second thoughts. Had he done the right thing—or had he been drawn into yet another trap by his amiable host? Mr. Snow had already tricked him over the building of Blue-Bird and had manipulated his relationship with Clearwater. That much was certain, indeed, the wordsmith had cheerfully admitted his part in both affairs. But Steve also suspected him of causing his radio-knife to disappear and of masterminding the destruction of the back-up squad. Unfortunately, to believe this meant accepting that, in spite of being given the whole story, Mr. Snow still did not trust him completely. He would be a fool if he did, thought Steve. But even as this cynical aside flitted through his mind, he sought to give the wordsmith the benefit of the doubt.

It was this ambivalence in their relationship that troubled Steve. From the moment of regaining consciousness in his presence, he had felt a natural affinity towards the old man that ran counter to his basic instincts for survival. He hungered for his friendship and counsel but lacked the honesty to confess his need; he wanted to believe yet was afraid to do so in case he became vulnerable. Maybe, he told himself, the wordsmith's motive was more benign. Perhaps Mr. Snow believed that by removing all means of

contact with the Federation he was eliminating a source of
pressure, putting him, in effect, beyond the reach of
temptation.

It was all pure guesswork. It was impossible to tell what
the wily old Mute was thinking or whether, as he loved to
imply, he really *did* know exactly what was going on inside
Steve's head. Or was it just his own imagination working
overtime? Had he become the victim of his own duplicity,
unable to trust, therefore unable to believe that others
might trust him, constructing labyrinthine conspiracies
against himself when, in reality, none existed?

There was only one thing of which he could be certain.
None of these lumps were the bone-heads he had first
taken them for. It was a lesson he had been slow to learn,
but in so doing he had gained a greater understanding of
his own character—and also a little humility.

Steve's main worry was that Mr. Snow had not been
telling him the truth about Clearwater and Cadillac. As a
master of devious game-plans, Steve foresaw a situation
where he could be on board one of the wheel-boats and
unable to get off while they were calmly disembarking,
courtesy of Yama-Shita, from another. Leaving them heading for home and laughing like coyotes while he was
carried off in the opposite direction.

It could be a neat way to get rid of him and would
ensure that he wasn't around to mess up their relationship
any further. But with Cadillac now aware of Clearwater's
true feelings, what price that relationship now? Mr. Snow
had hinted that the young wordsmith had been less than
overjoyed at what had taken place during his absence. It
was Cadillac's character which provided the answer to
Steve's present dilemma. The more he thought about Cadillac, the more convinced he became that Mr. Snow's
report of what Yama-Shita had said was the truth. During
the months of captivity, he had observed Cadillac's almost
obsessive preoccupation with status—what the Mutes called
standing. The young Mute was, in many ways, a mirror-
image of himself. Both were hungry for power, both had
the same, deep-seated need to win recognition, to *be*
somebody. Hence Cadillac's vain hope—dashed by Mr.

Snow—that he might have been marked out as the Talisman, a hope he had revealed to Steve in one of their many discussions. In allowing Cadillac to draw on his own accumulated store of knowledge Steve had, quite unknowingly, given him the means to acquire the status he longed for, had put him within reach of real power. But there was an additional factor to consider. In cloning Steve's memory banks, the young wordsmith had also acquired other mental processes that would influence the way he used this new knowledge. There was a strong possibility that Cadillac had become a split personality, able to think like a Mute *and* a Tracker. Not just any Tracker. But like *Steve*.

Viewed from that angle, Cadillac's wish to stay with the Iron Masters made sense. He was the first Mute to have taken to the air. He had then built a craft capable of powered flight, albeit it was with borrowed knowledge, had delivered it to the Iron Masters and had proceeded to instruct them in the techniques of its design and construction and perhaps, with their encouragement, had gone on to build other craft. Going east would have opened up fresh horizons, offered new challenges to his burgeoning intelligence. Cadillac had already alluded to the feelings of alienation engendered by his childhood experiences. As a straight, clear-skinned Mute he was already set apart from the rest of the clan despite the respect accorded him as Mr. Snow's chosen successor. Respect was not enough: Cadillac had to believe in his own worth, prove it by his own yardstick. And now he had a golden opportunity. Whatever he was doing had to be a lot better than the prospect of coming back home to watch your neighbours pounding buffalo hide. Yes . . . if he had been a Mute, that's just how he, Brickman, S R, would have played it too.

In his last briefing, Karlstrom had indicated the area the Iron Masters were thought to occupy, a section of the north-east coast running from Connecticut down to Virginia and including the Allegheny mountain ranges. But that was all. Karlstrom had not supplied any further details apart from suggesting that the Fire-Pits of Beth-Lem were probably located in the vicinity of Pittsburgh, a NavRef point in the pre-Holocaust state of Pennsylvania. This sole reference to the Iron Masters had come at the end of the session which Karlstrom then brought to a close, going straight into the "goodbye and good luck" routine without giving Steve an opportunity to ask any questions.

Steve was aware that it was standard Federation policy to disseminate information only on a strict "need-to-know" basis but he was puzzled by Karlstrom's reticence on the subject of the Iron Masters. He could understand why their existence had been kept secret from ordinary Trackers but he had returned knowing about them. Not only that, he was a member of AMEXICO about to embark on a delicate and dangerous overground assignment.

No matter. His latent hostility towards the First Family rose to the surface and swept aside any lingering doubts; gave him a renewed sense of purpose. What they did not know, or had declined to tell him, he would find out for himself. He would make the trip down the great river as a Mute journey-man. It would provide him with an opportunity to see the ominously-named Fire-Pits of Beth-Lem and the lands that bordered the Eastern Sea. He would go because of his desire to be reunited with Clearwater and his promise to rescue her, and because of Cadillac who would have to be brought back in spite of his expressed wish to remain in the east. If Mr. Snow died, Cadillac had to be there to take his place but there was more to it than that. The fruits of his work for the Iron Masters had to be utterly destroyed. A race with their craft skills and martial character could not be allowed to challenge the aerial supremacy of the Federation. And they could certainly not be allowed to develop flying machines with the help of someone calling himself "Steve Brickman." The First Family might not know exactly what the Iron Masters were up to but the full story was bound to emerge sooner or later. When it did, Steve knew he would not be able to escape the accusation of having started the ball rolling but he could limit the damage to his future prospects by making sure he got full credit for having stopped it dead in its tracks.

All of which was easier said than done. He was about to

embark on a journey into the unknown. All he had going for him was his incredible luck and—maybe—Talisman. Despite having silently vowed to give some credence to the idea of an invisible benefactor, Steve did not intend to leave everything to chance. He would take his combat knife and the bladed quarterstaff Clearwater had left in the care of Night-Fever. The bucket-jawed Mute might have forgotten the message that went with it but Clearwater had spoken to him through the staff. It was more than a token of affection and his reasons for taking it were far from sentimental. Behind the act of giving lay a deeper purpose that had become crystal clear when he had taken the staff in his hands to fight the back-up squad by the lake. It was then he had felt the wooden shaft come alive, pulse with a strange power that had flowed into his body, giving him an almost superhuman speed and strength. He had made a half-hearted effort to convince himself he was imagining it all but deep down he knew it was for real; a tangible manifestation of Mute magic. She, whose power had twice saved him from death at the hands of Motor-Head, was watching over him even now.

Mr. Snow had brusquely dismissed as impossible his suggestion about concealing weapons on the wheel-boat. It was certainly true his quarterstaff could not have been carried aboard during loading. The journey-men had been the only Mutes allowed up the walkways but before they could do so they had been obliged to strip naked, wash in the lake, then don an abbreviated loincloth made of white cotton that covered their genitals but otherwise left them as bare-assed as the day they were born.

As Steve had, at the time, not been one of them, he had been obliged to set down his loads on the beach but, when the boats withdrew each evening, he had questioned the loaders about what and who they had seen. From these conversations he was able to assemble a partial picture of the wheel-boat's interior. It was not as detailed as he would have liked but at least he would be able to get his bearings when he went aboard. Not with the other journey-men in the morning but that very night, while the wheel-boats were moored out in the bay.

He had also managed to discover that the Mutes from
the clan M'Call would be travelling on the left flank-boat—
the one coloured predominantly black and silver. The
captured renegades were to be divided between the boat
carrying, amongst others, the M'Call contingent and the
other flank-boat which was painted black and gold. Yama-
Shita's red and gold vessel, the most ornate of the three,
carried no human cargo.

Steve's plan was to swim out under cover of darkness,
board the black and silver wheel-boat and hide his knife
and quarterstaff in the safest place he could find. He had
absolutely no idea how long the journey would take or
what would happen on their arrival at the other end. That
bridge would have to be crossed when he came to it.
Burning with impatience, he reconnoitered a circuitous
route down to the shore, marked it with stones, and willed
the hours to pass quickly.

Throughout the afternoon, groups of white-stripes brought
sets of heavy iron chains down from the two flank-boats
and carried them up to the lines where red-stripes waited
to shackle the captured renegades. Each breaker had his
wrists manacled together by a chain running through a
loop in an iron belt fastened around his waist. The chains
allowed the arms to be raised head high but only one at a
time. A heavy anklet was clamped around one leg but they
were otherwise left free. Even so, escape was impossible.
Anyone trying to run away would quickly become exhausted and if they were foolish enough to jump overboard while at sea they would sink like a stone.

When Mo-Town had drawn her dark cloak across the
sky, Steve strapped the sheathed knife to his left forearm,
shouldered the quarterstaff and headed westwards away
from the lines without telling Mr. Snow, or anyone else,
what he intended to do. Picking his way along the stone
markers, he reached the shore some three quarters of a
mile north of the trading post. He undressed quickly,
placed his folded garments under a pile of stones and
slipped into the water. His pioneering swim across the
lake had given him more confidence but had not entirely

dispelled his fears of encountering some dreadful slimy creature.

The three wheel-boats, now moored out in the bay, stood out clearly against the surrounding blackness. The arched galleries running along the front, sides and rear of the upper decks were hung with lanterns in which pots of oil burned with a yellow flame. Other, bigger lanterns lit the fore and aft decks and the ships' external illumination was completed by a row of lanterns that hung out over the water on booms fixed to the wooden parapet running around the roof of the superstructure. Steve had seen these on previous nights but had failed to appreciate that their purpose went beyond mere decoration. Now, as he approached the boat with slow, silent strokes, he saw they illuminated a wide strip of water around each boat making it virtually impossible for a swimmer to reach the hull without being seen by the patrolling sentries.

The only solution was to dive under the water and remain submerged until he reached the side. The thought made Steve uneasy. Even though he had swum halfway across the lake in pursuit of Lundkwist and successfully covered an equal distance now, he could not bring himself to plunge below the dark surface for fear of what he might encounter. There had to be another way.

Withdrawing to a safe distance from the pool of light, Steve ran his eye along the ship. There was a patch of darkness under the square-cut bow but there was a guard stationed on the deck immediately above and there seemed to be no way to climb aboard except up the heavy anchor chain. The stern looked more promising, the huge wooden planks that formed the blades of the paddle broke up the light cast by the aft deck lanterns. If he were to slip through the rear blades he could climb round the inside of the wheel onto the deck. The smoke he had seen coming from the funnels has given him a clue to the boat's motive power. The pistons—huge beams of wood reinforced with metal straps—which drove the paddle wheels round had to be linked to a source of steam pressure. This was probably located somewhere within the lower levels of the hull. Steve wasn't sure how everything was connected up

but the point where the forward end of the pistons passed
below the line of the deck was covered by a sloping
housing. This, he decided, would be where he could effect
an entry.

So far, he had noted a dozen guards posted around the
ship, some guarding doorways, others patrolling in pairs.
There were bound to be others inside. Steve considered
how best to proceed once he was safely on board. The
visitors' masks provided a wonderful means of disguise but
their incomprehensible language made an effective imper-
sonation virtually impossible. And there was always the
chance that the Iron Masters might remove their masks
once they were inside the ship amongst their own kind.
Given those two factors, overpowering one of the guards
and taking his place was too risky. Not that his present
disguise—that of a semi-naked Mute—made things any
easier. He would have to rely on the element of surprise,
as with his swim out to the island. Safely ensconced on
their boats and surrounded by water, the Iron Masters had
little reason to fear an intrusion by their non-acquatic
trading partners. The real clamp-down would come tomorrow when the Mute journey-men and renegades came
aboard. From then on, the guards would be on maximum
alert to prevent the escape of any of their reluctant passengers; they would not be expecting anyone to come aboard
a day early and of his own free will.

Taking care to disturb the water as little as possible,
Steve circled the boat to check the galleries on the starboard side then came in under the stern.

Back in the lines, where the M'Calls were encamped, Mr.
Snow walked back and forth with an uncharacteristic nervousness, watched by Rolling-Stone, the impassive chief
clan elder, and Mack-Truck, a member of the trade council. All three were decked out in their ceremonial finery.
Steve's suspicions about Mr. Snow had not been entirely
without foundation. While he had not concealed anything
of substance, the wordsmith had not passed on the totality
of Yama-Shita's reply concerning Cadillac and Clearwater.
The chief Iron Master had indicated his wish to make a

further pronouncement on the subject and had invited Mr. Snow and two compaions to a private audience on board his ship; an honour never previously accorded to any member of the Plainfolk.

Mr. Snow had said nothing to Brickman about the invitation for all kinds of reasons. Protocol demanded that Rolling-Stone be one of the two who would accompany him and he had chosen Mack-Truck in preference to Blue-Thunder. The paramount warrior, although a worthy representative of the clan, was not the greatest brain around and lacked the necessary social graces the occasion might demand. Mr. Snow would have preferred to take Brickman because of his acute intelligence but he was too emotionally involved in the situation. If he spoke out of turn, things might get difficult. And that wasn't the only problem. The cloud-warrior's status was still that of an honorary Bear. To have taken him would have been a serious affront to Blue-Thunder and would have diminished his standing in the eyes of the clan. Hence the choice of Mack-Truck.

Even so, Mr. Snow had been wondering what explanation to give Brickman when the promised rowboat arrived to take them out to Yama-Shita's vessel. He was already apprehensive about what would happen when they got there; his nervousness was compounded by the thought of what Brickman might do when he found out what was going on—and that he hadn't been invited. The last thing he wanted was for the cloud-warrior to gate-crash the party.

The mental energy expended on Brickman was completely wasted. When he saw Mr. Snow decking himself out in his ribbon and bones he did not ask why and, by the time the runner arrived to announce that the rowboat had been sighted, Brickman had vanished into the night. No one in the M'Call camp had any idea where he was. Knowing Brickman, the news gave Mr. Snow something else to worry about. He borrowed the pipe that was being passed around a nearby group of Bears, took a few puffs to calm his nerves, then led his companions to the shore below the trading post.

*   *   *

Steve, now perched inside one of the giant paddle wheels, saw the rowboat leave Yama-Shita's vessel and head towards the beach. Lanterns hung from the ends of cross-beams supported by two posts that had been fixed to the side-rails fore and aft. The boat was crewed by its usual complement of whites, four oarsmen and a helmsman but the ornate red and gold cabin in which Yama-Shita travelled was not mounted on the deck. In its place stood an impassive masked samurai, legs splayed, arms folded. Behind him, in similar postures, were his two "red-stripes," both now holding slim, twelve-foot long poles topped with pennants bearing the symbol of their house. The boat passed within fifty yards of where Steve lay concealed. He followed it with his eyes as it slid across the wind-rippled water, its lanterns creating a soft-edged oasis of yellow light in the all-enveloping dark.

From where he now sat, at water-level, Steve could just make out the vertical line of the tall trading post, silhouetted against the orange glow coming from the fires of the more distant Mute encampment. The actual lines and the enclosed bull-ring were hidden by a rise in the ground. He saw tiny figures step out of the darkness to meet the row-boat then, after a short interval, it began its return journey. Steve was conscious of wasting valuable time but his curiosity was aroused and nothing was going to budge him until he saw who was in the boat. The samurai now sat cross-legged facing his three seated passengers, one in front, two side-by-side behind. Behind them, stood the two reds, their pennants fluttering proudly in the wind.

At a distance of fifty yards, in the warm fuzzy glow of the lanterns, it was almost impossible to discern the features of those on board but there was no doubt about the identity of the white-bearded figure who faced the samurai. The crafty old coot. So *that* was why he had gotten dressed up. What was he up to?

Steve was filled with a sudden urge to swim across and find some way to eavesdrop on their conversation but commonsense finally prevailed. If he was caught, armed to the teeth, on the big wheel's territory it might sour what were clearly private negotiations and put Mr. Snow and his friends in mortal danger—not to mention himself. The fate of Mr. Snow's two companions was of little concern but he could not risk losing the wordsmith at this stage of the game. There was still too much to play for. Steve waited until the rowboat reached its destination, watched Mr. Snow mount the steps and vanish with his samurai escort, then he turned his attention back to the problem of finding a way into the wheel-boat without being detected.

The samurai led Mr. Snow and the two-clan elders through a door in the rear of the galleried superstructure. They found themselves in a large area covered entirely in moist, sweet-smelling wood. The deep beams, which held up the planked ceiling were supported by huge square wooden pillars set into a latticed floor.

Mr. Snow, who had never been inside any man-made structure bigger than a Mute hut, found the wheel-boat's size and complexity rather frightening. And to judge from their expressions, so did his companions. To be within such a colossal construction awakened fearful folk-memories of another time when their ancestors had been trapped in flaming labyrinths of wood and stone, crushed under falling beams and cut to ribbons by jagged shards of frozen water—the Mute way of describing glass, itself a word that had been lost from the language.

Six big round tubs stood in a line, four of them filled with steaming hot water. Three attendants, stripped to the waist, stood waiting by each of the filled tubs. At their feet were several wooden buckets of cold water; a supply of rough-textured white cloths lay folded on a shelf running along the wall behind. Mr. Snow stared at the attendants in shocked surprise. It was not the sight of their small breasts that was the source of consternation but their faces. They were unmasked. He was looking on the true face of the Iron Masters, slant-eyed, flat-featured individuals without, as far as he could see, the slightest trace of body hair.

Mr. Snow exchanged a puzzled look with Rolling-Stone and Mack-Truck. They were equally surprised and also a little worried at what these four simmering cauldrons might portend. "What are they going to do?" whispered Rolling-Stone, "Boil us alive?"

Mr. Snow turned to the samurai, half-expecting to find himself looking into another flat, slant-eyed face. He was disappointed. The samurai, who had already handed his helmet to one of the reds, kept his features hidden. He stretched out his arms to allow the second red to divest him of his body armour and undershirt then, when his yellowish torso was bared, he pointed to the three Mutes then gestured to the steaming tubs. "You please to do the same."

Mr. Snow and his companions bowed as he addressed them. "Hai!" said Mr. Snow, venturing to use the only word in the Iron Masters' tongue whose meaning he had grasped. What he did not know was that, in the dead-faces' homeland, the use of the samurai's language by foreigners was absolutely forbidden under pain of death. Had Mr. Snow not been summoned by Yama-Shita, that brief pleasantry would have resulted in the instant removal of his head.

Straightening up, Mr. Snow saw that one female from each trio of attendants had removed her baggy pants and was now standing waist-deep in the hot tub wearing only a white cotton headscarf. The next move was clear even to a Mute. Their apparel, with its collection of bones, feathers and pebbles was laid out neatly, then they were invited to mount the steps and immerse themselves in the hot water.

It was a novel experience. In the thousand years since their traumatised ancestors had clawed their way out of the rubble, Mutes had never gotten around to wasting hot water on their bodies; the only time water ever got heated was inside a cooking pot full of soup or stew. But there was another surprise in store. The dead-face in the tub held a block of hard yellow fat that produced a white foam like soap-leaves but in much greater abundance. And she had a soft rock full of holes that could be squeezed in the hand and was used to rub the skin. Mr. Snow mastered his initial misgivings and submitted meekly to her attentions. It was not as unpleasant as he expected and, when she reached the parts that had not felt the touch of a woman's hand for several decades, Mr. Snow had to admit there was something to be said for the Iron Masters' brand of civilisation.

Once in the tub, the samurai removed his mask but kept his face averted. Before emerging, one of his reds brought him a fresh mask. When they had been thoroughly washed, the three Mutes were drenched with cold water then rubbed dry by the two attendants who had remained outside the tubs. They were then offered a cotton loincloth and loose undervest, a pair of black baggy trousers and a black and brown patterned wide-sleeve jacket fastened by a sash. Sitting on low stools, they had their hair dried and combed then expertly plaited and gathered onto the crown of their heads where it was secured with thin slivers of wood. One of the dead-faces then carefully dried the soles of their feet while a second guided their toes into short white cotton socks then fitted a pair of wooden sandals.

While this was going on, the samurai was receiving similar attention. They only difference was in his clothing which was patterned with threads of shimmering silver and bore the symbol of his house on the back. His face was once again concealed, a white head-scarf with a solid red circle centred over the forehead covered his hairless skull. Inserting his curving swords into the wide sash around his body, the samurai invited the three Mutes to follow him. Leaving the bathhouse, they came out onto the main deck then mounted two flights of open stairs which brought them onto the second of the upper side galleries.

The boat's overall structure was made of horizontal and vertical beams but its severe lines were softened by sculptured beam supports and cornices, richly decorated panels and pierced screens set between the massive uprights. Their guide turned right and passed between two masked reds guarding a passage running across the ship from port to starboard. A platform, some four feet wide, ran along the left hand side of the passage at calf height. Two more reds sat on the platform amidship, on either side of a

door. Like the walls on either side, the door was made up
of two panels of translucent white cloth stretched over
wooden frames.

At their approach, the reds hastily uncrossed their legs
and knelt facing each other. They slid open the door and
bowed low as the samurai stepped through. Mr. Snow
followed, passing between two more red guards stationed
immediately inside. He found himself in an even larger
rectangular space whose walls were made of identical framed
panels of white cloth. The floor was covered with straw
matting with not a speck of dirt or a leaf to be seen
anywhere. On the matting were several small dark brown
mats, three of them arranged in a triangle which pointed
towards a square dais at the far end of the room. Four Iron
Masters, dressed even more richly than their guide, sat on
the dais to the right and left of an ornate folding stool.

Following the samurai's lead, Mr. Snow and his companions dropped to their knees and bowed from the waist.
The samurai then took his place on the left-hand side of
the room. Mr. Snow knelt on the first mat; Rolling-Stone
and Mack-Truck occupied the mats behind him. A panel at
the rear of the room slid aside to reveal Yama-Shita instantly recognisable by his black mask with the bridge of
the nose and eyebrows picked out with three broad strokes
of gold. Everyone went forward on their hands and put
their noses to the floor then, when Yama-Shita had seated
himself, the Iron Masters on the platform straightened
their backs and adopted a cross-legged position. The junior samurai and the Mutes sat back on their heels and
awaited his first pronouncement. The chief Iron Master
addressed their guide with an unintelligible burst of sound
then leant forward with his right elbow on his knee and
focused his attention on Mr. Snow.

The samurai translated: "Lord Yama-Shita says your presence here is proof of the high regard he has for the
Plainfolk. Unlike those who inhabit the deserts of the
south, our two peoples, in their different ways, share the
same sense of honor and respect for valour. It pleases him
to know that the long sharp iron he has furnished will be
carried into battle by the most valiant of warriors."

Mr. Snow acknowledged this unexpected compliment with a gracious nod. Yama-Shita responded with another unintelligible burst for the samurai to pass on.

"Lord Yama-Shita wishes to speak again of the cloud-warrior you sent us and whose return you expected, together with that of his escort."

Another long string of nonsense words.

"He is aware of your disappointment and hopes it will not shadow the friendship between the Sons of Nissan and the Plainfolk. In order to remove any doubt about our conduct in this affair, he has summoned you here to seek the truth for yourselves."

Yama-Shita barked an abrupt order and looked at the wall to the right of Mr. Snow. Drawn back by invisible hands, the two centre panels parted to reveal an olive-skinned, dark-haired girl kneeling on a padded cushion in the room beyond. Mr. Snow was momentarily thrown by her strange appearance but the light that shone from her blue eyes was unmistakable.

It was Clearwater.

Dressed in the style of the Iron Masters, she wore a long multi-coloured coat the dead-faces called a kimono. It was held in place by a deep sash of smooth lustrous material wrapped around her waist and fastened at the back in a huge bow. Her hair—of which there now seemed to be a great deal—was drawn up into a stiff lacquered bun secured by long black combs. But it was not just her clothing that was different. Her face, neck and the back of her hands were no longer marked with the usual pattern of browns and blacks. She had taken a supply of the special pink scrubbing leaves with her in case of some unforeseen emergency. What had caused her to remove the dye from her body—and reveal her smooth unblemished olive-brown skin? Mr. Snow longed to know the answer but dared not ask for fear of how such questions might be received by his hosts—and where they might lead.

As her eyes met his, Clearwater bowed respectfully then sat with her hands placed submissively on her knees, her face devoid of all expression.

The two reds from the back of the room positioned

themselves on either side of the parted screens. Momentarily bewildered by Clearwater's presence on the boat and the dramatic transformation in her appearance, Mr. Snow exchanged glances with his companions then turned towards the dais uncertain what to do next. Yama-Shita gestured towards Clearwater then barked briefly in his native tongue.

"Lord Yama-Shita says now is the time to speak. You are both free to say whatever you wish."

The senior samurai on the right hand side of the platform barked an order. The nearest red padded over to a low lacquered cabinet and brought back a large hour-glass which he placed midway between Mr. Snow and Clearwater, in the centre of the open doorway. Mr. Snow had never seen such an object before and he did not know what it was called but, on seeing the fine trickle of sand fall from the upper vessel into the lower, he was quick to divine its purpose.

After being told that they were free to talk, Mr. Snow had expected Yama-Shita and his samurai to withdraw but nobody moved. They just sat there waiting, and with their faces hidden by the ferocious masks it was impossible to tell what they were thinking. Mr. Snow exchanged a long look with Clearwater. It was apparent that she also felt constrained by the presence of the dead-faces and yet they both submitted, even though they jointly possessed the power to call up a thunderous wall of wind and water that would have hurled the huge wheelboats ashore, crushing their great timbers as if they were breadstalks. Their minds were stilled by the thought of the absent Cadillac and the knowledge that they could do nothing which would imperil the vital trade links between the Plainfolk and the Iron Masters.

Referring to Cadillac as "the cloud-warrior," Clearwater began by explaining that he had asked to be allowed to prolong his stay in the east. She was at pains to stress that, while the "cloud-warrior" had made this request against her wishes, he had done so of his own free will. No pressure had been put on either of them by their hosts. As his appointed guardian, Clearwater felt she had no alternative but to remain with him until he could be persuaded to return. She confirmed that the "cloud-warrior" was in good health and that they were both enjoying many privileges. Her fine clothes and her presence on the boat were proof of the Iron Masters' generous hospitality. She was, she added, eager to take this opportunity to express, in the presence of her own people, her heartfelt gratitude to her principal benefactor—the great Domain-Lord, Yama-Shita.

At the mention of his name, she turned and bowed to the chief Iron Master. Taking his cue from her, Mr. Snow did the same. Rolling-Stone and Mack-Truck exchanged nervous glances then followed suit just to be on the safe side.

Clearwater than asked after her clan-sisters and Black-Wing, her blood-mother.

"Your name is on their lips and in their hearts but they do not weep." Mr. Snow paused then added, "Others wait and watch for word of your return in the stone."

He saw Clearwater's eyes react to the trigger word. "And what does the stone say, Wise One?"

Mr. Snow chose his words carefully, using a slight pause or a subtle emphasis to convey the real meaning of what he was saying. "The stone speaks of life and death, of going and returning, of hope and despair, of love and hate. What it has seen, has come to pass, what it foretold, is at hand. Visions shall take shape, dreams shall become reality."

Clearwater signalled with her eyes that she was beginning to get the message. She asked how the clan had passed the winter and for news of the spring planting.

"The seed which we thought was carried away on the wind has sprung again from the earth," replied Mr. Snow.

"And what of the scattered fruit?"

"Nothing is lost. With the help of strong sharp iron, all will be gathered before the Yellowing."

Very little sand was now left in the top half of the strange vessel. Clearwater turned to the right and used both hands to pick up a small black and gold lacquer box that lay close to the cushion on which she knelt. Measuring about nine

inches by six by six deep, it had cut-off corners and cham-
fered edges and was fitted with four little feet. Light
reflected from the golden images that covered its various
surfaces.

"Wise One, Lord Yama-Shita has permitted me to offer
you, my teacher, this gift as a token of my respect and
devotion. Only the Sons of Nissan could have fashioned an
object of such beauty. Knowing your love of such things I
used their unrivalled skills to create a design that would
please your eye. It expresses better than any words of
mine, the wonders and infinite riches to be found in the
Land of the Rising Sun." So saying, Clearwater reached
forward as far as she could without moving from the padded cushion and placed the box on the floor. She then
bowed again to Yama-Shita.

The Iron Master responded with a peremptory flick of
the wrist. One of the kneeling reds picked up the box and
set it down in front of Mr. Snow who, in his turn, bowed
deeply to the chief Iron Master then said: "Though our
daughter's hand is on this gift we know it reaches us by
virtue of your inexhaustible munificence. We are deeply
honoured to be the recipients of your bountiful goodness
and shall forever seek ways to be worthy of the respect
and friendship you have expressed for our people."

The junior samurai translated this for Yama-Shita's benefit. Mr. Snow was sure that the chief Iron Master could
speak the Mute language and understood it perfectly well
but for some reason—perhaps to enhance his already ex-
alted position—he chose to have everything relayed by a
mouthpiece.

Yama-Shita grunted his assent and stood up with an
imperious wave. Everybody below the dais put their nose
on the floor and stayed there till he had left the room,
followed by his entourage.

When Mr. Snow sat back on his heels Clearwater was
no longer visible. The invisible hands that had opened the
wall screens had now closed them cutting off his view of
the adjoining room. He felt a sudden pang of anxiety at
what would now happen to her but as he picked up the

box, he felt reassured. It contained a message; what she would have said had she been free to do so. He had understood that much from what she had said and the subtle inflections she had used in her replies. He ran his fingers over the painted surface of the wood and felt her presence within it. It was fortunate that the Iron Masters were either ignorant of, or did not give any credence to, the stories of Mute magic.

Returning to the main deck, their guide ushered them into an annexe of the bath-house where the female attendants who had washed them now stood waiting, fully dressed, to help them back into their own clothes. Mr. Snow found it strange that they had been allowed to look on the faces of the female Iron Masters but not those of the males. He reflected on the phrase "Sons of Nissan." Tonight was the first time he had heard it used. Did it imply that, in Iron Master society, all women were considered to be inferior beings. Or was it merely that these particular women were considered to be of lower standing than the samurai and his red-striped minions?

The two clan-elders said nothing until they were safely ashore then both threw themselves to the ground, hugging and kissing it, their fingers clawing deep into the fine round pebbles covering the beach.

Rolling-Stone was the first to rise to his knees. "What a night!" He gazed towards the departing samurai. "I still can't believe the size of that boat. Just think of the trees they must have killed to build it! And the whole time we were on board it never stopped *moving*. Didn't you feel it?"

"Yes," said Mr. Snow. "But it didn't affect me all that much."

The old clan-elder got up and massaged his chest and stomach. You're lucky. I feel as sick as a yellow dog."

"Me too," said Mack-Truck. He stood up and spat the bile from his mouth. "Why didn't you ask Clearwater why she was unskinned?"

Mr. Snow threw up his hands. "I didn't know how to. Since Yama-Shita didn't raise the subject I thought it

better, in the end, to say nothing. If he gets it into his
head that we tried to trick him we could find ourselves in
all kinds of trouble."

Rolling-Stone gave vent to a grumbling sigh as they
headed towards the lines. "I really don't understand why
we have to keep grovelling to these dinks."

"Especially when they're robbing us blind . . ."

"Look, Mack, before you start complaining just remember that, if it wasn't for them, most of us would still be
throwing rocks at one another and opening buffalo with
our bare teeth. Is that what you want to go back to?"

Rolling-Stone answered for him. "Life must have been a
lot simpler."

"What makes you think it was meant to be simple?"
grumped Mr. Snow. "You must try to *live* simply but to do
so requires a mental effort that is beyond most people.
Life itself is the most complex mystery there is. A tree
starts out as a tiny seed that can be carried in a bird's
beak. But if it doesn't get eaten does it stay that way? Of
course not. If it takes root and is favoured by the sun and
the rain it gathers strength and grows until it is twenty
warriors tall! And when it reaches its prime that *one* seed
can produce a whole sackful. In the days when Oakland-
Raider led this clan, the M'Calls numbered no more than
eighteen hands. Look at us now! Just as the tree stretches
its limbs upwards, seeking to touch the sun, so the Plainfolk
are destined to grow tall and strong in the light that is
Talisman."

Momentarily silenced by his eloquence, his companions
trudged alongside him through the darkness, their faces
bathed in the warm glow from the hundreds of camp-fires.

"I still think you overdid it," mused Mack-Truck. " 'Inexhaustible munifience,' 'bountiful goodness' . . . I don't
know exactly what it means but do you really think they
swallow that jive?"

Mr. Snow gave him a fatherly pat on the shoulder.
"Mack, you're here to do the deals. Just leave the word-
games to me. Come sun-up tomorrow the dead-faces will
be on their way and we'll be able to hold our heads high

for another year. Okay, so maybe we have to bow and
scrape a little but so do they. That's the way they operate.
I don't mind playing the grateful underdog for a week if it
means the clan gets what it needs to survive. Yes, sure,
they twist our arms a little but so what? It's better than
having them blown off by the sand-burrowers."

There was another lengthy silence. The noise of the last
night's festivities began to assault their ears. They picked
their way through the celebrations to the four turf marker
poles which indicated the area alloted to the clan elders.
Mr. Snow threw off his ceremonial finery and sat down on
his sleeping furs.

"What's in the box?" asked Mack-Truck as they sat
down facing him.

"Nothing." He opened the lid to show them the bare,
black-painted interior.

"Rolling-Stone looked puzzled. "I don't get it. Why
come all this way to give you an empty box?"

Mr. Snow let out a long-suffering sigh. "Don't you understand *anything* about magic? Haven't I explained to
you, over and over again, what summoners can and cannot
do?"

Rolling-Stone shrugged his thin, bony shoulders. "I don't
know. Maybe you did. I forgot. It happens."

Placing the box in his lap, Mr. Snow closed his eyes and
slowly rubbed his palms over the intricate gold images
that adorned the top and sides. When he spoke, his voice
had a distant, echoing quality. "It's not what is *in* the box
that is important but what is *on* the box." He opened his
eyes and raised the box, turning it around so they could
see the pictures for themselves. "Without understanding
what he was doing, the craftmaster who fashioned these
images has told us many things. When you examine them
in the light of day you will see they are pictures of the Iron
Masters' world. They show the land that lies beyond the
Fire-Pits of Beth-Lem, between the Buffalo Hills and the
Great Sea, the paths that lead to where Cadillac is to be
found—and this one shows the great hut by the falling
water where Clearwater is held against her will."

His two companions looked impressed. "Why did she not speak of this?" asked Rolling-Stone.

"She could not. Hidden behind each side of the open door where we could not see them were two more red-stripes with drawn bows, their arrows pointing straight at her heart."

The chief clan elder frowned, adding more lines to his deeply wrinkled face. "But what has she to fear? Does she not possess the Second Ring of Power? Could she not have willed the arrows to turn aside? If she and Cadillac are prisoners why does she not call upon the earth-forces to free them?"

Mr. Snow caressed the golden images on the box. "She dare not. Cadillac stays of his own free will. He no longer cares whether Clearwater goes or stays. She remains because she is pledged to do so but she is not free. She is held in the hut of a great warrior chief who desires to make her his body-slave. She does not use her power because Talisman has forbidden it. No Iron Master is to die at the hands of the Plainfolk. This is why the cloud-warrior was sent back to us. It is *he* who has been chosen by Talisman to bring Cadillac and Clearwater out of the eastern lands. Many dead-faces will die, their great huts and many of their works will be burst asunder but their anger and their desire for revenge will fall not on us but upon the sand-burrowers."

"Neat," said Mack-Truck. "I like it. What now?"

"We find the cloud-warrior and show him the box. This middle picture on the top shows what looks like a tree but it is much more. The branches and the trunk are rivers. The other lines show the run of hills and valleys as seen from the sky. He understands better than I what these marks mean. Once they are in his mind, they will guide his feet along the right path."

Mack-Truck accepted this with a nod. "Are you going to tell him Clearwater is here—on Yama-Shita's boat?"

"No. It will only complicate matters. Let him find that out for himself."

NINETEEN

STEVE'S HUNCH about being able to find a way into the ship via the piston housings proved correct. The forward end of the pistons ran down a sloping slab-sided shaft. There was just enough room between the stationary beam and the planked roof of the shaft to allow someone to crawl through. Like the blades on the huge paddle wheel they drove round, the two long wooden beams were reinforced with metal straps, pins and inserts. As with everything made by the Iron Masters, the level of craft skills employed was very high but the extensive use of wood seemed to indicate they were not yet able to produce heavy forgings. The Federation had gotten around the problem by developing SuperCon, a special formulation of concrete that had all the advantageous properties of steel and could be machined to the same fine tolerances; the big difference was that everything could be cast in cold moulds, without any need for giant furnaces, tempering or drop forging. It also didn't rust.

Unslinging his quarterstaff, Steve crawled forward in the shadow cast by the beam, wriggled into the housing and slithered down head first. Had someone been waiting at the other end he would have been totally at their mercy but, once again, his luck held. The lower end of the piston was connected to a massive cylinder and a cluster of valves

which provided the impetus to drive the paddle wheel.
The pipes that carried steam to and from the cylinder ran
downwards before turning at right angles to follow the line
of the floor below. They were uncomfortably hot but, as
his almost naked body was still dripping wet, the short
slide was not too painful.

Emerging from the lower end of the shaft, Steve found
himself in the darkened engine room of the wheel-boat. It
stretched from side to side of the hull and seemed to be
about fifty to sixty feet long. In the centre, in a square,
vaulted area rising through the deck above were two huge,
wood-fired boilers made of black riveted metal plates,
linked by an intricate web of copper pipes and brass valves
to the cylinder and piston assembly in the shaft above his
head, and to its twin on the starboard side of the boat.

The total structure rose some fifteen feet into the air,
the upper parts being encased in a framework of ladders
and narrow walkways. Split lengths of wood were stacked
in neat piles on both sides of the hull and across the entire
forward section of the engine room. The boilers were
alight but had been damped down for the night. Steam
hissed lazily from excess pressure vents. The air was moist
and heavy with heat, the aroma of woodsmoke and warm
oil. The sole illumination was provided by twelve small
lanterns which were moved about as required by the night
crew. The burnished metal work gleamed in the yellow
glow but, beyond the pools of light, everything lay in deep
shadow.

Steve counted six unmasked dead-faces sitting at a table
set amid-ships a few feet from the business end of the
boilers. They were eating food from a collection of bowls
with the aid of small sticks. Like Mr. Snow, Steve was
surprised to discover the flat faces and hairless heads of
the Iron Masters. Five were stripped to the waist, their
smooth, waxy skins glistening with sweat. All had a short
length of oil-stained yellow rag tied around their throats.
The sixth sported a red sweatband and wore a wide-
sleeved jacket. It carried no visible signs of rank but since
he was the only one so dressed he was probably the
crew-chief.

Crouched behind the vertical cluster of pipes, Steve could not be seen by the crew as long as they remained seated. But he could not rely on them sitting there for ever. He needed a safer place to hide while he worked out his next move. Keeping the pipes between himself and the crew, Steve moved quickly behind the tall stack of logs running along the port side of the engine room then climbed on top of it. The stack rose to within three feet of the beamed ceiling that ran around the central vaulted area, obliging him to lie flat on his stomach. Unless any of the crew mounted the walkways with a lantern and looked in his direction he would be able to crawl right around the engine room without being seen. He considered stashing his weapons behind the stacked wood but the risk of discovery was too great; the stacks were certain to be used during the voyage which would last several days at least, maybe weeks and, even if they weren't, it might prove difficult to get back into the engine room. He had to find somewhere better.

One of the M'Call loaders had told him that arrangements had been made to accommodate the journey-men on the main through-deck. Steve had a hunch it could be the one immediately above his head, where the out-going cargo had been stacked. Tonight was probably the last night when the guards would either be absent or at a minimum. But how to get up there? The only set of stairs he could see ran from the centre of the engine-room floor, up between the two boilers, to meet a walkway running across the vaulted section. From there, the upward journey was continued via a second flight of stairs placed at either end. From where he lay he could not see the top but, presumably, there had to be a means of access to the deck above. Simple enough, except he could not negotiate the stairs without being seen; the table at which the sweating engineers were feeding their faces lay across the bottom of the stairs and less than six feet from the first step.

Casting his eyes around in search of another exit, Steve saw a shadowy gap in the centre of the forward stack of logs and decided to investigate. He crawled along to the far end of the port stack then angled round over the main

store. The wood here was six rows deep. He kept close to
the wall where the darkness was almost complete then
carefully climbed down into the gap between the front
stacks. He had guessed right again. There was a sliding
door set into the forward wall of the engine room. He
opened it up a crack to see what was beyond. He could
see no lights nor hear any sound of activity.

Looking back towards the crew table, he saw that two of
them had begun to play some kind of a game with stones
and the others had crowded round to watch. The game
seemed to be a source of entertainment, triggering cries of
amazement and bursts of laughter from both players and
spectators. Steve waited for a particularly noisy outburst
then slid the door open and stepped through. When he
tried to close the door behind him it jammed half-way.
Shit . . . Fortunately, it was even darker here than in the
far recesses of the engine room but if any of the engine
room staff got bored with the game and wandered in his
direction he was done for.

Steve paused for a moment to tune into his surroundings. He was in a narrow passageway leading under the
bow deck. As his eyes adjusted he detected a feeble glimmer of light at the far end and what looked like a ladder.
He moved slowly towards it, feeling the walls on both
sides to discover if they contained any doors or recesses.
His fingers brushed across a series of rectangular panels.
Those in the bottom half of the wall had solid inserts;
those at the top were pierced screens of latticed wood.
Running his toes along the skirting, he located a groove
that indicated the presence of a sliding door. A door meant
access to a space beyond, a space that could be occupied
by a sleeping Iron Master. He put his ears to the screens
and listened intently. It was hopeless. Every piece of
wood creaked and vibrated in sympathy with the rest of
the boat. He tried easing back one of the panels. It slid
part-way open with what seemed an alarmingly loud noise.
Hardly daring to breathe, he poked his head gingerly
inside. Nothing. A black, impenetrable void.

Leaving the door as it was, Steve headed towards the
ladder, climbed up and peered over the rim of the hatch.

To the right and left, almost within reach, were sacks of grain and what, by their smell, appeared to be rolled buffalo skins. What lay beyond was as much of a mystery as what lay on either side of the passage below.

The light that had cast its feeble glow onto the ladder came through a latticed square in the ceiling above his head. Its source was one of the fore-deck lanterns. The light was eclipsed briefly as the guard he had seen standing near the bows walked overhead. Steve ducked instinctively then, as he raised his eyes level with the through-deck, he saw two bobbing yellow lights moving towards him. As they drew nearer, he saw they were lanterns carried by two patrolling guards. He shrank down on the ladder. Christo . . . where should he go? The guard's patrol area might include the engine room and the areas on either side of the passageway. He dare not risk staying where he was. He would have to get back on top of the wood stacks.

With a muttered curse, Steve retreated down the ladder into the dark passageway. Halfway along it he froze in horror. The sliding door at the far end was still only half-closed and now, two of the engine-room staff had begun to shift logs from the corner of the stack just beyond! He looked back at the hatchway and saw it filled with the glow from the approaching lanterns. The guards were now only yards away. *Move* Brickman! Flattening himself against the port side of the passageway to avoid being silhouetted against the light, Steve found the edge of the cabin door he had attempted to open and squeezed inside. He heard the guard's footsteps pass almost directly overhead. Crouching down below the level of the pierced screens, he laid the bladed quarterstaff on the floor and eased the sliding door towards him. To his heightened senses, it seemed to make even more noise than when he had opened it.

Drawing back against the wall, Steve came into contact with a corner of the room. He quickly unwrapped the strip of cloth that concealed the knife strapped to his left forearm. The guards climbed down the sloping ladder, lanterns swinging. As they passed in single file he could see them quite clearly through the small holes in the lattice.

He held his breath as the yellow light from their lanterns dappled his face and chest but they went straight on down the passage. Pressing his face close to the screen, he saw the light fade as the guards entered the engine room. There was a brief exchange of nonsense words and a burst of laughter. Steve uttered another whispered curse. He had been so intent on watching the progress of the guards he had missed the opportunity to take stock of his surroundings during the brief moment when they had been illuminated by the passing lanterns. Never mind. Too late now. Onwards and upwards.

He wrapped the cloth back around the knife but left the top part of the handle free—just in case. He had a feeling he had pushed his luck just about as far as it would go for one night. A smile crossed his face as he thought of Mr. Snow. When the wordsmith found out what he had been up to, his whiskers would catch fire. Steve planned to let the news slip casually when they said goodbye in the morning. The journey-men were due to board at first light; the wheel-boats leaving, as always, as the sun came up. Right now, the poor bastards would be whooping it up around the fire, getting sky-high on rainbow grass. Steve whose hair had already been dyed dark brown to enhance his disguise, wondered what Jodi Kazan would say when she saw him step off at the other end. He stooped down and slid his hand towards his quarterstaff. It wasn't there. Puzzled, Steve knelt down and searched the darkness with both hands. His fingers touched a pair of bare feet. He glanced up and saw a shadowy naked figure towering over him. Before he could reach for his knife or throw himself clear, something crashed against his skull. The blow registered as a jagged flash of lightning on the inside of his eyelids and a thunderclap of pain exploded inside his head. His last memory was of falling sideways, through the floor, into a black bottomless pit.

At first light, Brickman was still missing. Around the lines, the various clan groups were already astir as the small scattered groups of renegades were hauled to their feet and readied for their last walk on Plainfolk territory. The journey-men, not all of them males, went the rounds, bidding their clan-brothers and sisters a last farewell. As the two flank-boats nosed up to the beach below the trading post, a M'Call Bear brought word to Mr. Snow that the cloud-warrior's walking skins had been found neatly folded under a pile of stones on the beach.

It was obvious what had happened. Mr. Snow threw up his arms and cursed loudly. What an idiot he had been! Instead of worrying in case Brickman did something foolish he should have taken steps to prevent him doing so by having someone sit on his head until it was time to board. If he didn't turn up soon, the young Mute warrior whose place he had offered to take would have to make the trip as originally planned. All the journey-men and renegades had been issued with flat metal armlets which were threaded through a plaque bearing three convoluted signs representing the sounds of words in Iron Master's language. Fortunately Mr. Snow had put off making the substitution until the last possible minute so the unfortunate journey-man was still wearing it. Had the plaque been found to be missing by the tally-master there would have been some awkward explaining to do. The dead-faces were absolutely fanatical about head-counts and lists. Mr. Snow had envied their ability to write the signs for silent speech but having now reflected on the way their lives seemed totally dominated by an obsessive concern with organisational structures, administration and paperwork he was beginning to feel that the gift of literacy also had its downside.

The wordsmith paced up and down in a fine old fret. Brickman, running true to form, had jumped the gun and—if he hadn't already been caught and skewered—had stowed away on one of the boats to begin his rescue mission while he, Mr. Snow, was here on the shore with a complete set of instructions! His sole source of comfort was the knowledge that Clearwater had grasped the meaning of his veiled message—that the cloud-warrior had returned as predicted in the seeing-stone and was about to embark on a rescue attempt. But she had been forewarned of this already. The box, with its charged images, had not been intended for him but for Brickman. Things had not

gone quite according to plan but it was proof yet again that
The Path was already drawn and that Talisman watched
over his own.

The last of the journey-men filed aboard and disappeared into the bowels of the ship. Even though he had
witnessed the scene many times, Mr. Snow always felt the
same way. Their going—like the doleful task of despatching dying warriors after a battle—was an occasion for bitter
regret. This time, perhaps, when the cloud-warrior returned with Cadillac and Clearwater, they would finally
discover the fate of those who, over the years, had been
carried away across the great river. One day, when the
Plainfolk were one nation under Talisman, they would no
longer be forced to kneel to the Iron Masters. They would
march to the east in glory and bring forth their lost clan-
brothers and sisters.

Surrounded by the rest of the M'Call delegation, Mr.
Snow watched as teams of white-stripes laboured to wind
the walkways back up onto the decks of the two flank
boats. The M'Calls were only a small part of the huge
crowd now gathered on the beach for the final farewell.
Grey and white smoke belched from the tall thin funnels
as the huge paddle-wheels churned up the water beneath
their sterns. Once clear of the shallows, the two boats
turned about and took up their positions on either side of
Yama-Shita's vessel. Its bows were already pointed towards
the far horizon. As the sun passed through the western
door, the assembled Mutes heard a rumbling roar like the
thunder of falling water. It was the engines responding to
the call for full steam ahead. The great steel-bound blades
on the paddle-wheels knifed into the surface of the lake,
driving the boats towards the rising sun. All three boats
vented plumes of pure white smoke sending a shock-wave
of sound reverberating across the water. Vvvooooooo-
oommmmm . . .

"Heyy-yahh!" roared the Plainfolk with one voice. Lines
of drums pounded out an insistent rhythm, and the knives
that would soon kill each other and the turf-marker poles
which, in two short weeks, they would die to defend were

raised into the air in unison. Heyy-yahh! Heyy-yahh!
HEYYY-YAHH!"

The Iron Masters responded with a final explosive salute. Long stabbing fingers of flames and billowing clouds
of red and black smoke erupted from all three decks on
both sides of Yama-Shita's vessel followed by an explosive
burst of sound. A great rippling thunderclap that caused
many of the watching Mutes to think the sky was being
torn apart. Hundreds fell to their knees on beach as the
spreading pressure-wave washed over them like a great
wind.

BA-BA-BABOOOMMM-mmmoommm . . .

From a thousand throats came a hushed cry. " . . .
heyy-yaahh . . ." The Lord Yama-Shita was truly a man of
great power. A master, not only of men, but of sky-fire
and cloud-thunder.

The noise and flame came from the three tiers of ship's
cannon mounted on the side galleries of Yama-Shita's vessel. For this farewell double broad-side, the guns had
only been loaded with a flamboyant mixture of black powder and magnesium but, if required, they could spew out
a murderous hail of grapeshot or hurl balls of cast iron, the
size of a man's head, several hundred yards.

The sun, now a giant semi-circle of golden fire, framed
the three departing wheel-boats, its light eating into their
square outlines. Those near to Mr. Snow saw him shield
his eyes against its brightness but, in reality, the gesture
was a vain attempt to hide his tears.

Steve recovered consciousness to find himself lying in
total darkness inside what seemed to be a long narrow
box. He had been expertly gagged and bound hand and
foot and his body was wedged between bundles of cloth
that prevented him from kicking against the sides in an
effort to break out of confinement or attract attention—not
that that would have been a wise thing to do. As the hours
passed he gradually lost all sense of time, then his surroundings started to vibrate as the engines at the heart of
the ship sprang into life with a sonorous, accelerating beat.
He guessed, correctly, that they were heading towards the

shore to collect the journey-men and renegades. After an interminable wait, the engines began to pound with a new urgency. They were leaving! On their way at last! But not as he had planned. His sixth sense, which usually manifested itself in moments of stress or danger, had totally failed him. Caught unawares, he had been struck down and was now trapped, quite unable to move and completely at the mercy of his mysterious assailant.

From time to time, faint voices and the muffled sound of footsteps reached his ears, providing a fleeting counterpoint to the monotonous drum-beat of the engines and the thrumming of the water as it passed beneath the hull. The realisation that he was still in the bottom of the wheelboat provided some small comfort. He tried not to think that, at any minute, his captor might return—this time not alone—to drag him before the boat-master and . . . Steve tried to wipe the chilling images from his mind.

Gah-DOONG, guh-DONG, gah-DOONG, guh-DONG, gah-DOONG, guh-DONG. Each throbbing beat of the engines sent a vibrant pulse through the timbers beneath his body. As the day wore on, the noise ceased to be an intrusion and became part of his pitchblack world, seemed to seep into his bones. He dozed fitfully, grew hungry, thirsty. His tongue and throat dried, the air felt stale, he experienced moments of panic and periodic bouts of claustrophobia but he hung on, willing himself to stay calm.

Time passed, an eternity it seemed, then without warning the lid of the box was slowly lifted leaving Steve momentarily blinded by the light of a flickering lantern. A big evil-looking lumphead dressed in a sleeveless leather jacket and baggy trousers stood over him holding a knife; a long, slim, razor-sharp blade forged in the Fire-Pits of Beth-Lem and which now hovered dangerously close to Steve's face. He dragged his eyes away from the knife and gazed up at the owner. He had a folded band of red cloth tied around his shaved skull. It was a strange sight. Steve had never seen a Mute with no hair before. The lumphead motioned him to remain silent then cut loose the gag and offered him a drink of water. Steve raised his head and took a few sips. His jaw had been open for so long he was unable to swallow properly at first and almost choked.

"Easy, compadre," muttered the Mute.

Steve eyed him curiously. "Compadre" was not part of a normal Mute's vocabulary.

The lump squatted down beside him. "Okay, listen carefully. I had to tie you up for your own good. You were blundering around like a blind buffalo. And also because I have an investment to protect. I now propose to untie you. But stay right where you are. No smart moves—comprendo?"

Steve responded with a silent nod.

Placing the knife between his teeth, the Mute quickly untied Steve's hands and feet. He was a powerfully-built guy with a great bull neck but his movements had the suppleness of a snake. He rose and stepped back. "Okay, sit up."

Steve did so and found himself in a small bare wooden-walled cabin. The box in which he had been concealed formed the base of a bunk bed, the planked frame on which the mattress rested being the lid. The only furnishings apart from the bunk were a wall cupboard and a narrow shelf. He gratefully accepted another drink of water and a piece of flat-bread. "Are we safe here?" he whispered.

"Reasonably. It'll be some time before the guards come back."

"How long have I been here?"

"About twenty-four hours." The Mute's eyes never left Steve's face. "I suppose you're wondering what the Sam Hill happened."

Steve grinned. "The question did cross my mind. I've got a feeling that, if I wait long enough, you're going to tell me."

"That depends."

"On what?"

"On what you've got to say for yourself. There aren't too many straights around—especially with blue eyes. What clan are you from?"

"Does it matter?"

"It does to some people."

"The M'Call, from the bloodline of the She-Kargo—"

"—mightiest of the Plainfolk. Yeah . . . they've got quite a reputation. Even so, you were taking a big chance sneaking on board with a set of blades. What exactly were you after, friend?"

Steve didn't respond.

The Mute grimaced sympathetically. "I know how it is. After you've been living close to the engines for a while you get hard of hearing. I've already got problems with this one." He raised the middle finger of his right hand and pressed it against his skull just behind the lobe of his ear. "How about you?"

Steve hesitated for a moment then did the same. The pressure activated a tiny device carried by all MX operatives. Inserted just below the line of the skull in an operation under local anaesthetic that took less than fifteen minutes, it sent out a signal which caused a feedback in any similar device with a range of five to seven yards. Mexicans also had various passwords by which they could introduce and identify themselves. These could never be totally secure but nobody could duplicate the mosquito-like hum that now impinged on Steve's inner ear. And by applying an almost imperceptible pressure under the guise of a quite natural gesture, the device could be turned on and off allowing two mexicans to exchange brief signals in Morse code in the middle of a crowd of people. Steve did this now, sending the letters, 'MX.'

"Do you hear what I hear?"

"Loud and clear." The mex grinned. "I had you spotted when you came in the door. Mutes don't swim and none of them would have the moxey to break into a wheel-boat. You're lucky the guards didn't spot you. But then they're lucky too. If you were found now, half of 'em would lose their heads."

"Why didn't you tell me all this last night instead of breaking my head open?"

"There wasn't time to be properly introduced. I wasn't looking to get my guts engraved by some gung-ho artist with more balls than good sense." The mexican extended his hand. "Side-Winder. What's your handle?"

"Hang-Fire. Are my blades safe?"

"Yeah, that's been taken care of. Do you realise what would have happened to you if you'd been caught carrying?"

"One of several things, all of them unpleasant."

"Yeah, like having your asshole hot-wired. They can also skin you, boil you alive, chop you up into little bitty pieces, or feed you into the furnace of one of the boilers feet first—very, very slowly. You get the picture?"

Steve nodded. "So how come you're carrying a knife?"

"They trust me. I'm the head overseer in charge of the journey-men. There's six of us altogether. Our job is to help the dinks keep control during the voyage. A lot of these lumps are scared shitless at being on the water and there are others who don't take too kindly to the new routine. They have to be broken in. Having some of their own kind around helps ease things along."

"What happens to the ones that don't break?"

"They're strapped to one of the blades of the paddle-wheels."

"How long for?"

"For as long as it takes."

Steve sucked his breath in sharply. "Nasty . . ."

Side-Winder shrugged. "That's just for openers. There's worse believe me. These dinks are experts. But you know all that anyway. Before we go any further, am I right in thinking you *were* trying to hitch a ride?"

"Yeah—but I'd planned to be with the party upstairs."

"Better this way. Strange how things work out. I got a message to say you might turn up at the trading post but I didn't expect to run into you."

"Me neither . . . listen, there was a terrible explosion just after we got under way. What happened—did one of the ships blow up?"

"No such luck. That was Yama-Shita saying goodbye to your friends with a seventy-two gun salute. Muzzle-loaders. Thirty-six on each side, twelve on each deck. They're mounted on wheeled trolleys. Got a barrel this long . . ." He stretched both arms out sideways then brought his hands together and formed a circle with his fingers and thumbs. ". . . And they fire an iron ball this big."

Steve frowned. "I didn't notice anything like that when I swam out here."

"Only Yama-Shita's boat has them. Unless you're on board, you can't see 'em until they're wheeled out for action."

"Got it . . ."

"So . . . why haven't you been in touch?"

Steve gave him a brief explanation of what had happened to his radio-knife and the back-up squad.

Side-Winder listened impassively them remarked: "They must have been new boys . . ."

"They can't come much newer than me. How long you been on the boats?"

"Long enough. Before that I spent some time hauling barges up the Allegheny. That was what I was working my way up in the world. This could be my last trip. I'm just waiting for the nod then I'll be on my way home." He indicated the row of lumps on his forehead and cheekbones. "Can't wait to get these things out of my face."

"I didn't like to ask," said Steve. "Just how in the hell—"

"Silicone pads. Not bad, huh?"

"Fantastic."

"Yeah . . ." Side-Winder showed Steve the blotchy pattern on his left fore-arm. "Whether I'll be able to get rid of this so easily is another matter. How long have you had your paint job?"

"About a month. But I wouldn't have done it if I hadn't seen for myself that it came off. But those lumps . . . I don't know whether I could go that far. Must have been a tough decision."

Side-Winder responded with a lop-sided grin. "I think they call it 'service above and beyond the call of duty.' But then, you've got to be pretty dumb to be able to act like a Mute in the first place."

Steve bit his lip and let it pass.

"Okay, let's get down to the nitty-gritty. Just where are you headed, friend, and how can I help?"

Steve explained that his task was to locate and recover two Mutes—Cadillac and Clearwater. He did not reveal that they were both gifted unmarked straights or give any details of his overall assignment.

Side-Winder did not press him further on the subject. He just listened in silence then grimaced worriedly. "Sounds like you've bitten off a big one, compadre. With some luck and a following wind I can get you ashore but from there on in you're on your own."

"Are there any more of our people over there—amongst the Iron Masters?"

Side-Winder laughed drily. "Are you kidding? Lumps they can do but not even Rio Lobo can turn one of the good ole boys into a dead-face."

"What I meant was—are there any more like you?"

The smile vanished from the mexican's face. "If there are, they haven't told me. And if you weren't still wet behind the ears you would know not to ask. If this was meant to be a team effort you'd have heard about it."

"Point taken. Can you at least tell Rio what the score is?"

"Not immediately but yes, I'll see they get the word. Anything special you want me to say?"

"No. Just tell 'em I'm still on the case—and that I need a new back-up squad."

"I have a feeling they already know that."

Steve looked at the mex sharply. "News travels fast."

"Bad news always does. Anything else?"

"Yeah, there's the rifles."

"Rifles?"

"The M'Calls just took delivery of the first hundred. I gather there's more on the way."

Side-Winder frowned. "They didn't come off this boat."

"No, they came off Yama-Shita's. Special delivery." Steve gave the mexican a brief description of the weapon and its capabilities.

"Ahh . . . I wondered what the noise was."

"Where were you?"

"Down here. I'm not allowed to put my nose out of the door while the boat is run up on the beach."

"I see. Can you pass that information on to Mike X-Ray One?"

"I'll try," said Side-Winder. The new boy was so painfully keen, he didn't have the heart to tell him that the details of the new weapon had been despatched to Rio Lobo over twelve months ago.

"There's a couple of other things. I'm gonna need some clothes—and I want to know everything you can tell me about the Iron Masters."

Side-Winder met this request with a solemn nod. "I made a big mistake with you, friend. When I laid you out I should have thrown you overboard. Is that all?"

"Not quite. How long is the trip?"

"To Beth-Lem? Ten days. Did you get to see any maps while you were at Rio?"

"Yes. Mike X-Ray One took me over the ground himself."

"Lucky you. Okay, we ride the big water all the way to Lake Erie and make landfall near a NavRef point called Cleveland. The Iron Masters have joined up three rivers with canals and locks—"

Steve frowned at the unfamiliar words.

Side-Winder gave him a brief explanation of how canals and lock systems worked. "What it means is that these boats can sail right through from Lake Erie to the Allegheny—"

"Which runs down to Beth-Lem."

"Correct."

"Is that another name for Pittsburgh?"

"It is. And that's enough questions for tonight. Back in the box."

Steve lived in his narrow hideaway for the next nine days, emerging for an hour each evening and just before dawn when it was safe to do so. While Steve put himself through an intensive physical work-out, Side-Winder passed on what he knew about the structure of the Iron Masters' society and taught him the sounds and signs for several key words and phrases. Although he never admitted it, the big mexican appeared to have a fluent grasp of the strange tongue but, on several occasions, he warned Steve that he must never attempt to make use of it. He must always speak Basic, the language of the serfs.

Steve longed to ask Side-Winder how AMEXICO had managed to insert him into the Iron Master's trading operation but knew he would draw a blank response. His presence on the boats and his flawless disguise was clear evidence that very little remained secret from the First Family. He thought about Lundkwist's revelation that she had been recruited prior to entering the Academy. The Family had people everywhere. Was there no limit to their power and guile, was there any place beyond their reach?

Side-Winder explained that the Iron-Masters' language was called "Japanese" and that was also the collective name they gave to their race. Experts on the Iron Masters at Rio Lobo referred to them as "japs." Iron Master was a Mute-term. The japs also styled themselves as "The Sons of Nissan"—Nissan being their name for the lands they occupied. This too had an alternative name, "The Land of the Rising Sun"—the origin of the solid red circle that was to be seen everywhere. The Fire-Pits of Beth-Lem was another name conjured up by the Mutes and merely referred to that one specific location.

The japs were believed to have landed on the eastern seaboard some six hundred years ago. Their society, which was regulated by rigid codes of behavior, was ruled by dynastic succession. The leader was called the *Shogun*, and he was supported by domain-lords whose power, like the Shogun's was drawn from their territorial possession. The domain-lords were not unanimous in their support for the Shogun and there was an undercurrent of conspiracy which sometimes surfaced as a challenge to the central authority. The lords, who were the heads of "families" with names like Datsun, Honda, Hitachi, Matsushita, Mitsubishi, Nashua, Seiko and Toshiba, presided over a multi-layered pyramid of lesser ranks.

At the bottom of the heap or, more accurately, *below* the bottom line, came the captured renegades and the Mutes—in that order. Jap society was divided into six main categories which, in descending order of importance were samurai, the ruling warrior class, administrators, merchants, boat- and craft-masters, and the factors who managed the farms and mines.

Unskilled manual labour was supplied by Mute journeymen—male *and* female—and the renegades. Because Trackers were adapted to underground life most of these were sent to the mines; Mutes were employed on the land, tending fields, digging canals and irrigation ditches, as carters and porters and, because of their amazing endurance, as couriers delivering the never-ending stream of messages that flowed to and from the court of the Shogun. A few lucky individuals found employment as servants in the great houses. These, like Side-Winder, had shaven heads—a sign of their trusted status; the others were referred to contemputuously as "monkeys," or "hairy ones." The renegades were known as "long-dogs"—an epithet derived from their height and their angular features.

The Trackers were, of course, unable to reproduce without the intervention of the First Family but the Mutes were encouraged to have children and raise them in Mute-type settlements attached to the estates of the great houses.

Side-Winder's greatest concern was how Steve was going to move around carrying a knife and a bladed quarterstaff. All Mutes and Trackers were dressed in outfits identifying their job or status and carried armlets or neck-rings showing which estate they were assigned to. Apart from the couriers, the captive labour force only moved from one area to another under armed guard. Runaways were harshly dealt with and there was an absolute prohibition on Mutes and renegades carrying any type of weapon. Even he, Side-Winder, was not allowed to take his knife ashore; it was to be worn only on duty, when working with each new batch of journey-men.

Steve thanked the mexican for his advice and told him he appreciated his concern but he did not intend to proceed unarmed. The information Side-Winder had given him had alerted him to many of the dangers. He would not go looking for trouble but, if his luck ran out, he wanted to be able to meet it head on. The mexican accepted his decision with a philosophical shrug.

Ten days after leaving the trading post, the beat of the engines was stilled. Once again concealed in the coffin-like space under the bunk, Steve felt the wheel-boat shudder as it drifted sideways and crunched against the timbered wharf that lay to starboard. There was a moment of silence, then the air erupted with a muffled babble of voices, bumps, thumps and hurrying footsteps as the process of unloading commenced. He lay back and willed himself to wait patiently for night to come. As the hours passed, he was sorely tempted to get out and see what was going on but Side-Winder had shrewdly taken the precaution of battening down the lid.

Eventually, the mexican appeared and let him out. A flickering lantern lit the bare boxroom that served as his sleeping quarters. Between it and the central passageway lay the second half of Side-Winder's nautical estate—the equally small cabin which Steve had ducked into to avoid the guards.

Side-Winder handed him a few twists of dried meat and a hunk of flat-bread. "Okay, this is where you get off. End of the line."

Steve chewed on one of the twists. "The place feels deserted."

"It is. Apart from a skeleton crew, everybody's gone ashore."

"Where do you go from here?"

"Nowhere. This is where I live." Side-Winder swept a hand round his domain.

"Christopher! How do you stand it?"

Side-Winder laughed. "How many Mutes do you know who have got a two-roomed hut? And *two* buckets. One to crap in and one to drink out of." He saw Steve's expression. "Listen, I'm not complaining. If I couldn't hack it I wouldn't have drawn this assignment. It's not so bad. If I want fresh air or something to see I can go on deck and every now and then I get a few hours ashore. What I miss most is the video. The dinks don't have electricity. But even that has its compensations. At least I don't have to

listen to that moronic musical shit the Federation pumps
out. Mind you, the stuff the dinks listen to isn't much
better. To me, it always sounds as if they've missed out
half the notes."

"Okay . . . I'd better get going." Steve paused hesi-
tantly. You mentioned you might be able to, uh . . ."

The mexican went into the outer cabin and returned
with a set of walking-skins.

Steve gulped down the last mouthful of food and tried
them on for size. The skins were impregnated with the
smell of their previous owner. "Mind telling me where
these came from?"

"Side-Winder eyed him narrowly then relented. "Someone took a ride on the wheel and decided he didn't like it.
On a trip like this you always get a few cancellations." He
opened the wall-cupboard and took out two small ceramic
cups and a flask. Laying the cups on the shelf he uncorked
the flask and poured out two portions of a pale liquid.
"Here . . . one for the road."

Steve sniffed the cup cautiously. "What is it?"

"Sake. It's a, uhh . . . medicinal restorative. It'll help
keep out the cold." Side-Winder emptied his cup in one
gulp and smacked his lips. "Good stuff. Go on, it won't kill
you."

Steve raised the cup gingerly and let the liquid come in
contact with his lips. It was sweet flavoured with a slight
bitter aftertaste. Not wishing to appear frightened, he took
a deep breath and swallowed the lot. The sake hit the back
of his throat like liquid fire. He gagged in a futile effort to
stop it going any further, coughing and choking as it came
back up and entered his nasal passages. For one moment
his chest felt as if it had been stabbed with a hot knife then
the sharpness eased, blurring into a warm glow which
turned his ears pink and made him feel agreeably light-
headed. "Wowww . . ."

Side-Winder refilled the cups. "Alcohol. One of their
better inventions. This one is made from fermented rice.
Imagine what that would do to a wagon-load of Trail-
Blazers . . ."

"Well, I don't know how it works but it sure makes you feel good."

The mexican nodded. "It certainly smooths off the rough edges. Trouble is it, uhh . . . numbs your central nervous system and ruins your coordination. Two is the limit. Three leaves you legless and four puts you on the floor. I speak from experience. That's where I usually spend my off-duty hours. In fact if it wasn't for this I'd have taken a dive from the top deck long ago."

"No friends, no company?"

"None of your business, amigo." The mexican took Steve's cup and put it away with the flask in the cupboard. Loosening a panel in the timbered wall behind the bulk, he slid it to one side, stuck the whole of his left arm in through the gap and pulled out Steve's combat knife and quarter-staff. Steve strapped the knife back onto his left forearm, covering it with the strip of cloth.

"That's, uhh—my spare knife you've got there," said Side-Winder. "You'll probably find it more useful than the one you came on board with."

"Thanks. But if I call, who's going to hear me?"

"I'm sure somebody will. The Family always keep one ear close to the ground." Side-Winder led the way up onto the main through-deck and opened a small hatch on the port side. Beyond was a wide expanse of river. "You'll have to swim for it. The wharf's crawling with dinks. The other two boats are moored ahead of us. Let the current take you down-stream until you're well clear of the dock then make your way ashore."

"Okay." Steve crouched down by the hatch. "One last question. When you were unloading, did you happen to see a female renegade—medium height, dark hair, with a big slab of pink scar tissue down one side of her face and neck?"

Side-Winder cast his mind back. "Yeah, as a matter of fact I did. Funny thing . . . they usually march the renegades straight off to the mines but this time they lined 'em all up and asked if any of 'em were wingmen."

Steve's interest quickened. "And . . . ?"

"Two guys stepped forward. She was one of 'em."

"Did the other guy have red hair?"

"Yeah, he did."

Jodi Kazan and Dave Kelso . . . "What happened to them?"

"They were taken away by Yama-Shita's people. Which could mean they're headed across the river and down the east road. It cuts through the Allegheny mountains to the coastal plain beyond."

"Did anybody say anything—like where they might be going, for instance?"

"Nope. At least no specific place name that meant anything to me." Side-Winder made an effort to recall what he had overheard. "Wait a minute, I did hear one of the dinks mention something about "the Heron Pool.' "

"What's a heron?"

"It's a bird, compadre."

"How do you say 'Heron Pool' in Japanese?"

Side-Winder told him. "I can't show you what the sign looks like because I've got nothing on me to write with and even if I had it's too fugging dark to see anything."

"That's okay." Steve grasped the mexican's hand and shook it warmly. "Thanks. You've been terrific." He pointed across the river. "The east road is thataway—right?"

"Yeah. You'll see the landing stage for the ferry about half a mile down river. If I were you I'd keep well clear of the road between sun-up and sunset. Especially over the next few days. Yama-Shita and his crowd are due to travel that way tomorrow. There's going to be a lot of people gathering at the road-side to pay their respects as he goes through."

"Will you be staying here?"

"Me? No. These boats carry shipments all over the place."

"In that case, I may see you again sometime."

"Maybe . . ." Side-Winder uncoiled a length of rope and lowered it over the side.

Steve slung the quarterstaff across his back and slid down into the water. As soon as he let go of the rope, Side-Winder pulled it back in and shut the hatch. Steve swam to the centre of the river, then let it carry him past the other two wheel-boats—the second of which was Yama-Shita's. When he had passed the last of the warehouses lining the wharf, he struck out for the far bank and came ashore near a clump of trees that reached down almost to the water's edge.

Unrolling his walking skins he dressed quickly and took stock of his surroundings. Beyond the trees was a large patch of newly cultivated ground divided into neat squares. Keeping to the paths separating the square plots, Steve worked his way round towards the landing stage and took cover behind a cluster of wooden shacks with lighted windows. A small knot of people stood by the roadside where it sloped down towards the river. Edging closer, Steve saw they were unmasked red-stripes armed with swords and bows. There were four of them gathered round a fire burning inside what looked like a pierced metal bucket. The sight of them was a timely reminder that he would have to proceed with caution. There might be other check points further on.

Retreating into the darkness, Steve went down a path leading directly away from the river, climbed over a wall at the end and turned onto the road about half a mile from the landing stage. The road had a bare dirt surface. Across the river, beyond the line of warehouses and other building, the horizon was aflame. A flickering orange glow pushed back the velvet night and lit the undersides of billowing drifts of white, brown and grey smoke. The Fire-Pits of Beth-Lem. His visit there would have to wait. He had other, more pressing business to attend to. With a quickening heart, he turned east and strode forward confidently. Each new step along the road brought him nearer to Clearwater and a new adventure. He had been the first Tracker to return alive from the Plainfolk. If not the first, he would be one of the select few to return alive from the land of the Iron Masters. And this time, he would not return empty-handed.

As he pushed on into the enveloping dark, Steve had no idea that Clearwater, as a member of Lord Yama-Shita's entourage, was preparing to pass the night in considerably more comfort aboard his wheel-boat on the other side of the river. But she had sensed Steve's fleeting presence and knew they would meet again as foretold in the stone. Until that moment, the power she had poured into the quarterstaff would protect him.

In the Federation, Commander-General Karlstrom also had reason to feel confident. In the essential field-tests, Brickman had proved he possessed the required courage, endurance, dedication and ruthlessness required of every mexican. All in all, it had been a most satisfactory performance but the nagging doubts about his loyalty remained.

After learning from High Sierra about the destruction of the back-up squad, Karlstrom had become concerned at Brickman's failure to maintain contact even though he had the means to do so. His only consolation was that Roz Brickman, who was under constant surveillance, had not displayed any signs of physical distress since Brickman had successfully rejoined the M'Calls. There had only been one instance of psychosomatic wounding—when she had developed brief sympathetic skin lesions on her rib-cage and left arm. Her general condition and demeanour indicated that Brickman was still very much alive and the latest signal from Side-Winder confirmed that he was still on course. His meeting with Brickman had been most fortuitous. On Karlstrom's instructions, he had given Brickman a new radio-knife that contained an additional refinement. It automatically broadcast an intermittent signal that allowed its position to be accurately plotted—even if Brickman failed, or decided not to make contact. As long as he kept the knife in his possession the First Family would know where to find him.

Here is an excerpt from IRON MASTER, third book in the "Amtrak Series:"

The five sleek craft, under the control of their newly-trained samurai pilots, lifted off the grass and thundered skywards, trailing thin blue ribbons of smoke from their solid-fuel rocket tubes. Levelling off at a thousand feet, they circled the field in a tight arrowhead formation then dived and pulled up into a loop, rolling upright as they came down off the top to go into a second—the maneuver once known as the Immelmann turn.

There was a gasp from the crowd as the lines of blue smoke were suddenly severed from the diving aircraft. A tense, eerie silence descended. The first rocket boosters had reached the end of their brief lives. Time for the second burn. The machines continued their downward plunge—then, with a reassuring explosion of sound, a stabbing white-hot finger of flame appeared beneath the cockpit pod of the lead aircraft. Two, three, four—five!

The watching crowd of Iron Masters responded with a deep-throated roar of approval. Cadillac, who was positioned in front of the stand immediately below his patrons, Yama-Shita and Min-Ota, swelled with pride. These were the kind of people he could identify with. Harsh, forbidding, and cruel, with unbelieveably rigid social mores, they nevertheless appreciated and placed great value on beautiful objects, whether they be works of nature or some article fashioned by their craft-masters. Cadillac knew his flying machines appealed to the Iron Masters' aesthetic sensibilities. Like the proud horses of the domain lords, they were lithe and graceful, and the echoing thunder that marked their passage through the sky conveyed the same feeling of irresistible power as the hoofbeats of their galloping steeds. Here, in the Land of the Rising Sun, he had been taken seriously, had been given the opportunity to demonstrate his true capabilities, and had been accorded the praise and esteem Mr. Snow had always denied him. And his work here was only just beginning!

As the five aircraft nosed over the top of the second loop, leaving a blue curve of smoke behind them, their booster rockets exploded in rapid succession. Boooomm! Ba-ba-boom-boomm. Booom!

Cadillac, along with everyone else in the stand behind him, watched in speechless horror as each one was engulfed by a ball of flame. The slender silk-covered spruce wings were ripped to pieces and consumed. On the ground below, confusion reigned as the shower of burning debris spiralled down towards the packed review stand, preceded by the rag-doll bodies of the pilots.

Steve Brickman, gliding high above the lake some three miles to the south of the Heron Pool, saw the fireballs blossom and fall. It had worked. The rocket burn had ignited the explosive charge he, Jodi, and Kelso had packed with loving care into the second of the three canisters each aircraft carried beneath its belly. Now there could be no turning back. Steve caught himself invoking the name of Mo-Town—praying that everything would go according to plan.

General To-Shiba, seated on his left, was quite unaware of the disaster. Fascinated by the bird's-eye view of his large estate, the military governor's eyes were fixed on the small island in the middle of the lake two thousand feet below. It was here, in the summer house surrounded by trees and a beautiful rock garden, that Clearwater was held prisoner. The beautiful creature who was now his body-slave and who possessed that rarest of gifts—lustrous, sweet-smelling body hair. The thought of his next visit filled him with pleasurable anticipation. As a samurai, To-Shiba had no fear of death but, at that moment, he had no inkling his demise was now only minutes away. . . .

Announcing one hell of a shared universe!

OF COURSE IT'S A FANTASY . . . ISN'T IT?

Alexander the Great teams up with Julius Caesar and Achilles to refight the Trojan War—with Machiavelli as their intelligence officer and Cleopatra in charge of R&R . . . Yuri Andropov learns to Love the Bomb with the aid of The Blond Bombshell (she is the Devil's *very* private secretary) . . . Che Guevara Ups the Revolution with the help of Isaac Newton, Hemingway, and Confucius . . . And no less a bard than Homer records their adventures for posterity: of *course* it's a fantasy. It has to be, if you don't believe in Hell.

ALL YOU REALLY NEED IS FAITH . . .

But award-winning authors Gregory Benford, C. J. Cherryh, Janet Morris, and David Drake, co-creators of this multi-volume epic, insist that *Heroes in Hell* ® is something more. They say that all you really need is Faith, that if you accept the single postulate that Hell exists, your imagination will soar, taking you to a realm more magical and strangely satisfying than you would have believed possible.

COME TO HELL . . .

. . . where the battle of Good and Evil goes on apace in the most biased possible venue. There's no rougher, tougher place in the Known Universe of Discourse, and you *wouldn't* want to live there, but . . .

IT'S BRIGHT . . . FRESH . . . LIBERATING . . . AS HELL!

Co-created by some of the finest, most imaginative

talents writing today, *Heroes in Hell* ® offers a milieu more exciting than anything in American fiction since *A Connecticut Yankee in King Arthur's Court*. As bright and fresh a vision as any conceived by Borges, it's as accessible—and American—as apple pie.

EVERYONE WHO WAS ANYONE DOES IT

In fact, Janet Morris's Hell is so liberating to the imaginations of the authors involved that nearly a dozen major talents have vowed to join her for at least eight subsequent excursions to the Underworld, where—even as you read this—everyone who was anyone is meeting to hatch new plots, conquer new empires, and test the very limits of creation.

YOU'VE HEARD ABOUT IT—NOW GO THERE!

Join the finest writers, scientists, statesmen, strategists, and villains of history in Morris's Hell. The first volume, co-created by Janet Morris with C. J. Cherryh, Gregory Benford, and David Drake, will be on sale in March as the mass-market lead from Baen Books, and in April Baen will publish in hardcover the first *Heroes in Hell* spin-off novel, *The Gates of Hell*, by C. J. Cherryh and Janet Morris. We can promise you one Hell of a good time.

FOR A DOSE OF THAT OLD-TIME RELIGION (TO A MODERN BEAT), READ—

HEROES IN HELL®
March 1986
65555-8 • 288 pp. • $3.50

THE GATES OF HELL
April 1986 Hardcover
65561-2 • 256 pp. • $14.95

Here is an excerpt from George R.R. Martin's newest novel, coming in February 1986 from Baen Books:

Tuf drove through several kilometers of corridor in the small, three-wheeled cart. At every intersection he stopped, looked right, looked left, and weighed his choices before proceeding. He saw nothing, encountered no one. Now and again, the kitten Chaos moved in his lap.

Then Rica Dawnstar appeared up ahead of him.

Haviland Tuf stopped his cart in the center of a great intersection. He looked right, and blinked several times. He looked left. Then he stared straight ahead, hands folded on top of his stomach, and watched as she came toward him slowly.

The mercenary stopped about five meters away, down the corridor. "Out for a drive?" she asked. In her right hand she carried her familiar needler.

"Indeed," said Haviland Tuf. "I have been occupied for some time. Where are the others?"

"Dead," Rica Dawnstar said. "Deceased. Gone. Eliminated from the game. We're the end of it, Tuf."

"A familiar situation," Tuf said flatly.

"This is the last game, Tuf," Rica Dawnstar said. "No rematch. And this time I win."

Tuf stroked Chaos and said nothing.

"Tuf," she said amiably, "you're the innocent in all this. I've got nothing against you. Take your ship and go."

"If you refer to the *Cornucopia of Excellent Goods at Low Prices*," said Haviland Tuf, "might I remind you that it suffered grave damage which has not yet been repaired?"

"Take some other ship, then."

"I think not," Tuf said. "My claim to the *Ark* is perhaps inferior to that of Celise Waan, Jefri Lion, Kaj Nevis, and Anittas, yet you tell me that all of them are deceased, and my claim is surely as good as your own."

"Not quite," said Rica Dawnstar. She raised her needler. "This gives my claim the edge."

Haviland Tuf looked down at the kitten in his lap. "Let this be your first lesson in the hard ways of the universe," he said loudly. "What matters fairness, when one party has a gun and one does not? Brute violence rules everywhere, and intelligence and good intent are trampled upon." He stared back at Rica Dawnstar. "Madam," he said, "I acknowledge your advantage. Yet I must protest. The deceased members of our group admitted me to a full share in this venture before we came aboard the *Ark*. To my knowledge, you were never similarly included. Therefore I enjoy a legal advantage over you." He raised a single finger. "Furthermore, I would advance the proposition that ownership is conferred by use, and the ability to use. The *Ark* should, optimally, be under the command of the person who has demonstrated the talent, intellect, and will to make the most effective use of its myriad capabilities. I submit that I am that person."

Rica Dawnstar laughed. "Oh, really?"

"Indeed," said Haviland Tuf. He cupped Chaos in his hand, and lifted the kitten for Rica Dawnstar to see. "Behold my proof. I have explored this ship, and mastered the cloning secrets of the vanished Earth Imperials. It was an awesome and intoxicating experience, and one I am anxious to replicate. In fact, I have decided to give up the crass calling of the merchant, for the nobler profession of ecological engineer. I would hope you would not attempt to stand in my way. Rest assured, I will furnish you with transport back to ShanDellor and see to it personally that you receive every fraction of the fee promised to you by Jefri Lion and the others."

Rica Dawnstar shook her head in disbelief. "You're priceless, Tuffy," she said. "You know what I've been up to while you've been cloning yourself a kitten?"

"Obviously I do not," said Haviland Tuf.

"Obviously," Rica echoed sardonically. "I've been up on the bridge, Tuf, playing the computer and learning just about everything I need to know about the Earth Ecological Corps and its *Ark*."

Tuf blinked. "Indeed."

"There's a swell telescreen up there," she said. "Think of it like a big gaming board, Tuf. I've been watching every move. The red pieces, that was you and the rest of them. Me, too. And the black pieces. The bio-weapons, as the system likes to call them. I like the sound of *monsters* better myself. Shorter. Less formal."

"Fraught with strong connotations, however," Tuf put in.

"Oh, certainly. But to the point. We got through the defense sphere, we even handled the plague defense, but Anittas got himself killed and decided to get a little revenge, so he kicked loose the monster defense. And I sat up on top and watched the red and the black chase each other. But now, the key question."

In the corridor behind her, Haviland Tuf glimpsed motion. "Excuse me," he began.

Rica waved him quiet. "If they were prepared to turn loose these caged horrors of theirs to repel boarders in an emergency, *how did they prevent their own people from getting killed?*"

"An interesting quandary," Tuf admitted. "I eagerly anticipate learning the answer to this puzzle. I fear I will have to defer that pleasure, however." He cleared his throat. "Far be it from me to interrupt such a fascinating discourse. I feel obliged to point out, however . . ." The deck shook.

"Yes," Rica said, grinning.

"I feel obliged to point out," Tuf repeated, "that a rather large carnivorous dinosaur has appeared in the corridor behind you, and is presently attempting to sneak up on us. He is not doing a very good job of it."

The tyrannosaur roared.

WATCH OUT! THE COBRAS ARE BACK!

That's right: in the new hit sequel, *Cobra Strike*, the Cobras are back, with all of the excitement and hard-hitting action that made Timothy Zahn's *Cobra* an instant bestseller!

Cobra Strike continues the chronicles of the Cobras, the most powerful fighting force ever created by man. Cobras are, in effect, supermen, thanks to surgical implants that give them fantastic strength, speed, and agility. Their abilities are partially controlled by nanocomputers, and augmented by built-in weaponry including, among other devices, finger lasers.

In *Cobra Strike*, the Cobras must decide whether or not to hire out as mercenaries to their former enemies, the alien Troft. This time, however, it's up to Jonny Moreau's *sons* to carry on the honor of the

Cobra name—which they do admirably, through high adventure and political intrigue with more than a few surprising twists.

Available February 1986 • 352 pp. • $3.50

GRANT CALLIN

"Grant Callin's universe is a fascinating one; I look forward to seeing more of it."—*Larry Niven*

"Grant Callin is a pro who knows space like the back of his hand. With this book he shares the excitement of exploring our newest, greatest frontier."
—*David Brin*

"A very distant descendant of *Treasure Island*, but the 'treasure map' and the action it stirs up are thoroughly different from anything Robert Louis Stevenson could have imagined."—*Analog*

JANUARY 1986 • 65546-9 • 288 pp. • $2.95